GOD'S EAR

ALSO BY RHODA LERMAN

Call Me Ishtar
The Girl That He Marries
Eleanor: A Novel
The Book of the Night

GOD'S EAR

A NOVEL BY

Rhoda Lerman

HENRY HOLT AND COMPANY

NEW YORK

Published by Henry Holt and Company, Inc.,
115 West 18th Street, New York, New York 10011.
Published in Canada by Fitzhenry & Whiteside Limited,
195 Allstate Parkway, Markham, Ontario L3R 4T8.

Library of Congress Cataloging-in-Publication Data
Lerman, Rhoda.
God's ear.
I. Title.
PS3562.E68G64   1989   813'.54   88-13239
ISBN 0-8050-0413-0

Henry Holt books are available at special discounts
for bulk purchases for sales promotions, premiums,
fund raising, or educational use. Special editions or
book excerpts can also be created to specification.

For details, contact:

Special Sales Director
Henry Holt and Company, Inc.
115 West 18th Street
New York, New York 10011

First Edition

Designed by Susan Hood
Printed in the United States of America
1 3 5 7 9 10 8 6 4 2

FOR MY MOTHER

"Everything on this earth, in this universe, is absolutely intentional."

"God weaves your destiny from your choices."

"The purpose of suffering is to correct the distance between you and HaShem."

"The world is created by the letters and answered by the sounds."

—Rabbi Fetner
of blessed memory

GOD'S EAR

1

THE RABBI'S only son, Yussel, sold insurance, mostly life. He made a fortune because everyone in the Hasidishe world knew that his father, the Rabbi, and his grandfather of blessed memory, and his grandfather's grandfather of blessed memory, all of them stretching back unbroken in a golden chain from Far Rockaway to Horodenka, to Braslow, Chernobyl, Lublin, Tiberias, Jerusalem, to David, to Adam, all of them in the Fetner family, made prophecy.

"So, why are you here, Yussel?"

"To sell you some life insurance."

"Oy. What do you know?"

"Nothing."

"Today, this *particular* day, why are you here?"

"You're on my list. I come every six months. Your premium's due."

"The truth, Yussel."

"You're on my list."

"How will I go?"

"Bernie, Bernie, I'm just selling life insurance."

"Believe me, Yussel, if a Fetner comes to my door selling life insurance, I'm buying."

Behind his back his clients called him the Angel of Death. The Rabbi's son made a lot of money selling insurance. From Williamsburg, from Borough Park, from the Five Towns, they came to him to buy. As soon as he picked up the phone and said, "Guess who?" they bought. Life, accident, doubled their umbrellas, upped their homeowner's and liability. Everything.

Yussel married a beautiful sweet girl from Toronto, a rabbi's daughter. Although she spoke perfect Poylishe Yiddish she also had a slight British accent and looked a little like Patty Duke. He had a Mercedes, a house near the beach with moss-brick on three walls in the leisure room, two ovens, the Patty Duke wife, four Donna Reed daughters, one son who looked like him, which wasn't so bad but very Jewish.

"You know something I should know, Yussel?"

"Nothing, it's just time to look over your policy, Berel."

"Your father tell you something? Your uncles? Did you hear something? Maybe about the Almighty's intentions?"

"Berel, I don't know from HaShem's intentions. I know only from accidents, from the tables."

Yussel rolled his shirtsleeves up over hairy muscular arms—he played baseball with the Kneth Israel Cemetery Association, handball on Sunday mornings against the wall of the Yeshiva behind his house—took his pen from his vest, removed his Hasidishe beaver hat, filled out the insurance papers. His friend Berel watched Yussel shove his skullcap forward and backward, forward and backward. Everyone thought this was a sign he was doing prophecy. Berel began to sweat. His wife brought a silver tray of schnapps and kickel.

"How long does my Berel have, Yussel?"

"Your husband's terrific. Look at his medical report."

"How long do I have, Yussel?"

Yussel shrugged and took his hand from his skullcap. "As long as you have, you have."

Such wisdom from the Fetners. The insured discussed every word Yussel spoke, watched everything he did, read everything he gave them to read. They discussed mortality tables and immortality. They discussed HaShem's intentions versus random accidents. They discussed handball, baseball, miracles, how much chicken fat a man could eat in a lifetime, cholesterol levels, the possible sainthood of the Fetners, the Rabbi, his wife, this remarkable only son. They discussed prophecy. Everyone was waiting for Yussel to become a rabbi even though Yussel swore never on his life. Yussel showed his clients the Metropolitan Life Expectancy Charts, wouldn't discuss prophecy. He offered variable rates, good returns on single-life premiums, no predictions. He wore his beaver hat over his skullcap, tried to keep his hand from pushing it backward, forward on his head. The Fetners don't see everything and they can't control what they do see, but they can turn it off if it starts coming in on the screen. Which is what Yussel did when he went to sell insurance. Yussel didn't want to know from prophecy, from God's intentions, from reward and punishment. Yussel knew from insurance tables: chance, probability, accident. One in 1,500 skiers at Aspen breaks a leg; one in 10,000 drivers breaks an axle; one in 200,000 planes is bombed. He knew the tables by heart. The average nonsmoker female lives to 72; smokers to 73. His father, on the other hand, lived in a universe in which absolutely everything is God's intention, where there's no coincidence, where an angel stands behind every blade of grass, singing, "Grow, darling, grow." Yussel didn't want to live in such a universe because if there's an angel behind every blade of grass you have to watch every step you take. Yussel only wanted to be a wealthy Jew, sell insurance, live in his house by the ocean in Far Rockaway, be comfortable.

"For me, Yussel?"

Yussel found the line in the tables, the age, the life expectancy, showed Berel.

"For me? Here?"

"That I can't guarantee."

Yussel wasn't stupid. Yussel, like everyone else in the family— the uncles, the mother, the father, even the sister—was brilliant. He soared through theological seminary like an eagle, his teachers reported, and then cursed him when he left the Talmud for actuary tables. Yussel wanted no part of the soul, the law, the rabbinate, the lineage, the blood. He was thirty-six years old. What he had, he wanted; what he wanted, he had.

Yussel sometimes walked on the boardwalk, sometimes on the beach, sometimes climbed out on the jetties, and sometimes, when the tide was out and the moon was shining on the wet sand and he could walk on the moon, through the moon, those times he wondered for just a moment if maybe he should be a rabbi and continue the dynasty.

On Friday night, if a man goes to his wife with the correct sexual procedures in the creative act, if he pays attention to what it means, not how it feels, his child will come down from Heaven with a higher consciousness. His child will be delivered out of the waters of the evil inclination, out of Egypt, into Sinai. And when this child, with all these generations of consciousness behind him, when this child says, "To me it should be revealed," to him it's revealed. Each generation more than the one before. Yussel, although he insisted he didn't make prophecy, was a generation holier than his father, the Rabbi. And to him, therefore, more should be revealed, which was what his clients were thinking. And his son, Schmulke, only six, was one more generation holier than Yussel. Already, Schmulke could tell Yussel how much change was in Yussel's pockets, almost a year earlier than Yussel had been able to guess how much was in *his* father's pockets.

Yussel used to pat his father's pockets and know immediately how much. There was never much. His mother emptied his father's pants every night so, she said, he wouldn't give the house away. He had already given away almost everything else, which was one of the reasons Yussel was determined to sell insurance, provide abundance for his own wife and children, and stay far away from God's great gift.

"I'm flying to Belgium to buy lace, Yussel. Do I need more insurance?"

"It's a good idea, also to buy linings now."

"Oy."

Once, just after he'd been hired out of Seminary, a full rabbi, by Metropolitan Life, he'd sold a policy to a cousin of his mother's. The man dropped dead the next week. Yussel's reputation was carved in bronze. Yussel read *The Wall Street Journal*, *Women's Wear Daily*, knew a little here and there about cloth, lace, linings, packaging, gas and electric stocks, futures, electronics, hazardous wastes. So with his Talmudic mind, which was trained to see every alternative, every nuance of a situation, it didn't take much effort on his part to say, for example, "Buy linings. Cut velvet."

4

His father, the real Rabbi, did prophecy only when he was drinking. Except for Shabbas, Simchas Torah, and Purim, the Rabbi didn't drink. But when he drank, he really drank, mostly vodka. On Simchas Torah and Purim only did he drink to get drunk because drunk he might see God. In the Rabbi's house, no matter how little money there was, how many people had to be fed, on Shabbas the cup overflowed just as the mercy of HaShem overflowed. When the Rabbi poured wine it ran through his fingers onto the gabardine of his pants. When the Rabbi held the Shabbas cup, people said they saw the wine boiling in the cup as if it were on fire. When Shabbas came to an end, he wiped the wine on his eyelids and schmered it in his pockets to bring a good week.

And he made prophecy. For you, forget the film career. Get a job. For you, better not to marry her. For you, Yussel, don't go back to New York. Stay here in Kansas. Buy some real estate. No one knew what else he told Yussel, but he must have told him plenty because everyone in the congregation was well covered. Widows were never left without, sons always had money for college, daughters for braces and weddings. The Rabbi didn't make prophecy about his own death. Not because it was a bad thing, but because he had so many mishugge people hanging on him, they'd try to go with him before their time. Once when he was in the hospital, someone tried to trade his life for the Rabbi's life by slamming a milk truck into a telephone pole. Nobody died. Yussel paid for a new milk truck.

YUSSEL WANTED to buy life insurance for his father, to provide for his mother after his father's death. It was something Yussel fought with him about every time he called him on the phone, which was every day, and every time he visited him in Kansas, which was three times a year.

"Yussele, when I go, I'll go. I'm sick. You know I'm sick. HaShem knows I'm sick. That's enough to know. Don't push me."

"You're not covered, Totte."

The truth was, in order to get a policy his father would have to go to a doctor and take a physical, and if he went to a doctor, then the doctor would know and somehow his wife and his congregation would find out. His father went therefore uncovered. It made Yussel crazy.

"You're not covered."

"I'm covered." By the heat in his father's eyes, Yussel knew he meant covered by HaShem. His father operated on many levels of reality. He also spoke four languages. Yiddish with the sweat and joy of the body, when he fought with his wife or his Creator. American English when he was fund-raising, sometimes with a Yiddish accent, sometimes without, depending who he was fund-raising. Harvard with the Queen's English accent when he lectured on the finite and the infinite at Interfaith dinners. And Hebrew when he prayed. "You're the one who's not covered, Yussele. You're the one with the uncircumcised heart." That's how they fought. Yussel would bring up insurance; his father would fight back with Yussel's uncircumcised heart.

"You're not covered, Totte. I'm talking about insurance on your life. About medical expenses." When his father drove seventy-five, eighty, eighty-five miles per hour on the Kansas highways, with the ancient Honda rattling like a dreidl winding down at the end of its spin, about to quit, his father would yell over the roar through the rotted muffler, "Attached above, safe below." This from a man with a degree in Analytical Philosophy from Amherst, this stupidity. "Totte . . . so Mom has some money. Do it for her."

"Look, Yussel, let's talk business. You and I, we're here to kindle sparks. HaShem sends me the worst, the wet matches of the universe, shmegeggies, the lost of the lost. And asks me to light their fires. I do what He asks. I'm not so successful. He asks you also. You won't. So don't tell me what I should be doing until you begin to do what you should be doing. Until maybe you circumcise your heart."

This was the problem: who had and who did not have a circumcised heart. Yussel's uncles had uncircumcised hearts. Even though they were already rabbis, his uncles were also international world-class scholars—Jung, Law, Philosophy. They taught in the great Christian centers, paid their bills, made *Who's Who in American Universities,* lived in big clean houses. His mother referred to his father's brothers as the three little kings, said they should sell shoes. They were precise small men with long delicate hands and

6

narrow feet, neat beards, hard eyes, had wives even smaller than themselves. When you offered them something to eat, they'd sit in front of it—say a square of noodle pudding—and go through some amazing intrigue in their heads about themselves and that kugel. Yussel's father was the same size as his older brothers but he spilled over, filled rooms, lived such joy, agony, passion he was twice the size of anyone around him. He had a world-class circumcised heart. According to Yussel's father, Yussel's uncles did not; they weren't attached to God. They hadn't removed their spiritual foreskins. Which was what Yussel also refused to do. Which was the problem. His father was in love with HaShem and all of HaShem's creation. Yussel wasn't.

On his Bar Mitzvah, this furious, thirteen-year-old Yussy Fetner went through all the steps, but he wouldn't reveal his heart, wouldn't attach to HaShem, wouldn't allow his heart to be circumcised, because he already knew one thing and he knew it well: once the word goes out that you have such a heart, you're a victim. His father, with his world-class circumcised heart, was a world-class victim. Yussel wanted only to have a good job, live in a big house. He didn't care about *Who's Who*. What's What was what he cared about. Which was why he hocked his father about his insurance, so at least his mother would have what's what when his father died, which—the way he lived, the way he let people suck his blood—would be soon enough. His father was a world-class walking victim for every living thing except his wife, his daughter, his son.

NOT FOR YUSSEL the business of the zaddik, of signs, meanings, intentions, attachments, prophecy. Yussel had a telex in his basement, a fax next to it, a direct line to Salomon Brothers, thirty-thousand-buck-wholesale computer equipment from 47th Street Computer. He didn't want to turn around from taking a trip or making an investment because at the moment he was making up his mind, he saw a black crow fly into his backyard and eat three olives from the Russian olive tree. That's the way his father lived and his fathers before him, and Yussel wanted no part of such involvement.

THE BEST OF rabbis are lamps to their generation. Yussel's father was lightning. Some of his people were burned, some transformed. When Yussel's father was a few years out of graduate school, he'd already offended everyone in the frum world with his radical shtick, his new ideas, his difficult questions, his willingness to apply Torah to life instead of life to Torah. But what scared them to death was that he might lead their children away from Yiddishkeit, into the world. They thought he might because after Yeshiva, the Rabbi broke the rules and went to a university—to a campus, listened to goyishe ideas and sat next to thousands of unmarried shicksas. On the same seats. He came out quoting Nietzsche, Carlyle, God knows who, saying things like: "You have to break the statue to find its heart." Which everyone figured meant breaking the rules of the Torah. No one had to have prophecy to see trouble ahead. The Rabbi's own father of blessed memory said to his son, Yussel's father, "You're going to think on the frontier, you better go live on the frontier. If I give you my pulpit, even *my* people will kill you. In Kansas there is a pocket of spirituality, families fresh from Europe. Go help them bring up Jewish children in such a wilderness." So Yussel's father took a big mortgage on a little split-level in a decent neighborhood on the South Side of Kansas City. By the time Yussel finished Yeshiva, got a job, got a territory, got married, bought a big house, had enough money to pay off the mortgage on his father's split-level, you could smell bacon. The neighborhood had become a white-trash/Mexican neighborhood, with liquor stores, a drug-rehab center, six-pack trailer parks, water-bed motels, 7-Elevens. The children of the old Jewish families got rich, moved to the East Side, joined a fancy shul, even intermarried. His father held services in the basement of the split-level.

YUSSEL AND HIS father sat in the kitchen of the split-level. It was Yussel's Hanukah visit. His father was wearing his silk pajamas. He had two luxuries: silk pajamas and Zabar's French Roast. He had two pairs of maroon silk pajamas, walked around in them, looked more like a king in those pajamas than in his clothes, explained he should sleep in silk because if his soul were to travel at night, his soul should go up to the higher rungs clothed in silk. He did not consider his pajamas a luxury. His father had taken another loan out on the split-level to give money for somebody's sister's operation. He couldn't remember who. Yussel wrote another check. It was the fourteenth time he'd paid off the mortgage. His father made coffee. The kitchen was filthy. His mother had a headache. Yussel was still arguing with his father that he should take out life insurance. His father was still refusing.

"If I tell my people I'm going to die, they'll explode. They'll start early with their craziness. And your mother, she'll start early to sell my clothes to raise cash for the funeral. All that herring, all those hard-boiled eggs. Why should my last days be spent naked surrounded by shmegeggies already wearing my old clothes?"

Yussel laughed. "She'll rent your room."

His father nodded. "She'll rent my room before I die. She'll bake strudel for the shiva and not give me a bite."

"She'll fly everyone out from New York thirty days early on SuperSaver."

The Rabbi and Yussel hugged each other, tears of laughter sparkled on their beards. "I'll be naked, sitting on the sidewalk while the Salvation Army truck carries my bed from the house."

They held each other, like bears, Yussel great and hairy, his father small and fiery, and danced with each other into the dining room, around the living room. In the living room, his father stopped, held Yussel at arm's length, searched his face as if he were seeing it for the first time. "Yussele. Tottele." His voice was low. "I know you won't attach to HaShem. Believe me, I understand your reasons. But when you smile like this, Yussele, I see Him in your eyes. I see all the generations before you. You can't hide your heart, Yussele. You can try but you can't hide your heart. Deny it if you want, but someone will see it, someone will figure you out."

HE WAS NOT yet sixty. He had been ill for years and in pain and on drugs, and when he danced, maybe from the suffering, maybe from the drugs, maybe from the joy, they said his feet didn't touch the floor. And when he sang, his voice, they said, rang with the voice of David, and when he made prophecy, his shmegeggies wept to be in his presence and brought at least four more nonbelievers to supper, and when his eyes went into melt, he looked on his shmegeggies and his eyes burned holes in their hearts and their hearts were opened forever to the sweet Creator above.

Yussel himself had seen this and often he too was swept away by his father's passion. But there was a story in the family that always froze the passion in Yussel's heart. When his father told the story, Yussel wanted to be a great zaddik, he wanted to "get bitten by the bug," as his father would say. When his mother told the story, Yussel wanted to kill himself. Even when he was very young he wanted to kill himself when his mother told the story. This is how his mother told the story.

"Your great-great-great-grandfather of blessed memory on your holy father's side was very poor. No food, no clothing, no shoes for the children, no wood for heat. Poor. His wife, your great-great-great-grandmother of blessed memory, wept through the bitter winters and fought with him through the summers to sell the one thing in the house that would take care of them all for the rest of their lives. Tefillin, so old, so treasured, that the richest Jew in town had offered my holy husband's great-great-great-grandfather four hundred rubles. A fortune. Enough, believe me, Yussel, for food and coats and shoes and heat and a horse and a carriage and peace of mind for the rest of their lives." Here, his mother would sigh. "So it's Sukkos, and he needs, you know, a lulav, like from palm tree leaves, and an esrog, like a lemon. The lulav he has, but no esrog. Who knows why? The boat didn't come from Palestine? It was a bad year in the esrog trees? Esrogs cost a fortune, so how could this holy man find one and how could he have one? And then one day, he's walking, worrying about how he could have Sukkos without an esrog and there's a man carrying a beautiful firm golden perfect esrog. 'How much for your esrog?'

"The stranger looks him up and down, sees the poverty, laughs, walks away.

"'How much?' the zaddik shouts after him.

"'Four hundred rubles,' the stranger jokes.

"'Wait! Wait!'

"He runs home, gets the tefillin, takes them to the rich Jew, who is overjoyed, runs to the stranger, gives him the sack of coins, and goes home with his esrog and puts it on the table.

"His wife sees the esrog. 'So, where did you get such a thing?'

"'I got. I got.'

"'You sold the tefillin for this esrog?' And she picks up the esrog, throws it, smashes it against the wall, and it's ruined. And my holy husband's holy ancestor is so holy, he says, 'Already the Yetzer Hara, the Evil One, follows me. He has taken my tefillin, he's taken my esrog. But I will not allow him to take my Beis Shalom, the peace of my household. I will not invite him in this house by arguing with you, so,' he says, this holy man whose memory lives with us, he says to his wife who has grown old trying to make ends meet, he says, 'I forgive you.'"

Yussel had seen the tefillin in his uncle's house. They were inscribed by a scribe in the time of the Baal Shem, the founder of Hasidism. The Baal Shem himself said this scribe was the equal of Ezra the Scribe. The writing, in four hundred years, hadn't faded. No one remembered how the tefillin came back into the family. When Yussel's mother told him the story, she would look him in the eye and watch him to see his reaction. His sister said there were lines missing from the story. When his father told it, there was something about holiness. When his mother told it, there was something about life and death. Something terrifyingly bitter.

Grisha, his father's gabbai, Talmud expert, baby-sitter, maybe best friend, maybe worst enemy, often told Yussel another story at bedtime. When Grisha prayed or told holy stories about the dynasty, he held his father's pocket watch, so in case he was transported to higher worlds, he'd be reminded to come back. The Rabbi insisted Grisha was a holy man. The Rebbitzen insisted Grisha was nuts from mercury vapors when he had been in the business of making felt hats. The story gave Yussel nightmares.

"One day in the Ukraine," Grisha would begin, putting his watch to his ear to make sure it was ticking, "the Zaddik, Rabbi Elimelech, decided to go into exile for two years to elevate himself to a higher plane and clean up his sins. After two years of exile he came to the outskirts of his little village and heard that his son,

Eliezer, had been very sick, near death. He rushed to his house and asked his wife, 'How is my Eliezer?' His wife said, 'Your Eliezer is fine. He's out playing.' 'But someone told me he was sick.' His wife shook her head. Then she said, 'There is an Eliezer who was sick, but your Eliezer, Baruch HaShem, is in good health.' The Rabbi was overjoyed to hear his Eliezer was okay. Then he realized he had accomplished nothing with his exile, no higher rung on the ladder to HaShem, no elevated soul, because he should have felt about the other Eliezer who really was sick, near death, as he felt about his own son. So that same day he said good-bye and went into exile again for another year."

The first time Grisha told the story, Yussel asked him if the Rabbi Elimelech said hello or good-bye to his own Eliezer before he left for another year. Grisha said probably not. Yussel had a dream about eating the wax from his own ears. The wax tasted in his dream like ginger.

And then one more story. Who hadn't heard that when Moses went to cross the Red Sea, the waters parted for the Israelites? Every Passover they heard it. In school, at home. Also they were told that every Passover the waters all over the world part at the same moment the Red Sea parted for Moses thousands of years before. And then a kid in Yeshiva, whose father hated Yussel's father, leaned over Yussel's desk, hissed, "The Red Sea was at low tide." Yussel tried to beat the kid up that afternoon, but the kid gave Yussel a bloody nose for his defense of the Torah. That night when Grisha was putting him to bed, Yussel asked Grisha if the Red Sea had really parted or was it just low tide. Grisha shrugged and said, "Nu? HaShem doesn't make the tides?" and turned off the lights.

Before Yussel had hair on his face, he'd learned that in the world of the zaddiks, husbands betray wives, fathers betray sons, and even the Torah betrays little boys. So why should he get involved? Still, they found him. They came like old gray gulls to pry open the shell of Yussel's soft heart.

2

BY THE TIME he was a teenager, Yussel wanted no part of a rabbi's life. Neither did his mother. The Rabbi fought all day and wrestled all night, not with the Angel of God, but with his wife who wanted him to get the schlemiels, the goniffs, the no-goodniks out of her house, out of her kitchen, stop giving them our last cent, stop feeding the world, stop stop stop. She would yell, her husband would look at her with those burning eyes, she'd have to turn away. So she took care of the bill collectors and the telephone company when they turned off the phone. She dressed up in her best clothes, went fund-raising to the rich oil dealers and grain suppliers in Kansas City who belonged to fine congregations. The Rabbi shrugged and said things like, "If the check bounced, HaShem wanted it to bounce." And danced and made prophecy, and people wept to be in his presence and stray children were saved and marriages reconsecrated and hysterical women made calm and somehow the bill collectors went away satisfied or amused although without money and the schlemiel bricklayer and the out-of-work bookbinder and the acupuncturist and the masseuse and the flower children who'd drifted to the West to find themselves and got lost in Kansas, somehow they were all fed every Shabbas and somehow the cup overflowed.

Not, you should know, Yussel would tell you, through magic or miracle, but through the guts of the Rabbi's wife, who one day finally left. This is how it happened.

It was after the Rabbi's nasty little congregation walked out on him. All the fancy Jews had Reform congregations—for who of substance would come all the way to Kansas, become rich, become American, become right-wing, and remain Orthodox? The shleppers who stayed couldn't pay the Rabbi his salary, so he sold the little shul on the corner, turned the split-level basement into a shul. His wife demanded a door separating the shul from the rest of the house except for the kitchen. With his own hands he built her such a door. Then she demanded a door separating her kitchen from the shul because the kitchen had strangers like New York City had cockroaches. They fought about the kitchen door. They fought about the strangers, the drifters, the sleep-overs who stayed months, maybe swept a floor once a week to pay off their room and board. The strangers kept coming. The Rabbi kept defending them. The Rebbitzen retreated, welcomed a few guests. But one morning, when the Rebbitzen came down to her kitchen, there was a flower child in a bathrobe, the Rebbitzen's bathrobe, drinking coffee from the MOMCAT mug, which her granddaughter, Bloomke's daughter, had given her for Mother's Day. And a flower child whom she had never seen before, although she looked and smelled of musk and sweat like all of the other lost souls, this flower child looked up at her and said with no emotion on her face, "You're out of toilet paper." The Rebbitzen went upstairs and packed. In two days the Rebbitzen was in Haifa with her Bloomke and her rich relatives on her mother's side. No one had to tell the Rabbi.

They always knew these things about each other. In fact, Yussel wondered if it was the toilet paper or if his mother had already watched on the screen in her head that Flower Child in her husband's bed. And merely recognized her.

So the Rebbitzen left her husband to his mishugas, his mishagoyim, his craziness, his crazy people; to New-Age Natalie, who expected to give birth to the Messiah once she found the right guy; to Dirty Ernie, the out-of-work bricklayer who played practical jokes with whoopee pillows and wind-up dentures until he put his wife into a permanent catatonic fit by pressing her hand with an electric hand-buzzer; to bitter Babe, the Rebbitzen's best friend; to Grisha, their live-in bachelor who played solitaire morning to night when he wasn't davening, who insisted God owed him nine thousand bucks, but he'd collect in the next world; to all the drifters, loners, losers, shnorrers, God knows who else came, ate, drank the Rabbi's blood. The Rebbitzen left the Flower Child, who had two holes burned through her forehead from the eyes of the Rabbi and would soon offer to marry him, even though he was sick, possibly dying. "Who isn't dying?" she asked, and the Rabbi was so struck by her new-age ease as well as her flesh, her little South African accent—she said her father was a racist school-teacher in Pretoria, but she also said her father worked for the Delaware and Hudson in Oneonta, New York—he squeezed in his mind her little parts even before the Rebbitzen called to have him mail the candlesticks to Haifa. In Yiddish he apologized to HaShem for bothering him so much about sending intelligentsia and students with worldviews, and although he could not understand why HaShem would send him such a young ripe thing—certainly children were not a consideration here—he would honor his duty to her and try to satisfy her as a husband if that were HaShem's intentions, which it seemed to be. The other Kansas rabbis threw him off the Rabbinical Board, wouldn't invite him anyplace anymore. Even Grisha left temporarily to live with the Lubavitchers, whom he despised.

When the Rebbitzen called the Rabbi from Haifa, neither of them said what they meant, although they each knew what the other meant. He meant he was going to marry the Flower Child. She meant over my dead body. "A Fetner doesn't do such a thing," the Rebbitzen said.

He said, "How do you know? You're not a Fetner. I am."

His daughter said, "This is a terrible mistake."

The Rabbi said, "It must be for the best."

The Rebbitzen said, "Maybe you're just getting even because I left. Maybe you should ask me to come back?"

The Rabbi said, "Maybe HaShem wanted to protect you from the suffering, from having to help me die, from those last days." The Rabbi suggested softly to the Rebbitzen, "Maybe HaShem is lengthening your life."

To which the Rebbitzen replied, "Maybe He's shortening yours." And hung up.

Undersea cables boiled, stars shrank, satellite disks trembled as the Rabbi howled through the empty lines: "Nothing is a mistake.

You hear me? I know you hear me. Nothing is accidental. Everything on this earth, in this universe, is absolutely intentional!" The Rabbi hung up. He could still hear his wife and daughter shrieking at him from Haifa. "There is no accident!" he yelled back at them. "Everything is intentional!"

His brothers called from Yale and Brown and Oxford. They had all agreed it was the pain drugs, a cumulative effect over the years, and could he go off the drugs and bring his wife back and get rid of the girl?

"I couldn't bear the pain."

"Your wife? Or your illness?"

"Both." It was a conference call. They all four hung up at once. The uncles called Yussel.

AFTER HIS MOTHER left his father, from Hanukah to Passover, Yussel sat in his three-story house on Ocean Avenue in Far Rockaway and spoke to no one. Next door to Yussel lived Chaim, a young rabbi Yussel had no use for. Chaim was the only child of Holocaust survivors. They'd carried him around on a pillow for most of his childhood. He was brilliant, egotistical, and referred to Yussel as arrogant, from that arrogant family. He claimed to make prophecy as well but never to use it for his own advantage. To others he would point out the moss-brick and the Mercedes and the Florence Eiseman outfits on the five kids and the Calvin on Yussel's wife. Yussel would never invite him over, even though Shoshanna, his wife, would say weakly, "Simply to remove his wrath, we could invite him." Everything with Shoshanna was simple.

Yussel crossed the street when he saw Chaim coming and taught his children to cross the street also. If Yussel saw Chaim walking toward him on the boardwalk, he'd turn around and walk fast in the other direction. If he saw Chaim's old Chevy station wagon parked near the beach, he'd drive home. But now that Yussel didn't move from his house for all those months because of his parents' tzuros, his children didn't bother crossing the street when they saw Chaim's children. Instead, they all walked away together. Worse, his wife, his own Shoshanna, would stop on the sidewalk and speak with Chaim's wife, Ruchel. Yussel would watch them laughing, nodding in agreement, exchanging things, kissing each other on the cheek. But worst, ten times a day, Chaim himself walked by Yussel's front door and waved energetically each time, as if they too were best friends. And Yussel, behind the drapes, the shade, hiding, would curse Chaim. "I'll get you in the bathtub." Or, "Your teeth should be like stars and come out at night."

Yussel sat in his three-story house and spoke only when necessary. No one reached him on the phone. His clients were happy because the Angel of Death wasn't knocking on their doors to sell them insurance.

Shoshanna answered the phone and took the messages. "Asher says your father told him once that on Rosh Hashonah, HaShem determines how much money you'll make for the next year. So if it's all set, he wants to know how many hours a day should he work this year."

"Tell Asher I don't make loans."

"Levy wants to know if he'll break his neck at Aspen."

"Tell Levy in the tables at Aspen Mountain the odds are one in fifteen hundred. One in ten if he eats pork." The last part was a joke. Levy didn't get it.

"Is he that *one,* he wants to know."

"Shoshanna . . . tell him . . . oy . . . to leave me alone."

"Levy," he heard Shoshanna say, "the Rabbi says simply 'only you will know that.' And be sure there's a minyan in Aspen."

"I didn't say that, Shoshanna."

"You should have."

He could see his father and the girl in his mother's bed where he'd slept between them as a baby. He could see his father davening on top of her, their arms and legs spread in a star, the sixth point thrusting the mysteries of the universe into her. "What did you call me, Shoshanna? Rabbi?"

"You are, aren't you?" Later she brought him coffee and two of the rugelach her mother made, sat beside him. "Remember the day you brought Schmulke to cheder? His first day, when he was three? We cut his hair. The teacher put a dab of honey on the book and he licked it off so he'd know learning was sweet. You came home, your face was like the sun. You looked exactly like your father."

"I look like my mother's side, the peasants. My father's side looks like kings."

"I mean your eyes, your mouth. For a minute you looked just like your father."

"Poor Schmulkele, learning isn't so sweet. Look what it did to my father's stomach. The bee gives honey but it also stings."

The first girl they'd brought Yussel to marry was as tall as his mother. She was also the daughter of a rabbi and very pretty in a big healthy generous way. She wore a flower in her hair. Yussel turned down the arrangement immediately. He wanted someone shorter. His parents shrugged, brought in Shoshanna. Yussel agreed immediately. He saw his mother give his father a look, ignored it. How should he have known then that it wasn't short he wanted; it was control.

After a while he stopped speaking to Shoshanna, spoke only to his children.

Some of his friends with whom he'd gone to Seminary wrote letters begging him to take care of himself, to maybe stop selling insurance, to become a real rabbi, have a real congregation, that's why he was in such bad shape. Maybe because it's in his blood, he shouldn't fight it. Once a Fetner, always a Fetner. His father wrote, left emergency messages on the service. Yussel didn't answer. His bills were paid every month. He never paid interest on his MasterCard. His wife ordered two eighteen-hundred-dollar jackets from the Soho designer Linda Evans took from. He sent a thousand dollars a month to his mother in Haifa. She was very bitter, but her stomach had settled. Everyone sent in their premiums, most increased. Yussel ordered a 450 SL for Shoshanna from his friend Bernie, the auto broker. Yussel watched from the living room window as Shoshanna picked up Chaim's Ruchel, helped Ruchel shlep groceries from the trunk of the gleaming new car. Yussel's screen showed Chaim looking out his window with envy. Yussel didn't mind. When Yussel was unhappy, it felt good to have other people unhappy, except for his family. His father used to say, "If you could feel about other people the way you feel about your wife and kids, you'd be a saint, like your ancestor Elimelech, may he rest in peace." Yussel was exceedingly careful not to feel that way about other people. Shoshanna would tell Yussel when his father called that his father was well, that his father was happy. Once in a while Yussel broke his silence for his father's calls. "Ask my father if his flower child is happy." Shoshanna shushed Yussel, bubbled on to his father.

"He wants to see you, Yussel. He says you should come out soon."

Yussel froze, got a cramp in his stomach, saw them in the bed, returned to his silence. He studied the stock market. He invested in a Tofutti brownie cheesecake you can eat with meat, a Ben & Jerry's, waste removal plants, cheap haircut chains, walnut trees, crypts, sent a form letter out to his clients advising them to increase their household liability. All but five of his clients mailed in the papers and he mailed papers back. But he didn't speak, except to his children, at night, to tell them a story, to ask about school for the girls, Yeshiva for Schmulke. He wouldn't let his children suffer. Shoshanna was a different story. She wanted him to be a rabbi. Her parents were after her to get after him.

In the spring he knew something was about to happen, but when the screen became clear before his eyes, he blinked and made it go away. He did not do prophecy. Also he couldn't tell what was prophecy and what was fear. Finally, just before Passover, he flew out to Kansas City to help his father make shmura matzoh in the oven in the backyard, to help cook for Pesach, to fight with him about his mother. "How could you do it? What kind of man are you? You give everyone everything, nothing to her. All she wanted was a door."

His father rolled the shmura matzoh. The two men rolled, cut, washed, sanded the rolling pins, rolled, cut, washed, sanded the rolling pins, timed the eighteen minutes between this dough and that dough, yelled "L'Shem! Matzoh! Mitzvah!" to each other, in loud voices, long into the night. They stood before the flaming oven, pulled out the baked matzohs, dropped them into straw-filled boxes. Their echoes could be heard at the 7-Eleven. And they yelled at each other. "Why?" "How?" "What is intended? To do what you *want?*" Yussel had not seen the Flower Child yet. He had seen a white blouse in the laundry that was printed with large black ants, three inches long, her ants. His father must have sent her away when Yussel visited. Yussel didn't want to see her. He'd been seeing her in his head since Hanukah. The hippies were everywhere in his father's house. They didn't look in his eyes.

His father bent to the oven. Flames danced on his face. Yussel saw his father's face melting like wax. Weeping, he said to his father, his hand on the infant-thin shoulder, "Why do you fight with me, Totte?"

His father pulled out a large, round matzoh, dropped it into the straw, looked at him in surprise. As his father turned, the fire of the flames slid from his face and the cold of the moon spread wax over it. His father said in Yiddish to the sky: "This son should not understand everything I have in my own mind? This son who need only ask that it be revealed and it is revealed, even more than for myself? *Why* do I fight?"

"Yes."

"We're here to save souls, Yussel, to kindle sparks, to bring the world closer to the Creator. You and I come from a dynasty of holy men, of souls so kingly, so intelligent, so keen, we get killed for it. Why do we fight?"

"Yes. Why?"

"Oy, Tottele, selling insurance isn't good for your mind."

"Why? You fought with my mother and you fight with me. All your knowledge, you couldn't make peace in the family?"

"Who learns from peace?"

"We couldn't discuss things? Other families discuss things."

"Yussel, what happens to you when we fight?"

"I get cramps in my stomach."

"If it was only in your head, you wouldn't remember it so long."

His father was right. The question so torments, only the right answer brings relief to your gut. "Okay, me you're teaching. What about Mom? Why do you fight with her?"

"I'm marrying again."

Yussel turned his back. He wept and saw himself reflected in the picture window, the moon over his shoulder. He was young, rich, strong, and he wept. What should he ask for? What could be revealed to him that would help? "Why marry? Why embarrass

Mom? My accountant says if I'm going to fly it or drive it I should rent it."

"So?"

"So maybe you could just rent, Totte? Not buy?"

"This is what you learned from me? You should go to Hell, Yussel. This is a lovely human being."

"So is my mother."

The world revolved around his father. His father could make it stop, start, change directions. His father fought with God over His decrees, shook his fist at Him on Yom Kippur in front of the whole congregation, accused God of being a bad father. If his father wasn't fighting with God for his people, he was fighting with his people for God. He was always alone, always fighting. His father said that when a Jew knows the universe and how it works, knows the Creator and the Words, knows the Torah, he isn't a victim of the stars. He makes them move, sometimes. Sometimes he can figure out how things happen. Sometimes they show beforehand on the screen. His father didn't mean go to Hell the way ordinary men meant it. He meant go to Hell so you can learn from your errors.

"You're telling me I should go to Hell, Totte? I'm telling you, you're going."

His father handed him a matzoh from the oven. It burned Yussel's fingers. "Yussele, the fires of Hell are only the shames you've created for yourself in your lifetime. I have no shame, Yussel."

"You should." Yussel took his airplane ticket from his pocket.

"If I should, I would. And you? Shoshanna says you aren't nice to your neighbor, Chaim."

"He's a user."

"Aren't we all, Yussel, aren't we all?" His father dampened the flame. They went into the kitchen to wash their hands. "I said I'm marrying her. I sleep every night in Babe's old garage, not under the same roof. I have nothing to be ashamed of."

Yussel said nothing. He handed his father a clean dish towel. He knew exactly what his father would say. His father knew he knew but said it anyway. With a shrug, as if he were throwing something away. "The first marriage is not made in Heaven. Even so the stones of the Temple weep when there is a divorce. The second marriage, that's made in Heaven."

As his father said Heaven, the screen appeared for both of them. Yussel saw his father in action with the Flower Child. Maybe that's what his father saw also. They both blushed, turned from each other. "I need a cup of coffee," the Rabbi said to Yussel.

"It's bad for you."

"If they tell me I'm going to die by fire, I don't have to worry about water."

Yussel pounced. "You've been to the doctor?"

His father said nothing. Yussel followed him inside. The hippies were back. Greasy knapsacks and rotting sneakers filled the foyer. His mother's wallpaper was flocked with chicken fat. Dead plants were lined up under the dining room table. The drapes his grandmother gave to Yussel's mother were black at the tops from Sabbath candles, memorial candles, holiday candles. His father sat at the dining room table, rolled beeswax candles from slabs of wax. Yussel thought his father was mad, holy, a genius, an ass. He hated him, he loved him. His father's face lit up at something behind Yussel. Yussel froze.

The Flower Child was buxom, succulent, might have once been Christian. Everything was as he had imagined. She came in with a tray of brownies and coffee in Styrofoam cups. She looked him over carefully, the way a woman looks at a man. He didn't like women who made him feel like a man. He only liked men who made him feel like a man. She laid her arm over his father's back. His father took her hand, lifted it off himself in the presence of his son, gave it a pat. She giggled, then spoke to the Rabbi with a little lisp and a very slight English accent. "I'll be right in the kitchen if you need anything. You're warm enough?"

His father said to Yussel, "Some people in this world know they are angels, that they are here to give. This is one of those people. Except of course for her temper and her little crises. Now, sheine maidela, pretty little girl, go keep busy while we talk."

She gave him a slow sweet dimpled smile. There was something absolutely childish and beguiling about her. She put the tray down and left. Yussel and she were the same age. He should not look at her, ever.

"She's not such a flower child," his father apologized. "She just acts like one."

Later she set up an easel in the dining room, hummed little waltzes, painted cats with a large Japanese brush in great confident strokes.

YUSSEL COULDN'T forgive his father for what he'd done to his mother, his mother for what she'd done to his father, both of them for what they'd done to him. He'd never be a rabbi as long as he lived.

"It is more true . . ." His father exhaled, looked at him over the rim of the Styrofoam cup, and Yussel knew he'd read his mind. ". . . It is more true that you will never be a rabbi as long as *I* live."

Yussel was used to this. His mother knew when it would rain. His father never called into his room when he was masturbating, which was a sin but according to his father, to the horror of everyone in the Yeshiva, was perfectly natural for a young boy. Yussel bent his head under the weight of his father's words. "HaShem should give you long life, Totte."

His father rolled another candle, kissed it when its shape was finished. So did Yussel. His father rocked his head side to side. "I've already had a long life," his father said, shrugged, his neck disappeared, his shoulders covered his ears. "Come here, Tottele." He blessed his son and touched his forehead with his finger. Yussel felt the fire of his father's eyes burning into his own. "I speak your name twice, Yussel. The first time I talk to you, to your animal soul. The second time I talk to your Neshama, your higher soul. Yussele, Yussele. As long as I have, I have." He smiled up at his son. "Go back to your wife, go back to your clients, protect the widows and the children. Protect the trust funds. Say hello to your mother when you talk to her. Tell her I'm okay. Tell her I'm even a little happy."

"I can't tell her."

His father shrugged again. "She'll know without you. Save your money from the phone calls."

"You should be ashamed."

"If I should, I would. HaShem doesn't make mistakes."

"Men don't?" Yussel smoothed the plane ticket on the tabletop.

His father's voice was soft. "You're going back then?"

Yussel nodded. "First thing in the morning."

"You want to come sleep in the garage with me? I made a nice little place."

"I'll sleep here on the couch."

"You'll come back soon."

Yussel didn't know if it was a question or a prophecy. He didn't want to know. "Even if you die, I won't be a rabbi. You understand that?"

Deep in his own chest, Yussel felt his father's sigh.

EARLY IN THE morning he rose from the couch, stretched, walked toward the night-light at the bottom of the stairs in the narrow hall leading to the bathroom. She was just coming down the stairs. They met at the bottom. They were less than a foot from each other and there was no place to go. She gave a startled "Oooh!" Then she smiled a sweet sleepy smile at him. Yussel was in his pajamas and very embarrassed. They stood there for a moment, both not knowing which way to move. She smelled of baby powder. Without her makeup, without her scarf, she looked much younger. She had a huge old-fashioned head of hair, all ringlets and curls and tumbling darkness around a sweet wide-eyed small-mouthed pale face. She looked like the girl on the couch in some famous painting. She looked like someone you feed chocolates to. "Oh, my God. I didn't know anyone was here!" She grabbed a shawl from the closet and threw it over her head. Yussel smiled. He couldn't help smiling. If he had been awake, he wouldn't have smiled or even looked.

"You have your father's smile," she said.

Yussel stood there at the bottom of the stairs by the night-light, trying to remember the painting, trying to wake up. She took a step one way, he took a step the other way. They kept shifting but couldn't get past each other. She wore the strangest pajamas he'd ever seen. Unless they weren't pajamas. They were yellow cotton printed with black guns. She wore a loose white sweater over the pajamas. Her toenails were polished pink. Yussel cleared his throat, determined to say something, like, "Your turn." But she flung her arm out to her side, toward the bathroom, and, like

Charlie Chaplin, danced a little two-step, crossed in front of him, and went into the bathroom. She closed the door behind her. He heard her lock it, heard her turn on the water so he wouldn't hear her. He went back to the couch until he heard her flush, unlock the door, heard the bare feet with the pink toenails padding softly up the stairs. He called after her, "A religious woman doesn't leave her bedroom with her head uncovered."

"And a religious man doesn't look."

The bathroom smelled of baby powder. Yussel stayed up the rest of the night. He could understand why his father would want such a new-age fairy-child. He couldn't understand what the fairy-child could see in an alte cocker like his father. He couldn't understand that wordless gesture of apology for her weakness, that she must do something human like using the bathroom in the middle of the night. He could understand why the Federation kicked his father off their board.

HIS FATHER'S Honda had 110,000 miles on it, was peeling and rusty. He called it the Shanda, which meant the shame. They drove it to the airport. His father ran a stop sign, a red light. "She's a good girl."

"You should rent."

A jeep with college kids swerved away from them, screamed to a dusty stop in a 7-Eleven parking lot. "You almost had an accident."

"Everything's intended. I can't have an accident."

On the highway, his father wouldn't yield to the oncoming traffic; trucks peeled around him.

"I'm not so well attached, Totte. Slow down."

"Maybe you want some insurance, Yussel?"

"Me? What for?"

At full rattling speed, his father, ignoring an oncoming cement truck, turned to Yussel. "Moving is expensive. It's like a fire."

"I'm not moving. I like the ocean. By the way, I left an envelope next to the telephone in the kitchen."

"So, HaShem provides."

"*I* gave it to you, Totte. It's *my* money. *I* earned it."

The Rabbi looked at his son in astonishment. "My river is mine and I made it? Where do you think you got it? HaShem gives. He also takes."

Yussel looked out the window. The sun was rising on his face. He didn't want to hear how HaShem takes. Gelt, gilt, and guilt. At the airport, his father handed him a brown paper bag of beeswax candles. They kissed each other's cheeks, hugged, cried. The other red-eye specials stared, smirked, pointed them out to each other: the two Jews in the long coats, beaver hats, the old one in cowboy boots.

SHOSHANNA WAS shopping for duvets and drapes on Delancey Street with Ruchel. She'd left a note in Yussel's study. "Your father called, very excited, and said you should come quick."

"I just got home," he said to his father on the phone.

"Come quick."

"You okay, Totte?"

"It happened, Yussele. It happened. I heard from HaShem."

"From who, Totte?"

"HaShem. Yussel, I heard! You must come."

"Did He, blessed be His name, did He tell you when . . . you uh . . ."

"No, Yussel. The message was for you!"

It was three in the afternoon. Shoshanna would be back because the kids would be coming home from school. "Could it wait until tomorrow, Totte?"

"Yussel! Shame!"

"I haven't slept."

"Yussel, your father hears from HaShem and you haven't slept? You'll have eternity to sleep. And pick up some Chinese? The little pancakes with the plum sauce, chicken."

One thing, they didn't lie to each other. They never lied. He didn't change a thing in his suitcase. He laid the beeswax candles on the kitchen table, said a prayer for his journey, and left. A message for Yussel. Don't fly? Get plenty of sleep? Your father is going crazy?

His uncles were wrong about the drugs. His father was no less sane, no more sane than ever. Yussel said evening prayers in the back of the plane. A lot of people watched in case he was a hijacker.

His father's first words when Yussel stepped from the cab: "You should take all your money and buy land." Then: "You brought the Chinese?"

"What?" Yussel handed him the plastic container.

"In Kansas."

"HaShem knows from Kansas? How did he say Kansas in Yiddish?"

"Hebrew."

He saw the Flower Child slip up the stairs. Coffee bubbled in the kitchen. The drapes were down. New ones were up. They were Shoshanna's, from the dining room. Shoshanna was in cahoots with this. Yussel was furious with Shoshanna. The dead plants were gone. New ones blossomed brightly. His father looked worn. There were crayons on the floor. His father ate moo goo gai pan, glat kosher.

"I didn't hear Him. The words came. 'He should take all his money and buy land in Kansas.'"

"God help me. Totte. Totte."

His father shrugged. His neck disappeared. Then his father turned on his eyes and looked at Yussel and he felt the eyes burning. "I work all my life. I pray. I live in poverty. I study Talmud, Nietzsche, Carlyle, anything that might help the shmegeggies. I turn my pockets inside out for them. I lose my wife. I love. I give. I wait. And finally . . ." his voice thundered, roared with power. "Finally, Yussel, I am given illumination. Yussel, illumination. Yussel, I heard." His father danced. His father stretched his thin arms above his head, his forefingers pointing to the ceiling, and danced to God. His feet didn't touch the floor. He wept; he sang.

"I am given as Abraham is given, the Voice of the Lord, and I heard Him and He tells me my son should take all his money and buy land in Kansas with three palm trees and a tent." His father dropped into a chair. His chest heaved. "And my son, the insurance salesman, doesn't believe me."

"You saw?"

"I saw light."

"You heard?"

"Only in my head." His father threw himself at Yussel's feet, clutched Yussel's ankles. "I trembled. I fell to the floor. My stomach burned but I think that's my prostate problem. I, oh, Yussel! Yussele, I heard." The Rabbi wept. He loosed Yussel's ankles and buried his face in his hands and wept and his hands trembled and he hit his head against the floor next to Yussel's feet.

Yussel rubbed his beard. "When?"

"Last night, when you left."

"When?" Yussel saw it all on the screen. "When, Totte?"

"With her."

"With her?"

"What can I tell you?"

"I don't want to know, Totte."

"But you know."

Yussel sat on the floor and stroked his father's head. "You spent a lifetime praying and it happens . . ." Yussel shook his own head. "With a woman? You think it's *because* of her?"

His father sat up and leaned against Yussel's back. They spoke away from each other, slowly.

"I don't know."

"It couldn't have been with Mom?"

"She didn't give me backrubs. Also I'm now married to this one. A month."

Yussel felt his father pull himself up, watched him walk to the picture window. With his back turned, he shook his head slowly. Yussel decided it wasn't a good time to ask about the crayons. He was embarrassed for his father.

"So, tomorrow morning we go look for the land, Yussel."

He was worried for himself. In his wildest imagination he could not imagine this. "I should move to Kansas? I should take all my money and buy land? I'm not going to." Yussel felt something pressing on him, squeezing him like an olive. It felt like time. "I don't tell you what to do, you don't tell me what to do."

His father sat down against him. He could feel the old knots of his father's backbone pressing into his own strong back. "He says you should. All your money."

"He says?"

"Bite your tongue."

"I'll sleep at a motel. How could you marry her?"

"It's not up for discussion."

28

3

THEY DROVE around the block, around the causeway, across the river, out of the city. Factories gave way to airports, to silos, to nothing. They took matzohs, herring in cream, herring not in cream, hard-boiled eggs, jars of borscht, a bottle of schnapps, thermoses of water, school lunch packs of tuna fish you can pull open like a Coke can, cold meat loaf for sandwiches.

"Three tents and a palm tree?"

"Three palm trees and a tent."

"Egypt. He wants me to buy Egypt."

All the farmers in Kansas had emptied out their barns and spread the winter's collection of manure across the plains. The sun beat down on it, steamed off. Great brush fires burned far from the highway. Lightning split the sky. The highway wavered and swam before Yussel like a serpent. "Did He say coconut palms or date palms?"

His father shrugged.

Miles later, Yussel said, "Maybe He doesn't know from Kansas. Maybe He meant Kuwait."

"Three palm trees and a tent." His father sang Polish Army marching songs, kept time with his fist on the dashboard. They zigzagged around the state for three days. The signs weren't good. "Don't worry. If it's intended, we'll find it." And he closed his eyes. "Relax."

Yussel couldn't relax. "Don't give me *intended*, Totte. Please."

"You hear about your friend Mayer Pinsky, who messed around with his models and got cancer of the testicles?"

"Totte, I'm doing this. I don't want to hear anything else, okay?"

"And Rudi Gernreich, who designed the topless bathing suit, he didn't die of lung cancer? And Malcha Lieberman, who had an illegitimate kid? And the kid grew up, goes to find her mother, but Malcha won't see her? Six months later, guess what kind of cancer Malcha gets." His father slapped his thigh with great satisfaction. "Uterine. Why the uterus? To remind her of her daughter. That's how HaShem works. Intention. No accidents!"

"Please."

THEY SLEPT IN the car, washed up as well as they could in gas stations and Pizza Huts. His father swiped Sweet 'N Lows every place they stopped. The Shanda trembled above forty-five. Yussel trembled but for him it was anger. All my money. Two million. He was personally worth two million. Nothing, as far as he could see in the flat baked horizon, was worth—could cost—two million. The whole state? Then they came to a mountain range. Two. One on one side, one on the other. Yussel didn't like the looks of the mountains. The air was thin and dry. Sand chipped away at the windshield. It was no place for palm trees. He had a feeling they'd been climbing, although the road was flat and straight as a ruler. Like heads, tumbleweed rolled across the highway. Jewish heads, exiles, rootless, fine-boned heads. There was nothing to hold on to out here, nothing for comfort. It was all too big, too quiet, too goyishe. Now and then Yussel passed a bone-white tree, a vulture nest, nervous grasses by an irrigation ditch. They came to a historical marker. HERE CORONADO, SEEKING GOLD . . . Yussel couldn't read the next lines.

The mountains looked like construction-paper scenery ripped out of the flat earth, went on forever.

"Okay, Totte, let me give you one. Last week Berel fell on the way to the office, broke his leg in four places. When he got to the office he found someone had robbed it over the weekend. How do you explain that?"

"Easy. There's a piece missing. He was going to take a trip that week; the plane crashed, but he wasn't on it because of his leg and his cash flow."

"How about Betty Weinstein? Betty Weinstein never sinned in her life. Nothing bad went into her mouth; nothing bad came out of her mouth. Her husband and children were happy, well, prosperous. Betty gets breast cancer. The doctors said she ate too much dairy. Do the rabbis say she deserved it?"

"If your platform was higher you'd understand why Betty Weinstein suffered."

"Why?"

"I don't know. My platform isn't high enough."

Yussel jammed on the brakes. "Yeah, Totte, well how about Hitler? What was God's intention?"

"Some people," his father said softly, "some people say we shouldn't have gone to Palestine, we should have waited for the Messiah before we went back to Israel. I wonder about that." His father poked him in the ribs. "But listen, how about Chernobyl? Thirty miles away is Babi Yar, the mass grave for thousands of Jews murdered by the Russians. The nuclear plant blows up and gets the children of the murderers of the Chernobyl Jews."

"Totte, the fallout also went to Sweden."

"So they must have had some Jew killers left in Sweden."

This was an old argument. It was a mistake to get started. Yussel tried not to yell, tried to sound patient. "My company doesn't cover acts of God because no insurance company can come up with statistics, probabilities about acts of God. You can't be rational about acts of God."

"I'm not talking about rational. I'm talking about how He works. After five thousand years, we can figure out how He works."

"The fallout landed on Sweden, not because that's the way He works. Because that's the way the wind blew. Period. Random."

"So Who makes the wind blow?"

"I'm arguing with a wall."

"If you knew how to listen, I wouldn't be a wall. We going to start driving soon? I don't have so much time." His father coughed once, hard, wiped his mouth with a stained handkerchief, slept with his mouth open.

Later his father yelled, "Back up. Back up!"

Yussel thought he was going to get another lecture. He jammed on the brakes, backed up along the highway in a cloud of dust, and when the dust settled he was looking at a roadside inn called the Arizona. Three palm trees were painted on its window. His father turned off the ignition.

"Baruch HaShem, palm trees."

"No tent." Yussel turned on the ignition.

His father turned off the ignition.

Someone had scrawled *Closed* under the palms. Yussel shook his head, just sat in the car, shook his head. "Can't be. No tent." Yussel turned on the ignition, put the car in forward, took off.

"What are you doing?"

"Goddamnit, I'm leaving. I'm taking you back and I'm leaving. What am I, some kind of Isaac you're going to sacrifice in the wilderness? You, some Abraham who promises to kill your son?"

"I heard Him!" His father's voice thundered. "I heard Him!" His father started to weep.

Yussel backed up, turned off the engine. From behind the Arizona, a ragged, small, filthy Indian weaved toward the car. He wasn't drunk. He walked in another pattern. Yussel couldn't tell what he was.

"You folks wanna look the place over?"

"Yes," snapped the Rabbi. "Yes, yes, yes!" And leaped from the car. Yussel began to sweat, to sweat seriously. The Indian examined the beards, boots, and beaver hats. The long coats in between didn't catch his attention.

"Beaver?"

"New York." His father skipped behind the Indian.

"Figures."

They walked around the Arizona, his father skipping, Yussel worrying already that his father's enthusiasm would triple, quadruple the price. They came to a tent. The Rabbi punched Yussel in the ribs and then coughed on the dust rising from their footsteps. A milk snake the width of Yussel's muscular forearm slithered into a hole beneath the tent. Ahead of them lay nothing. Flat dusty nothing, some scrawny wind-twisted pines like bushes, knobs of cactus, gashes in the land. Far in the distance three peaks towered above the land.

"Holy land. When world comes to end will be lake."

"No kidding?" Yussel was being polite for the Indian, critical for his father.

"Those mother mountains. Here is sacred lake beneath our feet. When world comes to end, you have water."

They walked around although there was nothing more to see except the snake holes as large as grapefruit and the scratchings of a clawed animal against the boards of the Arizona. The Indian bent down, smelled the ground beneath the claw marks. "Cat! Big. Big cat."

His father fell to his knees, thanked HaShem. His father really knew how to negotiate a deal. Yussel could hear the adding machine clicking in the Indian's head. "So, you want to buy whole reservation?"

"Whole reservation?" Yussel choked on the dust.

"You got two million?" Something was out of synch with the Indian's teeth. Yussel felt faint. His father continued to pray on his knees.

"That's too much, huh? You wanna look inside?" Indian Joe made an arc with his arm as if the Arizona were the Taj Mahal. It was a long building, with a front door, a side door, a dumpster.

Yussel said, "I don't want to look inside. Also, I don't want to look outside."

Indian Joe weighed this. "I know you're the right people soon as I saw you. I know. These people I sell sacred land to. Okay with my tribe, all yours. And you got water. No one else for miles got water. Fifty thousand acres, maybe seventy-five thousand. This land . . ." The Indian walked over to talk to the Rabbi. He knew a good customer when he saw one. "This land belongs to all of us. This land is Mother Earth." His father stood.

Yussel put his hand on the Indian's shoulder. "So, tell me, Cochise . . ." His teeth were very expensive. ". . . if this land belongs to all of us, how is it you're asking two million bucks for it?"

"Commitment. You give me two million bucks, I know you're committed to Mother Earth."

"Yussele," the Rabbi whispered in his ear, "think of the wilderness and Who is exiled in the wilderness and Who do we do the commandments for to bring Her back to Him?" Yussel didn't know his Kabbala well. But he knew he was hearing the real mysteries. "Think, Yussele, think. Think Moses, Yussele, leading his people to the Promised Land."

"Yeah, Pop, think Abraham, sacrificing his own son in the desert."

"Shame, Yussele."

"We don't have water until the world comes to an end, Totte."

"So, then it will be worth a fortune."

"Sure, Totte, and when they get rapid transit out here, we can all retire."

Yussel grabbed his father's arm. The father and the Indian grinned at each other. The Indian picked up a feather and stuck it into the brim of the Rabbi's hat. "Eagle."

"Eagle," his father repeated.

In the car, Yussel handed his father his Swiss army knife. "Here, slit my throat now. Tell HaShem you'll sacrifice me. Forget the ram. Slit my throat."

"Sacred land, Yussele. Three palms and a tent, Yussele. You could mortgage . . ."

"I'm not doing it!"

"Yussel!"

"Did He tell you what I need it for? Did He tell you why?"

"I should go back and ask? He told me, Yussele. He spoke to me and told me. Intended is intended." His father had a coughing fit, let his head drop on the back of the seat, slept. Yussel drove back to his father's house. Something told him he'd have to buy cowboy boots for Shoshanna. And then he hit his fist as hard as he could against the dashboard. "No!"

In his sleep, his father said, in Yiddish, softly, "I told him. It's okay. Not to worry." Hours later, just as they passed under the light a block from his father's house, his father stirred, whispered faintly in Yiddish. "He's a good boy. Not to worry."

Yussel slammed the door of the car. He was inside the house with the Flower Child in front of him, wearing the white blouse with the three-inch ants, with her luminous eyes examining him when he realized his father was still in the car. They both raced to the car.

_____

34

THE FLOWER CHILD called the Burial Society. Yussel called his mother in Israel. She already knew. The Flower Child answered phone calls, gave people directions to the house. The Flower Child threw her arms around Yussel, wept against his chest. He shoved her from him. She sat huddled in a corner, weeping until he yelled at her to answer the phone and make coffee and do things.

"What things?"

"Things!" he screamed.

"What?" she screamed back.

Yussel called his mother in Israel and asked her what the Flower Child should do.

"Yussele, put her on the phone." His mother was also a saint.

There are some things, Yussel told himself, which exceed our earthly emotions. Death is one of those things. His father's feet were very large. They stuck up. He bathed him, right side, left side. He thought there was a smile on his face. One of the members of the Burial Society said it happens as they stiffen. Yussel was certain he saw a smile.

"Why not?" the member answered and went for more water.

Yussel looked down at his father. There it was again. They said his feet didn't touch the floor when he danced. They said he was a saint. They said he did prophecy. He said he heard the Voice of HaShem. Yussel was thinking his father had some kind of joke, was laughing at him, dead, laughing at him. He looked for the last time on his father's face, pulled the shroud cap over it, broke down.

SHOSHANNA CAME with the children. She took one look at the Flower Child and for some reason Yussel would never understand, unless his wife also was a saint, or women had secret understandings men would never know about, Shoshanna put out her arms and held her to her bosom. Chaim and Ruchel flew out. The world came. Yussel was so tired he couldn't see straight. He spent most of his energy avoiding the Flower Child, in his head, in the kitchen, in the dining room.

AFTER THE FUNERAL, Yussel called his attorney, his accountant, his broker. And then he told his Shoshanna.

"I'm not sure. We may have to move."

She raised her chin high. "I am proud to be a woman in your family. I will do what is to be done."

"This family? This family is crazy, Shoshanna. Sick, from generations, sick."

"Your father was a saint."

"I'm not."

She shrugged. "You could be."

"The snakes are the size of my thigh."

"Yesterday you said forearm."

She looked like his mother. Would he ever hear HaShem's voice with her? He saw his father's back at the window. He saw the slow sad shake of his head. He kissed his mother, his sister, his uncles, good-bye at the airport. The next day he flew home to Far Rockaway to the three-story house near the beach. From there his uncles questioned him closely. Gimbel, Dean of Humanities at Brown, and Nachman, Dean of Law at Yale, and Moses, at Oxford in Abnormal Psychology. They had a conference call.

"He said he saw light?"

"Yes."

"Not lights?"

"No, light."

"And he heard?"

"No, he heard, but didn't hear. His body was about to break."

"And there was a language?"

"Hebrew."

"And physically?"

Nachman from Yale hung up when he told them when it had happened. Moses from Abnormal Psychology said it was all right what happened and when.

Gimbel said, "If Abraham can hear Him when he's killing his son, certainly when a man and woman are loving each other is a far better time."

"How did he tell you, Yussel?"

"He wept and held my ankles and kissed my shoes and begged me to believe him."

"Did you?"

"Moses, don't be a fool." Nachman was back on the phone. "What choice did the kid have?"

36

Yussel's uncles offered money.

"It isn't the money. I don't want to live in the wilderness. I don't want to be a rabbi."

In the silence, he could hear them shrug.

"Look," Moses' voice was calm. "If you don't do this, could you live with yourself?"

"Yussel, you don't have to answer him . . ."

Yussel knew the answer. But he said, "I could try, Uncle Moses."

"So try," Gimbel decided. "Give it till Shavuos. Then you do it or you don't do it."

"Sit on it," Nachman said. "As they say."

So Yussel sat. He read books on restoring the desert. His father's learning-disabled called him every five minutes, wrote him letters, those that could write. When they called, he'd say to Shoshanna, "Tell them, when I come I'll be there. No sooner." And he sat. And when the lawyers read to the family his father's pathetic will, there was a terrible line in it. "And to my only son, Yussel, I leave my heart."

4

YUSSEL DOUBLED his coffee intake, went up to two packs of Chesterfields a day, played handball right after lunch, ate pastrami on rye with Russian dressing, rugelach by the pound, chocolate cheesecake, all the cholesterol he could find. He thought maybe he was trying to kill his heart. When there were still no shooting pains up his arm, no shortness of breath, no fibrillations, he shouted to the bedroom ceiling: "What do you mean you give me your heart? What do you mean?"

Then it began. First a letter came from a friend of Ernie the out-of-work bricklayer. "I am writing this letter for my friend Ernie he wants to know if he can build a house, not too big. So when he goes there he has a roof." Someone had signed it with an *x* in ink, tried to erase the *x*, drawn a circle in the inky schmutz. Yussel had Shoshanna write a letter back saying that the deal wasn't made, don't spend your money, he hadn't made up his mind.

A second letter: "My friend Ernie says he built the house already."

"Where does Ernie the out-of-work bricklayer get money to build a house? How does he build it in a week, ten days? What's happening?" Anxiety, irritation, no shooting pain, no blue in the fingernails, no shortness of breath. Shoshanna wired Ernie at the Rabbi's shul, care of the Flower Child. "Please explain."

And a penciled letter came: "I'm writing this for Ernie. He built the house, not too big, so when he goes there he has a roof. Also two others."

And from Grisha, his father's sidekick: "Dear Yussy, We have a real problem. There is a person lives above us by the name Lillywhite, up in the hills, not exactly the mountain, and she has a sound system. It plays music like an orchestra and she sings along. It isn't right that we listen to her. The sound comes right down on our heads. Yesterday I called the Saguache County sheriff and he said there was no such thing as a noise ordinance, but he called her up and then he called me up and said she said to leave her alone. So I explained to the sheriff how it's against our religion for a man to listen to a woman sing, so he said he'd call her again, but we should know he's heard she dances naked in a room full of books, so we shouldn't expect much from her. So then he called me back and said he told her about how it's against our religion and she said, according to the sheriff, that's why she's singing. Exact words, you should know. So maybe she's even Jewish? Everyone's stuffing their ears with cotton and those little things swimmers use but it doesn't do any good. She also sings terrible. Bing Crosby, the Mills Brothers, sad stuff. What should we do. Grisha. P.S. She turned it up louder. It just comes right down here, the sound, her singing. Please answer asap."

YUSSEL WROTE back, thanked Grisha for his concern, wondered if he was still playing solitaire, wrote a check for a thousand dollars, told him to order a sound system himself and play "Hatikvah" until it drives her out of the hills. Ernie called to say he found some Jewish aerobics music but what should he do about Shabbas. Is it better to play or worse to listen? Yussel told him to turn it off on Shabbas but have everyone sing loud, and hoped it would be okay. Ernie said it depended on how the wind blows off the mountain.

Yussel couldn't understand why they were already out there. The land didn't belong to them. He called Grisha. Grisha explained that Indian Joe invited them, told them it was just a matter of time before the deal went through, told them the land needed religious people to live on it. Yussel told Grisha he should be prepared to leave. He had no idea whether he was buying it or not. Which, after he said it, made him realize that now he was seriously debating the purchase. Before, it was an absolute no. Then a letter from Natalie. Could she maybe make some curtains for the Arizona? Then the Flower Child called Shoshanna to ask her to please make him make a decision because everyone was driving her crazy and she personally didn't know what to do. Also there was a problem with money. Yussel sent her five hundred dollars and stayed up half the night wondering about the crayons, which had just entered his head like bullets, all of them, reds, blues, greens. He didn't answer the Natalie letter. He called the insurance company home office and asked if he could take a leave of absence for a year or two, what would they do about his home territory. Could he keep it and come back? Neighbor Chaim wanted to discuss buying homeowner's policies from Yussel. Yussel refused to do business with him. Yussel was fighting with the Burial Society. They wanted to move his father's body to the Arizona, maybe near the mountains or onto some high ground near the road.

YUSSEL DREAMED a dream about the Flower Child. In the dream he followed her into the bathroom. For three days afterward he didn't drive his car, something could happen to him for such a dream. He called his lawyer. It was his right to leave the body, of blessed memory, where it was as long as he was paying the plot upkeep. Then the lawyer called back. "On reexamination of the will, it is duly noted that the deceased wishes to be interred. . . ." Yussel chewed a handful of Maalox tablets. His heart attack went away. He called his Uncle Moses. "I'm surprised, Yussel, that you are acting in this self-destructive way." Yussel hung up. He felt a little pain. Nothing shooting, nothing biological. When you bequeath, you bequeath! He flung a fist at the ceiling. How could he curse his father when he should be praying his father's soul higher and higher with each word he uttered? Nevertheless, he cursed. And then something strange happened. His heart told him to invite Chaim for Saturday lunch. "No!" He banged his fist on his desk. He called Chaim.

"It's about time."

Yussel kept his mouth shut. Chaim came from morning services at his shul. Yussel walked with Schmulke from his uncle's shul, a half-hour on the boardwalk. Very slowly. Chaim came in a gorgeous blue satin caftan. He had brought Carmel wine over before the Sabbath. Yussel didn't bring it out.

"Something's wrong with my wine, Yussel, that you don't use it?"

Yussel's children and Chaim's children looked at one another in some silent agreement.

"I drink only Kedem."

Chaim blanched. "This week I told my congregation about interpreting dreams." He went solo until they sat down. Chaim started in again, expounded on Kabbala.

Yussel, with an eye on Shoshanna, interrupted Chaim. "That's the sort of thing you aren't supposed to teach to more than one person at a time, Chaim."

"It's a new age, Yussel." Then he asked himself questions and answered his questions until everyone left to wash. After Yussel made kiddush, with the wine and the challah, he took Shoshanna into the kitchen and said, "Make him leave."

"You invited him."

Yussel and Shoshanna whispered, snarled together.

"Litvishe gangsters, Borough Park bagmen, refugees from the Satmars, rejects from the Lubavitchers. The original anything-anybody-ever-said-bad-about-Jews-is-true guys. That's who he has; that's who he is. And I should sit with him? At my table?"

"Fancy people come to him, from the Upper East Side they come, professionals."

"His court, Shoshanna. I'm talking about his court, his inner circle, his goniffs, his thieves, who murder one another for the crumbs off his plate, who feed him grapes, suck the bones from his fish, brush him clean, run for his cigarettes. If his yarmulke slips off, they put it back on."

"This is the way they treated your ancestors."

"Chaim's a nobody. He has no line. You know what he is, Shoshanna? He's Father Divine with Jewish room service. You've seen some of the wives?"

"They're very frum."

"Converts."

"So? They raise their children right. They keep kosher. They observe the Sabbath. What's so bad?"

"Not a spark of Jewishness in them. Denise and Wanda became Zipporah and Rivkeh. They change their names, buy wigs— they're Jews? No inclination to Yiddishkeit, no spark. Sexy shicksas the goniffs wanted. Too stupid to be even kapore chickens, Shoshanna. You know where they find them? When they deliver traif meat to Catholic nursing homes on Staten Island. They take home the Polacks who work in the kitchen and wear nets on their hair. And Chaim converts them, makes them Jewish so his criminals can reproduce. That's what's sitting out there at my table I have to be nice to. Scum. Saloon boys." Yussel's voice rose. "You hear about his mixed mikveh, men and women together in the pool before Shabbas? You hear about that? Together? Undressed?"

"Together? Undressed?" Shoshanna's face went white. Then she caught herself. "That's just gossip. Ruchel never told me such a thing."

"You think he'd tell his wife? Hah!"

"Number one, Yussel, if it's true, which it isn't, you should help him, guide him. Number two, such words should never leave a rabbi's mouth."

"I'm not a rabbi."

"You're a Fetner."

"Whose side are you on, Shoshanna?"

Shoshanna put her hands on her hips.

"Your hands light the Shabbas candles. I love your hands. Your hips make me children. I love your hips. But your mouth, Shoshanna, God protect me from your mouth."

"Then tell me, Yussel, why does Chaim have such a big congregation?"

Yussel shrugged. "He's charming when he wants to be."

"He's brilliant and he has power."

"Yeah, well he uses it wrong . . . he uses it for his own benefit."

"And which is better, using it wrong? Or not using it at all, like you?"

Sometimes Shoshanna saw things too clearly. Yussel felt pain.

She saw his pain because she took his hand in her own and led him from the kitchen. "He's insecure." Shoshanna was taking a psychology course in the mail from Empire State College. She wanted to be a social worker. Maybe Chaim was her first client. "He's trying to impress you. He's lived next door seven years and you haven't ever invited him. Also who are you to criticize him? When you have a congregation, then you can criticize."

In the dining room, Chaim, Ruchel, all the children were wreathed in smiles. Shoshanna smiled too. There was something going on among all of them. "I hate the guy," he whispered to Shoshanna. She smiled benevolently at him. Yussel passed a plate of cholent. He put it in front of Chaim, who pushed it around with his fork.

"You lose something, Chaim? A tooth from too much smiling?"

Chaim looked at Ruchel and then at Shoshanna. Now Yussel was certain they shared a secret. "I don't eat lima beans," Chaim explained.

"Oh."

It was a long incoherent lunch. After sponge cake there was a moment like a thud in the attic: both families stared at Chaim as if he should make a speech. Finally, Shoshanna said, "Go on, Chaim, tell him."

Yussel was ready to kill his wife. Ruchel said, "Tell him, tell him."

Chaim stood, cleared his throat, put his arm around his wife, which made Shoshanna draw in her breath sharply, and put on a wedding cake smile. "We purchased a house."

"Yes?" Yussel responded politely. He would even wish them well, to get them out of the neighborhood. Him and his hippie, new-age ideas. Banjos in the shul. The mixed mikveh he wasn't so sure about.

"Near yours!" Ruchel said.

Shoshanna giggled. Yussel felt everything in him tighten. This is what comes from dreaming of the Flower Child. This conspiracy between my wife and my enemy. Maybe Chaim with all his hockma with dreams and magic, maybe he's making me dream this Flower Child dream to weaken me. Chaim's eyes were squeezed almost shut, his shoulders raised as if for a blow from Yussel.

Shoshanna said, "Oh, that's wonderful! Isn't it wonderful, Yussel? Near us."

"Shoshanna, Chaim lives *next door. Already.* How much nearer can he get?"

Chaim laughed. Ruchel laughed. Shoshanna laughed. They were giddy like kids with their laughter and their secret. Yussel drank his coffee, one cup, two cups. Chaim sat there with his eyes pinched, his shoulders raised. Yussel sat spellbound. Shoshanna poured into Chaim's cup, but her eyes were fixed on Yussel and the coffee flowed out onto the linen tablecloth. She wiped it up with seltzer.

"So, ask, Yussel, ask." Chaim was ripping at a fingernail with his teeth, viciously. When he removed it, he put it in his pocket to burn at home.

Chaim, Yussel said to Chaim's fingernails, I hate you. I'm sorry I invited you into my house. "Ask what?"

Ruchel exploded. "Ask *where*!"

All the faces, his wife's, Chaim's, Ruchel's, were raised expectantly. "Come on, Yussel." Shoshanna stood behind him, her hands on his shoulders. She had such little pink hands. Was she dumb or mean? Chaim was playing tricks with her mind. He was capable. "Ask," she whispered, and squeezed. She never touched him in public. What was breaking loose here? New age? New age, I'll give you new age. "Okay, okay. So." Yussel leaned back in his chair, took a deep breath. "So where did you buy a house, Chaim?"

"Out there."

NO MATTER what Shoshanna said, no matter how Chaim pleaded from outside the door of his bedroom, Yussel would not come out. He heard hushed whispers, at last the front door, the screen door, footsteps on the sidewalk. Shoshanna didn't come in. Yussel beat at his heart. It remained whole.

IN THE MORNING, Shoshanna said only, "Next to you is miles away from the Arizona. In a town. He paid a fortune for it."

Yussel shouted. "What do you want from me? All of you. What

do you want?" He knew Shoshanna knew he was not shouting at her. At the world. Never her.

At the dining room table, Yussel buried his head in his hands and wept. Shoshanna and the girls watched him. Schmulke leaped around the table in new cowboy boots. "What do you want?"

Shoshanna touched his arm. She was frightened and he was sorry. The look on the girls' faces made him sorry also.

"What should I do, Shoshanna? What?"

Shoshanna stroked his arms. "It's simple. It's simple. Do what's in your heart."

He hit his forehead and his heart with a fist. His head rang with the impact. Shoshanna took the girls to school in the car.

Yussel called Bernie the auto broker, ordered a bus.

"A bus, Yussel?"

"A bus, Bernie. Sleeps eight, two sinks, two refrigerators, like the rock stars have."

"You have a lot of company coming? You're parking it on the lot?"

"To drive to Kansas."

"Kansas?" Bernie started to laugh.

"We're leaving right after Shavuos."

"Listen, you want the back window should have a picture of the ocean?"

Yussel hadn't realized he was leaving the ocean.

THAT NIGHT he heard someone downstairs, late. He found a black man with a ring of keys, a flashlight in his pocket, a ski cap in May. "Welcome," said Yussel. "I own nothing in this house. Everything is yours."

The thief looked at him, shined the flashlight in Yussel's face.

"You crazy, man."

"So you shouldn't sin. If I tell you everything is yours, then you haven't stolen anything, so when you die . . ." But the thief was already gone in whatever way he'd come. Yussel could not believe he had done such a crazy thing. He decided not to tell Shoshanna. She would be scared. Also for other reasons he would not tell her. He went back to bed. He thought thoughts, his thoughts thought thoughts, he slept. His father came to him. He was wearing silk charmeuse pajamas in black-and-white zebra stripes, over them a silk charmeuse quilted smoking jacket with a shawl collar. The smoking jacket was leopard print in black and red.

"YUSSELE, DO YOU remember the story about the hiccups?"

Yussel remembered. In the morning he wished he'd asked about the pajamas.

"You drive, Yussele."

Yussel drove. They were in the Shanda. His father held his beard with his right hand, laid his head back on the headrest. "When my grandfather of blessed memory was a teenage boy, his grandfather was a great rabbi, with a big court, horses, servants, a chair of gold. So great, hundreds, thousands came to him with their troubles, with their requests, a marriage, a son, a cow sick, even Gentiles, once a count with a barren wife, which is how we finally got out of the country and came to America. Everyone came. But mostly it was the poor, his Jews, who came. Crowds of them. Such angst, Yussel. Such pain his people gave him. One day my great-great-grandfather of blessed memory he got the hiccups. The Great Rabbi. For days. Nothing stopped the hiccups. He couldn't eat, drink, sing, pray. So he agreed to go to Kiev to the University where a learned professor was curing hiccups. My grandfather of blessed memory who could speak Russian went along to help because the Great Rabbi couldn't speak Russian.*

"The professor said, 'Tell your grandfather to take off his shirt.' He told his grandfather and he took off his shirt. 'Tell him now to sit still no matter how this hurts.' The grandfather nodded. From behind the Rabbi the professor heated an iron until it was red-hot. And he touched the Rabbi's back. The Rabbi didn't move. But still he hiccupped.

"'Tell your grandfather I'll try again.'

"'Grandfather, he'll try again.'

"The Rabbi nodded. This time the professor heated the iron until it was white-hot and touched the small part of the Rabbi's naked back. Still the Rabbi sat and said nothing.

"'Tell your grandfather he's a remarkable man. Just before he *came, a Cossack came, also with hiccups. When I touched the Cossack with the red-hot iron, he screamed and jumped from that window and ran away half-naked into the snow. There's his coat and shirt. With white-hot, your grandfather sits still, makes no sound. Doesn't he feel the pain?'*

"So my grandfather of blessed memory told his grandfather of blessed memory what the professor had said. 'The professor thinks you're a remarkable man. A few minutes ago a Cossack sat here and when he felt the red-hot iron he jumped out the window and ran away. There's his coat and shirt. But you sit still and make no sound. You don't feel the pain?'

"When the Great Rabbi heard this he said to his grandson, 'So. Tell the professor his pain is nothing compared to the pain I feel every day from my Jews. That's pain.'"

In his dream, Yussel shook his head.

"Yussele, tell me, do you feel pain?"

"No way, José," Yussel lied. "I'm not a rabbi."

"You don't feel pain even for poor Chaim and his envy eating him alive?"

"No."

"Aha."

That was all his father said. *"Aha."*

"It's not written against pleasure, is it, Totte?"

"No, but how does one distinguish pleasure until one knows pain?"

"I'm not buying."

"Believe me, you will." The Rabbi sighed, peeled an egg, threw the shell pieces from the window. *"It's in your blood. Pain, rapture. You don't remember from your blood?"*

Yussel knew the message. Eggs you eat for mourning. In his dream, his father mourned because his son felt no pain. "I never asked, Totte, did he get cured?"

His father shrugged. *"I don't know. What I do know is he never got rid of his Jews and when he died they followed him to Heaven, still to torment him."*

Yussel woke up in a cold sweat as if a great fever had broken in the night.

5

SHOSHANNA AND Ruchel made lists, brought home library books about the Wild Wild West for the children, shopped for denims, made orders, spent, spent, spent. Chaim took his court, his ten men, flew them west, left them there to get things ready. He didn't say what things. Ruchel told Shoshanna. Shoshanna told Yussel. Yussel didn't want to hear what Chaim was doing. Yussel saw on his screen a yellow sky, a salt-encrusted landscape. Ruchel told Shoshanna Chaim had eighteen houses already, a regular neighborhood, and Yussel better buy quick if he wants anything decent before the houses are all gone. Shoshanna noodged Yussel to call Chaim to find out about houses. "Just in case you change your mind, Yussel."

"I told you already. You'll live in my father's house. It's only for a year. We'll drive the three hours to the Arizona for holidays and Shabbas. That's why I'm buying a bus, so we can sleep at the Arizona on the bus."

"Please, Yussel, just in case."

All week Shoshanna begged Yussel to call Chaim. "Just call and tell him to keep an eye open."

"I don't want to get involved with him with money. It's a bad combination. The man is like death, he can't get enough. Also I don't want to live in his neighborhood. He has the only minyan in America that's on parole."

Finally she cried; finally he called. "So, Chaim, I hear you're buying a lot of real estate out there."

"Yeah, yeah, a regular neighborhood."

"Shoshanna asked me to call maybe you saw something she'd like just in case. A two-story with plenty of bedrooms."

"They got a two-story out there. It's the old whorehouse. By the dump. Nobody wants it. You can still see the numbers on the bedroom doors. It's got a lot of bedrooms. Ha ha."

"Well, if you hear of anything. And the prices?"

"High, low. Six families I had to make rich. They loved me."

"And twelve you had to make poor, they hate you?"

"Anti-Semites."

"Chaim, we have to live out there."

"They moved." Yussel could see Chaim shrug. "Listen, Yussel, before you make your judgments on me. First I offered everyone forty grand. Okay? No one would sell. They didn't want Jews. So then I offer six of them a hundred grand. That they can't refuse. So then the other bloodsuckers want a hundred grand. So I wait. I string wires so we can carry on Shabbas in the neighborhood and I wait."

Yussel had a headache slicing from above one ear to above the other. He pressed his forefingers into the pain, held the phone with his chin against his shoulder. "Go on."

"They complained about the wires. They complained how we dress, how we don't say hello, how we talk a foreign language, how we leave the garbage outside the wires on Shabbas, how we throw stones at their dogs who pee on our lawns, at their wives who walk around in front of us, up and down, in pants yet. They made a lot of trouble for us. Finally they took what I offered and left."

Yussel thought maybe he was allergic to Chaim. His head pounded. "How much?" Blood would soon gush from his ears.

Chaim mumbled, "Twenty-five." Then he blurted out his excuses. "But it averaged out, Yussel. It averaged out to a fair price for everyone."

"You squeezed them out?"

"They didn't like living near Jews."

"You forced them from their homes?"

"They haven't forced us? For two thousand years they haven't forced us from our homes?"

"HaShem can take care of His own justice. He doesn't need you."

Yussel wanted to hang up, go to the mikveh and purify himself, take a handful of Maalox. His heart made him continue. Someday he'd get even with his heart. "Chaim, where do you get such money? That's maybe five grand a month in mortgages, a big nut to crack, Chaim. There's no jobs out there."

"I'm setting up computers so we'll have jobs."

"Malcolm Forbes adopted you, suddenly you have for eighteen houses and computers?"

"HaShem provides."

"Yeah, He also provides pogroms, Chaim."

"I don't see it that way. Also I'm not asking you for advice. You called *me!*"

"For that I'm sorry." Yussel conquered his heart and slammed down the receiver.

He told Shoshanna she'd have to make do with his father's house. She might have been unhappy. He didn't know. He didn't care. Probably her mother was pushing she should have a nice house, be a rabbi's wife. Yussel was busy figuring out where Chaim could get so much money, where his goons could get so much money. Eighteen houses and a main-frame empire. The schlemiel.

Chaim called back. "Ruchel says you told Shoshanna I was playing with fire. I want to know if you really are worried for me. I would like to know a Fetner is worried for me. It would make my heart swell. Also, I have to tell you, it came to me in a dream I should buy the neighborhood, so what could I do? A dream's a dream."

"I hate to disappoint your heart, Chaim, I'm worried about myself, that what you and your zoo do out there I'll get punished for."

"You're calling my court a zoo? At least my people pay me a salary. Who did your father have? Certifiables who couldn't scrape two pennies together. That's what you'll have."

Chaim was still talking when Yussel slammed the phone into its cradle.

HIS UNCLES came, wished him well, blessed him coldly. His Uncle Gimbel from Humanities took him aside. "Get yourself a rich congregation, build a fine synagogue on the best side of town, make a place for yourself in the Rabbinate, write articles for *The Observer*, travel, make speeches, get respect, write best-sellers on why smart people die. Your father of blessed memory killed himself with his radical shtick. You don't have to grovel, Yussel. You don't have to host the halt and lame of the universe like your father did. You don't have to reinvent Judaism, rewrite the Torah. You understand? You don't have to do what your father did."

This Yussel understood.

His Uncle Nachman from Law took him aside. "You don't have to sacrifice yourself. Your father was a little crazy sometimes."

"He was a saint, Uncle Nachman, a zaddik."

"So where is he now?"

Moses from Abnormal Psychology joined them. He lit a cigar, blew the smoke to the ceiling, spoke with consideration. "We're all saints. But your father, tackeh, he was crazy."

Nachman finished the advice for them all. "Look, just don't get involved. You feel you have to go out and help, get his congregation on their feet, okay. But don't get involved the way your father did."

Shoshanna came in with a tray of coffee and chocolate-covered mandel brot. Her face was small with fury. "Leave him alone. He knows what he has to do."

They all left without taking a sip of coffee, a crumb of cake. Yussel stood over her shoulder as she poured the coffee into the sink. "A year, Shoshanna. A year. That's all. Don't expect any more from me."

THAT NIGHT his father came again to him in a dream. Yussel had been lying in bed listening to Far Rockaway. He heard ocean, the clang of the buoys, the long cries of silver-tipped gulls, a girl screaming "Tony!" under the boardwalk, sirens. He was comforted by the sounds. He fell asleep thinking how much he loved Far

Rockaway. His father was wearing vanilla silk pongee pajamas under a mandarin-collared quilted vanilla silk pongee robe. They were in the Shanda again, on the highway, in the desert. They passed the sign about Coronado. Yussel read the first line, still couldn't read the second. Kansas was too quiet. He was eating a meat loaf sandwich as he drove. A bit of aluminum foil stuck in a molar.

"I came to tell you a story about your great-great-grandfather, may his soul rest in peace." Yussel's father held his beard with his right hand. *"He had in his congregation a very rich Jew, a Jew so stingy he used other men's handkerchiefs. With a wife so terrible he wouldn't wish her on his enemies. Cold, mean. One day near Rosh Hashonah the Jew goes to the Rabbi and says, 'Rabbi, I want you to say a prayer my wife should die in a year.'*

"The Rabbi, you can imagine, is shocked. 'I can't do such a thing.'

"'Rabbi,' the Jew pleads. 'She won't give me a divorce. She never cleans, cooks. She never gives me to eat what I like. She shrieks at me day and night. Please, Rabbi, I can't bear her anymore.'

"'Impossible.'

"'I can't go on. I'll kill myself or her.'

"The Rabbi thinks hard. 'The Talmud says if a man pledges charity and doesn't make good on his pledge, someone close to him will die in one year. So make a big pledge to the shul and don't pay. In one year, she'll be dead.'

"Of course the rich Jew pledges a thousand rubles, what does it matter? He dances home he is so happy. When he sees his wretched wife, his face breaks into a smile. He sings songs through a miserable supper of groats and watery soup. Once he notices she's looking at him. The next day she makes a delicious kugel. Weeks pass. He sees a gorgeous dress in a shop in Kiev. He thinks at least she should look good for him and at the end of the year he'll find a pretty young thing to wear the dress. His wife is very surprised to have such a gift from him. Now his pillows are fluffed up. She makes strudel all the time. His house is clean. A few months pass. He sees a gorgeous diamond ring in Kiev. A ring is an investment. In a year he can sell it maybe even for more than he paid. So he buys it. She kisses him on the cheek. She dances around the house in her new dress with her new ring. The house sparkles like the

ring. She looks younger than he remembers. More time passes, win-
ter, spring. He forgets the pledge. He thinks of nothing but this
lovely human being who cooks wonderful food, brings in fresh flow-
ers, sweeps ten times a day, warms his bed. And then suddenly it's
Rosh Hashonah and he remembers the pledge. He runs to the shul.
'Rabbi, Rabbi, what should I do? I don't want her to die. She's my
life!'

"'So pay the pledge.'

"Without thinking he pays the thousand rubles, an extra five
hundred just in case.

"'You see,' says the Rabbi, 'now you're not only like a bride-
groom, you are also a generous man.' You see," Yussel's father con-
cluded, although Yussel knew the conclusion, *"Perception creates*
reality."

Yussel pulled the dream car in front of a dream Texaco station. His father got out, stretched, bought a Hershey's bar with
almonds, swiped some Sweet 'N Low. *"You'll feel better about this*
once you get started. So, listen, get started."

"What's to listen? I'm doing it, aren't I? Right? Right." In his
dream he was surprised at his own anger. "The feelings I can do
without."

CHAIM RETURNED. He brought home cowboy hats for his children
and for Yussel's. He was full of himself. Yussel wouldn't listen to
him. Yussel was going to leave right after Shavuos. The day before Shavuos, Yussel packed the bus. Both families stood around
the bus while Yussel packed. Ruchel gave the kids a box of
Raspberry Joys for the trip. Chaim nailed a mezzuzah to the front
of the bus and stuck a HONK IF YOU LOVE JESUS bumper
sticker to the back. Yussel didn't think it was funny. Everyone
else did. "It came to me," Chaim explained, "that you should have
protection."

"Funny, Chaim," Yussel said from the corner of his mouth so
Shoshanna wouldn't hear. "It didn't yet come to *me* that I should
have protection, particularly from *you.*"

Chaim spread his hands. "A dream came to me that you needed
protection. A dream's a dream."

"Don't put your dreams on me. Do you hear?"

"Okay, Yussel, okay." He stretched out a hand to say good-bye.

Yussel mumbled something, refused Chaim's hand. Yussel took his client list, their phone numbers, addresses, the deeds to the Arizona, put them in a briefcase, slipped the briefcase under the front seat. Schmulke wanted to wear his Darth Vader suit on the trip.

"No."

"Why not, Totty?" Schmulke hung on him.

Yussel had a lot of things on his mind. Yussel had to take the SL to Bernie who'd promised to sell it. Then he had to make out the lease for their beautiful three-story house near the beach. He was ripping up roots. Why did he listen to his crazy father? A man could be crazy when he's dead as well as when he's alive. Also it was possible Chaim did have a dream that they would be in danger crossing the country. Sometimes dreams don't predict events but create them. Yussel knew Schmulke was upset, didn't want to hear his tzuros, his troubles. Yussel had enough of his own. The answering service wanted him to call two clients who were having an argument over next season's skirt length. The home office said if the new agent replacing Yussel worked out, the territory belonged to the new guy. They offered Yussel a territory in Kansas, which was worth beans.

"Why not, Totty?"

"You can't wear your suit because I said no. And I'm not going to argue with you because you can argue the schmaltz out of a matzoh and I haven't got the strength for that today." Yussel wondered what Chaim had dreamed, whether he should ask him. There was a midrash about a dream that created danger. Twice a woman went to a rabbi and said she dreamed her house burned down. Twice he told her she'd have a baby. Twice she had a baby. The third time she had the dream she went to ask but the Rabbi wasn't home. Some kibbitzers in the Rabbi's house told her the dream meant her husband would die. Her husband died. The Rabbi found out and told them they'd killed an innocent man. Dreams have power. Now Chaim has a dream that Yussel needs protection. Yussel felt his kishkes turn over. What was ahead for them all? Maybe Chaim's making danger for Yussel like the kibbitzers did for the woman?

"Totty, there's no schmaltz in matzoh."

"Right, Schmulke. Think about it."

"*Why* can't I wear my Darth Vader suit?"

"Because we Yiddehlach are strange-looking enough without bringing along Darth Vader."

"Why are we strange-looking? Maybe they're strange-looking?"

Yussel sighed and sat down on the steps of the bus. Shoshanna brought him iced tea and said he should have shook Chaim's hand. He told her he didn't like his business of dreaming and manipulating people. Yussel took Schmulke on his lap. "Schmulkele, out there it's a different world. You know that. When your grandfather came to America, they called him an Oriental, like a Chinaman. Those who stayed in Europe, they called them junk people and killed them. Here they call us Christ killers."

"They're all dumb anyway. Every shaigetz is a moron."

"They teach you that in Yeshiva?"

"It's true. Everyone knows." Which meant no, they did not teach that Christians were stupid. Maybe they taught that Christians had no souls, which was just as bad.

"That kind of talk is going to get you in trouble out West."

Schmulke looked at him crookedly, climbed from his lap. Yussel wondered what was coming next. Every generation increases its perception, but they don't learn any better to live together. Schmulke, if it were possible, was a tougher kid than Yussel had been.

Yussel could feel Schmulke rummaging around in his Talmudic head for an angle. He had to have a Kissinger for a son.

"Look, Schmulke, Tottele, out there you don't rub that you're different in their faces or they could rub it in your face. Don't make trouble. Cool your Yeshiva ideas, okay? We have to live with these people."

He could tell by the look on Schmulke's face that he'd found the angle. "So that's why I want to wear my Darth Vader suit so I'll look like everyone else."

"Go help your mother."

Schmulke shouted from the front porch. "I wear it or I don't go. I'll live with my grandma."

"All right, all right. If together we see one other kid who looks like Darth Vader, you can wear yours."

"She put it on top of the bus. I want it in the bus, in case I need it."

"If you need it, Tottele, you'll have it."

Yussel checked his client list, shoved it even farther back under his seat. Maybe the new guy wouldn't work out.

AT THE REAR of his great-uncle's little shul in Arverne, a rat hole of a town up the beach, Yussel sat in the weak sunlight filtering through dirty windows. He sat on an oak bench sculpted from wear. Columns of dust hung like searchlights. There was an old smell of incense, smoke, mildewed prayer books. A samovar bubbled in the hallway. The caretaker, who knew him from the day he was born, greeted him. This caretaker, in Liga, when he was a boy, as he was marched off to the camps, he saw his father's head in a butcher shop window. Yussel sat in the dark, wove the letters of one Name of HaShem with another Name of HaShem, something he'd learned from the great-uncle. Yussel didn't ask HaShem for any favors, like messages, foresight, revelation of danger. He knew if he asked, he'd have to pay back from his heart and he didn't want to start that kind of relationship. It was the first step to circumcising your heart. When something came in on the screen, something that would protect his wife and kids, not even himself, then and only then would he listen.

Sacred letter by sacred letter until his breath grew short, rhythmic, he weaved, waited for the screen, thought about his ancestors, the whole line, the melancholics, the saints, the nuts. Schmulke already bore all the marks of the Fetner generations: anger, allergies, weak eyes, impatience, great generosity. Anger was the wrong word. Wrath was better. The first Nachman Fetner of blessed memory, when he ascended to a higher rung, he came down and wept for weeks. The fourth Nachman Fetner of blessed memory saw a cow's skull at a tannery, went home, climbed the stairs to his attic, and didn't come down until they carried him out of the house on the Shabbas table. It was healthier to stay off the rungs, play football, eat ice cream, marry, have kids, be a good Jew, but stay off the rungs. Maybe Schmulke should stay with Shoshanna's mother and go to Yeshiva in Toronto. Maybes,

maybes. Yussel had to start weaving the Names all over again. This time he concentrated, saw thunderstorms over a lake, decided to go by the southern route. He went home, called AAA to change the TripTik. His mother called from Haifa to tell him to avoid Chicago, also to avoid someone named Chaim.

The AAA people also told him there would be storms over the Great Lakes. Yussel marked the maps with pink underliner late at night before they were to leave. The pink underliner was almost to Harrisburg, when Dina, the eldest, eleven, soft and lovely, day by day more secretive, climbed into his lap. She wanted to see Safari Adventureland in New Jersey. She was in her pajamas with red spots of sleep on her cheeks. "Lions, Totty, monkeys, zebras." She rocked on his lap, chanted baby dreams, reminded him he'd already promised he'd take her and he'd forgotten and she'd never have a chance to go to Safari Adventureland again, that he always promises, always forgets. He carried her up to bed. "Lions, monkeys, zebras," she hummed as he tucked her in. He went downstairs to his study, redrew the map so Dina could go to Safari Adventureland.

6

SHAVUOS IS A two-day holiday. On the first day the ancient Israelites brought their first fruits in seven baskets up to Jerusalem. On the second day, they sacrificed animals on the altar. In Far Rockaway, on the second day, Yussel realized he was taking his family and himself—the seven of them—and offering them up for sacrifice on the altar of his father's wilderness. He tried not to think about the coincidence. On the day after Shavuos, Shoshanna, standing behind him as he started up the bus, had to remind him. "The finest produce of your land, you shall bring to the House of the Lord your God."

"They meant Jerusalem, not Kansas. And I asked you not to quote."

"I'm a rabbi's daughter. I quote."

They crossed the bridge from Far Rockaway, left the ocean behind. Shoshanna showed pictures of lions, monkeys, tigers to the children. The baby yelled, "Ti, ti." Everyone ran around the bus shouting, "Ti, ti!" growling, roaring except Shoshanna, who sat by herself at the foldout table and rolled an apple from hand to hand.

"What's the matter, Shoshanna?"

"I have something to say you don't want to hear."

"Okay."

"Don't you think it's significant that in the month Moses went into the desert to make a covenant with HaShem, you're going out also, making a covenant?"

"You're right."

"I really think so, Yussel."

"No, you're right I don't want to hear it. Also I think it's more significant that yesterday was the day for the slaughtering of the sacrifices."

Shoshanna rolled the apple and cried. Didn't she know she shouldn't have said it? Didn't she know he hated her quoting at him? So why did she start? "Come, Shoshanna, come sit by me."

And she came to sit and he listened as she wept about no neighborhoods, no cleaning women, no wig makers, who'll teach the children, where would Schmulke go to school, what about rednecks, how would Schmulke get along. She was so sweet, helpless, had clearly contained all her worries all this time so she wouldn't bother him when he was busy, even though he had another week before he could touch her, he took her hand, held it, drove with one hand on the wheel. Why was it, the more helpless she was, the more he adored her? He couldn't imagine what it would be like to be so helpless.

The farther they were from Far Rockaway, the more cars honked. The more people honked, the colder Shoshanna's hand grew. Some caught up and stared in his window, saw Hasidim, instead of Born Agains, sped away. The kids waved, raced from window to window, made peace signs.

"It'll be okay."

"I always wanted to be a rebbitzen."

"So?"

"But with a house and a congregation and fresh flowers on Shabbas and interesting people in a Jewish neighborhood."

"You could also be a rebbitzen like my mother, leaving my father over a kitchen door."

Shoshanna ignored this. "Who will I talk to? Who will I go shopping with? My mother will never come to Kansas."

"Ruchel moves out soon, doesn't she?"

"You won't talk to Chaim. I can't have them over."

"I'll talk to Chaim."

"There's no Loehmann's. I can't buy wholesale."

"You'll fly home whenever you want, like a Texan from the ranch, to shop."

"You must think I'm so foolish, Yussel."

He squeezed her hand. Women are like another species. Their concerns are so different. He felt very sorry for her, wanted to hold her.

At the gate of Safari Adventureland, Yussel's bus took its place in a small convoy of cars, wagons, and vans. Everyone had kids inside, luggage outside. Warning signs lined the narrow dirt road. DON'T FEED THE ANIMALS. KEEP YOUR WINDOWS SHUT AT ALL TIMES. UNDER NO CIRCUMSTANCES LEAVE YOUR VEHICLE. KEEP YOUR VEHICLE MOVING. WARNING! THESE ARE WILD ANIMALS. College dropouts in pith helmets and bush jackets checked windows. Yussel pushed the forward lock. The rest of the windows snapped into place. "We'll work it out, Shoshanna. We'll add a big kitchen and family room to my father's house. You can take the kids to your mother whenever you want."

"Where will we get the money?"

"Shoshanna, believe me, if you need money, I'll get it for you. Believe me."

"Don't make promises you can't keep, Yussel."

THE CONVOY rolled slowly along the dirt road past large meadowlands. A young man in a safari hat waved at them. He had a metal hook for a right hand, a glass eye, a ponytail, a matted beard and mustache. The kids waved back.

"Is that a shaigetz?" Schmulke beat Yussel on the back. "Is that a shaigetz?"

"No, he's a Vietnam veteran."

Schmulke exploded. "Shaigetz, there's a shaigetz!"

"Cool it, Schmulke."

"Don't yell at him, Yussel. He's just a little scared."

"Monkey! Monkey!" Hanny, the middle, yelled. The kids raced to the monkey side of the bus, side to side, back and forth. The bus rocked. The monkeys were wise guys. One jumped on the front of the bus, rode the hood, looked into the window, spread his lips against the glass, kissed Shoshanna. She forgot her tears, laughed, made faces at the monkey who made faces back at her. Yussel tooted the horn to get him off, washed the windows, shpritzed the monkey. The monkey grabbed the windshield wiper, broke it off.

60

Yussel felt a cold slice of fear, like a piece of watermelon, in his chest. He didn't know from monkeys.

Hanny was the first to see a lion, very distant, grazing on flat land. The baby yelled, "Ti, ti!" Shoshanna screamed and laughed with the children.

Yussel's hands turned white on the wheel because he didn't know what to do about the monkey brandishing the windshield wiper at him. Yussel opened his window, grabbed at the furry leg. The monkey screeched. The last Yussel saw of him were his blue underparts as he scrambled up the window and disappeared on the top of the bus. Yussel could hear the click of his feet on the aluminum of the roof.

To get the wagon in front of them to drive faster, Yussel leaned on his horn. The man spread his arms. He could do nothing. There were no side roads. Once he saw a pith helmet, opened the window, yelled to him. "There's a mon—"

The guide blew a shrill whistle. "Close that window, sir. Close that window. Keep it moving."

Yussel's neck turned red with anger. "Shaigetz."

"Just close the window, Yussel. We'll be out in a few minutes."

He heard more feet on the top of the bus, running back and forth, like a basketball team. The kids started to watch the ceiling. And then he saw a suitcase descend from the top of the bus, bounce off into the New Jersey veldt. And another. And then socks rolled into balls, like snowballs they flew from the bus across the scenery, and then pieces of Calvin, Custom Shirt Shop shirts drifting, nightgowns. Shoshanna began to scream and the kids began also.

"My pink Reeboks!" Yussel did not know from Reeboks either.

"My pajamas!"

"Totty's tallis!"

"Yussel! Do something!"

"I have another."

"Mama!"

"Stop the bus! Stop the bus!"

"Yussel, do something!"

"I'm stopping. That's it!" Yussel stopped the bus, jumped out on the road. He heard the shrill blast of whistle.

"Yussel, it's against the law to endanger a life for anything less than a life. Come back!"

"Don't quote at me, Shoshanna. Don't quote." He heard the baby yelling, "Ti, Ti!" He heard the horns blaring at him. He saw the man in the car behind the bus pointing. He heard Shoshanna screaming and he looked at a very athletic rugged male lion looking at him. One small pink sneaker, which clearly was what was meant by a pink Reebok, dangled from his mouth. Yussel leaped back into the bus. Not a Daniel. Into the stricken silence he said, "It's okay. We'll buy new. It's okay." His heart demanded out from his chest but now was a bad time.

A monkey with Dina's new Benetton sweatshirt over his head swung on a tree limb along the road. Hanny shrieked. Schmulke screamed. His family clung to one another, weeping, begging him to do something. What could he do?

"We'll buy new," Yussel shouted into their noise. "Everything. Don't worry. Don't cry. Shah. Shah." He tried to be funny. "So, now everyone's seen a lion, even Totty." No one laughed.

They were almost at the exit gate when Yussel saw what could not have been his briefcase sliding down the front window of the bus and onto the ground and four monkeys surrounding it, ripping it apart, pulling out the papers, eating them. With one hand he reached beneath his seat, pulled out Darth Vader satin. Schmulke was already crouched under the foldout table in the back of the bus. Shoshanna was hysterical. Yussel knew he couldn't be, that he must keep calm and get them out, that he had to take care of them. "Don't cry. Don't cry. It's okay." His client lists. He was wiped out. Wiped out. He could not believe his son would betray him. Yussel balled up the Darth Vader suit, shot it vehemently behind him.

At the exit gate a golem in a pith helmet told him blandly that they would mail whatever they could find, that it had never happened before, that it must have been something about the bus the monkeys didn't like, and his eyes slid to the mezzuzah and he half smiled. "Maybe it was too shiny."

THE BOX OF prayer books and the underwear suitcase were untouched. "This is not an accident," Shoshanna announced with conviction. She sat under the table with Schmulke, comforting him. "This is not an accident."

Yussel said to Shoshanna, "A year. We pack up the shmegeggies, we sell the desert, we come home."

Schmulke, with a look of cold fury, came forward, retrieved his Darth Vader costume from the floor, took it back with him under the foldout table.

"He couldn't take it when I was off the bus? He had to wait until I could see?" Yussel asked Shoshanna. She shrugged.

Driving, he saw his father dead on the pallet and the smile. *"Let me put it this way, Yussele, you keep doing the right thing. Someday maybe you'll do it for the right reasons, maybe you'll feel it. In your heart."* He could walk out. He could find another life, disappear into the Other Side of sin and evil inclination where the Yetzer Hara reigned, or run off with his father's flower child, shed his clothes by the side of a reservoir, leave Shoshanna all the money, what was left after he bought the desert. "My own Schmulkele betrays me. My own son." He sounded like his father.

"Don't yell at Schmulke, Yussel. He's only trying to control things because he's scared."

And why wasn't she comforting him? I shouldn't yell at Schmulke because *he's* scared? *I'm* not scared? Chaim's dreams? Lions? My client lists gone? Maniac monkeys? Maybe intentional. "Listen," he called back to Shoshanna, "one year, one year, that's it. I'll send them to a kibbutz, I'll get them institutionalized, or I'll bury them. All of them. All my father's shmegeggies."

THEY OUTFITTED the kids in a Sears Roebuck near Harrisburg. Dina turned her nose up at everything. Shoshanna said the quality was terrible. Yussel said not to worry, nothing had to last very long. Schmulke kept his Darth Vader suit on, agreed to change his underwear. Hanny, the middle, was already sneezing.

Abe and Berel had left urgent messages with the answering service. Yussel finally reached Berel at 5 A.M. They were fighting about next season, midi or mini. What did Yussel see?

"I see nothing. I'm in the basement of General Lee's Headquarters in Gettysburg. It's dark."

"Abe sees only the midi. I told him in one season the midi killed more Jews than Hitler. I can't go along with the midi. What do you see for next season?"

"Berel, a religious man doesn't make immodest garments for women. A mini is immodest."

"And a religious man has to eat, to feed his family, to dress them for the holidays."

The kids had cried all night. Yussel had decided to drive through. Shoshanna was still curled up under the table with Schmulke and he has to tell clothing manufacturers about their next season.

"Berel, make graduation gowns, wedding gowns, duvets. Make for simchas, for joyous times."

"Yussel, what do you see for next season?"

An uncle, way back, a great-uncle, could tell the meaning of the week's news from the Torah portion.

"Berel, you know the parsha for this week?"

"Sure."

"Calf."

"Calf?"

"Moses, in the desert, golden calf."

"Calf! I love you, Yussel. Yussel, I can quote you to Abe? You say calf for next season? Above or below?"

"Always better above, but not too much, Berel. Don't forget what happened to Rudi Gernreich." Yussel was joking. "You shouldn't ski if you make the skirts too short and show too much leg."

"Vey iz mir."

"I'm joking, Berel. I'm just joking."

"Vey iz mir. How do you guys know this stuff?"

SHOSHANNA WAS cooking eggs and beef strips on the bus.

"Wrong, Yussele." He imagined he heard his father. *"Wrong."*

"What did the monkeys mean, Totty?" Dina stood behind him as he drove.

"They meant we shouldn't wear label clothes so we don't call attention to ourselves, so we don't make people who don't have feel bad."

"And why did HaShem take away your client list?" Shoshanna called from the stove. Yussel sighed. It was such a deep and painful sigh, he was sorry to have sighed it before her. "Maybe he wants me to pay attention to my new clients."

Schmulke crept out from under the table.

"Was it a sign?"

"Who knows. A sign's a sign. To stop, to go on, to pay attention. I don't know."

"Zeide would know." Schmulke was coming closer.

"He was a saint," Shoshanna helped out.

"Is he in the Heavenly Court, with the angels, Totty?"

It would be a long trip. Yussel could use it to teach his children, to draw them close. He could also go crazy from having them close. He needed a cigarette but couldn't smoke because of the kids' allergies. Schmulke touched Yussel's back tentatively. Yussel jumped. "So, is Zeide in the Heavenly Court or not?"

Yussel didn't mean to yell. He wasn't yelling at Schmulke. "He's right here! On my back! And if he doesn't get off my back soon I'll stop saying Kaddish for you, Totte! You hear that? And you're gonna be stuck wherever you are right now because I'm your only son and it's only me saying Kaddish. So watch it! You hear?"

"Let's all let Totty drive." The children climbed under the table with Schmulke and played Scrabble, even Shoshanna.

Someplace at a gas station, they saw a large stuffed rabbit with horns. Hanny wanted Yussel to buy it, fell in love. The attendant said it was a Jackalope. Hanny loved the glass eyes. Schmulke said it looked like the shaigetz in Safari Adventureland. Hanny threw a tantrum about leaving the Jackalope behind. Dina drew her a picture. Schmulke ran around the bus with two hot dogs for horns. It took miles for Hanny to settle down. In Kentucky, his father sat next to him. He was wearing black-on-white polka-dot pajamas under a white-on-black polka-dot bathrobe. He had a chrome pipe through his ears and on either end of the pipe, two large doors, like wings, doors that folded on piano hinges, the kind of cheap veneer doors you buy legs for at Sears to make coffee tables if you live in a trailer.

"Kitchen doors, Yussele. What do you think?" His father knocked on his doors. *"Knock knock, who's there?"*

"Don't do that!" Yussel's hands were slippery with sweat.

"You wanna come in?"

"That's not funny."

"Kitchen doors, your mother's kitchen door. That's what they got me for."

"They didn't get you for the Flower Child?"

"You they'll get for the Flower Child."

"That's not funny."

"You're telling me."

"Is that a curse, a threat, or a prophecy?"

"Yussele, I want to tell you a little about where I am, what I'm doing."

"I don't want to know. It's not my time to know."

His father knocked on his doors, called, *"Come in, come in. Who's there? Come in. Yom diddle yom diddle ai diddle dai dai."*

Yussel was terrified. He might drive off the road. "You trying to take me with you, Totte?"

"I'm trying to be funny."

"I told you, it's not funny. A man comes back from the dead is not funny."

Hurt, his father folded his doors across his chest, lay his head on the headrest. His voice was muffled by the doors. He pushed his hat back off his head.

Yussel reached over and felt the pajamas. Silk pongee. Even in pajamas, even with the chrome pipe through his ears, and the veneer doors, he looked like a king. With the bottom of the top of his pajamas he polished a doorknob.

"You're bored up there? They don't have shuffleboard for the alte cockers?" Alte cockers meant old shitters. Yussel hoped the kids hadn't heard him.

"I come back like this to teach you, Yussele."

"It's a little late, Totte. When I was a kid and I had questions, you shoved me away with both hands."

"You didn't run with both feet?" His father drew a Q-Tip from his pajama pocket and reamed out one ear, then the other, then his keyholes.

"So, how did you take your pajamas along with you?"

"They give you, you should feel at home." His father spread his

lips backward with two index fingers and displayed for Yussel a new and pearly set of teeth. *"I know a guy he gets his own brand of Havanas. From before Castro yet and Church's shoes."*

"You eat?"

"For now. Later I won't need teeth and he won't need cigars. Just like you don't need your SL."

Yussel bit his lip to keep from responding. He felt very bad about the SL, hoped Bernie would sell it for a small fortune. "So, I take it they're pretty organized where you are?"

"Sulphur, Windex, we run out. Everybody steals the Sweet 'N Low from each other." His father cackled. *"Half the place is crooks, the other half is murderers."* Then he lowered his voice, touched Yussel's arm. His touch was like a mosquito lighting. *"Listen, Yussele, about the desert, it's worse than I thought."*

Yussel didn't want to ask. As far as he knew the dead get judged, go to Gehinnom, get a year to work out their flaws, their errors, their sins. If they work them out, they go on up to the Heavenly Court to live with the Angels and study Torah at the feet of HaShem for eternity. A son says Kaddish for eleven months to move his father up a little quicker, to earn merit for his father. Yussel said Kaddish three times a day. He was committed to take care of his father's debts, his people, his two wives. How much worse could it be? "How much worse, Totte?"

"It's not enough you bought the land. It's not enough you're taking care of my people. I had to make a deal."

Yussel's testicles shrunk, withdrew from life. "I don't want to hear it."

"A deal concerning you."

"A deal in Heaven has no authority."

"You want to test such a statement?"

"How much worse?"

His father sighed a terrible sigh. *"You do good, I go to Heaven. You don't do good, I stay in Hell."*

"Who said?"

"We're starting that business again, who said?"

"Yeah, who said?"

"He said."

"So you're asking me to die the same death you died because you got what you deserved? No. The answer's no. I'm taking care of your people, I bought the place. I'll get them settled. That's it."

His father left. Yussel took Maalox, didn't believe what he'd heard, seen, imagined, decided he'd better stop early. When they crossed the Mississippi, which everyone spelled until Yussel shut them up, even Shoshanna, who got it wrong, his father came back. *"I thought maybe you'd changed your mind about doing good with my people. I know it's in you, Yussele, all that goodness, all the sweetness."*

"I'll do what I can. If it's good, it's good. If it isn't, then I guess you get what you deserve, don't you?"

His father swung his doors, sulked. Yussel could hear the doors squeak against the pipe joint. "I guess that hurts, Totte?"

"Listen, my darling son, if they give you a choice between dying of shame and dying of cancer, any kind, the worst kind, take the cancer. Oh, Yussele, be a good boy. Do a good job out there with my shmegeggies."

Then he came back, on the hood, like the monkey, but far more frantic. *"About the Kaddish. . .you won't forget? Even if you get mad, you won't forget? You gotta get me out of here!"*

That night Yussel dreamed a strange dream. His father stood in a long line of people. He held a piece of paper. He was waiting to see the king. His father wore a silver fox coat to his ankles over black pajamas. A strong wind rippled the fur like waves. In his dream, Yussel understood that his father was in Heaven, already fighting with HaShem. He woke up happy.

7

YUSSEL TOOTED, rubbed his eyes. The yard was brown, grown over. The Flower Child who was now his mother opened the door, broke into huge sobs, and then Schmulke capped the diaspora by shouting, "Where's my real bobie? I wanna go home. I wanna go home right now!" Yussel also. He hadn't remembered how she smelled. Baby powder. Yussel made absolutely certain he didn't smile at her. Which was easy because behind the Flower Child stood a clone of Safari Adventureland man. A woman alone, Yussel heard his heart, a woman alone with such a burden. How would she manage? Yussel felt his heart turn over, forced it back in place, forced the thoughts from his head. Yussel couldn't wait to tell Schmulke that the grown boy on disconnect, with eyes frozen like the eyes of the Jackalope, lower lip adangle, hair in a ponytail, a toy car in one hand, a box of Crayolas in the other, that this person, he would use the term loosely, was Schmulke's new uncle and he would have to be nice to him. Yussel felt a rotten pleasure. "And your new grandmother."

The girls whimpered. Shoshanna tried to shush them. They clung to her skirt, hid behind her.

Yussel addressed his father. "That you should do this to my family! The kitchen doors and the pipe through your ears, they aren't enough. You hear me? They aren't enough."

Hanny, following in late, took a look at the boy and shouted,

"The Jackalope!" The Jackalope grinned sideways at her, showed her his new crayons. Yussel gripped her thin arm, held her back. Shoshanna hugged the Flower Child, hugged the Jackalope. Yussel's soul screamed. When the Jackalope touched Schmulke's shoulder, Schmulke swung around, yelled "Feh!" Yussel allowed himself a cup of coffee, wouldn't eat the strudel, wouldn't sit down. He said prayers in the basement shul. He could smell the Flower Child's baby powder wherever he went in the house.

"We'll go with you to the desert, Yussel," she said softly. "My son can run a tractor."

"No."

"He was brought up in a kibbutz."

"No."

"What do you mean 'no'?" Shoshanna asked.

"What do I mean 'no'? I mean no. She should stay here. In the house."

"I want to be where . . ." the Flower Child burst into tears. Shoshanna held her, stroked her head. Why do women cry? Why do they all cry so much? Yussel knew then that his father had already been moved out to the desert. And he knew he'd have to take the Flower Child and the Jackalope with him.

Even though the rooms were ready, Yussel said they would sleep on the bus. Shoshanna put the kids into their new pajamas, curled up under the table with Schmulke, who was very upset and hated his father forever.

"This I understand, Schmulke. Believe me." Yussel called back to him.

THE NIGHT was warm. The moon hung over the acacia tree on the corner, spread like cream cheese over the Shanda. "It isn't enough already? A half-wit?" The roots of the tree had broken the sidewalk. The Jackalope watched him through the windows of his father's house. Their father's house, Yussel reminded himself, shook his head, waved, climbed into the bus, where he fell fully dressed into his bed. Beyond, Shoshanna slept as peacefully as an angel. Such a pretty face. How could she touch that kid? Had she washed? Yussel, sleepless, sat finally outside on the steps of the bus, smoked half a pack, maybe more. A curtain drifted from a second-floor window. The Flower Child was watching him. He stubbed out the cigarette on the broken sidewalk, climbed inside the bus, locked the door softly so no one would wake up. He kept himself awake by praying. He didn't want to have any more sex dreams, not when he had to drive to the Arizona with all the kids in the bus and maybe her. Shoshanna sighed, curled up. Yussel sighed back.

The dirt road of Safari Adventureland wound before him on the ceiling. His client lists and securities drifted into the veldt with the socks. He heard monkeys on the roof, sat up so fast he smacked his head hard on the fold-down bookshelf. It was rain.

Sometime near midnight he heard his father say, *"Yussele, you gotta help. I can't stay here. It's no joke."*

FINALLY HE decided to go by himself to the Arizona. Sometime before dawn he washed, davened, made three meat loaf sandwiches, wrote a note to Shoshanna, took his father's hand-drawn map, wished he'd bought a real one. He was wiping dew from the Shanda's windows with a squeegie when the Flower Child, wearing a red housecoat with black Zorro z's all over it, the baby powder smell all over her, put her hand on his arm. Yussel warned himself not to feel anything. He felt plenty. He jerked his arm away.

"I'm family," she insisted, touching him again, hurt, whispering, secretive.

"Not by me you're family." Yussel took paper towels and Windex to the rear window. She followed.

"You aren't at least curious about me? About me and your father?"

"I already know too much."

Her voice was soft. "My first husband was a very old beautiful man. I was eighteen. He was more than seventy. We shouldn't have had a child. But I wanted to save him, somehow, preserve him, so we made a baby. I knew he'd die soon. From his deathbed, he taught our son how to daven. From his deathbed he made a miracle. But his son never could speak."

Lights went on inside the bus. Yussel fled to the passenger-side windows of the Shanda, squeegied as fast as he could. She followed.

"Our son's silence is his father's silence. When he is silent, I hear his father speaking to me. When he davens, he davens like an angel and I hear his father sing. He's a good child, Yussel, but I don't know what's to become of us. You see . . . " She made that same wordless gesture of apology for her weakness that she made the night on the stairs when she had to go to the bathroom, an apology for having to do something human, like worry about the future and a retarded son. She smiled. "There's so much I want to tell you. I feel you'll understand."

"I've got four or five hours. I better get going."

"It's much longer than that. You don't have a map?"

"What are you talking about? I'm not going to Colorado, for God's sake." Maybe the Flower Child was stupid after all. Shoshanna never ever went outside in her housecoat. Yussel slipped past her into the Shanda, turned on the ignition. He could feel the heat off her body, off his, rising like the steam from the manure the first time he took this drive with his father. He could see her on a bed with his father, bodies sweating. He wiped at his eyes with the paper towel. The Windex burned.

"What's to become of me?"

"We'll work something out. Don't worry." He'd find a husband for her, quick. Someone would turn up. Who wouldn't want to marry her?

The lights went off in the bus. Yussel roared into the Kansas night, the Shanda shookeling, losing flecks of paint like the space shuttle each time he hit a pothole. He wished he'd had some sleep, that she'd leave him alone, that he had his SL. Yussel drove west, passed all the one-diner/four-church towns scribbled on the line of his father's map. His father's hand on the map wavered like an EEG. Here and there it paused, slowed, refueled itself with some kind of power, grew more firm. And went forward. Near the destination, an *x* called Moffat, he was to look for the historical sign about Coronado. Yussel had already taken the trip in a dream, a second time in this world with his father, and now a third time. Did other men live inside such magic? He only wanted to live in a world where he could think straight, where what you see is what you get, where there are no angels in the grass.

YUSSEL STOPPED at a bakery with a counter. Mercury lights carved blue planets out of the night. A man with flour on his nose gave him coffee in a Styrofoam cup, wouldn't take money, called him Reverend, told him there had been others dressed like him passing through who would drink only from Styrofoam cups, asked the name of his ministry, his destination, handed him two fried cakes in a wax paper bag that sucked lard even as Yussel held it, examined Yussel's little map, told him he wouldn't hit the Colorado border until ten or eleven, that he'd be in Moffat about six that night.

Yussel had never been so close to such traif food. He squeezed the bag into a lump, tossed the lump onto the seat of the Shanda, thought about how you kill a dead person, cracked his knuckles twice, three times, every knuckle, wished they were his father's bones, wondered if his father had bones or what.

His father was sitting on the fried cakes. He wore elegant maroon pajamas with black fleurs-de-lys, a black velour bathrobe with smaller fleurs-de-lys in the lining, black velour mules. Moonlight shone on the doorknobs. *"Who's saying my Kaddish while you're traveling?"*

"Uncle Gimbel."

"Listen, if you don't have ten men at the Arizona, you'll go to Chaim's to say Kaddish, okay? As soon as I can, I'll get you a minyan."

Yussel grunted. "You daven alone. Why can't I?"

"I daven by myself because I want to be alone with HaShem. You just want to be alone. You'll daven in a minyan when you can. Yussele . . ." His father's fingers brushed over Yussel's shoulder *". . . even from where they put me I'll hear you when you say my Kaddish, Yussele. The angels will sing along with you. Your voice will extend to the highest Heaven, to Atzilot, it extends, when a son says Kaddish for his father."*

"Maybe." Yussel watched his father from the corner of an eye. His father held what might have been his breath. "Maybe in Colorado I don't say Kaddish for my father. A father who betrays you from the grave, maybe he doesn't deserve Kaddish." Yussel didn't know where that was written but it should have been. "Maybe you made up the whole cockamamy shmegeggieville-in-the-desert megillah."

"Maybe I'll tell your mother if you don't say my Kaddish."

"And maybe my mother would say it would take seven sons seven generations to say enough Kaddish to get you out of where you are."

"That hurts, Yussel. I love your mother."

"She said it." Yussel didn't care what hurt. He himself hurt.

"Maybe I'll tell your Schmulke on you."

"It's none of Schmulke's business."

"Hah!" That was all his father said. But he said it triumphantly.

Yussel parked underneath a plane tree. He poured water from the thermos over his hands, wrapped tefillin, put the tallis over his head, his shoulders, davened while a thin strip of pink dawn drew itself up over the horizon.

Once, when Yussel was six or seven, his father had vanished. It was Havdalah, the last ceremony of the Sabbath, when the Sabbath Bride departs. Everyone rubs a bit of the blessing wine onto their eyelids and into their pockets, so Her blessings stay with them the rest of the week. That week, when his father rubbed his eyelids with the wine, he vanished. Yussel screamed. Grisha picked him up. "Shah, shah." And then his father was back at the bimah as if nothing had happened. Yussel didn't know what he'd seen. But he did know, from then on, with his father anything could happen. And also that he himself, Yussel, could make it happen. Because the morning of the night his father vanished, Yussel had taken a dime from his sister Bloomke's nightstand drawer. So on the Shabbas, Yussel had not only touched money, stolen money, carried it outside the house, bought a Raspberry Joy, but made his father vanish because of his sin. And someday, he knew, from then on, he would make his father die. If he was a good son and became a rabbi, he'd kill him by taking his place. If he was a bad son and didn't become a rabbi, he'd kill him by breaking his heart. Either way he knew he'd kill him. That's what he'd lived with as a kid.

When Yussel was back in the Shanda, driving, his father said, *"I didn't make anything up about what HaShem told me. Maybe I was hearing things. But I doubt it very much. I think I deserve that much respect, my son should believe me."*

"I'm *doing* it, aren't I, Totte? I don't have to believe you."

In the rearview mirror the strip of sunrise, spread wider, pushed the night from the earth, turned fiery, backlit the murderous young mountains. The sky flushed rose, then peach, paler. Still there was no sun to see. As much as he didn't want to understand, to think this way, Yussel understood that the sun he couldn't yet see filled the sky with light the way HaShem, Who can't be seen, fills the world. He thought about teaching a class out in the desert, watching the light fill the sky. "No!" He heard himself shout.

"No, what?" His father cleaned both ears around the pipe with a Q-Tip.

"No whatever you're trying to do to me. No, no, no."

"Do? I came to tell you a story."

Yussel said nothing.

"You mind?"

"A man comes back from the dead to tell me a story, I should stop him? Leave out, however, Kansas, Colorado, the circumcision of my heart, my SL, intention versus random."

The Rabbi tipped his head on the back of the seat, folded his arms over his thin chest, took his beard in his right hand, crossed his doors, and spoke from behind them. *"So. Once there was this poor Jew who lived in misery. We'll call him Yitzhak Isaac. Yitzhak Isaac had a horse, a cart, an ax. He worked hard. But one day he heard the Rabbi say, 'Trust in HaShem and HaShem will provide.' So he put down his ax, tied up his horse, his wagon, went to shul, and prayed. For days, for weeks. 'Nu?' his wife screamed. 'Enough! Go cut some wood. Earn some money. Buy some food.' 'HaShem will provide,' was all he said and went back to shul. His wife had to sell the horse. Then she sold the cart. Finally there was nothing to sell. Yitzhak Isaac kept praying. And then one day there was no food and no money, so the wife left to go to her mother and took the children so there would be to eat. And Yitzhak Isaac kept praying. In the meantime, who buys the horse and the cart? A thief, a robber. He's filled the cart with jewels and gold stolen from Christians. He goes to hide the jewels and gold under a tree. Comes a storm, comes a limb from the tree, hits him on the head, kills him. So the horse, naturally, being a good horse, goes home to Yitzhak*

Isaac's house, taking with it the cart and the jewels and the gold.

"Well, after that everyone in town stops working and goes to shul to pray. The Rabbi sees this and sends them home. Why did the Rabbi send the others home? Because they already knew what to expect so their trust wasn't complete. Trust, Yussele. Trust completely. Forget the details: Kansas, Shmansas. The details don't matter. Trust, Yussele, and HaShem will provide."

"HaShem I trust. It's you I'm worried about."

His father found the Windex, polished his pipe and his doors with the paper towels. Yussel felt for his father, felt he deserved better doors, maybe walnut, carved, with a fancy brass plate and his name in script. Also a better son.

"Totte, you want to explain to me who's going to worry about the details?"

"Women." His father cackled with his joke.

"Yeah, yeah. Tell me who's going to figure out where I get the money to buy another house now that I find out the Arizona is in Colorado, twelve, fourteen hours away from the house in Kansas. Maybe I should wait for my SL Bernie sold to come back to me loaded with cocaine?"

"I don't understand, Yussele. Where's all your money?"

"My money? Of blessed memory, my money. You have a pencil, Totte? Two million for your mishugge Indian Joe. Maybe a hundred grand to pay off the personal loans you made for which the world calls you a saint. For which the banks you borrowed from call me a debtor. You know how many people I had to feed for your funeral?"

"I saw. I saw. That was something." His father, having cleaned, shined, polished himself and his accoutrements, was napping like an old lion, a little wounded.

Yussel went on anyway. "Some more for the move across country, the rest for the kids, which I won't touch. I have to pay attention to the details. But I'll manage. I can borrow. I have friends. It's only for a year."

His father stirred, smiled, nodded.

"Totte," Yussel spoke softly, apologetically, almost hoping his father wouldn't hear, wouldn't wake up. "I'm an ordinary guy, Totte. Even though I'm your son. I'm good with numbers. I sell insurance. I was once a wealthy Jew. I hope to be again. That's it."

His father snapped awake. *"Bite your tongue, Yussele!"* His father shouted, gasped between shouts. He broke his Q-Tip in three places. It was orange with wax. *"A Fetner talks like this? A prince talks like this? A man with generations that go back to the Baal Shem of blessed memory, back to David, back to Adam, talks like this? When you ask that it be revealed to you, Yussel, it shall be revealed to you!"*

"I'm not asking." Yussel winced at his own words. He was a very coarse seed.

"I'm asking." His father closed his eyes.

"The answer's no."

"It's in you, Yussele."

"No."

Yussel drove west toward the Rockies, then picked up a two-lane road following the mountains. The land dried up, flattened out, turned to burlap. Barbed-wire fences lined the road, the sun warmed the car. The morning was brilliant blue. The shadow of the Shanda slid along the land. The fourth time Yussel's father cleaned his ears, Yussel exploded with a venom that surprised both of them. "You know why a dead man has wax in his ears? You know why? Because when he was alive he never listened to anybody! He never listened then and he doesn't listen now! So listen to me! I'm not going to be a saint for you!" Yussel's veins danced against his temples.

His father looked at him, eyes widened, said evenly, *"Wax in my ears? I'll buy that. At least you're thinking like a Jew."* He shrugged. *"By your ears you have sinned; by your ears you are punished."*

"You or me?"

"Both of us."

8

NEAR THREE in the afternoon, Yussel, who was driving as fast as the Shanda would allow him, picked up a familiar line of mountains and headed southeast. Something was wrong with the time. The drive from the Arizona back to his father's house, with his father in the car, using the same scribbled map, had taken three, maybe four hours. Now, in the opposite direction—from his father's house to the Arizona—it had already taken ten hours and he wasn't there yet. Why was it taking him four times longer to get to the Arizona? Maybe his father had the Baal Shem Tov's charm for swift travel. That's how the alte cockers would explain it. They'd shrug, raise their hands, palms up. "Why shouldn't it take him three hours? Your father was a saint. Insurance salesmen it takes longer."

The road snaked as it had the last time he'd driven it. He saw a double rainbow in an orange sky. Three lakes became mirages. Three mirages became lakes. Umbrella irrigation systems spread over endless stretches of spinach fields. Warehouses collapsed beside rusted ore cars. Above the road, in corrugated cliffs, old gray timber sluiceways swung loose against mine entrances. The road pounded in Yussel's head. Bolts of pain zapped his shoulders, his neck, his thighs. At last he passed the historical marker about Coronado, backed up, pulled in, turned off the engine. The last line on the marker read: CORONADO, FINDING NO GOLD,

NAMED THE MOUNTAINS, AND RETURNED TO MEXICO.

He looked around to see what Coronado had seen. The sun crept low through the pines like an animal, hit a clearing, splashed its last rays against the flanks of the mountain range like blood, which was of course only something red in the rock. Standing right here, maybe seeing this moment, Coronado probably didn't intend to name the mountains the Sangre de Cristos. Probably he was cursing them. "Blood of Christ," Coronado said. "Let's go home. Blood of Christ, where's the ocean?" Coronado couldn't find gold, couldn't sell bananas, packed up his mules, went back to Mexico. And Yussel, the schlemiel, goes on. To what? To the shmegeggies who killed his father, waiting now to kill Yussel, and a handful of newcomers who'd learn fast how to suck a rabbi as dry as the land, spit his blood out against the mountainside, order up a fresh rabbi from the Yeshiva, put up a triumphal arch: THIS IS WHERE YUSSEL THE RABBI GAVE UP, TURNED AROUND, WENT BACK TO FAR ROCKAWAY. The Sangre de Yussel. Yussel washed his hands from the thermos, made a blessing, ate the last meat loaf sandwich, did not pack up his mules, did not turn around, drove on.

Golden aspens followed the snow-melt down mountain folds, fanned out into meadowlands, lost themselves in cottonwood groves, died alone at the edge of the high desert land.

FROM EACH utility pole along Moffat's main street, a basket of dead geraniums hung like a vulture's nest. Yussel passed boneyard railroad beds, rotted freight cars, hundreds of white-faced cows waiting in yards to be slaughtered. He thought about Auschwitz, shivered, stopped at the Texaco Station, bought two Hershey's bars with almonds from an attendant with a yo-yo for an Adam's apple, who didn't seem at all surprised at Yussel's prayer cap or beard, bought a map of the Southwest to find out where he really was, where he'd come from, called Shoshanna to tell her he'd arrived.

THE PHONE rang in his father's house. Yussel opened the map. Four states on the map had Moffats. Moffat this and Moffat that.

Especially and particularly Kansas had a Moffat. Yussel laughed. He laughed harder until he laughed so hard he had to lean against the door of the phone booth and hold his stomach. He remembered Chaim at dinner saying, "Out there." The joke was on Chaim. If Yussel didn't know the Arizona was in Colorado, Chaim didn't either. They both thought it was in Kansas. Only his father had known. So now all of Chaim's money was tied up in Kansas real estate and Yussel was free of Chaim the Parasite.

The Flower Child answered the phone. Tapioca slid through the wires. He saw her stretched out in bed, lifting her arms, reaching for the phone. She tried to make conversation. "Yussel, how was the trip? Are you okay? Are you there yet? What's so funny?"

"Get Shoshanna. I don't have much time." A Jewish man doesn't make conversation with a sex machine.

Shoshanna had to come to the split-level from the bus. He waited, hummed a table song that was once a march from Napoleon's army, "Lai lai lai, de lai lai lai." He cradled the phone under his chin, with one hand made a fist and marched on the phone book with Napoleon as he crossed the wintry steppes of Russia, with the other hand ate both Hershey's bars.

"Yussel?"

He adored Shoshanna's little voice. "Listen, Shoshanna, wonderful news. I'm in Colorado. The Arizona's in Colorado!"

"Yes?" Sometimes Shoshanna was slow.

"That schlemiel Chaim bought his eighteen houses in Kansas. Kansas, Shoshanna! He had to outsmart me, see? He had to do what I did. He should lose a fortune on it."

Her voice was very soft, very small. "Words like that should never leave the lips of a Fetner, Yussel. You're a rabbi."

"I don't want to hear what a Fetner should do or not do because you aren't a Fetner and I'm not going to be a rabbi."

"You will be for a while. I may not be a Fetner, but I have to share in your destiny." Her voice dropped to a whisper. Something was wrong. "The Flower Child thinks I should shave my head."

"Why?" Yussel didn't want to talk about the Flower Child. He could feel his breath getting short.

"She says things will fall apart with your father gone so it's up to the women to be more observant, more frum, and we should all shave our heads." Shoshanna was crying. "When she gets to the desert, she's going to make everyone shave their heads."

"Don't bother me with the Flower Child. Nothing's falling apart. I'll call you tomorrow."

"You don't have anything more to say?"

"I have a headache. I feel faint. I think it's the altitude or the meat loaf."

"It's not my meat loaf. Do you miss me?"

"Of course I miss you. What kind of husband would I be if I didn't miss you? I'll call you tomorrow."

FIRST HE smelled Lemon Pledge. Then he saw his father's huge dark eyes reflected in the phone booth glass. His father was slouched fashionably against the phone booth, hands stuck in the pockets of a gorgeous paisley smoking jacket with a fringed silk belt. Underneath he wore black satin pajamas. He had his hat pushed back, looked worried, knocked on the glass. *Be nice, Yussele. Be nice.*

And then he saw the reflection of Shoshanna's SL pull in behind the Texaco sign. And then he saw Chaim the Parasite. How did Chaim get Shoshanna's SL? Bernie sold the SL to Chaim? It wasn't just a reflection. Chaim wore a white beaded cowboy hat with a big brim, his side curls tucked away. Yussel hit the phone book with his fist. If the phone book had been a brick, it would have powdered under Yussel's blow. Instead something crackled in his hand, flew up his arm, into his chest. He cheered his heart on. Go on, attack. Better you than them. Go on.

Like a tennis champion Chaim leaped over the door of the SL, reached into the phone booth, tried to hug Yussel, tried to pull him out and hug him. Yussel gripped the door jamb of the phone booth, wouldn't budge. Yussel tried to close the phone booth door. His father pushed to keep it open. Chaim pushed to keep it open. Chaim reeked of Brut. "It came to me you would be here today. It came to me. Oy, Yussel, my friend, am I happy to see you!"

"Sure, Chaim, you must be out of blood." Yussel turned his back to Chaim, wouldn't look at him, wouldn't look at the SL.

"You promised Shoshanna you'd talk to me out here, Yussel."

Yussel smashed one fist into the other palm not to hit Chaim in the face. "I'm talking to you, aren't I? You want to talk? Let's talk about greed. Let's talk about envy."

Chaim put on his visit-to-the-dying-face: a little pain, a little concern. Everyone learned it in Yeshiva, that look. "So, these things are troubling you, Yussel? You want to talk about envy, greed?"

Yussel remembered Waterloo. The horses pounded inside his head. With whatever he'd torn up punching the phone book, his hand pounded in time to the horses. He couldn't control his face. What showed, showed. His father climbed into the phone booth. Yussel shoved past him, closed the door, leaned against it so he was out and his father was locked in.

Chaim leaned back against the door of Yussel's SL. His head was shrunk into his shoulders, expecting a blow, brows knitted, eyes pinched, shoulders tucked in. His whole body said, "Hit me." He, however, said, "I also think we should talk about charity, Yussel."

"Charity, Chaim? Charity? Maybe I should have *given* you my SL?"

Chaim wet a finger and wiped off a spot on the chrome of his door handle. "You'll get Bernie's check, you'll see. You *did* give it to me."

One move, Yussel would really give it to him. In the face. One move, maybe tipping his cowboy hat forward, maybe touching Yussel on the arm.

"You having trouble breathing, Yussel?"

"What's it to you?"

"I care. It's wrong to care?"

"It's the altitude."

"Baruch HaShem. I thought it was your asthma."

Yussel's father yelled from inside the phone booth. *"Yussele, listen. If HaShem wanted you to have the SL, believe me you'd have the SL."*

"He wants Chaim to have it?"

"If HaShem didn't want Chaim to have it, Chaim wouldn't have it."

"Don't give me your trick Jewish logic, Totte. You sound like Kissinger."

"Trick logic? I'm giving ancient wisdom, the Ari, Akiba, the Baal Shem Tov."

"Okay, don't give me your ancient trick Jewish logic."

"It's truth, Yussele. Everything's intended. There are no coincidences."

"This *universe* is intended? Hah!"

"It's truth. Hitler, hot dogs, camels. Even Chaim is intended."

"And what about free choice, for God's sake?"

"Yussele, maybe you should think about whether free choice is also intended?"

"This is no time for such a discussion."

"Sure it is. You have murder in your heart."

"Not to worry, Totte; it's intended."

"Oy, Yussele. Do we have a long way to go."

CHAIM TALKED fast. The Brut made Yussel woozy. Chaim's hands rotated in little mechanical circles as if what he was saying had nothing to do with what he was doing. "I'm laying all my cards on the table, Yussel."

Yussel hadn't heard a word. "Yeah, yeah."

"Listen, Yussel, you'll come over to my house . . ."

"I wouldn't step a foot in your house. Also I have to get back. I have problems." Yussel watched Chaim's face. First he saw pain from the insult. Then he saw pleasure that Yussel should have problems. The smell of Chaim's Brut reminded him of the baby powder on the Flower Child. An idea came to Yussel. Chaim looks at women. Yussel had seen him looking at women. Also the story about the mixed mikveh was going around. Also Yussel had to defend himself. So he would put his dreams on Chaim. Why not? Yussel didn't owe Chaim a couple of bad dreams? "Chaim, you know how lonely widows are. She's too young to be a widow. I hate to leave her alone too long."

"Filth, Yussele, filth. You're asking for it, Yussele."

"Listen, Totte. I went to Yeshiva too. To save somebody's life you're allowed to do anything. I'm saving my life. See the shrunken shoulders? That's a disguise. He's after me and I have to protect myself."

"Vey iz mir."

Chaim's mouth was open a little. "I've heard your stepmother is a wonderful woman, very beautiful."

"He drives my car, Totte. He sucks my blood. Why shouldn't he dream my dreams? Better him than me."

Yussel smiled down at Chaim. "The moon and sun beautiful. And very frum. A little too sexy if you know what I mean, but that's not her fault. She's a wonderful human being with a broken heart. I told her about you."

"I'm a married man," Chaim protested too mildly.

"Who isn't?" Yussel held his hand up. "Just kidding, Chaim, just kidding." Yussel had him. You want to talk about envy, Chaim? I'll show you envy. The horses stopped running around in Yussel's head. "You'll meet her. She'll be here. Maybe we can find her a husband."

"Yussele? It's my wife."

"Stay out of this, Totte."

"My own son bargaining off my wife? I'm hearing this?"

"Maybe it's intended, Totte, huh?"

"Gottenyu."

Chaim forgot to shrink his shoulders. He gripped Yussel's arm. "Yussel, my friend, before you go. I need some homeowner's on the new houses here. I'm offering you *business.*"

Yussel shook loose, retreated to the side of his father's car. "I don't do business with you."

"I offer you business and you refuse? You're a pig, Yussel. Who do you think you are? You wouldn't recognize charity if it danced down the street in a shroud. You with your three stories and your moss-brick and your wife and her designer clothes and your . . . your fancy name."

"And my gorgeous stepmother. Don't forget my gorgeous stepmother, Chaim."

"Stay off my property, Yussel."

"Don't cross my threshold, Chaim." Yussel climbed into the Shanda, slammed the door. The handle fell off.

Chaim picked it up, smiled. "See? A sign. You don't do mitzvahs, the Gates to Heaven are closed to you." Chaim flipped the handle from one hand to the other. Yussel wrenched it from Chaim and left.

YUSSEL DROVE for ten minutes before he looked for Chaim's house. The streets were named for minerals. He passed an elementary school, a Woodpecker's Hardware, a superette, a Rexall, a Sears, a diner, more waiting white-faced cows, a bank. Big FOR SALE INQUIRE WITHIN signs sat on the overgrown lawns of a lot of houses. Some of the signs had blue stars on them.

Chaim's SL was parked in front of the biggest house in town on the corner of Molybdenum and Carbon. New wooden fences were built around Chaim's property and a dozen other homes.

Chaim's house had red roof tiles, blue stucco walls, a kennel with an electric fence, the kind to keep schvartzes out in the city and cattle out in the country. It was a nice house, one of the $100,000 ones for sure. Yussel could no longer afford such a house. Except for the rental on his Far Rockaway house, he had no income anymore.

Yussel pushed his hat back, lay his head on the neck rest, closed his eyes. They were burning. Then he pushed his skullcap back and forth, pressed his eyes inward with his thumbs. On his screen the SL was burning, smoke, fire, fire engines lined up outside, cars with blue gumball lights, a crowd watching, a blazing red pickup with ROSEBUD painted on its door panel in loving golden tendrils, the SL melting, men running around, a sofa that looked like a grilled cheese sandwich. He thought he saw Chaim's goon, Mendl, from Rikers Island. For some reason, the firemen were standing around, drinking coffee, strangely inactive. He decided with shame that he was seeing what he wanted to see, not real information. So he shut off the screen and headed for the Arizona.

9

THE THREE jaundiced palms glowed in the dark. Red and green Christmas lights outlined the long building. Behind the Arizona rose a new cluster of snowy white tents. The flagpole clinked with greater melancholy than the first time Yussel had heard it, perhaps because under it lay a rectangle of grave marked by flowerpots and large stones painted white. Everything else was the same: brutal, isolated, bleak. Yussel switched his headlights off, then the engine.

"Yussele, your grandfather told me once about a ladder to Heaven by a little railway station in a barren field in old Russia where crowds of Jews climbed up to a fiery cloud. I think possibly it looked like this place."

He tapped his fingers on the dashboard and tried to calm his chest. A cold wind blew off the mountains behind the Arizona. On his screen, Yussel saw blizzards, a tractor in a ditch, a car stuck in the mountains. His father watched also. They saw a stray mountain lion, sixteen phone poles knocked over by a chinook wind, their wires great lacy scallops along a field of snow, the skies howling white. "It snows up here, Totte. It's seven thousand feet high. Over there the mountains are twelve, fourteen thousand feet high. Men die on them."

"You're the ladder, Yussel. Feet on the ground, head brushing Heaven. You lift yourself too high, you let go of the world, you lose your people. A zaddik holds fast to the lower and the higher, to

Heaven and to earth, lets the mercy come down, lets the souls go up."

Yussel heard his own voice crack. "Totte, I'm no zaddik."

A light inside the Arizona turned on. An old coconut face hung among the three palm trees: Grisha, returned from the Lubavitchers, yelling, "Someone's here! Someone's here!"

"Totte." Yussel shook his head. "I can't do this." He was going to cry.

His father put his hand on Yussel's arm. His touch was gentle. *"These are sweet good people, my shmegeggies. Stupid, self-involved, stubborn. But decent. Torah Jews. Together me and my congregation learned by the Torah, died by it, grew by it, came from death to life by it, had such satisfaction. Believe me, Yussele, such satisfaction. I'd go back in a minute."*

"They killed you."

"There are worse ways to die." His father sat up, shook a finger, took a little notebook from his bathrobe pocket, opened it to a scribbled list with lots of x's, exclamation points, underlines, question marks. Yussel's name had big question marks around it. *"Listen. Babe's here because your mother wanted her to be. And Bingo. Who drove the cab? Who put the buzzer in his wife's hand and scared her to death? Make sure he keeps up his payments. She's a boiled potato in a nursing home. Bingo sleeps. He wakes up if you mention sex. Grisha's here because this is where he dreams. Natalie because she hasn't finished fighting with me yet. She's also waiting for the Messiah. Except she thinks she's going to be His mother. The others—little families, seekers, people who need, people who have a little spark in them for you to light. Listen, Yussele, you watch out for Babe. Babe's got so much money if you counted it by thousand-dollar-bills for a year, you wouldn't be finished. But if you take a penny from her, you're dead in the water and she's running the boat. Don't take a red cent from her. And no advice from Grisha. He's sore because he isn't the Rabbi, that he has to take from a kid, so he'll sabotage you the first chance he gets."*

"Totte," Yussel's voice cracked. "What are you doing to me?"

"Your mother would say it's terrible what I'm doing." His father pushed his hat back on his forehead, interlaced his fingers, cracked his knuckles. *"Maybe she's right. Maybe you should forget the*

dynasty. Drive away now. Get your Shoshanna, pack her up, go home, be a wealthy Jew. A zei gezunt. Go, live civilized. You're right, Yussele. How can I do this to my only son?"

As if he were slitting both their throats, his father drew two heavy lines through Yussel's name, climbed out of the car, doorknobs gleaming gold in the blue-dark like cat's-eyes. His father yawned, belched, stretched, swung his doors back and forth as if he were exercising them, folded his doors around him from the cold, called from inside them, *"Look, my grave,"* and then stood long, tall, dark, sadness cut in every line. Yussel had the remarkable thought that his father was peeing on his own grave. *"On the other hand, as Jacob wrestled through the night with the angel, as you'll wrestle with Chaim, my shmegeggies need to wrestle with you, to change themselves, so they can see the dawn. You're their angel. So, come, Yussele, come."*

"I THINK IT'S Yussel!" It was Grisha yelling. "Yussel, is that you?" More shapes came out and stood in front of the building.

"Yussel?" Grisha called into the dark again. "That you?"

"Luftmensch! Grisha! Turn off the inside lights so we can see who it is." It had to be Babe.

Yussel stayed in the car.

"So then, go home, mein kindt. Save yourself, Yussele, while you can. I deserve what's coming to me."

A tight knot of people were moving out by inches toward them, hands shielding their eyes from the glare of the mercury lights.

"Who's there? Who are you? What do you want?"

When Yussel didn't answer, they backed away. Yussel started up the car, pulled out, hit the highway, turned on his headlights, rammed his foot to the floor. Sand and dust rose behind him. Just like Moses in the desert: a cloud by day and by night a pillar of fire. He'd give them Chaim's phone number in Moffat, give Chaim Indian Joe's deed, go home, put his client list together again, buy another SL, send out letters, get his territory back, buy two cars for his Shoshanna.

He tore across the desert, snaked around the bottom of a mountain, then into a deep canyon. His father deserved what was coming to him, the way he sacrificed his family. So his life was over, so what. So he was getting his share of punishment in the World to Come. It wasn't Yussel's problem. He had his own life to lead. Better he should handle his finances, make sure his wife and kids have in abundance instead of sacrificing them for the lost souls at the Arizona. All those poor shmendricks waiting for him in the desert. What would they do out there without him? "Look," he said to his father who might or might not have been listening. "If I stayed, I'd be a worse disappointment."

His father said, *"What will become of them? What will become of you?"* He also meant what will become of me but was smart enough not to say it.

At the Riverside Cafe, which was on the other side of the mountain, Yussel bought two cartons of Chesterfields, two half-pound bags of Reese's Pieces, listened to the water rushing below the parking lot, ate his candy, smoked a cigarette. It was a big empty wide-open night. There was plenty of water on the other side of the mountain. Why hadn't his father found a piece of real estate with water? His heart was running ahead of him like a diesel engine, pulling him along back over the mountain, betraying him. He lit up two cigarettes and put both of them in his mouth. His father coughed from the backseat. Yussel started up the mountain.

His father's doors made a tent. Smoke rose from his keyholes. *"You nervous, Yussele?"*

"Why should I be nervous? They're your congregation, not mine."

"My first day, my first congregation, I didn't know what to say, what to think, what to do with my hands, my face. My face seemed so big, like it was going to blow up and show everybody what was going on inside. Please God you should do better than me."

"So I can die younger?"

Yussel's father unfolded his doors, leaned over the front seat, clutched Yussel's shoulders. The road curved, abysses hung right and left. Yussel couldn't see through his own cigarette smoke.

"Grisha's very depressed. I'm really worried about him. The little couple from Santa Fe, she needs to get pregnant. The butcher Slotnik, his son's on coke. Slotnik won't give you any trouble. He studies all day. Natalie. Oy, Natalie. A good man would help. Also

Ernie's taking blood pressure pills—too many. I think maybe he could be violent. And there's a woman from Denver who . . ."

"Okay, okay." Yussel pulled directly under the mercury light and tooted the horn. Like a moth, Grisha fluttered in circles under the light. "He's here. Yussel's here!"

Suddenly his father grabbed him by the collar, talked very fast, hard-sell fast. *"Look, Yussele, before you go in. I have to tell you something. This is more serious than you think. Yussele, I don't get into Heaven unless you do good in there. I don't get into Heaven, Yussel. I stay outside the Gates forever."* His father's voice broke. *"It's all riding on you. I couldn't tell you. It's . . . it's a terrible thing. But, Yussel, forever. I'm with murderers, thieves. A Fetner. I'm the only one in my whole Yeshiva class, Yussele. The rest of them already entered the Gates. You understand?"*

"I understand. You already told me. However, even I know they don't sentence you to Hell over a kitchen door."

"Fetners they do. Other men they'd forgive." His father gripped his arm. *"Would I kid you about this? They gave me my judgment and said my son could help me out of it. The only way I could get out of my judgment is if my son helps me. I said 'Look, my son doesn't know enough. I would have to teach him.' They said, 'Try dreams.' But, Yussele, your poor soul drowns in the filth of your dreams. Your Neshama, your soul, she can't hear me. So I went back and told them, 'Look, I can't do it unless I go back and be with him for real.' So, Yussele . . . what can I say? Be nice. You hear me? Be nice. Because if you don't make it here, I stay there forever."*

"I thought you were just sort of waiting around to get clearance after the obligatory year."

"I'm already sentenced. I'm not waiting at the Gates, Yussele. I'm not near the Gates. You're my only chance."

"I thought you wait in line to change decrees that HaShem has made. I thought you were at least nearby Him."

"On Shabbas when they let us out I go ask for your family they should be healthy and live long lives and for my congregation. Someone's sick, someone's going to be hurt, go bankrupt, the decree is written. I go fight the decree for them. We all do. Listen, Yussele, if you don't make it here, I stay there forever."

Yussel removed his father's hands from his shoulders. "Just what do you mean by 'make it here'?"

"Do good."

"Go on."

"Be a great leader. Light sparks."

"Go on."

His father looked at the palms of his hands. *"Become a zaddik."*

"That's what you promised them?"

"What else could I offer?"

"My life. You promised them my life." Yussel turned away from him. "So you could get into Heaven, you promised them my life."

"Yussele, please, try to understand. So I can get out of Hell."

"I understand. You haven't changed a bit. I understand completely."

10

THE ONLY WOMAN in the world who was more bitter than Yussel's mother, was Yussel's mother's best friend, Babe. Babe was barren. She said she wasn't; she said her husband was, you could tell from his poetry. Babe treated her bad luck like the family jewels. Yussel used to try to imagine Babe when she'd been a girl like his sister Bloomke. Tall, heavy, square-jawed, dark, dog-eyed, sharp-tongued, loving—the kind of woman who slits your throat with one hand and feeds you chocolate pudding with the other. She'd sit in the kitchen and carry on about her husband, his poetry, and Yussel's father, who referred to her as Mrs. Mouth behind her back, would ask nobody in particular, "You know why Jewish men die early? To get away from their wives." Babe didn't have a sense of humor. She also carried a sharp-edged H.O. gauge miniature train track in her apron pocket.

His mother called her a balabusteh, a real power and doer around the house. His father called her a ball-buster. She used to beat Yussel with the H.O. track. Once she chased him up the street, screaming at him for touching her husband's poetry notebooks, beating him on the shoulders in front of everyone in the neighborhood. When his mother went east to visit her mother, Yussel went to Babe's house. For five bucks a week she also gave him piano lessons. He didn't practice. He argued that for every half-hour he practiced on the piano, his IQ dropped ten points. She said if she didn't know him better she'd have thought he practiced all the time. Then she'd flatten his knuckles on the keyboard with the H.O. track.

Babe's father was a refugee rabbi who was deaf. When he met Babe's husband-to-be, a poet who was a mumbler, the Rabbi asked, "So, what do you do you should marry my beautiful Sonya?"

"Poetry," the poet mumbled.

"Tackeh. The chicken business is a good business. My Sonya will never be without."

Babe always said she should have said something then and there, but what difference would it have made? It began the big lie of their lives: the poultry farm they didn't have. Even though they were always up to their necks in hock, like Rothschilds they carried dozens of fresh-killed kosher chickens to her father's house for Shabbas and told him the farm was too far for him to drive to, one excuse after another. Babe's father gave chickens to everyone, a big mitzvah. Sometimes Babe and her husband ate cornflakes for supper while her father was giving chickens for charity.

Babe's poet never worked a day with his hands. He wrote his poetry in Yiddish and English, together, filled his notebooks with poems about the Dallas Cowgirls, Dunlop tires, raccoons, frankfurters, garbage cans, God. Once he spent a week and a half looking for a word in Yiddish that rhymed with Dunlop. He never found it.

Finally her father, the Alte Reb, retired, moved to Israel, bought a little flat in Safat. A year later he called, said he was coming back because he wanted to bless the farm before he died.

Babe sold a menorah and candlesticks from her mother's side, a tea set from her father's side. She bought two hundred chickens, a little land, a little fencing, went, in four days, into the poultry business for real. After her father went back to Israel, she decided poultry wasn't such a bad idea after all. She liked land. Land, unlike a husband, you tell it what to do, it does.

Babe worked hard, registered Conservative, stuck a bumper sticker on her Ford pickup: KILL A COMMIE FOR YOUR MOMMY. Nearby farmers gave her advice, feed, seed, once a loan. Soon she started to sell little pieces of farmland for this farmer, for that farmer, sold larger pieces of land. And then one day, her husband the poet rhymed Dallas with tallis and thought the world had come to an end. Babe laughed in his face. He left immediately to live with a woman artist—from where, from what, how did he know her, what would he live on?—in an adobe shack on Indian land outside Los Alamos, because he couldn't write his poetry with all the noise from the chickens.

Babe was head of the Women's Holy Burial Society. She prepared bodies. She used to whisper to each dead lady, "See? I told you so." She came to Thursday night classes only to ask the Rabbi questions about suffering. Yussel, still on the edge, a kid, sixteen, seventeen, would sit in the kitchen, preparing kugel for Shabbas, peeling potatoes, grinding potatoes, breaking eggs, mixing eggs, potatoes, listening. It was all slippery. The lessons, the potato peels on the floor, the eggs. Each week, with his chin, his father would motion from the dining room for Yussel to join. Yussel wouldn't come sit with the shmegeggies. He wanted, he said, to learn separately.

"Rabbi, why do I suffer? What have I done I should suffer like this?"

"Babe," the Rabbi would answer her. "What can I tell you about suffering you don't already know?"

"What am I waiting for? Why isn't HaShem coming to me?"

"Because you haven't trusted Him."

Everyone would nod. Babe hadn't trusted. They went through this a dozen times a year with Babe.

"How do you know?"

"Number one, I know. Number two, if you trusted, HaShem would have provided."

Yussel wanted, even then, to shove a potato down his father's throat. Greek logic turned inside out by the Jews. Jewish thought turned inside out by Greek logic.

Babe couldn't be fooled. "Okay, I trust. He provided. He provided a nebbisheh poet, a life that's a lie, a barren man, mishugge chickens who peck each other's eyes out." She held up scarred hands. "Bloody fingers from making them masks. So, I trust. You know what I trust? I trust nothing will change. That's what I trust."

No one could look at the other. Yussel turned his back to the dining room, the class, his father. Babe had spoken the truth.

THEN BABE sold a racetrack near Phoenix. No one understood how. What would she do now without her bad luck? The day they heard about Babe's racetrack, Yussel had come home from Yeshiva. Everyone was sitting around the kitchen table, heads hanging between their shoulders, his father's lower than the others. Two brown wigs curled up in small boxes, like cats, were on the kitchen table. Yussel thought Babe had dropped dead. He exulted. "What happened to Babe?"

"She got a new wig," his sister Bloomke answered sourly.

That morning Babe had flown in a snowstorm to New York in someone's Lear jet to collect $800,000 in commissions and accept a partnership in an Orthodox real estate firm in TriBeCa. Yussel's father had driven her in the Shanda to a private airport. She was going to be picked up in New York by a limousine. Just before she left, Babe gave the Rabbi her polyester wigs to give to his wife. Babe, Yussel's mother told them, bought a blond wig of human hair that dropped straight to the shoulder and came, for $400, all the way from Paris. Also an entire new wardrobe and a sable jacket, used but sable, which Yussel had always thought was a kind of whitefish you eat at Bar Mitzvahs. And Babe left. "Just like that," his mother snapped her fingers, threw the wigs into the garbage can. "Babe was never really my friend, anyway," his mother mumbled, which wasn't true at all.

From the kitchen table, his father flung a fist at the ceiling. "You're all going to kill me. All of you." When the Rabbi quieted down, Bloomke, who was by then engaged to a rabbinical student and knew she'd be hungry the rest of her life, retrieved Babe's wigs from the garbage can and took them up to her room.

Two days after Babe left, one day after Yussel's Bar Mitzvah, five minutes after the Rabbi and the Rebbitzen had had a furious shouting match over a stack of bills the Rabbi had left/lost/it wasn't clear, in an old blue-enamel turkey roaster, the Rabbi had his first heart attack. Yussel knew his father had the heart attack because Yussel had done too well at his Bar Mitzvah or because he hadn't done well enough. His mother knew it was because Babe, who didn't deserve, didn't learn, didn't trust, had received.

The next Hanukah, Yussel's father, who had recovered miraculously and was back smoking, screaming, working forty-eight hours a day, found in the mail a leather-bound gold-edged book of Babe's husband's poetry, which she'd published privately, which she'd mailed without an explanation to the Rabbi. Who after reading, threw the book in the garbage. "His father-in-law of blessed memory was right. He should have stuck with the chickens."

"LOOK AT THIS. Our new Rabbi who can't even smile after twenty years he sees me!" Babe, half the size Yussel remembered her, calves no longer meaty, arms no longer rolling pins, stood at the door with her hands on her hips, a high-gloss bonded grin, tears and green contact lenses in her eyes. From shoes to eyelids, everything on Babe was lizard-green except for the nine-millimeter pearls swinging at her pupick. Yussel knew they were nine millimeters because once Shoshanna took him to Tiffany's to show him what she wanted when they were rich enough, which now they'd never be. Babe had a new nose, leathery skin from face-lifts. Support hose hanging off the back of Jane Fonda workout calves. "I changed his diapers for him, he can't smile at me." Babe still talked out of the side of her mouth, like an auctioneer. "You can't come in until you smile."

He should have accepted the offer on the spot. But he didn't. He smiled. Even people you hate, to see them again after a lifetime, you're sentimental, you smile.

"The kid hasn't changed. Maybe you're even handsome. You look like a hockey star."

"You watch hockey?"

"I watch." She shook her head. "You should have your mother's constitution, not your father's." She walked around him, examining him. Yussel tried to turn with her. She was already in control.

"Before you enter among the thieves, Yussy, your mother, who thinks you're crazy to do this and that your father of blessed memory should be arrested for kidnapping, your mother sends her love and wishes you only good luck with your new congregation, who you will, God willing, meet tomorrow. So now . . . " She moved aside so he could pass. "Welcome to the Arizona." Babe swept the floor with her bow, like she was greeting an angel. Babe didn't believe in angels. It was the sarcastic bow of an executioner. So Babe bowed and Yussel walked into the Arizona.

"I'll make coffee."

"I don't want coffee. I already had too much today."

She closed both eyes, nodded once. Yussel remembered that well. "You look terrible, Yussy. You need a cup of coffee. Sit. Look around." Babe wore green-gold high-heeled slippers that clattered on the floorboards of the Arizona as she made her way to the kitchen. She still moved like a battleship.

Yussel sat, looked around. Babe must have told everyone at the Arizona to stay away. Babe used to tell Yussel's mother what to do. She may have told his mother to leave his father, maybe gave her the airfare to Haifa.

The Arizona was pretty much what it had been when Indian Joe had shown it to Yussel's father: a long rectangle with a stage at one end, a dance floor in front of the stage, a kitchen and restrooms at the far end, a bar padded in orange Naugahyde in between. The bimah was on the stage. The ark was a gun case with a ruffled kitchen curtain over it. The dance floor was split by a shaky latticework divider so the men could sit separate from the women during services. Kitchen curtains were stretched over the latticework so the men and women couldn't see one another praying. The men had two-thirds of the space. The bimah faced the men's space. As Yussel passed the ark/gun cabinet, the curtains moved. His father would say the Torahs were alive behind the curtains. Yussel of course wouldn't. The idea had scared him to death when he was a kid. Everything had scared him to death when he was a kid. Yussel waited at the bar while Babe made coffee. He couldn't imagine why she'd come out here with all her money, with all her outfits. His mother told him Babe put her suitcases into a coffin when she traveled. It was always first on, first off, never got lost, never got opened.

"Where's Grisha?"

Babe pointed to a door off the kitchen. There was a light on in the room. "In Lala Land, playing cards. Go, knock."

THE DOOR WAS open a crack. Yussel pushed it a crack more. Grisha wore the same navy blue gabardine suit, the ancient snapped-brim hat, yellowed shirt, stained tie, sat on a stool, hunched over a dresser, and, under the light of a green gooseneck lamp, played solitaire with a greasy pack of cards from the railroad before it was Amtrak.

Grisha looked like he'd been peeled off a Russian icon, a holy man losing his material dimensions, drying out, flaking off. His beard and hair were paper white. His cheeks had red cherry spots on them and his skin was parchment, very thin, stretched and taut. Yussel hadn't seen him for a dozen years. He was sixty something. He looked eighty. His face was smaller, his ears as big as griddle cakes. The waistline on his pants was gathered up in a belt yellow with scars. His shirt collar stood away from his neck, which looked like the lamp neck. He'd become one of the seedy ghost-Jews who hang around cemeteries and say prayers over the dead for a buck. Grisha was a bachelor, therefore a virgin, therefore could never climb to the full heights of holiness because he wasn't married. Grisha swept up the cards, reshuffled them, didn't look up, pulled apart the cards as he dealt.

"Who's ahead, Grisha? You or God?"

"Baruch HaShem, He owes me."

"You know I'm here?"

"I'm busy. I'm praying for you and I'm not getting an answer." When he didn't find the right cards, he ran the deck through a second time, shrugged, wiped his hands on his pants, grabbed Yussel, pounded him on the back, kissed him on the cheeks, took Yussel's arm, led him to the main room. Grisha smelled of cigars, onions, stale, a leftover gabardine mold smell, a thrift shop scent, a man without a woman, growing old. His cheek was sandpaper when he rubbed it against Yussel's. He whispered like a conspirator. "You better be nice to Babe, Boychickl. Babe's a business lady. She didn't have to come here."

Babe brought tuna fish sandwiches, coffee.

Grisha swept a half-sandwich from the tray, put all of it in his mouth, spoke through it. "This is a rich lady, Yussel. You should see her bus. It sleeps eight. On her arm, her name in diamonds in English. On her neck, her name in diamonds in Hebrew. Some stuff. Her outfits . . ." He rocked his head from side to side. "Like a movie star." Something flashed on Yussel's screen, showed him Grisha as a very very old man, old and fat, his mouth open, snoring, stretched out on a La-Z-Boy.

Babe turned to Grisha. "So, what do I have to show for a lifetime, some shmatas and a bus?"

Yussel wondered what his own mother had to show for her lifetime. What Shoshanna would have; what she wanted. "And you, Grisha?" Yussel inquired.

"You don't have family, you live longer."

Babe scraped her chair back angrily. "I'll defrost some Entenmann's."

Yussel started to refuse, knew it would be futile.

Grisha dealt his cards. "She make you turn around? She likes backsides. She watches football, baseball, hockey, backsides." Yussel's father hadn't allowed anyone else to play cards. Only for Grisha, because Grisha was on a higher rung, cards weren't sinful. Yussel's mother always objected, went flying to her husband. The Rabbi said, "He's talking to God. Leave him alone," the Rebbitzen scoffed, "please." The Rabbi said, "Who are you to say he isn't talking to God?" "Me?" asked the Rebbitzen. "I'm only saying it's against the Law what he's doing." "Behind the Law," answered the Rabbi, "behind the Law beneath the veils, there's a mystery that's more sublime than the Law. Leave him alone." So the Rebbitzen gave Grisha so much housework to do, he didn't get much time to play cards. He kept a journal as greasy as the deck of cards, charged himself fifty bucks a game to play, earned from himself five bucks for every card he turned over. When Yussel left to get married, God owed Grisha over fourteen thousand bucks.

Babe brought out two squares of cheesecake for the men, a sliver for herself. Babe's nails were long and plastic, the kind of nails they put on in special shops. The first fingernail on each hand was gold. Shoshanna wanted such nails. He wouldn't let her. Babe tapped these nails on her coffee cup, mopped her brow, sighed, said to no one, "So, this is our new Rabbi."

Yussel's father sat on top of the mirror. It was ornate, gilt, like a whorehouse mirror. Yussel had never been in a whorehouse, but he was certain this would fit, this and red velvet sofas. His father wore a red velour robe over black-and-white tiger-skin silk charmeuse pajamas, was now the size of a small goat with a large beard. He wore old slippers, Dearfoams, lined with plaid flannel. He'd had them for years. He nodded at Yussel formally as if business were about to begin. Yussel had a very reliable thought. No matter what his father said, no matter what he, Yussel, said, no matter what Babe and Grisha said, he'd leave in the morning and go back to Far Rockaway, buy his territory back if he had to. He'd sit and think these things if they started in on him. Yussel sat back in his chair, spread his hands on the table. "Well, what has to be done? What's new? Who's here?"

"You'll see, Yussel. In the morning. Ernie built adobe huts. A new girl, a blondische, sewed regular Navajo tents. The kitchen's terrific, fully equipped. Tomorrow you'll kosher it. Everything's organized. And we dig for a mikveh soon." She pointed upward toward the mountain. "Also you have to talk to Music Minus One up there to turn herself off."

"What's Music Minus One?"

Babe jerked her thumb toward the mountain. "This woman who torments us. She had an entire honest-to-God orchestra on tape. It's a sing-along system that does background music. You bought the sound equipment to cover it. It doesn't cover."

"Okay. What else?"

Grisha put down his sandwich, wiped his mouth with his navy blue gabardine sleeve. "Listen, what would your father of blessed memory say about the place? We did a good job? Wouldn't he say we did a good job?"

It was cold, empty, cheesy, worse than the basement in the split-level. The ark was an insult, maybe even a sacrilege with its kitchen curtain. His father shook a warning finger. *"Your father of blessed memory, Yussele, would say, thank you, you did a good job, you touch my heart."*

That's what his father wanted him to say. So Yussel repeated,

"My father of blessed memory would say thank you, you did a good job."

Babe and Grisha smiled smugly at each other. Maybe they thought he was going to be a grateful, gracious, obedient rabbi, a good kid.

"And you touched my heart."

"Sorry, Totte. We leave my heart out of this."

Once, not long ago, a week, he was a successful businessman with opinions, clients, experience. He leaned back again, spread his hands out on the tabletop again, made believe they were asking him for a loan. "So, then, what are your major problems? What do you need?"

Grisha gave a little nod of approval for the question. "First, extra prayer books. For visitors."

"For visitors?" Yussel laughed. Not a big laugh but enough of a laugh. Looking back, Yussel thought it might have been that moment, that question, that turned everything sour. He'd been there fifteen minutes. Up until then, they'd welcomed him. Babe raised her eyebrows at Grisha; Grisha sighed a long moist shuddering sigh. His eyebrows flaked bits of dandruff into his coffee. He stirred them in with a spoon. Babe said to Grisha, "See, for the rich the birds sing. On the poor, they shit."

Grisha made a square mouth, lips out and forward as if he were tasting something rotten. "We expect from Kansas, Fort Greeley, Durango, Santa Fe, maybe Denver. Who knows? Also, right now we need four more men for a minyan."

"You don't have even enough for a minyan? How can you have Shabbas? Where are you davening?"

"We go to Chaim's."

Babe added, "Chaim charges fifteen bucks a head, includes three meals. On Shabbas the men sleep on the bus. The women don't go. He's a regular sweetheart, your friend Chaim."

"I have to see Chaim twice a day?"

Babe rocked her head from side to side. "It's not so terrible. We'll get a minyan soon. It's just a matter of time."

Grisha leaned forward. Since Yussel could remember, Grisha breathed shallow breaths, and just when Yussel, even as a little kid, thought Grisha was dead, Grisha would take one big long moist shuddering sigh. Now he took one big long moist shuddering onion sigh. "Listen, Yussel, shmendrick, if it's intended, we'll have a minyan. That's what your father would say. If it's intended, they'll come. Visitors, a minyan, donations." Yussel could see the inside of his lips. The gums had white bumps. "So, Mr. Yussel Prophet, what do you see? We're going to make it? Be a congregation?"

"I don't see anything, Grisha. I don't do prophecy."

"Yeah, yeah. We all know about that, don't we? So you don't see a big shul? A Bes Midrash? Brisses, weddings, Bar Mitzvahs? Hundreds of Jews dancing at Simchas Torah? Mercedes lined up outside?"

Yussel leaned, tipped the front legs of his chair up, leaned back, watched his father in the mirror. His father was twisting his doorknobs, nervous. "An airstrip, Grisha, and stretch limos, and the Macy's Parade. A regular Castle Garden."

Grisha stood up as if Yussel were dismissed. "You see? What did I tell you? This is not a mensch."

"Grisha, at least he came. He bought the place and he came."

Grisha walked across the room, looked at the prayer books in the bookcases, looked at the altar, looked out the front door to the Rabbi's grave, spread his cards on the bar. "So why did you come anyway? Why are you here, Yussel, if you don't see a future?"

"Me? I'm here to help my father's . . ." —He had to keep the word shmegeggies from rolling out—". . . my father's people."

There was a long ugly silence. Babe looked at Grisha. Grisha looked at Babe. Babe shrugged, looked at her gold nails, examined each nail for imperfections, found a little chip. Grisha shuffled his cards. Finally Babe spoke, "You're here to help *us*?"

The Rabbi slid off the mirror, put on his Dearfoam slippers, climbed onto the stage, hid inside the gun closet ark. Yussel could see his feet under the white ruffles. Yussel wanted to kill him. "Is that a problem for either of you? That I'm here to help you?"

"No," Babe said diplomatically. "Who could refuse a little help?"

"So?"

Babe twisted her strand of pearls, swung them back and forth, decided. "Before he died, your father of blessed memory told everyone to come here and help you be a rabbi. Except me. He didn't want me. Your mother wanted me here."

Grisha slapped cards down. "He asked *us* to help *you*."

The kitchen curtain covering the ark sucked itself inward.

"Before he died? He *knew* I'd buy before he died? It was all arranged?" Yussel stood, knocked over his coffee, made a vague gesture with a paper napkin to wipe it up, went as casually as he could toward the ark.

The ark said, *"I do prophecy, Yussel. You know I do prophecy. I can see things going to happen, places, you know that."*

"They call it lying. Since when do we lie to each other?"

"Don't get excited, Yussele. It's not a lie. It's just a matter of timing. When the Baal Shem Tov told a story that wasn't true, it didn't matter because he could make it true. We'll talk later. You be nice. We'll talk. Can't we talk? Listen, you want a minyan? I'll get you a minyan. Tell me what you want."

"I want to go home."

Yussel smashed his fist against the wall. The overhead lights swung back and forth. The divider swayed dangerously.

"Vey iz mir. He hasn't changed, Grisha."

"If I stay—if—I want you to know, I don't want any advice from you, Grisha. Nothing. And from you, Babe, I don't want a penny. Not a red cent. If I'm going to be the Rabbi here, I lead. I don't follow. So if you want me to stay, you better understand the rules. Understand?"

Babe put on Sophia Loren glasses, examined her nails again. Grisha played his cards. Yussel stood on the stage. "You hear me? I'll give you a few minutes to discuss it. Then I want an answer."

Babe turned to Grisha. "He hasn't changed much since he was a kid, has he?"

"Maybe it's the altitude. Your head hurt, Yussel?"

"Forget the altitude. At sea level he was like this." Babe and Grisha sounded like they rehearsed. "Remember his pole? How he hid in the garage and when some poor kid who'd hurt his feelings came along . . . he'd come charging out like a kamikaze pilot flying a forklift. His mother used to worry he'd kill someone. Take an eye out, God forbid."

Yussel remembered the bamboo pole. From a carpet.

"We called him Zipper because he never zipped his fly and that's how we reminded him." Babe made the sound of knife on bone, which generically could be called laughter. Babe looked up at him.

"His fingers were too fat for the piano. When did you get fat, Yussel? Before or after you stopped wetting the bed?"

"Wait. Wait. Remember how he ran around in his mother's underwear? How everyone worried?"

"That's a lie!" Yussel shouted, hated himself.

"A lie? Yussy," Babe smiled slowly, crookedly. "You don't remember how I went after you on the sidewalk with the little train track? You came outside in her corset, Yussy."

Yussel remembered the H.O. track beating on his shoulders, Babe chasing him down the sidewalk, screaming. He didn't remember wearing his mother's corset. He did remember looking at the poetry notebooks because they had cutouts of the Dallas Cowgirls with shorts so short he could see the fold of tushy. He thought Babe chased him down the sidewalk because of the tushies. He didn't remember ever even once putting on his mother's corset.

Yussel turned to the ark, checked his fly because he couldn't help himself, because maybe Babe was right, said to his father, "These are lovely people, Totte. Filled with Torah. How many years did you give them, working on their souls, teaching them to do mitzvahs, to respect, to love, to give charity, kindness? Look at your handiwork. What they're doing to me I wouldn't do to a dog, not even to Chaim. Maybe to Chaim, a little. This is what I should give my life and soul for?"

"These are souls, Yussele. One goes, we're all in trouble. Like bricks in a building. You lose a brick, the whole building weakens."

"These are vampires, piranhas. They live on the taste of blood. First yours, now mine. I stay until morning. That's it." Yussel left the ark, stepped down from the stage. "You're on your own, Totte."

His father hopped down from the stage onto Yussel's neck. Yussel started to tilt, held the edges of reading tables, worked his way over to a chair. The whole father, doors, all of him on Yussel's neck, his hat tilted back like it used to be when he had a real problem, the forehead like a blackboard, the letters of pain scratched into it, the eyes hot, the long white side curls adrift, beard electric, potent. *"Don't quit on me, Yussele. Don't quit!"*

"Get off my back." Yussel fell onto a chair at a table.

"Forever's forever, Yussele. Have a heart." His father wrapped his legs around Yussel, put his Dearfoam feet on the plastic sheet protecting the tablecloth, which had been Yussel's mother's tablecloth. Under the plastic, in the linen, like scar tissue, Yussel found a patch. He remembered his mother darning her tablecloths, Bloomke's underwear, his father's socks, saying to Yussel, "I'll never have new. Maybe your wife will have new. You've got your father's eyes, his smile, maybe his soul." Tears splashed on the darning egg. "God help you. Whatever you do, sweetheart, don't be a rabbi."

Babe said to Grisha, "If he doesn't want my money and he doesn't want your advice, so what?"

"And if he comes to us?"

"We refuse." Babe turned to Yussel. "Okay, Yussy? We refuse."

"So, it's a deal, Yussel?"

"On one condition."

"Yes?"

"In regard to the rest of the congregation, you treat me with respect. No matter how you feel. For example, I'm not Yussel. I'm Reb Yussel."

"Rabbi? You need this title?" Grisha bent heads with Babe.

"Yes. If I'm the Rabbi, I should be called the Rabbi."

Babe made circles with her teacup. Grisha flattened his cheesecake with his fork. Finally Babe said, "We decided not yet for Rabbi."

Grisha banged his fork down. "I warned you about taking over, Babe. That's not what we agreed. We agreed when Yussel acts like a rabbi, we call him Rabbi. It's that simple. After all, he's already a rabbi whether we like it or not."

"Not to us."

Grisha was trying to smooth things. It was too late. "Look, Boychickl, you're just not our Rabbi *yet*. See?"

His father dug into Yussel's back, by the kidneys, and chopped away with the heels of his Dearfoam slippers. *"Be nice, Yussele. They mean well."*

Yussel dug his manicured nails into the soft palms of his hands. "Bone-breakers, shnorrers, alte cocker marrow-suckers. This is the first test, Totte? If I pass this, if I don't kill them, run them through with a broomstick, I get to stay?" In the mirror he could see his father's face. If Yussel had the kind of heart his father wanted him to have, one that could be touched, wrenched, torn to pieces like carrion, it would have been so torn to pieces from the agony in his father's eyes. They pulsed in the mirror like live and separate creatures, frightened, rolling around, looking for a way out. *"Don't quit on me, Yussele."*

"They can't call me Rabbi? I'm not a rabbi?"

"I'll call you Rabbi. Don't worry. We'll work it out. I'll get you a minyan. Tell me what you want. I'll get it. I've met someone he'll give me his place in line. Ask, I'll get for you. Just don't quit."

Yussel slapped both hands down on the table hard enough to alarm his father, hard enough his father jumped off Yussel's back, but the pressure stayed and his head felt like someone had axed it. Maybe it was the altitude. He felt as if he was having the bends. But he didn't feel anything else, for any of them, even his father, and he was glad.

11

GRISHA LED Yussel out to the absolute brink of a desert night. Yussel didn't make conversation with Grisha. His head was splitting. He was nauseated. This would be a terrible place to die of altitude sickness, pulmonary edema, all that. Also he could die from fear, from no sidewalks, from the dark, from the big cat claw marks he'd seen on his first visit, from the snake holes the size of his thigh. What would Shoshanna live on if he died in the next ten minutes? Yussel scared himself so much he had to talk to Grisha. "So, you had a problem about a woman singing? I haven't heard anything."

"She's out. She's sleeping. You'll hear."

"I don't want to hear, Grisha. Nobody should hear."

"It's Ernie's job to turn on the new speakers you gave us, but he falls asleep."

Cold moonlight waxed the ridges of the corrugated roofs, the sides of the Navajo tents. The sky was a wall, stars buckshot all over it. Where were the clanging buoys, the waves, the drunks and lovers under the boardwalk, the shouting, the horns, the fire engines? A tall wooden water tower sang old oak songs in the wind, sounded like his father's table hymns. Candles flickered inside Ernie's little adobe house, through the pale skins of the towering tents. Chickens cackled from somewhere behind the tents. Yussel smelled feed and shit.

"Babe's chickens on your right. We're getting a slaughterer once a month from Wyoming, from the Federation. The mountains are on your left. There's a dirt road out there. It cuts across the flats to the foot of the mountains. You'll see it in the morning. Babe's bus is out there in the trees. And her new Lincoln. You should see her Lincoln."

"Somebody's following us, Grisha."

"Probably Babe. She doesn't want to miss anything."

"What if it's not Babe?"

"Then she'll miss something."

A girl pulled up the flap of a tent, ran out to them, stuck her hand out. She was shivering in the cold air. "I'm Alma. I made the tents."

Yussel leaned backward to avoid her touch. "Alma, I don't shake with such pretty girls." Chaim had pencils for such occasions. On the pencils was written DIAL-A-JEWISH-STORY with a phone number in Far Rockaway. Yussel had seen a lot of Chaim's pencils all over New York. A lady puts out her hand to shake, Chaim sticks a pencil into it. And doesn't have to touch her.

Yussel heard whispering from the tent. "He's a hunk, like a bull." "More like Alex Karras with a beard." "I think the guy on 'Barney Miller' with the curly hair, a little bigger." And then in a significant whisper, "I say he looks like Moses." And everyone fell quiet.

"God, I am *so* embarrassed." Alma was rubbing her hands together.

"So now you know for next time."

"I knew your mom in San Francisco, Rabbi. I mean she was older than me but I sort of knew guys she knew."

"My mother?"

"Yeah, LaDonna."

Yussel's ears turned red, fiery. Possibly other things also. He could see the Flower Child LaDonna with the cloud of curls rising behind her, straddling a Harley, straddling a Hell's Angel, wearing a HARVEY MILK FOR MAYOR T-shirt. Guys she knew? Who names a kid LaDonna? No schoolteacher from Pretoria. Maybe the railway man from Oneonta. No one Jewish, that's for sure. So the Flower Child was a convert. Imagine. Yussel imagined.

Her mother was someone from a dump like Cedar Rapids, someone who runs away from home, takes the Trailways to L.A., works at McDonald's, has yeast infections, abortions in clinics, a kid out of wedlock, names her LaDonna. Nice going, Totte. LaDonna/Madonna makes herself over, reverses the course of religious history, becomes a Rebbitzen. "Oh. My stepmother. You must mean my stepmother."

"Yeah, LaDonna. Well . . ." She giggled. "Hasta mañana." Alma ducked into the tent. Giggling exploded into belly laughs.

"Shah!" Grisha hissed at them.

Guys she knew. Alex Karras. The guy in "Barney Miller" with the curls. Women in a tent, giggling, thinking he looked like a football player, Moses for God's sake. Yussel knew what he looked like: a big peasant with a long beard.

"Craziness," Yussel said to Grisha.

"They have to get married soon. Maybe some kibbutzniks who want American citizenship." Grisha led Yussel to his tent. "Look, Yussel, no matter what goes on between us, you, me, Babe . . ." Grisha cleared his throat, sighed a long moist sigh, spat. "I just want to say, to tell the truth, okay? We're happy you came."

"This your tent?"

"Before Babe made me move inside the house." Grisha gave Yussel his flashlight, went in, lit a candle. Guys she knew. Yussel didn't want to go in, didn't want to be alone with himself, with the flagpole whacking off in the wind, with the terrible sharp loneliness of all things.

"I want you to know, Grisha, just so there's no misunderstanding, no false expectations, just to tell *you* the truth, I'm not happy I came at all. And probably I'll leave in the morning. You can hire someone cheap out of Yeshiva."

Grisha said, "Listen, Boychickl, maybe it's the altitude the way you feel. Shluf. Sleep." Grisha sighed his long moist shuddering sour sigh, shuffled away into the dark.

YUSSEL SAT ON the edge of the bed, listened to the dark, listened to his heart pumping in his ears, wondered if he'd strangle in his sleep, turned the flashlight on. The sheets were clean, so was the pillowcase. God knows how old the blankets were. Yussel didn't like sleeping in another man's bed, especially Grisha's. Next to the bed on the floor was a milk crate and on it a basin of water, a towel to wash his fingertips off in the morning, because sleep is one-sixtieth of death and you have to wash it away. In Grisha's bed sleep might be closer to death than one-sixtieth.

"Yussel? You sleeping?"

Yussel leaped up.

"I won't bother you, if you're sleeping." Babe talking from the side of her mouth.

"Babe, if I was sleeping you wouldn't be bothering me."

"So am I bothering you?"

"I'm not sleeping."

"I want to give you a little advice."

"I thought we agreed—"

"From me we agreed you wouldn't take money. Anyway I'm doing this for your mother not for me. Okay. Listen. . ."

"You want me to come out, Babe."

"No. I'll stand here in the dark."

"I'll come out."

"You don't want to come out. I can't come in."

"Don't be ridiculous. You're my mother's age. You can come in." He knew she wouldn't. Yussel lay back on the bed. The mattress sighed a long moist shuddering sour sigh. Everything smelled like Grisha. "I'm listening."

"You're not coming out?"

"Why should both of us freeze?"

"Okay. Listen. Chaim's here."

"I know."

"You heard about his house?"

"It burned?"

"It didn't burn. Why did you say such a thing?"

Yussel shrugged.

"Worse, Yussel, believe me. Chaim's gabbai, Mendl, from Rikers Island, has a brother-in-law, a real-estate agent, a real goniff. He sold Chaim's house in Far Rockaway. Next door to your house. It was worth three hundred. He listed it for two and sold it seven times to seven families, who thought it was such a great bargain they dropped dead to sign up fast. The brother-in-law has now a million, four. Moving day, seven vans pull up on your street. Furniture goes in, furniture comes out. Men fighting, kids fighting, women crying, and Mendl's brother-in-law vanishes with the money."

"Nebbuch."

"I know. It's terrible. That's why I'm telling you. I'm not sure. So Ruchel and the kids, who were supposed to live off the money from selling the house while Chaim's getting settled out here, she has to go to her mother. So where's the money? So where's Mendl's brother-in-law? So how does Chaim have enough money for eighteen houses in Moffat, Colorado? I ask you. What's the connection?"

Yussel got up and went outside. "Chaim wouldn't let his wife and kids go hungry if he had the money. I don't think so."

"I'm not so sure."

"What are you telling me, Babe?"

"As your mother's closest and dearest friend, I am telling you you should steer very clear of your friend Chaim. Go daven, but that's all."

Yussel pulled back the tent flap and went inside. "I promise." In the morning he'd steer clear all the way to Rockaway.

YUSSEL REFUSED to think about Chaim. He tried to sleep but inside his eyes the Flower Child was riding around under his eyelids like a circus performer on a motorcycle, upside down, round and round, in the double rings of both closed eyes. He tried to squeeze her away. He blinked, she went round and round. Outside, the flagpole beat at itself, girls giggled in the night. He was glad he was married. An unmarried man would be tempted out there. He didn't want the girls to think about him, to talk about him; he didn't want to think about them. God forbid he should smile at them. He closed his eyes. The Flower Child was back, under both eyes, going in different directions. Guys she knew. The desert air was dropping to winter temperature. It was sharp, bit inside his nose when he breathed deeply. He resisted thinking about guys she knew. He resisted thinking about resisting, which led him directly back to her and the women giggling about him in the tent, fifteen, twenty yards from Grisha's tent, talking about him. "Shh, he'll hear!" He'd leave first thing in the morning, before anyone else woke up. He thought about his father, his father and the Flower Child, his father.

It had been some kind of emergency, some kind of tzuros, everybody up in the middle of the night. Maybe his father had been sick or Yussel was sick or his mother or Bloomke gained a pound. Yussel remembered being much smaller than the door. Maybe he was seven, eight. He remembered standing at the bedroom door; his father stood at the closet reaching for something. A light was on in the closet so it must have been Shabbas. There was no light on in the bedroom. Yussel saw a flash of his father's thighs, white with blue veins, little, thin, delicate, like veal, but between them his father's member, raw, large, red, determined, wet, glinting, pornographic, although he did not then know such a word. Maybe he was nine, ten. No more. Boys, sons, even in the Torah, shouldn't look on their father's nakedness. Yussel remembered shutting his eyes, dizzy between the blue-and-white weakness of the thighs and the secret red power, like some terrible fruit, of his father's member.

Yussel decided then and there he could never be a man like his father, would never want to be burdened with such a thing, with its rules, its demands, its prohibitions, its evil inclinations, which he'd already heard about in cheder. He imagined walking around with such a thing, putting it in the right place, trying to turn around in a phone booth, changing a tire, going through a subway turnstile. To make children with such an instrument, to make generations, to sin. Such dilemmas, such choices.

He imagined then moments like these in the tent, the son equally fruited as the father had been that night long ago, girls giggling in the other tent, the Flower Child zooming around under his eyelids. LaDonna/Madonna and the guys she knew. Yussel rolled over, looked up into the point of the tent, smelled Lemon Pledge. His father towered above him. His doors touched the high roof of canvas. He wore creamy silk pajamas with little interwoven *CD*'s for Christian Dior and a brown cashmere robe with gold-and-silver trim around the neck and sleeves. *"To faint from such a bathrobe?"*

Yussel groaned, pulled Grisha's moldy pillow over his face.

"I have to tell you something."

"I only see liars in the morning."

"You think we have a shuttle bus?"

Yussel buried his head with his arms and the pillow. The candle flickered, died, renewed itself like a joke birthday cake candle. His father's shadow leaped and shrank along with the candle, across the four walls of the tent, four fathers, eight doors, one son trying to hide himself and his thoughts. His father sat down on him. The candle flickered, burned bright. The doors were killing Yussel, their points in his heart, his groin. Every place he had ached, he now ached worse. His father lay down beside Yussel, folded his doors, put a thin arm around Yussel, his head on Yussel's big chest, almost as a woman would. Yussel gave him some blanket, a little pillow.

"Oy gevalt!" The steam of his breath quivered in the air, bent the candle. They lay together for a long moment without speaking. Even if his father betrayed him, lied to him, ruined him, this was as beautiful a moment as Yussel could remember in his entire life.

"You comfortable, Totte?"

"Here? Sure."

"And there?"

"There? There, Baruch HaShem, I weep to enter the Gate."

"For that you thank God?"

"Who else should I thank?"

"You visit Mom?"

"She's still sore. She won't listen."

"I'm sorry."

"It works out. If she doesn't listen to me, I don't have to listen to her."

"Somehow that's not funny."

"I know. It never was." His father blew out the candle, settled in deeper.

The Flower Child no longer zoomed around under his eyelids. The girls no longer laughed in their tents. Yussel decided not to ask whether his father visited the Flower Child. His father pulled the blanket from Yussel, snuggled.

"I'm not staying."

"They were out of line. It'll work out."

"They couldn't even call me Rabbi?"

"They're still mourning for me. Give them time."

"What am I doing here if I'm not the Rabbi?"

"Yussele, maybe for a nice Reform synagogue in Santa Fe for nonobservant Jews, maybe for them you're a rabbi, do a little service, a lot of weddings, talk politics on Shabbas. But for us you have an uncircumcised heart. You aren't attached. Somehow Babe and Grisha know this. Subliminally."

"They know they can't make me suffer?"

"They know you don't feel their pain. A real rabbi feels pain. I told you. The hiccups."

"I don't want their pain."

"So why should they call you Rabbi? When your heart is broken, then you'll be a rabbi."

"Maybe I don't feel pain, but God knows I've sacrificed a lot to come out here, to help. They don't even think I'm here to help them. That little gem I hold you responsible for."

"How could I get them out here if they thought it was because they were insufficient? I had to give them a cause."

"And you had to give me a cause. So what's true? Who's insufficient? Me or them?"

"Let me tell you a story." Yussel's father took his beard in his right hand. "The first Bobover Reb, this is about him. He's eating a fish. A Hasid comes up to him with a request his barren wife should have a child. The Bobover holds the fish in his hand and he tells him a story. He doesn't give the Hasid to eat. He just gives him the story. He tells him that there were four young men who were very poor. They wanted to make a trip for the holidays to Lublin to stay with the Seer but they had no money for food, horses, lodging. So they decide if one dresses up as a rabbi and one dresses up like his attendant, they'll get rides, what to eat, where to sleep. So they dress up. And it works. They are welcomed at an inn. They are given fine rooms, good food. Then the innkeeper comes to the Rabbi, weeping, and says his little girl is very sick, could the Rabbi help. The four young men look at one another. The one who is making believe he's a rabbi knows he has to go to help, although he knows he has no power to heal because he's only making believe. But how can he say no? So *he goes in and leans over the little girl in the crib and says prayers. So he prays to HaShem to make the little girl better. Then he goes as fast as he can to his room, tells everyone to get dressed fast and get out of there. On the way out the innkeeper runs after the four and gives them money, he is so grateful. They finally get to Lublin to the Seer and spend the holiday with him. Then it's time to go home. On the way home, they pass the inn, although they dare not stop there. The innkeeper runs out. They are so scared. He tells the make-believe Rabbi that his child is well, thank God, and he is so happy. He insists they come in and let him give them a fine supper and fine rooms. What can they do? They eat and sleep like kings. In the morning the innkeeper gives the make-believe Rabbi money.*

"This is all too much for the other three. They want to know what happened, maybe their friend is a rabbi in disguise. What did he do? What did he say? Finally he says, 'I don't know any more than you do. But when I went in and saw how sick the little girl was, I said to myself: "You're a fake. But the innkeeper, he's a Hasid, he's a good man, he believes. Why shouldn't HaShem do something for a good man? He doesn't have to do anything for me. I'm worthless. But this innkeeper who is weeping and this child who is dying, for them He could do something. So I said a few prayers. I don't know any more than that.'

"So the Rabbi, who was still holding the fish, told his Hasid, 'I'm a nothing but you're a good man. Why can't HaShem do for you?' And within the year the Hasid had a child.

"So, Yussele, give it a year. Maybe you don't have to be a rabbi the way they think you should. You can still heal the baby." Then his father rolled over, snapped his fingers at the candle, which relit itself, leaned over Yussel, and ripped a hair from inside Yussel's nose. *"All stories are true. Even my lies."*

The pain rode up his nose, exploded like horseradish through the universe of his head, his body. He rocked over the pain, held his nose, said through it, "What did you do that for?"

His father stood above him, holding the single hair between thumb and forefinger like a treasure in the light of the candle. *"I'm bringing it back. See, I'll tell them, my son feels pain. Believe me, my son's okay."* His shadow slipped upward into the point of the tent, disappeared.

YUSSEL COULD still feel the thin arm across his waist, his father's tired head resting on his shoulder. And then, because he couldn't stand to think about where his father had come from, where he was going back to, Yussel, a pious man, a married man, allowed back into his head, into his bed, into the hollow where his father had been, the Flower Child in her HARVEY MILK FOR MAYOR T-shirt and the guys she knew and he was the guys she knew and he felt the hot honey of his teen-age days pouring into the wounds his father had left in his soul and then he really couldn't stand himself. So he washed, said prayers, got back into bed again, thought only of Shoshanna's little hands stroking his forehead. Sometime that night he dreamed something large was sliding over his waist where his father's arm had been and that the something large curled into something round and slept next to him for warmth.

12

YUSSEL WOKE up too early in the morning, felt a lump in his stomach, found himself prone, which isn't a kosher position, rolled over onto his left side, which is not only kosher but good for digestion. The lump didn't go away. He couldn't tell if it was heartburn or depression.

He sat up on the edge of Grisha's bed, sighed, rinsed his hands, mumbled the Eighteen Benedictions, thanked God he woke up with a lump in his stomach and not in his pants, thanked God he wasn't a woman, thanked God he was going back to Far Rockaway, stuck his head out of the tent, and, as they say in the Torah, lifted up his voice in a voice that shook the land, and yelled for Ernie. "Ernie!"

What had woken him up was a woman presenting a Music Minus One "Gong Show" live from the mountain. "I've Got You Under My Skin." She didn't know all the words. It was a sin for Yussel to listen to a woman singing live. Her voice blasted, bounced off the mountain, aimed for his tent, sank into his stomach. She sang something very intimate he shouldn't hear.

Yussel tossed his blanket over his head and shoulders, went outside, yelled for Ernie again. The morning was cool and dark, like standing inside a glass of iced tea, the flagpole clinking, the moon still in the sky, not a star missing from the sky. The woman's voice cracked and scraped against the rocks. Babe's chickens woke up, joined in. There was nothing seductive about her voice. It was the loneliness in it, like a wolf cry in the wilderness, that gave him a lump in his stomach. "Ernie!"

Ernie came running, stumbling, rubbing his eyes, buttoning buttons on the fly of a pair of wool khaki army pants.

"I don't want to hear a woman singing! I bought you a sound system, didn't I?"

"I didn't hear her."

"How could you not hear her?"

"Stand still," Ernie whispered in awe. Ernie grabbed Yussel's arm.

Yussel grabbed Ernie's arm. Something large and leather-cold slid between his legs, over one bare foot, out of his tent.

Ernie whispered again. "You know how many sandwiches you could get from her if she was a salami? Jesus, I wish she was an Isaac Gellis salami."

So did Yussel. All of it passed over his foot in a slow slide into the dark. Maybe six feet long, as thick as his arm. Yussel's hand was white on Ernie's arm.

"She likes Grisha." Ernie laughed a dirty laugh. "She thought you were Grisha. So, what do you want to hear? 'Hatikvah,' *Peer Gynt,* Jewish aerobics?"

Yussel washed his hands again, poured the basin water over his polluted foot. "Hatikvah" blasted into the dark morning, the lights went on in the Arizona, in Babe's bus. He heard voices in the tents. It had been a mistake to turn on the music because now everyone was waking up and someone was sure to see him leaving, try to stop him, plead with him to stay, carry on. Yussel groped for his shoes, his clothes, tossed his pajamas into his overnight, looked both ways out the tent door, and took off.

Very softly, he walked around the tents, around the adobe huts, over snake holes the size of number-ten grapefruits. Just as he ducked around the far side of the Arizona, a woman stood in his path. His heart stopped. It was still too dark to see her features. He smelled musk. Why do women have to smell?

She whispered a significant whisper. It was the same voice from last night that said he looked like a Moses. "I know who you are, Rabbi. Don't think I don't know who you are." Natalie, saying what she used to say to his father, whom she'd decided was the Messiah.

"Sure you do, Natalie. I've known you since we were kids."

"That's not what I mean."

Yussel didn't ask what she meant.

"I'm right, aren't I?"

He shouldn't have said, "Don't tell anyone." He was being funny.

"I knew it." She wrapped the shawl tighter halfway up her face, turned away from him melodramatically, pregnant now with their secret.

YUSSEL HID behind the Arizona, waited until she was gone. It was growing lighter. Natalie hated men because she thought they all had one big secret that would give her inner peace. Someplace she'd heard about the wonder Rabbi in Kansas who was giving out answers, so she'd walked to Kansas, arrived at the door of the shul, filthy, ragged, with amebic dysentery they found out later. "If you don't let me study with you I'll go out into the world and be a sex machine." The Rabbi said okay but she'd have to wear a skirt, be clean, keep kosher. Then she could study with him and not be a sex machine. He threw her clothes into the garbage can, gave her Bloomke's favorite sweater and skirt. Ever since Yussel could remember, her fingernails were chewed to the bone and now and then she'd have bruises on her neck, sometimes new and blue, sometimes old and orange. A bride of violence, his father called her.

When Natalie fought with the Rabbi because he wouldn't tell her the secret, she'd disappear with this or that dark-haired acned kibbutznik who'd come from Israel to Kansas to see the wonder Rabbi with the answers. "So tell me, Rabbi, I've been waiting a lifetime . . ." she'd say to his father. Nothing the Rabbi could tell Natalie satisfied her because she knew he was holding back the answer. Once she ran away to be a sex machine with a Moroccan Jew who sold fake Gucci bags from the trunk of his taxi, who beat her, whom the Rabbi told her to stay away from or he wouldn't teach her Torah. The last time Yussel saw Natalie, he'd been visiting his father. She'd come in drenched from a thunderstorm, her hair matted, a bloody nose, a holy book clutched to her chest. The Rabbi didn't stand up, didn't approach her, kept rolling the wax into a candle. "Didn't I tell you to stay away from the cab driver?"

"I had an accident in my kitchen, Rabbi. On a cupboard door."

His father had turned his back on Natalie. She still clutched her holy book; he rolled his wax. "So?"

"I have a problem, Rabbi."

It was the line that led straight to his circumcised heart. He turned to her immediately, his face softened, he smiled. The room lit up with the sweetness of that smile.

"In the Torah it says . . ." She flipped, panic-stricken, through pages. She'd been studying with the Rabbi for a dozen years. She was pushing thirty-five, still knew nothing. "You know about milk separated from meat? You want me to read it to you?"

"I know it. I know it. What's your problem?"

"Do I need a garbage can for meat and a garbage can for milk?"

His father stood, faced Natalie, looked at her with those terrible majestic eyes. "Tell me, why do you have a bloody nose?"

She left, slammed the front door angrily. All night it rained like a monsoon. At daybreak when Yussel got up from the sofa to pack, he looked out the picture window. Natalie was halfway up the small acacia tree on the corner, up in the branches. He could see the soles of her boots. He woke his father. The Rabbi came to the window in his pajamas. He cranked open the side window. "One garbage can. You hear me? One." Yussel remembered saying, "Why don't you just send her over to the Lubavitchers?" And his father had answered with pained patience, "Because there's a soul inside all that confusion. Because someday I may break through. Because someday she may understand. Because that's our job." Natalie had climbed down, shook water from her hair, brushed leaves from the suede, gone home.

Yussel slipped past the Arizona unseen, crossed the last hundred feet of flats, climbed the little spur to the mound of highway, tossed his overnight in the backseat of the Shanda. Mishugge people. The lump in his stomach was hardening, sending out vines. He put the AAA TripTik map into his head, thought about what route he'd take back to Far Rockaway, looked around one last time just in case he was making a mistake, which he knew he wasn't.

A small deer chewed on dried flowers on his father's grave. The sky blushed pink behind the mountains. Banks of clouds rolled against them, hit the peaks, dropped over them in smoky bagels. The peaks glinted like knives in the rising light. Under the water tower, a silver mirage shimmered like a lake. It was no place for him or his family. He couldn't find his keys although he was sure he'd left them in the car. They weren't under the seats, in the overhead, on the floor. He was on his hands and knees in the back of the car when Grisha banged on the side. Yussel jumped up, banged his own head on the roof of the car.

Rust flaked off the car, dandruff from Grisha's eyebrows. "Nu?"

"Keys."

Babe climbed the slope up to the highway, rubbed her eyes. You could read by the diamond ring she wore. She saw Yussel's overnight. "What's the matter?"

"He can't find his keys."

"You leaving, Yussel?"

"I'm leaving."

Grisha banged the side of the car again. "What's taking you so long?"

"I can't find my keys."

Babe gave Grisha a dirty look, smiled sweetly at Yussel. "Yussy, you have to kosher the kitchen before you go. At least that much."

Yussel searched in his pockets for the third time. "The kitchen's not kosher? How do you eat?"

"Cold food, sometimes from the microwave, paper plates, plastic stuff," Babe said.

Yussel tapped his fingernails on the cracked plastic of the steering wheel. "Just to kosher, that's all. Not for Shabbas."

"Also to negotiate about the mikveh when the well-digger gets here. Today, he'll be here today."

"You can't negotiate with him, Babe?"

"He doesn't do business with women. It's the West. Men are men. Women are women."

"So, Yussel, what do you say? Okay?" Grisha's fingers dug into Yussel's forearm.

"The water's already boiling for the koshering, Yussy."

"Okay, okay, koshering and the well-digger. That's my limit."

Babe took the car keys from her apron pocket. "You'll miss Chaim's morning service. Go."

YUSSEL DROVE to Chaim's house. On the way, Grisha passed him in Babe's Lincoln and Yussel passed his father standing next to a flood ditch, one door gleaming in the sun rising over the desert. Yussel backed up. His father smelled of linseed oil. He wore a creamy satin robe piped in navy blue, a navy blue silk handkerchief folded into his pocket, navy blue silk pajamas piped in cream, navy blue slippers with his initials on the fronts. The other door was lead. His father knocked on it. *"A little token of my son's esteem. My son. Packs and leaves and thinks filthy thoughts about my wife."*

"I'm not going to feel guilty. I'm not staying and that's that."

"Tricks, filth, Yussele. Other men's sons, they're giving charity, studying Talmud, earning merit for their fathers in the World to Come. My son . . ." His father banged on the lead door. *"My son packs and leaves and thinks filthy thoughts."*

Yussel could feel the banging zing down to his toes, up and into his nostrils like a tuning fork. He could feel where the hair was missing in his nose. "Don't blame me. You put yourself there."

"You can get me out."

"You put your money on the wrong horse, Totte."

"If there were another horse, Yussele, believe me, I would have bet on him. My lovely beautiful saintly Bloomke can't help me. If she'd been a son. . . . Some horse. A mule, a jackass, I have for a son."

"You want to walk?"

His father knocked with his knuckles on the doors, then on Yussel's head, which rang because he hit it with precision on the spot already sore from the Shanda's roof. His father sighed. *"If I were a priest, I wouldn't have a family. If I didn't have a family, I'd be a saint today. I'd be sitting today at the feet of HaShem instead of shlepping around with a jackass son. I'll wait in the car."*

Chaim's maniac dogs screamed, hurled themselves against their fences. Yussel shielded his eyes from the bright sun to look through a square of thick shower-stall glass cut into Chaim's front door. Swimming behind the glass, Chaim and his lump-faced low-browed stump-legged Miracles of Creation, who looked as if they'd been grown underground in manure, davened the morning service. Grisha, Feldman, Bingo, Slotnik, Ernie were with them. Seventy-five dollars a week, add Yussel, now it was ninety dollars a week; 360 dollars a month it cost to daven by Chaim.

Chaim, a nobody who came from nothing, living like a prince with his Jewish room service, Yussel's SL, a cathedral-ceilinged bunker, ebony woodwork, his velvet Maurice Villency matching everything covered in clear plastic, a turquoise bar, picture windows draped like brides in ivory satin, track lighting, a rosewood bimah, a backlit china closet with more silver than Grand Sterling. All of this on a sidewalk and seventeen other houses on sidewalks, near shopping for the wives when they came out, a computer programming business already set up so his people could earn a living in the wilderness. Yussel had goornisht mit goornisht, nothing with nothing.

Most of Chaim's court Yussel knew from Far Rockaway. Zipper Pinsky; Fifey the Kluger, which meant Fifey the Smart because he was so dumb; Johnny Atlas, which wasn't his real name; Velvl the Shecter; Mendl Weiss from Rikers Island. Mendl had served on Rikers Island for selling hot TV's in boxes that had no TV's inside. But "only to goyim" was his defense, except the judge wasn't a Jew. He was paroled early when he demanded a kosher kitchen at the jail and Corrections wouldn't pay for it. One thing, garbage or not, Chaim's court was strict to the letter of the law. Only when it came to anybody outside the congregation were they crooked. Yussel was outside the congregation.

Yussel was dazzled by the silver of the crowns on the Torah, the gold embroidery on the satin covers, the gorgeous spice boxes, the Torah pointers, the menorahs. He couldn't wait to see if the turquoise bar was really turquoise, if the leaves on the ficus trees were really silk, which would mean the trees went for three hundred bucks apiece in the Flower District, plus delivery.

Yussel pressed a button. Electronic chimes rang the six notes of "Ain Kaloheynu." The dogs went up an octave to the edge of the sound barrier. The davening stopped. Lights flashed on and off on the second floor, as if someone were signaling Paul Revere. Mendl, wearing a Patagonia shell of gray fleece under his crumpled black gabardine jacket and probably a bulletproof vest under his fleece shell, came to the door, looked with narrowing eyes through the glass, yelled over his shoulder to Chaim, "You want Reb Fetner?"

"Fifteen dollars a week. Three meals on Shabbas," Chaim yelled back.

Yussel was out in twenty minutes. Real silk, real turquoise. Chaim must have *something* he gives to his congregation that they give him such gifts. Something rotten but impressive. On the way to the Arizona, Yussel passed a jackrabbit crucified on a barbed-wire fence.

"See, a sign. Out of fear and impulsive action, the rabbit traps himself. There, Yussele, is a rabbit who didn't pay attention."

Yussel shrugged a shoulder halfway. "On the other hand, there's a fence that by standing in one place, things come to it. I don't like signs, Totte. I don't want to live in your crazy universe."

"Two Jews out here in the wilderness, you should be nice to Chaim. You depend on each other."

"I owe him nothing."

"You owe every Jew, Yussele. Fetners especially owe. Didn't I tell you already? Just as the Angel who wrestled with Jacob, Chaim comes to wrestle with you until you see the dawn. Until you see the light. Maybe that's Chaim's job. To get you through the night. Maybe that's the only reason he exists—to challenge you."

"Yeah, yeah. I exist so he can have my SL, my blood."

"Cuchem! Wise guy! You think you're not being challenged? HaShem's putting pressure on you. Harder and harder. Measure for measure. I know how He operates. You ignore HaShem at one level, believe me He'll get you at the next level even worse. So I'm telling you, you're being asked to be kind to Chaim."

"Why doesn't HaShem ask Chaim to be kind to me?"

"Something in you needs correction."

"In *me?* The guy's out for my blood. I should be kind to my own murderer? I'm only human, Totte."

His father found Q-Tips, cleaned out his ears, his keyholes. *"Maybe that's your problem. Maybe you've forgotten you're more* than human, that man is more than man. Maybe you don't know who you are."

"You think I'm something else. I know who I am. I'm an insurance agent from Far Rockaway. Period."

His father sighed a terrible sigh, pushed his hat back, leaned against the seat, held his beard with his right hand, folded his doors. *"Listen, a who-you-are story. One day to the Maggid of Trisk, your ancestor, the famous Rabbi Urula, came for Shabbas. When Reb Urula sat down with the Maggid for the evening meal on Friday night, he saw that the Maggid didn't eat.*

"'Why don't you eat?'

"'I don't eat because I don't feel well.'

"'And why don't you feel well?'

"'I don't feel well because I don't sleep.'

"If it weren't that Reb Urula was the son of the illustrious Meor Vashemesh, the Maggid of Trisk wouldn't have even answered this much.

"The next day at the second Shabbas meal, the Maggid didn't eat. Reb Urula asked, 'Why don't you eat?'

"They go around again with I don't eat because I don't feel well. I don't feel well because I don't sleep. So by the third meal, the Maggid still has not eaten. Reb Urula, who was after all one of the elders of his generation and deserved respect even from so famous a man as the Maggid of Trisk, was persistent. Finally the Maggid told Reb Urula the truth. And this is what he told him:

"'Long ago when I was a very little boy, my father of blessed memory woke us up and told us to get dressed warm because we were going to take a ride in the wagon into the forest. This was very strange. It was so early we knew he hadn't even davened yet. Something very important was happening. The sun wasn't even up yet. The forest was pitch black. Steam rose off the horses' backsides. Frost was on everything. We drove very fast and very far into the forest, deeper and deeper. The road ended. Still we went on. Finally we came to a small hut, one room, maybe a woodcutter's shack. My father stopped the wagon. He told us to stay in the wagon and be quiet and watch for an old man with a long white beard and when he comes we should tell him our father is waiting for him in the little hut. So my father left and went into the hut and

we pulled blankets around us and huddled into the straw. We could see a little sunlight come through the pines. The sun came up higher and higher and then sure enough a wagon came into the forest and stopped behind our wagon. There was an old man with a long white beard and sad eyes. He said to us, "Children, where is your father?"'

"'We pointed to the hut and he went into it. Now it was almost noon. The sun was overhead someplace but the forest was still dark and cold. We ate bread, cheese, waited. They were in the hut for hours. There was no sign from them, no sound. We waited some more.'

"'Finally the old man came out of the hut and walked to his wagon. His back was bent over as if he had a heavy pack. Just as he was about to climb into his wagon, he paused and gave a sigh, a terrible sigh. Then he climbed in and drove away.'

"'My father came out of the hut and took up the reins of the wagon, turned it around, and drove home very slowly. The old man with the white beard was the Messiah. My father had to tell him not to come because the generation wasn't ready for him. From that deep sigh, I don't sleep.'"

Yussel's father lifted his hat, scratched his head with both hands. *"That, Yussele, that's who you are, who we all are, from the generation that saw the Messiah and told Him the world wasn't ready. No small potatoes. I told you this story so you too can know here in your forest, in your generation, who you are, what you can be. Maybe it will be your generation and you'll have to tell the Messiah you aren't ready. Maybe you'll be ready."*

"Yeah, yeah. He'll tell me he has a message: Sell your kids; buy Kuwait."

"Why are you fighting this? Circumcise your heart, Yussel. Make a relationship with HaShem. Attach."

"I believe in Him. That isn't enough?"

"Yussele! I believe in Evel Knievel. But I don't have a relationship with him."

Yussel pulled up in front of the Arizona, helped his father out. His father listed to the side with the weight of the new door, dragged a foot, worked out forward motion downhill, rotated his arms like propellers to balance himself as he climbed down the spur, collapsed at his grave. *"I'll wait here in case I have visitors."*

126

———

YUSSEL'S CONGREGATION—mostly young women—was crowded into the kitchen and beyond in the social hall to meet him and help kosher the kitchen. Yussel said a sullen hello to people he knew, to people he'd never seen before, would never see again. Mostly he said hello to sneakers, hiking boots. He made sure not to smile.

"You want me to take your coat?"

Yussel shook his head no, kept his coat on, nobody should think he was staying.

The kitchen was as trim and sleek as a dining car. The stove had burned on high all night and now people cleaned white ashes from the ovens and burners. Steam from the boiling pots formed drops and slid down the windows. Babe mopped her brow, sighed, snapped orders. Yussel poured a cup of coffee, lit a cigarette. Babe told him to go outside if he had to smoke. Yussel put out his cigarette, banged around, already sore, slammed drawers, grabbed handfuls of silver, piles of pots, plunged a fire-hot brick into the boiling water, dumped in forks, knives, spoons, pots, pans, everything, swore mightily at his father. His congregation watched him, studied him, looked away when he looked back at them. They washed, dried, cringed, avoided Yussel with little steps, backward, sideward, gave one another big looks. Slotnik, tall, slouched, shook his hand, mumbled something about studying, left. Natalie stared hungrily, nodded knowingly when Yussel glanced her way. He was burning up in his coat, dying for a cigarette.

When he finally took a break, he found his father in the pantry off the kitchen, sitting on top of boxes of noodles, sacks of brown rice, bags of potatoes. Yussel took off his coat, lit a cigarette, saw the Flower Child in the smoke.

"Hah! Look! Mr. Lump-in-the-Pants himself. Someone should take down your pants, Yussele, and make you stand naked in front of your congregation. You, such a filthy person you are, that you should criticize me! With your thoughts? Filth! You better watch yourself about my wife, Yussele, putting such ideas into Chaim's head. Don't think I forget."

Yussel exhaled slowly. "You tell me, where does filth come from, Totte? And where do thoughts come from? And where does

127

lust come from? I should only thank Him for good thoughts? I should only thank Him for wealth, not poverty; for health, not sickness; for life not death? He's the One Who sets up the longing, the desire, the evil inclinations." Yussel jerked his thumb Heavenward. "Don't blame me. Blame Him!"

"A little willpower goes a long way, my darling son."

"What good is willpower when He's already given me diarrhea?"

"Vey iz mir. Vey iz mir. I don't have enough shame with a lead door? I have to have shame from my own Yussele, my blood? I should have two lead doors, maybe a ball and chain? What do you want, Yussele?"

"I want only to be comfortable. Me and my family, period. In spite of you. In spite of everything."

"That's not even Jewish, comfortable."

"I'm going to drive up the mountain, dip the pots and pans in a stream, finish the koshering, drop everything off back here, leave. I just want you to know. I don't want my wife to pay the price. I don't want my family to hate me. I don't want my wife to leave me. I don't want to live your life. We'll be home in a week. You want to take a ride up the mountain?"

"No, no. Think your filthy thoughts by yourself."

Somebody changed the "Hatikvah" tape to Jewish aerobics. Between beats of rock and roll, women on the tape shouted, "Oy gevalt, two-step, turn." Anything was better than "The Gong Show" from the mountain. The rhythm speeded up the work.

Grisha refused to help in the kitchen, sat at the bar, dealt the cards. Yussel wanted Grisha to help in the kitchen. "Who's ahead, Grisha?"

"Baruch HaShem, He owes me."

"You couldn't talk to HaShem while you're drying dishes?"

Grisha grunted. "Slotnik studies. I'm studying." And dealt another twelve piles of cards in a circle, with one in the center.

Yussel didn't have the time or the strength to argue. All morning he worked furiously so he could get on the road before dark, get home in the morning, finish packing, drive to Far Rockaway.

Just before lunch, a strange car pulled up, left. He heard the little lisp. She wore her big turban like a white cloud around her head and a long white dress, loose, almost a robe. She looked like a

Jamaican priestess who kills chickens and reads their guts. She herself wasn't so extraordinary. It was the sense she had of herself—the way she walked, the way she held herself, the way she stroked herself, the softness, the juiciness of everything. Yussel felt his apron rise, smelled baby powder.

"Man!" the Jackalope screamed like a parrot. He carried suitcases and an easel. She was planning to stay.

Babe swooped in like the wrath of God. "What are you doing here?"

"Who are you that I should ask your permission?"

A door slammed. Natalie ran in, wild-eyed, arms winding up like a baseball pitcher, her face twisting into one dread mask after another. The Blondische, who was right behind her, trying to stop her, stepped between Natalie and the Flower Child, threw her arms round the Flower Child. "Don't you lay a hand on her, Natalie!"   .

"The Black Widow's here. What are you doing here, Black Widow?" Natalie yelled. "We don't want you here!"

The Flower Child pushed the Blondische's braid from her own face to answer Natalie. "I belong here."

"You killed him."

"That's a lie, Natalie."

"House! Lady!" the Jackalope shouted at Natalie.

The Blondische turned to Natalie and Babe. "Why don't you leave her alone? It's not her fault. She has every right and more to be here. It's not her fault."

"People like *you* killed my husband, Natalie. If it wasn't for people like you, he'd be here today."

"Like me? You killed him. You . . . with your . . . your body and your demands, your crises. *You* killed him. *And we do not want you here!*"

"Lady!" The Jackalope screamed a parrot scream. His mother grabbed him by the arm, dragged him into the kitchen. She held her head high, but her lower lip trembled. "You can't defend me, Yussel?"

Yussel shrugged. He couldn't look at her. Of course he should look at her, be kind to her, but he couldn't. She wasn't his problem. His mother was his problem, his own wife was his problem but not his father's extra wife. Also she was a big girl. Also he didn't want to have weeping women around. Also, he didn't want a sexpot around because he couldn't handle it, that much he'd admit. He couldn't handle it. Hadn't she managed for herself before she met his father? She'd manage for herself again, find her friends in San Francisco, or something. It wasn't Yussel's problem.

She set a green eyedrop bottle on the table. "Chlorophyll for the altitude. It will help. And some Chinese tea for flatulence."

Yussel grunted, read the directions on the bottle.

"Your father used it when he came out here."

"He came out here?"

"We both did, a lot. He said it was holy land. You didn't know that?"

"My father was a liar."

"Your father loved you. He told me that many times. You must never say anything bad about him to me. I'm his widow." On which word her voice hardened as if she'd hit a switch. "I have a role here, Yussel."

"We'll have to talk about it."

"There's nothing to talk about. He told me I had a role here and you had a role here. He expected me to be here and I'm here. It was his wish. I'm going to sleep with my friends in their tent. My son can sleep with the men."

"Uh . . ." Yussel could feel his ears turn red. He didn't want her around. Yussel handed the Jackalope two potatoes. He banged them together happily.

"He's very excited to be on a trip, to see you. He won't be any trouble. He'll sit for hours."

"Didn't I ask you not to come?"

The Flower Child stretched both arms out at her sides, palms up, empty, to show him she came without weapons. It was the gesture of a dog rolling over and offering up his belly. What she didn't understand was that she was all weapon. Yussel felt very sorry for her. Just in his father's memory he should be kind. He couldn't. She moved closer, smiled her little smile. "My house is full of tears. Death comes up into the windows. I long for your father as a hart longs for a flowing stream. Here there is life. Here I have friends. Also a student of Chaim's was bringing down meat from Kansas City and staying for Shabbas."

He looked at his watch. "You drove through the night? It's forbidden to be overnight with another man, even in a car."

"I had my son. Nobody was alone." She smiled, opened her eyes wide. He didn't want her here. Maybe it was only to protect his own ass, maybe it was to protect Shoshanna, maybe it was to protect the community from the fighting, but he didn't want her here. He didn't care why.

"Shoshanna's the Rebbitzen here. There's no place for two of you. It creates too many problems. Shoshanna wouldn't be able to handle it."

Her eyes grew big with tears. He felt the lump in his stomach expanding. He couldn't handle having her around. He felt terrible for her, but he couldn't handle it. The tears ran down her face. She licked them up with her tongue. He just couldn't handle it. Women. He turned his back. "It just won't work."

"Look at me, Yussel. I drink my own tears like wine, Yussel. You're my family. You're all I have. What's to become of me? You won't even look at me."

He knew she was standing behind him, staring at his back, maybe doing her Charlie Chaplin step, her apology for any human traits she might have by mistake. Yussel wouldn't look at her. "What do you want from me? It won't work."

After she left, his father came to him. *"You sure what you're doing is okay?"*

"It's okay with me. She's a big girl. She'll make a new life."

"You don't think you're kicking her out?"

"If that's what you want to call it, I'm kicking her out."

"You couldn't let her stay and ignore her a little, try to work it out?"

"She's not the kind of woman you ignore."

His father clucked his tongue. *"Listen, you're also a big boy. You know your heart."*

"You think I'm wrong, Totte? She'd ruin the community. She'd wipe out Shoshanna with a swat. She'd be all over me."

"You have to weigh these things. What's wrong for you may be right for me. Who knows? One thing . . ." The Rabbi came closer, leaned with his elbows on the counter, pinched his eyes and looked hard at Yussel. *"One thing, HaShem weaves your destiny from your choices. So make sure you're making the right choice."*

131

"So how do I know I'm making the right choice?"

"You won't know probably until it's too late. Only HaShem knows the consequences."

Yussel called his father's house. "I'm coming home. Pack everything. We're leaving for Far Rockaway. It isn't going to work."

Long pause. Yussel smelled trouble.

"I've made up my mind, Shoshanna."

Longer pause.

"I have to get out of here."

"A Fetner would stay for Shabbas."

"I've made up my mind."

"Don't be melodramatic, Yussel."

Long pause from Yussel. He couldn't expect her to understand sex, lust, filth. Even him, the way he was right now. "No. I'm leaving tonight, as soon as the koshering's done. I'll be home for Shabbas. That's final."

"Nothing's final except death."

"It should only be."

13

A BLAZING RED pickup with stainless-steel vertical exhausts, a four-man cab, balloon tires, ROSEBUD tendrilled in gold paint on the door panel, pulled up on the highway. Yussel wiped the steam from the kitchen window, watched a side of long-haired pork roll out of the pickup, roll down the spur toward the Arizona, roll as if all his parts worked on ballbearings. Natalie wiped her own circle of steam from the window, exhaled, "God help me."

The Indian had metallic eyes that burned in the sunshine. Yussel had never seen such eyes. The women had never seen such flesh. His jeans were so tight you could tell he wasn't circumcised, which was an exaggeration but so was the Indian. He wore one long dangling turquoise earring, a beaded necklace, a French braid instead of a ponytail.

"Your eyes," Natalie breathed.

He grinned a great American hero grin. "Reflector contacts, ma'am."

Yussel said, "No shirt, no shoes, no service."

He left, came back in a MILK DRINKERS MAKE GREAT LOVERS T-shirt in which he still looked worse than naked. The women offered him coffee, admired his beads, stared into his contacts, saw themselves double, called him Rosebud. Yussel sent the women to the kitchen, put on his coat and hat to negotiate. Yussel could see himself in the reflector contacts. He was pleased he'd put on his hat and coat.

"Rosebud your name or your truck's name?"

"Me, Your Highness, and all my trucks. I like trucks."

There was nothing to negotiate. Rosebud guaranteed water, called Yussel Your Highness.

"You guarantee water in the desert?" Yussel wondered what the chances were, what his tables would say. One in fifty thousand, one in a million?

"Yep. No water, Your Highness, no deal."

"You do this for a living, Rosebud?"

"I don't get many calls."

"How much if you hit water?"

"By the foot. If I dig deep you come out ahead. Shallow, I come out ahead. Moneywise."

"It's not the other way around, moneywise?"

Something moved under the reflector contacts. The Indian adjusted his testicles, considered the question. "Must be the other way around, moneywise." Rosebud handed Yussel a bill from Woodpecker's Hardware for a three-and-a-half-inch pipe and a number-four cap. Yussel questioned this, that they didn't match. He was a patient, respectful Indian. In spite of his pants, Yussel liked him. "Look, Your Highness. Three and a half inches inside. Quarter inch on each outside. Adds up to four inches. Four-inch cap. See?"

"Why don't they call it a four-inch pipe then?"

Rosebud readjusted his testicles for a possible answer. Grisha whispered to Yussel to leave him alone in case he changed his mind. Yussel decided since the Indian wouldn't find water, Yussel wouldn't ask him how deep, how long, at what point he'd give up digging.

As they talked, the Flower Child drifted around the Arizona, smiling secret smiles, lifting things, putting them down gently as if they were alive and she were the angel standing behind them telling them to grow. Yussel hoped the Indian kid wouldn't see her, wouldn't be polluted by her, that she wouldn't bring him a glass of milk.

ROSEBUD HAD sticks to shake to find water. The sticks had long narrow red, blue, and green ribbons. Grisha told him according to Oral Tradition the mikveh had to be under the water tower to catch the rainwaters from Heaven and mix them with the waters from earth, so go and shake anywhere, but dig under the water tower. Rosebud stroked his ribbons, himself, told Grisha and Yussel that a man needs a hundred gallons of water a day, a cow thirty, a horse ten, a bathtub same as a cow, and isn't this going to be a bathtub? A hot tub? A pool?

Babe came out with coffee and Entenmann's, shooed the Flower Child out of sight. "A hundred chickens need four gallons, right? Be sure my chickens get enough water too."

"Four gallons? That's all?" Yussel asked. It was such a basic fact of creation, more fundamental than his actuary tables.

"Out here, Your Highness, you can't have too much and you can't have too little. Tricky place." Rosebud waited to eat until Yussel took the first bite of coffee cake. Yussel hoped Schmulke would grow up with such manners, couldn't get over the precision of the fact that a hundred chickens need four gallons of water.

Grisha explained the mikveh. "What we're going to build here is actually a ceremonial bathtub. To purify."

"A kiva. We got the same thing."

Everyone laughed, the Jews arrogantly, the Indian with pleasure. Yussel went on. He liked this boy. "As you said, a man's volume is about a hundred gallons. According to our law he needs twice his volume to be purified, so the mikveh should contain two hundred gallons of water."

"You got it, Your Highness."

"And for my chickens." Babe wiggled a finger at the Indian. After they shook hands a lot, after Rosebud climbed into his truck, Yussel decided to make a potato kugel. He didn't know what made him decide to make a kugel except it was Thursday and it was what his father would have done on Thursday. Also he wanted an excuse to stay around a little longer to watch the well digging. If he left by dark, he'd have plenty of time to get back to Shoshanna for Shabbas. If he hit water, he'd invite Chaim over. Chaim would plotz with envy if Yussel hit water. Yussel peeled potatoes, chopped onions, thought with satisfaction about Chaim plotzing with envy.

The Flower Child wandered around with her secret smile. Damp ringlets slipped from her turban, along the nape of her neck, on her forehead, by her ears. She pushed them back under the turban, twisted them absentmindedly around a little finger. Yussel wondered if she were thinking about his father, or him, or the Indian. Dreamily, she set up her easel on the bar, took out brushes and inks from a backpack, painted her cats. Yussel rolled a potato around in his hand. She was making him crazy. He needed to touch something. When she started to hum her waltzes, Grisha slapped his cards on the table, escaped to the kitchen, said he'd grind the potatoes.

GRISHA MADE a mess of the grinding. Pieces of onion and potato skins were all over his shirt and pants, also the floor. Black juices leaked from the grinder onto Grisha's shoes.

"What do you think, Grisha? She should stay?"

"In Yeshiva they told us to cross the street if we saw a girl on the sidewalk, never to talk to a girl, never, God forbid, to touch one, even by accident, and never to touch ourselves. They said we'd get over such strange thoughts once we got married. I'm not married. You are. What do you think?" He held up a potato. "Don't tell me. You think like your father thought. I don't want to know."

Yussel dropped his voice even lower. "Grisha, you ever dream about women?"

"You mean a sex dream? Sure."

"It didn't worry you?"

"When I dream a sex dream I know it's a sign my soul is traveling up into higher places. There my soul she'll hear prophecy, even revelations, collect important meanings. When a kid like you dreams a sex dream, it's a sex dream, not the wanderings of your soul. A sin."

"What if you remember your dream during the day?"

"During the day, if you allow yourself to think strange thoughts about a woman, your pants should be pulled down in front of the whole congregation."

"What's the difference, day or night?"

"I don't know." Grisha shrugged, cut a potato in quarters with karate chops. "Passion's passion. For God, for a woman. Who knows? For me, it feels the same. I'm sixty. It feels the same." Then he cocked his head toward the Flower Child bent over her drawings. "For example, a zaftig maidela like that one. Who wouldn't want to make Shabbas with her? You know what I mean?"

Yussel thought Grisha was dead already. He wasn't. Yussel's apron rose in a little tent. He pressed against the sink to hide himself.

MID-MORNING, drying cats spread along the bar, the Flower Child came to the kitchen, filled a thermos with Red Zinger tea, took it outside, spread a blanket on her husband's grave, wrapped her arms around her knees, wept, talked, sang, laughed. Yussel thought he might see his father talking to her. He made four thousand trips to the garbage cans.

Finally the Flower Child, rubbing her eyes, drifted into the kitchen. Her cheeks were bright red spots. "I saw your father, Yussel," she whispered to his back as he stood at the sink, his hands in water. "He has a silver fox coat. He must be a rich man in Heaven."

"Don't tell me lies."

"I saw him," she insisted. Yussel let the sink drain. She started to cry. He ran the water. She left.

YUSSEL HEARD the little lisp on the phone. Later, he saw the easel was gone, she was gone, but not the Jackalope. Yussel didn't care. He was very depressed. He could still smell baby powder. He put his hands to his face and breathed in onions until he couldn't see. He didn't understand what women saw in him, what they wanted from him. Worse than that he had learned in the past few days that he didn't understand what he wanted from women. Didn't he have a perfectly good wife? What was wrong with him, his penis going up and down like a flag every time she walked into the room, this Flower Child?

"Yussel," Grisha whispered. "You know why God gave women vaginas? So men would talk to them."

"Grisha, what do women see in me?"

Grisha looked at him with both eyebrows in the air.

"Robert Redford you're not."

"So what do they see? The Flower Child? The girls in the tent?"

Grisha shrugged. "Same as your father. He couldn't shake them off. They looked in his eyes, they saw five thousand years of wisdom, the sweetness of a soul, a prince, a man who has God's ear. That's all."

"Please."

"Listen, Boychickl, even *I* see it and *I* think you're a dumb shmuck."

"It makes trouble."

"Look what it did to your father. Listen, Yussel, play it safe. Don't smile, don't look in their eyes."

LILLYWHITE, who lived on the mountain, picked up the Flower Child on the highway, not far from the Arizona. She had a small suitcase, her easel. Her breasts were wet with tears. Lillywhite just pulled up, opened the door. The woman climbed in. "I'm going to the house of the Rabbi in the village of Moffat." Her jaw turned sideways as she talked, as if she ground her teeth at night, making a great effort to be at peace with herself. "I'm the widow of a rabbi. I visited with his son. He's throwing me out because he thinks I'd be a lot of trouble and he doesn't want any trouble."

"Would you be a lot of trouble?"

"Yes. A lot."

"And this new Rabbi?"

She turned her head, watched the landscape.

Lillywhite persisted. "And the Rabbi in Moffat?"

"Since my husband died, he's the first person who's smiled at me, the first person who's offered me so much as a drink of water, the first person who even asked me a question."

"So this new Rabbi will be nicer?"

She shrugged. "I'll tell you something. The tent of our forefather Abraham had four doors, so anyone could enter, no matter where he came from. I hope that where I am going there is such a door for me. Anyway"—she smoothed her turban, tucked loose hair under it—"if it's intended, it will work out."

Lillywhite drove silently, thinking about the son. The Flower

Child sniffed and wept. Lillywhite found Kleenex in the glove compartment. "Tell me about the doors in Abraham's tent again."

"Abraham's tent had four doors, so anyone could enter. No matter which direction he came from, he could enter his father's house. Are you married?"

"No. No men, no mortgage."

"When a holy man loves you, he loves all of you. There is no part of yourself that isn't good enough. You don't have to hold your soul apart. He hears you. He listens to every moment. What I had . . . I have no more." She sighed, she shook her head. "Have you known such love?"

Lillywhite shook her head, said nothing, hoped she'd hear more.

"He took me into the center of the universe."

Lillywhite changed the subject. "Do you have children? Aren't you people supposed to have lots of children?"

"From my first husband, I have a son. I'm coming back for him . . . in a few days."

"I have a big house. You could stay with me, think it through. I'd take your son. Whatever."

"I have to go where I belong. To belong is very important."

Lillywhite swallowed hard. "I never wanted to belong to anything."

"My husband of blessed memory would say to you, that's why you're not free."

Lillywhite tried to sound casual. "How about his son? Is his son like his father?"

"His son? His son is like a beautiful woman who wears a veil. A veil of knots and angry colors. A thick veil. He hides from himself, from his own humanity. His father of blessed memory wasn't frightened to be human."

Lillywhite pulled up in front of the blue-roofed adobe house. The dogs barked. She ripped a deposit slip from her checkbook with her name and address on it, jotted down her phone number. "Tell your kid. If you need anything. You don't have to . . . to go begging."

"This is where I belong." She pulled an end of her turban across the bottom of her face. She was from another desert, another time. "Will you promise me something?"

Lillywhite nodded. She wanted to go home and dream about the son, about what was under the veil, about loving a man who can see into your soul.

"Tell no one you saw me."

"If you promise to call me or come to me if you get into trouble."

"Agreed."

Lillywhite hesitated. She wanted to hug her. She didn't know if she should.

The Flower Child hugged her, squeezed her very, very hard. "I see worry in your eyes for me. Don't worry. What's intended will be."

ROSEBUD RETURNED with a mint-condition sky-high yellow rig and winch on the back of a huge truck. The door panels also said ROSEBUD. Everyone stopped work to watch him bring the truck down the hill from the highway inch by inch, brakes squealing, right next to the water tower. He took off his shirt, shook his sticks. Yussel yelled at the women to come back inside and get to work so he could leave by sundown, be home for Shabbas. Indian Joe arrived, sat on the Rabbi's grave, arranged sticks in geometric patterns, sometimes shook them.

The drill punched and screamed. Rosebud shouted directions to Bingo and Ernie, who had also removed their shirts. "Okay. Move that kelly. Okay, take out the kelly. Okay, move the kelly." Every now and then, Rosebud stopped, shook his ribboned sticks, scratched his well-hung self. Sometimes he passed the ribbons to Ernie who shook them, who danced around to the Jewish aerobics. Yussel started to jump around the kitchen to the music, wanted to be with the men.

When the Shanda was filled with all the pots and pans and silver and dishes for dipping in running water, Ernie gave Yussel directions to a deep stream up in the mountains. Yussel's father was curled up on the bags of potatoes, snoring deeply. Yussel took a blanket from Grisha's bedroom off the kitchen, covered his father, who said, *Where did you send my Flower Child? Why are you sending her away?* Yussel pulled the blanket over his face the way he'd pulled the shroud cap over his face.

YUSSEL DROVE past Babe's bus, into the cottonwoods, to the base of Kit Carson Mountain, up a rough road to a line of aspens, into a dark notch of pine and cliffs of red rock. The muffler clunked against the rocks in the road. The kitchen goods rattled, shook, scraped. The wheels spun out in ruts in the road. The car smoked, stank. Rubber burned. Yussel thought about the chickens and the four gallons of water. He understood that the rabbis made up the law about the mikveh. He just couldn't figure out who determined the law about the chickens. Higher and higher he drove until the road ended where a powerful stream of snow-melt crossed it. Yussel took a deep breath of fresh air, parked the car, stepped over large amounts of animal droppings, burnt orange sprinkles of wild-flowers, tree roots, found a point in the stream where it converged with the snow-melt to form a pool. He threw in a stone. The water seemed deep enough. He hoped the droppings were from a horse, not from anything he'd seen in Safari Adventureland, not from anything that would bite.

At a little lift, a little edge, he looked out over the desert below, then up through the black pines in the blue-eyed sky, wanted to pray, maybe even dance to God, right here on this spot. And then he thought maybe he should talk to God. So he did. "Listen." He had never done anything more than pray prayers, sing songs, never went direct since he was a little pisher and wanted a teacher to drop dead. "Listen." Pines swished like ocean waves. Birds made bellsounds.

"Listen, if a hundred chickens need four gallons of water, why put them out in the desert where there's no water? Why don't You just give the chickens enough water in the first place? Why don't You give all of us enough? You can't do a budget? My *wife* can do a budget, for God's sake. You put the chickens in the desert so they can learn about death? So they can learn to be grateful? So they can learn who's boss? So they can be challenged and become rab-bis?" Yussel rubbed his chin. "If You need the water someplace else, reduce their need to two gallons. Maybe You want us to want? Maybe you want me to want? Is that why You're shooting me up with strange and filthy thoughts about my father's wife?

Okay. I'm going to make a deal with You. I'll stay for Shabbas on two conditions: One, You give the shmegeggies plenty of water; two, You get rid of the Flower Child . . . out of my blood, out of my head, out of my sight." Yussel felt really stupid. He should be asking to win a lottery not to find water in the desert. With a lottery, at least there's a chance. "Okay? Okay, that's all I have to say. I know it's crazy." He stepped down from the rock, climbed back up again. "Listen, You set it up, don't blame me. None of this was my idea."

Yussel stepped back down, climbed back up. "All I ask for myself is that I'm comfortable, me, my family, comfortable. Amen."

It made him feel good. It made him feel so good he went back to the pool by the side of the road, stripped, stood for a moment in the scatter of sunlight, then plunged into the icy water. The tips of the pine trees scratched his destiny in the parchment of sky. It was his father's universe. Under he went. On his knees he could get his head in, every last hair. Except that it was freezing, it was a perfect mikveh. Every hair, every bit of his 613 parts, under for his dreams, for his thoughts. It was the right thing to do, to cleanse himself. He held his nose and stayed under. He said the name of God, intertwined it with other names of God, looked on his screen to see which way he should drive back to Far Rockaway, examined the route across Kansas up to Chicago, to Buffalo, over to the Thruway, south to Far Rockaway. There was heavy rain on the Thruway, a slow-moving convoy, so he drove the southern route across to Knoxville, then up to Pennsylvania, onto the Palisades Parkway, across the George Washington Bridge, until his lungs felt like bursting and he popped up and just as he popped up he felt the ground shaking and a mass of flesh, muscle, red hair, belly, hoof hitting his head—like the Behema—blotted out the sky, his screen, the George Washington Bridge. Yussel yelled.

A woman yelled back. A horse whinnied. The horse landed on the other side of the stream, reared up. The woman, who looked like part of the horse—her hair the same red as his tail—yelled over her shoulder at him as she struggled to pull the horse down. "You think this is funny, Minchas Pinchus?"

Yussel scrambled out of the water, but his clothes were on the other side. So, what does a Jew do in the wilderness, bare-assed, kicked in the head by a horse, freezing, a stranger accusing him of perversion? He smiles. Yussel smiled, pulled one shoulder up in a shrug, spread his hands, and smiled. "I'm sorry. I'm really sorry." He really was.

She stared for a moment at his face. Looking back, he could swear in a court of law she'd never looked down, just at his face, not at his body. Also that she was the most beautiful woman he'd ever seen. She shook her head No! as if he'd offered her something, which he hadn't except for the smile, wheeled her horse around, took off in a storm of mud that rained on Yussel. He jumped into the pool. The hoofbeats pounded through the forest, turned into runaway heartbeats, so he pulled himself out of the water. His skin was blue; his baitzim shrunken like a little boy's. He'd been run over by a horse, a half-inch more he'd be dead. So why was he apologizing? Why was he smiling? Because he was Jewish.

Shaking, looking in his head for his screen, his head pounding like Con Ed, he dried off with the dishtowels, squeezed out his beard, despised himself for apologizing, for giving her even a smile, wrapped his side curls back into their little anchovies, tucked them under his hat, put on the rest of his clothes, lay belly-down by the pool in a bed of pine needles, dipped all the kitchen goods into the pool, piled everything back into the car, drove down the mountain road across the flats toward the Arizona. He tried to reactivate his screen but couldn't get anything on it, worried that maybe he had a concussion from the horse. Maybe HaShem was taking away his gift of prophecy, which was okay with Yussel because if he lost his gift he wouldn't owe Anybody Anything. Yussel decided that Jews didn't belong in such a place. Everything was larger than life: Indians, redheads, horses. People who dunk in the ocean don't get kicked in the head by horses.

As he left the dark of the woods and headed out on the dirt road of the flats, he said to the redhead, under his breath, "Pig. Anti-Semite pig." From the phone at the Riverside, he said to Shoshanna, "Shoshanna, Shoshanna." With the first Shoshanna he was talking to her; with the second to her soul because maybe her soul would hear what he was really trying to say and he wouldn't have to say it. "Shoshanna, Shoshanna. I don't care what you say."

"So why are you calling?"

"So you can start packing."

"What will people say, a Fetner running away?"

"You don't understand."

"Explain, then."

"You won't understand. It's very complicated. I just don't want to get involved. You don't understand how involved this can get."

"You should at least stay for Shabbas."

"I can't."

"Please, Yussel, don't be melodramatic."

"Okay, Shoshanna, okay. Okay, I'll see." He'd drop the pots off, talk to no one, walk out. Just like that. Fetner or not. You want to see simple, Shoshanna? I'll show you simple.

What he was saying to her soul was that the horse kicking him in the head just as he came up from the pool was too precise to be an accident. That losing his screen was too intentional. That he had a horrible feeling he'd moved over into his father's universe and he was going to be trapped in its infinite cause and finite effect, in its decision-and-punishment routine, in the chaos of his father's universe that he wanted no part of. Hadn't he thought just before he dived in that he was in his father's universe? This was the way his father wanted him to think, to be afraid, to look for signs. This was the trap. Gorgeous women, wild horses. He didn't need any such tricks. He was leaving.

His father sat beside him in the Shanda, happy, shaking his head, beating both of his fists on the dashboard. *Yom diddle yom diddle ai diddle dai dai.*

"You're happy I got kicked in the head?"

"Maybe that's how HaShem gets your attention. The lady has, God help you, two legs. The horse four. He hit you over the head with a two-by-four. Yom diddle yom diddle ai diddle dai dai." His father cackled at his joke and sang and banged his fists until the Shanda reached the highway, then he sat up straight, alert for something Yussel could not yet see.

14

TRAFFIC ON THE highway was backed up like the FDR Drive at rush hour. Yussel maneuvered the Shanda around cars, trucks, Winnebagos, a horse van, hundreds of people. "Sacred lake," someone shouted at Yussel, pointed down to the Arizona, to a smooth shallow lake rippling on the flats. Yussel could see how the universe worked—with mirrors. A tower of water shot up under the water tower, reflected back into the lake, crashed on the roof of the Arizona. Babe's chickens were belly-up. The lake lapped at the Arizona, the adobe houses, the tents. Grisha held forth like a prophet, claimed a victory for HaShem. Rosebud stood in the middle of all this, scratching himself, his head. The Arizona listed, tilted at a crazy angle. His father was yelling from the water tower, dancing in the water tower, laughing, praising, dancing to HaShem, swinging his doors. His pipe glinted in the sunlight, his face lit up like the moon. Now he wore red silk pajamas with a black velour hooded robe, embroidered with green-and-yellow mallard ducks, a large hand-painted mallard duck on his pocket. The water tower had a leg up in the air as if it were about to pee. Yussel covered his eyes with a hand, rubbed his forehead, rubbed his eyes, dropped his head onto the cracked plastic of the steering wheel. Was HaShem in on this one? He asked for water, he got a flood. He asked to get rid of the Flower Child. He expected soon to see her belly-up with Babe's chickens.

"WHAT I WANT to know is how you did this!" His father swept his arm over the disaster below. *"I don't know how you did this but you did this. With the power that's in your blood, Yussele."* His father shook his head. *"We shouldn't let you walk around loose. You could be dangerous just by not paying attention."*

Yussel knew how he did, if he did. He knew precisely how he did, if he did. But he doubted if he did because even though the shmegeggies got their water, when he closed his eyes the Flower Child was still zooming around on her motorcycle under his eyelids. So HaShem hadn't really answered him. Right? Right. The little flood was pure coincidence, accident, stupidity, not part of any cosmic computer program. Yussel had not made it happen. However, Yussel decided, if it were even vaguely possible that such a mess as was below him was the kind of answer he was going to get if he talked to God, he was finished talking to God. He didn't want the power; he didn't want to have to pay attention. He didn't want to be involved.

Grisha descended from his stool, carried it over his head, moved like a small snail through the water, up the slope to the highway toward the Shanda, his eyes glazed with ecstasy. "Hear oh Israel. The Lord is One and His name is One!"

The folks leaning against the cars, watching the water, chorused, "Amen, Brother. Amen."

"Bless the Lord for the miracles of His creation."

The six-packers took a look at Grisha's wispy side curls, the fever-red cheeks, the white beard, the ancient gabardine suit, crossed themselves, took off their shoes and socks, offered him Gatorade, a Dos Equis, rolled up their pants, tucked up their skirts, ran down to the new water, the sacred lake, hung around waiting for Grisha to come back and baptize them, but from baptism Grisha did not know.

YUSSEL DROVE the Shanda down the slope through hubcap-high water to the kitchen door of the Arizona, kicked off his shoes, rolled up his pants, shlepped kitchen goods inside, holy goods outside. The tower of water hammered on the roof of the Arizona, slid off its sides down into the new thin blue silvery lake rising fast around the Arizona, spreading faster toward Ernie's huts and Alma's tents.

He thought about Pharoah's chariots. If he were Moses, he'd split the water. He thought about the River of Paradise, the heavens opening, the ground opening, male and female waters copulating. He thought about unplugging the freezer, the speaker system, the telephones, the Indian. He wondered why no one else had thought these thoughts, done anything.

Grisha danced with his stool. "Yom diddle yom diddle ai diddle dai dai." A cowboy tried to get his attention. He wanted a blessing on his bad back. Grisha was beyond listening.

Yussel ran by him. "You can't help?"

Natalie had her skirts tied around her hips, danced in circles, made paddlewheels with her arms. Yussel had no time for her. Babe he told to call the fire department before the phones died. Babe told him they don't come unless you've joined and for fire, not flood. Yussel told her to call anyway.

"Right now I should call?"

"Yes."

"You're crazy . . ."

"Don't tell me what to do, Babe."

"So who will?"

"Just do what I say and call the Fire Department."

"You're telling *me* what to do, Yussy?"

"I'm asking."

"Don't get upset, Yussy. You'll get cramps."

"I've got cramps."

From her pocket, Babe gave Yussel a handful of Godiva chocolates in the shape of acorns.

HIS FATHER leaned over the great bucket of the water tower. *"Yussele, watch my remains they don't get loose."* Roof tiles floated in the lake. Ernie's adobe shacks were collapsing into pancakes. The tents worked at their ropes. Like corks, stakes popped out of the ground. The Blondische organized onlookers to dig ditches with spoons, shovels, their hands, tried to direct the water away from the Arizona. Grisha's tent was on its side, picking up wind like a sail, cruising out toward Babe's bus and the cottonwoods.

Yussel worked his way through the people, passed Indian Joe, who was arranging his sticks as fast as a kaleidoscope, sloshed through the water, arrived at Rosebud, who stood like a statue in the middle of the tower of water, grinning, yelling, "Sacred lake, sacred lake!"

Yussel punched him on his back. "Hey, Cochise, turn it off!"

"Can't, Your Highness. Needs a four. This here's a three and a half." Rosebud moved his testicles steadily from one side to the other as if such movement would have an impact on his understanding of fractions.

"You said you had a four!" Yussel shouted over the crash of the water.

"Then we need a three and a half."

"Why didn't you get the right size in the first place?"

"Goddamn. Goddamn, Your Highness, how was I supposed to know I was going to hit water? Goddamn." And scratched himself at the peculiarity of the world and how things happen.

"You Tonto shmuck! You *have* a four. You need a three and a half!"

"I'll get a four. You wait. I'll be back." He sloshed through hip-high water to his truck, revved up, rammed it up the hill and down the highway, left a great white wake, the likes of which hadn't been seen in the desert in a million or more years. Someone, something gorgeous with a lot of red hair, maybe the other part of the killer horse, stood in front of Yussel, speaking very softly with great calm. "You've hit the aquaclude. You need a pump. Do you want me to get you a pump?"

But it was at the precise moment Yussel saw a corner of his father's shroud lifting from the grave, the casket opened at its pine seams, the piece of shroud floating in a pool of water, so he could do nothing else but charge past her. "Excuse me. Excuse me. My father's grave. My father." He reached his father's remains as it/they/he was slipping off the spur into the lake.

His father screamed from the water tower bucket, *"Yussele, my remains!"*

Yussel tossed his father's remains, shroud and all, into the front seat of the Shanda and turned on the engine. He was turning the car toward the highway when he had a brainstorm to back up, turn around, and drive into the tower of water.

"Not the Shanda!" Grisha stood between the car and the tower of water, banged fists on the hood. "Not his car!"

"Out of the way, Grisha!"

"It's almost sacred, Yussel. It's family!"

"So, it's a sacrifice." Yussel said good-bye to the Shanda, thanked it for its years of loyal neurotic service, drove straight into the tower of water, and stopped the Shanda over the well. The car rocked. The water split in half, went this way and that way but no longer onto the roof of the Arizona. His father sat in the car next to his remains, lifted the hood over his face as gently as Yussel had pulled it down, measured his dead beard against his grave beard, *"Look at that. A half-inch I grew in the grave. Will you look at that."* He shook his head over his remains. *"I wasn't such an old guy. I look pretty good. Maybe because it's so dry in the desert. Look at that, Yussele. No decomposition. Will you look at the beard I grew. How about this beard?"* He fluffed the beard, squeezed water from the bottom of the shroud, brushed dirt from the feet.

Yussel didn't want to look. Half-inches were becoming a new organizing polarity for the universe. He was crawling with half-inches. A half-inch too much, a half-inch too little, not enough this, too much that. Maybe the half-inch on his father's beard came out of the cap for the pipe or vice versa. You get involved in this kind of thinking you can go crazy. Also, if you start watching for half-inches you find them.

"I must be a saint."

"They don't have saints in Hell."

"Maybe that's the trouble with Hell. Maybe they need saints. Listen, Yussele, you'll have to bury me again when nobody's around. And wash yourself, your clothes, from my putrefactions."

"I know."

"You see how HaShem works?"

"I see how shmuck Indians work."

People were still digging trenches. The books were up on the highway, the chairs, the altar, the Torahs, boxes of noodles, electrical appliances. The torrent was a graceful double fountain, with a shimmer of colors promising a rainbow. A bird had already landed on the hood of the Shanda. His father was pointing at the woman with the red hair. His father was jumping up and down, pointing at this woman.

"Look, look. You think all this is an accident? You want to see intention? You want to see purpose? You want to see the cosmic computer grinding away in your program, Yussel? Right in front of you, you can see how the computer works, every detail, every second. That's no accident. That is pure living breathing juicy intention. HaShem doesn't put together a package like that without a good reason. Is that something?"

The woman who had said "aquaclude" to him had hair like the horse. She was saying something about a pump to him. She held a geodetic map. She wanted to show him the map. He stared at her. She smelled of horses and wore shiny black leather boots. She had amazingly long legs, riding pants like skin, amazingly short underwear. Yussel wanted her off his property, out of his sight. She recognized him as he recognized her. She smiled. "You nearly killed me."

"You nearly killed *me*. Look." He pointed to the bump on his head. She reached to examine it. He moved backward. "Also I didn't mean to scare your horse."

"You'll learn not to joke around out here. A half-inch more my horse would have killed you and maybe me. You, of course, first."

"Yeah, yeah, and a half-inch tighter on your pants you'd have a cleft palate." Where had that come from? He'd never said anything like that to a woman in his life.

She flushed. She was so beautiful. "I'm trying to help you."

Yussel pointed to Grisha, turned his back on her. "Go tell him. He's in charge."

He shouldn't have sent her away because he watched her walk. From where does a pious man say such a thing about how tight a woman's pants are? From where does he think such a thought? Only the Yetzer Hara. Only.

"You brought that one on yourself, my darling son."

"What are you talking about?"

"Her. You did this, Yussele. I know how He works. With my lovely young widow you did this. Now I know what you did, how you did. God help me."

"A shmuck Indian brings the wrong size cap and I did it? Please."

"Feh, feh, Yussele. I'm talking about the lady. Your platform isn't high enough. Someday maybe you'll figure it out. Maybe in time."

Yussel closed his eyes, looked under his eyelids. No one was zooming around on a motorcycle. The Flower Child was out of his head. The shmegeggies had water, Yussel had talked to God, God had answered him. He could do without such answers. HaShem gave him water, took the Flower Child from his head, put in a demon, a succubus.

"Watch her, Yussele. This is very important."

"If you were such a terrific prophet, Totte, you wouldn't be in Hell."

"I'm telling you. That package comes direct from intentional. Believe me."

She was showing Grisha her map, moving her hands, swinging her hair, pointing to the mountains, drawing long sweeps with her arm. Grisha concentrated on the map. He had no idea what she was talking about. Yussel walked closer until he could hear.

"So it must slope up around here, under the old lake bed. And the angle of fracture in the rocks up there"—she pointed to the notch in the mountains where Yussel had taken his bath—"that angle must be repeated down here. So there's a pocket and it slopes and you hit underground water. You need a pump to contain this. You know what fresh water's worth around here? You know how much money this land is worth now?" She swung her hair around again, caught Yussel in her net. Her eyebrows jumped up and down on her forehead. She was very excited about the water.

Grisha looked at the map and said, "Blessed art Thou oh Lord our God, Ruler of the Universe, who performed wondrous deeds for our ancestors in days of old at this season."

Yussel said, "Amen."

She said, "What's the matter with you guys? You're losing your building and you're wasting water. I'm offering you a pump!" She didn't wear jewelry. She was filled with light, cut with such swells, prisms, curves, facets, she was fire herself. She had the pale white skin redheads have, with little blue veins, hot blue eyes. Yussel thought of the Shabbas candles burning, the white shoulders of the candles, the blue flame, the hot blue center of her eyes, the flaming face of Sabbath. Why would a shicksa make him think such thoughts? He'd never seen a woman with so much fire in her eyes. Except for his mother when she battled with his father. No woman had ever looked at him with that kind of fury. Maybe his father was right; maybe she wasn't an accident.

She looked at Yussel. "Listen, I didn't try to kill you. You didn't try to kill me. Let's start over. Okay?" She thrust out a hand, "Lillywhite, Stevie."

He jumped back from her, sent out little waves. The waves rolled back around his legs like lassos, around his ankles, beat against the shores of his heart. "I don't shake hands with such pretty girls." He wished he had one of Chaim's pencils that said DIAL-A-JEWISH-STORY.

"You're calling me a girl?" She laughed. "I'm not a girl. I'm not pretty."

Looking back, Yussel always thought that's when it started. When she said I'm not a girl. I'm not pretty. Yussel, knowing the arguments, was prepared. You say woman. They don't like to be called girls. All right. "So, I don't shake hands with such beautiful women."

Time slowed down. The horizon buckled around like a jump rope, dropped away in great hunks like the clay on Ernie's adobe huts. The water tower swayed, creaked, groaned. The Arizona was tilting on its side, Yussel stared at her. She stared at him. Yussel was locked somehow in this moment arguing with this woman and he'd already told her she's beautiful and he could see the fury burning in her eyes, hatred, and he didn't know what he'd done, except maybe she thought he tried to kill her on purpose this morning or maybe even expose his business to her. She smiled a wicked smile. "And what would you do about touching me, Rabbi, if for example I were drowning?"

"Baruch HaShem, you're not drowning." How stupid he

sounded. How could she know a line from Talmud? The Yetzer Hara taught it to her, that's how. The Yetzer Hara made up this woman and that line just for Yussel, just for this moment. In all fairness a woman like this is not something God should do to a married man, unless He had a very good reason.

She leaned forward, her voice clear, softer. "Actually, it's you who's drowning, Rabbi." And then she lay her hand on his cheek and pressed hard, somewhere between a slap and a stroke, more like a trembling rolling pin, she drew her hand over his face slowly until she reached the bottom of his beard. Her eyes burned. Candles. Blue-hot fires. It wasn't amusement. Yussel didn't know what he had erupted in her, in him. She wasn't playing. He was so startled by the touch, the audacity, the putrefaction, the intention, the smell of horse, of woman, the pure loose-wire power, he stood still under her touch.

"Answer me, what would you do?" Her eyes were dark pools. Lightning streaked in them like a new kind of reality. She pulled his beard. Nobody had ever done such a thing to him. In his life. Lillywhite Stevie. What kind of name is Lillywhite Stevie? He remembered the black-and-white ceramic tiles of his mother's bathroom floor, buckling, coming loose, breaking up the inlaid stars. His mother kept the loose tiles in a jar, hoping someday to put the floor back together. It only became worse.

So he swung a left to her jaw, punched her, laid her out in the water, was about to fall on her, punch her again, except his men were grabbing his arms and yelling at him. They couldn't touch her. She stood up, shook herself off like a dog. Her nose was bleeding. She licked the blood, wiped it with her sleeve, grinned at him. No one wanted the sin of touching her. So it was Yussel they tried to pull away. He fought with them to get at her. Then she went for his beard again. But this time she touched his face lightly, stroked his beard, grinning all the while, rolling a pink tongue over her lips, tasting her own blood, breathing hard. Yussel struggled to free himself, to kill her. She watched him for a moment. He was the prisoner. They were both dying to get at each other. He wanted to taste the blood running from her nose.

"I own most of the land around here. So I think you can treat me like a nice person if only for your own benefit."

"You're telling *me* what I should do? You're telling *me*?"

That's when she laughed at him, tossed her head back, laughed. He wanted to bite the length of her neck. Grisha, everybody, was screaming at her to go away, to get off their property, to call the police, to turn a hose on her. For a swift moment Yussel could see what was happening, the paradox of his situation, but then the moment slipped and he was standing on the other side of a boundary. The floor was gone, the tiles in jars, no longer stars, everything realigned. In that one second. It wasn't the touch, the legs, the eyes, the hair, the blood, the sting of her hand on his beard. He didn't know what it was. Because once he'd crossed that boundary of perception, she could have been cockeyed, crippled, an idiot. It wouldn't have mattered. It was too late.

"Oy vey, Yussele, my darling son, does He play for keeps! What did you say to Him He should do this to you? Poor Yussele. The water may be up to your ankles, but you are up to your neck. Both of us. My lovely young wife wasn't enough. He had to send in His first team your heart was so hard, your neck was so stiff. Oy gevalt. I'll never get to Heaven. Not now. Never."

Grisha cleared his throat, rolled something around in his mouth and spat at her. His spit landed in a wad at the top of her gleaming boot. She looked down, smiled at Yussel, dipped water over her boot. "I'll send a pump and a crew."

Yussel felt the air sucked from his world, pulmonary edema creeping into his chest. She started up the road, splashing, the gray riding pants, the line of bikini underwear. Yussel, who wouldn't even watch TV except for documentaries on Jewish subjects, watched her run. Grisha was praying fast, desperately.

The water tower creaked louder and louder. Two legs hung in the air. Lillywhite Stevie, jogging, looked up, saw it, stopped, pointed at an electric wire the water tower was now leaning on. The tower was coming down slowly, stretching the wire as it came. "Everybody out of the water," Lillywhite Stevie yelled. "The distributor line's coming down. Get out of the water. You'll be electrocuted. Get out! Get out!" She dragged Grisha by the arm. He shook her off. She grabbed his stool and pulled him out as the tower swayed and pulled at the line. Everyone was out, screaming at everyone else. Yussel ran also. "Turn off the power," she yelled at him. "Turn off the power. Where's the switch?" The power line dropped into the water, hissed, snapped around.

"Power's off, Lillywhite," Rosebud yelled from the road.

But it was too late because Babe had stopped to pick up a chicken and now she was facedown in the water. Grisha and Yussel looked at each other, weighing the situation. Yussel was paralyzed. He couldn't touch her. Well, if her life's in danger. But then maybe she's dead and so her life isn't in danger. Into the absolute silence, with only the hiss of the wire jumping around in the water, Natalie whispered, "You mean nobody's going to get her?"

Lillywhite ran down the slope into the water, pulled Babe up onto the land. Yussel watched as if it were a movie. No one would go in, no one would touch. Lillywhite listened to her heart, her pulse, raised her fist above her, smashed her in the chest, listened again, then lay on top of her, chest heaving into Babe's, mouth on Babe's, forcing her body up and down as hard as she could to bring Babe back. Once she called out, "Someone call an ambulance. There's a phone in the Bronco."

Yussel was watching the redhead on top of Babe. That was all Yussel could see: the redhead on top of him, heaving and humping and squirming, the behind up and down in the tight pants. Grisha stood beside him, weeping.

Lillywhite stopped, exhausted, listened to Babe. "Call the fucking ambulance!" No one moved. Natalie finally ran up the spur to the Bronco and made the call. The men weren't moving. Lillywhite was humping, thumping, bumping, grinding. Their blouses were transparent, nipples, hairs, belly buttons—now and then, you could see it all on both of them. The possibilities weren't lost on the men who stood, biting their lips, trying, Yussel was sure, as he was, not to see what they were seeing. Lillywhite stopped, listened, finally turned her head sideways like a swimmer, body still heaving.

"Okay," Lillywhite shouted triumphantly. "We've got her. We've got her."

Grisha came alive, punched Yussel into the present. "She saved her. Babe's alive. She saved her."

Babe moved an arm, then jerked, focused on Lillywhite, croaked, sighed, "Where's that nice little Indian?"

Lillywhite fell back against the ground, legs and arms spread, chest heaving, laughing at Babe. "Where's that nice little Indian?" There was nothing of her body Yussel couldn't see, every curve, every valley. The ambulance came, men and women in shiny green jackets ran down the hill, carried Babe up, roared away. No one looked at Yussel. Yussel couldn't look at anyone. His ears burned with shame. His heart wasn't his anymore.

Grisha walked beside Yussel toward the Arizona. "I'll bet that's her."

"Who?"

"The one who sings."

Something was closing in on Yussel. A dead chicken clung to his ankle. He shook it off. It drifted after him a little as if it needed to talk to him.

"Nisht shlect, Yussel. Not bad. We've got water for a mikveh. They're going to think you're a saint, Yussel, finding water in the wilderness."

"Who's going to think?"

"Everyone."

"You?"

Grisha's voice went up an octave. "Me?"

THE FIRETRUCKS came behind the ambulance. The Moffat Volunteer Firemen wore bright yellow boots and slickers, wanted to save the Shanda. Yussel told them to leave it where it was. They served coffee and cheese sandwiches, offered to put everyone up in the high school overnight, used fancy suction machines to get water out of the house, driers on the wall plugs. Most of them had long full beards like Yussel, big beer bellies. They gave Yussel a slicker, shook his hand, congratulated him for hitting water, told him all he needed was a beer belly and a pickup truck and he could join up. Yussel took a minute to forgive Schmulke for wanting to look like Darth Vader when he went into the wilderness.

By dusk, the Arizona sat flat on the ground again. Mops and rags were laid outside to dry. Floors were dry, appliances plugged in. The fountain was off. Trenches carried excess water out into the desert. A lovely lake shimmered under the water tower, over a steady supply of pure underground water. Soon they'd have a mikveh. The land was now worth what Yussel had paid for it. That part at least, Yussel could acknowledge, was a miracle.

YUSSEL SAT behind the bar with his head between his knees. He was exhausted, near tears. His hands trembled. He couldn't catch his breath, settle his nerves. All he wanted to do was go home and hide. But he knew he couldn't leave such a mess. He drank a glass of milk and thought about the redhead on top of Babe, breathing life into Babe's mouth, the power of it, the control, the competence. A woman who saves lives, with those legs, the streaks of lightning in her eyes, her touch. He shook his head, couldn't understand how such a thing could happen to him. His father came. His red silk pajama bottoms were soaked. The hem of his mallard-duck robe was muddy. He poured water from the brim of his hat, pushed it back on his head.

"Yussele, in the right vessel the wire gives heat and light. You put it in the wrong vessel, the water, it kills. HaShem is showing you abundance. Some things can't take His abundance . . . they are not the right vessels . . . too weak, the wrong build. They break. They become the evil shells in the universe. Maybe He's trying to make you His vessel, trying you out to see how much of His abundance you can tolerate before you break, to see if He shows you His Face whether you can endure Him. If He breaks you, He loses you and you become evil. If you can endure Him, you attach. All that water, all the woman . . ." His father shook his head. *"Can you endure all this?"*

"I'm going home."

"I think it's too late. I think you're already on the path." The Rabbi shrugged. *"I may be wrong."*

"I'm not on any path."

"You don't think this happened because you kicked my Flower Child out of your house?"

"I told you, it happened because of one shmuck Indian. That's how it happened."

The moon scattered the clouds. His father sat for a while, watching him, sighed. *"I was once so dumb. Once I thought because I knew all the letters, I understood the alphabet."* He shook his head, left. Yussel smoked one cigarette after the other, kept closing his eyes, kept looking for the Flower Child on her motorcycle. She wasn't there. The redhead's crew came, installed a fancy pump, pipes, valves, clamps, he didn't know. They left an envelope. Yussel didn't want to look at the bill. Grisha still had ecstasies around his eyes. He sat at the other end of the bar, playing his cards.

"What do you think, Grisha?"

"Bashert. Intended. Now you have to stay for Shabbas."

"I can't leave you with such a problem."

"Also you can't leave because you want to see what happens next."

Yussel thought about that. "Could be. Maybe."

"Me too. That's why I play cards." Grisha dealt his cards in a circle, turned up a king in the center, looked at it as if it were a message from HaShem, made a blessing, kept turning up the right cards. "See, Yussel? See how He works?"

"She saved Babe's life."

"She's dirt."

Something in Yussel rose to defend the redhead. Yussel throttled it fast. He opened the envelope. There was no bill, only a note on ecru linen with little bits of hair from his beard. The note said, in a scrawl, "I know you have to burn these." Yussel showed the note to Grisha.

"She's Jewish," Grisha declared. "She knows too much. Listen, Yussel," Grisha walked over, talked very softly. "What did Babe mean, 'Where's that nice little Indian?'"

"I guess she wanted the redhead to be a man."

"Babe?"

"Babe."

All of us, Yussel said to himself.

Grisha, too high to sleep, the red spots on his cheeks flashing like numbers on an alarm clock, played cards long after midnight. Slotnik came in with his books. He'd driven up into the mountains so he wouldn't be interrupted by the excitement. Babe was in the clinic on the other side of the mountain, perfectly okay. She'd be home the next evening. The others found beds—some in the high school in Moffat, some at Chaim's, some even in the tents. The night was still, big. Yussel sat in the bar and wondered what he was feeling. Whatever he was feeling he had never felt before. He smoked one cigarette after the other, drowned the butts in coffee cups, lit up, poured another cup, tried to activate himself, couldn't. He was drowning in the redhead. The Flower Child had been in his blood. This one shook his soul, tore at his roots. He could see Shoshanna's little hand on her throat, trying not to cry. How terrible he should have looked at that woman, felt her touch. How terrible to do such a thing to his Shoshanna. He loved her more than anything in the world, in the whole world, even in the World to Come. But on the other hand, looking at a woman as he looked at the redhead, feeling what he felt, thinking what he thought, he wouldn't have to worry about becoming a saint. Yussel knew he'd have sex dreams if he went to sleep, so he said he'd finish the kitchen, told Grisha to go to sleep. Grisha grunted, shuffled off to sleep.

Yussel mixed dough for the challahs, laid three strands of dough out on the cutting board, thought about breasts, squeezed the dough, thought about legs, braided the dough, thought about why the redhead was in his blood. Maybe she was a lost Jewish soul and he was supposed to light her spark? Jews are sent into exile to wander the earth to find lost souls, to bring them back. Sometimes these souls, these Neshamas, are parts of the same old soul who stood on Mount Sinai and received the Torah from HaShem. So maybe the redhead was such an old part of his soul. Maybe like magnets their souls were supposed to be drawn together. Maybe she was actually intended? After all, why else would she exist? Why had they met? Maybe it was intended that he should confront her, deal with her, get to know her? Maybe it was even intended he should descend into sin in order to bring her back? Maybe he had to open her soul? Yussel punched the end of the braid into the bread, gave it a kiss. Maybe, God forbid, he just wanted a little action. Yussel tore off a piece of challah, made a small bread, put it aside. It was already four in the morning. What would be the point of sleeping now?

In the freezer, Yussel found old challah; in the pantry, cans of fruit salad; in the refrigerator, eggs. He broke up the frozen challah, opened the cans, cracked the eggs, one by one, poured each egg into a plastic glass, held it up to the light to see if it had any spots of blood, found a spot, dumped the egg down the sink. If someone had held him up to the light, this night, feeling what he felt, they'd find spots of filth and rot all over his soul like mold on a shower curtain.

While the challah and pudding baked, Yussel went outside to re-dig his father's grave. It wasn't until he was finished, until he covered the grave, laid out the white painted stones, that he heard a car start up, just above him, and realized someone had been watching him bury his father.

Yussel stretched out on the sacks of potatoes and flour and slept. He dreamed of her spread out, with lightning between her legs. An alarm went off in his dream: he wasn't dreaming about his soul. He was dreaming about the redhead in the Bronco. Yussel leaped from his bed, fell over a carton, yelled at God. Weeping, he yelled at God. "What do You mean? What do You want from *me?* Why did You put such immodesty, such filth, in front of me?" He smashed the wall of the storeroom, put his fist through it, swore he wouldn't think about her until after Shabbas, and, of course, at that moment, he was already thinking about her, blood hot, mind blind. Afraid to sleep, afraid something would happen to his wife, to his children, if he dreamed such dreams, Yussel went back into the kitchen, turned on the ovens, put the challahs in to bake, the priest's bread in to burn because there were no priests of Aaron to eat their portion. He wondered where his father would get four men for the minyan; if he really would, if they'd be human.

15

"LISTEN, YUSSEL." Grisha was worried. "It's almost Shabbas. Where's your minyan?"

It was the longest Shabbas in the year, 176 verses in the portion. Shoshanna said on the phone that morning, "Don't you think it's significant that the first Shabbas after the Torah was given should also be your first Shabbas?" Yussel had said, "No. I think it's significant that I who get sick to my stomach whenever I have to get up in public should be given for my first Shabbas the longest one in the year. So stop quoting at me. Also perhaps it has slipped your mind that not only is this my first Shabbas but also it is my last Shabbas. Don't start making plans." Yussel said to Grisha, "If I said there'll be a minyan, there'll be a minyan."

"Ernie, Feldman, Bingo, you, me, Slotnik. We need four more."

"I can't count? They'll be here."

"I thought you didn't do prophecy."

"I don't." Yussel lied, didn't lie, apologized in his head to his father. "I had a message others were coming."

"You better be right because the sun's gonna set soon and we won't be able to drive to Chaim's."

"No kidding. So that's how it works." Shoshanna would kill him if she heard such sarcasm. "Maybe you'll go find Ernie for me, Grisha? I really need Ernie."

"You don't know how to find Ernie? Maybe I should draw a picture so you'll recognize him?" Shoshanna wouldn't kill Grisha. She'd say, "The poor soul is miserable, forgive him." Yussel would say, "I'm miserable too." She'd say, "At least you have a choice." He'd say, "Hah!"

YUSSEL KNEW what to do, but he'd never given a sermon, never led, only followed. Shoshanna would say, "Simple, Yussel." Simple. Everything is so simple for a woman because they don't have to do anything. His stomach churned. Also he couldn't find Ernie so he couldn't find out if the electricity, which was supposed to be left on, was left on, that which was supposed to be turned off was turned off. And since he had been preparing the Shabbas food in the kitchen, keeping the soup warm, baking the cholent, mixing the tuna fish, he had no time to look for Ernie, to check the speakers, the lights in the bathrooms, the mercury lights outside, or even to have one last cigarette before Shabbas to calm him down. Also maybe he'd been a fool to believe his father would really deliver four men for a minyan.

Nevertheless, the first of his father's promises arrived, a couple in their seventies, deeply tanned, rich. The wife handed Yussel a Tupperware tuna salad with apples and onions cut in, the lady explained, and a two-quart jar of herring and onions in cream sauce. The man handed him a check for three grand. He needed three more men.

"We knew your father," the man said meaningfully. They were both wearing creamy cashmere jackets. It was all Yussel could do not to feel the goods. She was either anorexic or cancerous. What she'd lost in weight she wore in gold.

"I'm very glad you could come."

He heard the Jackalope scream his parrot scream. "Car! Lady! Man!" He was running backward in circles. Why hadn't the Flower Child taken him with her? Where the hell was she anyway?

"We're happy to see you've taken on your father's work."

Yussel felt shame. He should give the check back, tell them the whole thing's only temporary. That tomorrow night right after Havdalah, he'd be gone.

"My wife is not a well woman. Cancer. Six months, maybe less."

162

"I'm sorry."

"She wants you to pray for her."

"Me?"

"Your father did."

"Well . . ." Yussel nodded. He had no idea what to say. "Of course. You know Babe?" He needed Shoshanna by his side. He was tongue-tied.

They moved off to the far side of the Arizona where Babe was fighting with the Blondische over how a tray of cake should be laid out. The Blondische had cut the cake, put it on the tray. Babe took it back off the table, rearranged it, complained she didn't have time for such things, couldn't anybody else do anything, did everything have to be on her shoulders? The Blondische argued that cake wasn't a dead person so what was the fuss. The rich couple stood by, listening. Yussel put his hand in his pocket for Maalox, felt the check, wondered if he should give it back, wondered if a person has cancer, should you eat her tuna fish?

Grisha shuffled in.

"You find Ernie?"

"Forget Ernie. What about Shabbas, Yussel?" He swung his pocket watch in front of Yussel's face. "Seventeen minutes. We don't have a minyan. We can just make it to Chaim's if we leave now."

"Car!" The parrot scream cut through his head, split it apart. "Man! Baby! Baby!"

A Volkswagen held together with wire and gaffer tape pulled up on the highway. Slotnik appeared, shook hands with his son, the son's little wife, did not look at the new baby because it was a girl. Their car was filled with boxes, suitcases. They were staying. Slotnik's son had a job delivering mail in Alamosa. They'd live for a while with Slotnik himself. *God help the mother if the baby cries.* Yussel's father, still buttoning his shirt, stood next to Yussel. *Give her permission to use contraceptives. Unhappy women shouldn't have babies.* Yussel looked under the blanket at the little girl, tickled her chin. The little wife, who had been a lieutenant in the Israeli Army, burst into tears at the kindness. She looked as if Slotnik's son hit her a lot. Yussel turned away to the kitchen. "Natalie?"

Natalie came running, cheeks flushed. "Rabbi? You need me?"

"Go find Ernie for me. Tell him to check the electricity, what should be turned off, what should be turned on for Shabbas."

"He's got a friend visiting. They took a walk."

"A man?"

"Don't act surprised. If you said we're getting four for a minyan, we're getting four. Remember, I know who you are."

"Please, Natalie, just go find him."

"Fish. Go fish!" The Jackalope put two words together and the jar of herring came apart. Yussel heard the crash of glass, the splat of herring and onions in cream sauce.

Grisha grabbed Yussel's sleeve. "Nu, Yussel, you got nine and no time. Now what?"

Yussel put his arm over Grisha's shoulder, Yussel jerked his chin toward the Jackalope, on his knees, who was snagging chunks of herring as they slid in their cream sauce across the kitchen floor. "Ten."

"That's ten? Nine and a half I'll give you."

"I say that's ten, it's ten."

Grisha shook Yussel's arm off. "So let's begin."

The sourness rose into his mouth.

Natalie came running in. "Ernie's back and he forgot to turn off the sound system and he says now it's too late."

"Terrific."

"Nu, Boychickl, your father always started on time."

"Enough, Grisha."

Yussel ran outside to hear the sound system. The Sangre de Cristos were bloody with the sunset. Over the sound system, he heard the Jackalope shouting, "Go fish!" He heard Grisha saying to someone, "Shmendrick, he thinks because he has a fur hat and a famous father, he's a rabbi." He heard a girl saying, "He looks cute in his hat, don't you think?" It was too late to turn the sound off. Depending on the way the wind blew, everyone in the valley and on the mountain had heard/was hearing/would hear all the tzuros of getting ready for Shabbas, the fight with Grisha, the Jackalope screaming, God knows what else, and soon would hear the whole terrible service, with him whimpering, whining, crackling, stumbling on the words, depending on the wind. The drunken cowboys down at the

Riverside, the encampment at the Baptist Retreat, the Assembly of God. And then he was struck between the shoulders with the weight of shame, like a great stone. Because he thought about Lillywhite. He thought about her hearing him.

The sun dropped out of sight. Yussel threw his father's tallis over his head and ran inside. Ernie the Betrayer was smiling at him. Yussel gave him a look for what he'd done. Ernie smiled at him, at his friend, as if he'd intended to leave the system on, to show off their new rabbi to the world of Moffat. So Yussel, on the day that had been the first Shabbas for the Israelites after they'd received the Torah, after they'd made their marriage with God, Yussel began his first Shabbas. But Yussel wasn't going to make such a marriage. This was for him a one-night stand.

YUSSEL LOOSENED his belt. How could he sing like his father? His father could go from agony to joy in three notes. The only agony Yussel felt was for himself, not for humanity, and he sure didn't feel joy for anyone. He wondered if the cowboys would come up and set the place on fire for fun. The women arranged themselves in the seats on their side of the divider, the men on the other. His father, in full Shabbas dress, sable hat, black silk caftan, his face scrubbed pink, his beard white as a cloud, stood beside him, straightened Yussel's tallis. His doorknobs glowed under the Eternal Light. Yussel had never seen his father proud of him, was happy his father was with him, also wished he wasn't. It felt like Yussel's Bar Mitzvah. *"Sing loud, my darling. And this time, put in a little feeling. You never put in feeling. Now you need feeling."*

"Feeling is mayonnaise, Totte? You can just add a little? You have to get it from someplace. Where am I getting it from?"

"Ask. He already gave you a flood."

Grisha snorted just below Yussel's shoulder. "In case you forgot, the souls are freed for Shabbas from Gehinnom. You should remember millions of Jewish souls are waiting for you to start Shabbas. Millions."

"Enough, Grisha. Enough. You're getting me nervous."

"You think *they're* not nervous? Five thousand years' worth of Jews waiting to get out for a day? The sun's set, Boychickl. Begin!"

"When you stop, Grisha, I'll begin."

His father was delaying things. *"Listen, Yussele, I have a suggestion. What you could do is add a little sex. Not so much an erection. Just lose a few wrinkles."*

"Sex is out of the question. It would only make me more nervous."

"Sex is not out of the question. Think about Lillywhite. You climb with whatever you've got. Think about wanting. You need to cleave to HaShem. Seek Him and cleave. Attach. Make believe Lillywhite is God. Want her. Make believe God is Lillywhite." His father slammed his doors together and hid behind them.

Yussel knew better than to work with sex. It takes over. The big rabbis, they knew how. The big rabbis took two parts of Adonoy, the unspeakable parts, which are male and female, and prayed with madness, devotion, that the two parts be unified, that HaShem and his Glory copulate because that's when mercy descends to earth. That's a real Shabbas.

His father cracked his doors slightly. *"If you can't think about sex, think about wanting a cigarette, a Raspberry Joy, an egg cream, some moo goo gai pan . . ."*

He had 176 verses in the portion of the Torah. His voice would give out. His headache would blind him. "I'll do what I can."

"If you did what you could you could change the world."

"Totte, please. Why do you keep hocking me?"

Finally Grisha hit his hand on the bimah and started the davening. Like greyhounds they were off. Grisha set the pace. He went breakneck speed, no words, rising, falling, humming. Maybe if Yussel had started first he might have slowed them down. The congregation davened faster and faster trying to catch up to Grisha. Yussel floundered in the middle. He always thought if God was going to hear, you should say every word carefully and understand what you were saying. The alte cockers davened as fast as they could; the new ones struggled with the Hebrew words. Some just made believe so they'd finish in time. The young men shouted in thin voices, trying to get ahead of the alte cockers, like Bernie and Bingo and Feldman, especially Grisha. Now and then the alte cockers stopped to lay in a big Amen! and take a breath. Grisha finished the benediction, glared at Yussel until Yussel finished. In the

Psalms, his voice was thin, weak, his hands icy. Grisha banged on the bimah, snowed dandruff on the Torah. "Hecher, Yussel, hecher. Louder!"

Yussel forced his voice over Grisha's. His tongue felt as big as a cow's in a deli. The congregation watched him like nurses watch an ICU machine. When he came to the happy "Welcoming of the Shabbas Bride," the music was as familiar as his breath. His throat opened. His voice lifted.

His father sang along, nodded his head from his perch over the ark, swung his doors to the music. *That's my boy, Yussele. Sing with your soul, eat with your soul, pray with your soul, everything with your soul. Be like David. Attach, attach, attach."*

Loud he could be, but no soul, no mayonnaise. Yussel thought about the soft scented back of Shoshanna's neck. He wondered about Lillywhite's bikini underwear. A few wrinkles went. His voice rose. Other voices rose in strength behind him. The alte cockers dropped back.

"Shtark, Yussele, shtark!" His father wished him strength. He allowed himself to think of Lillywhite's candle eyes. He sang at the top of his voice.

"Don't stop, Yussele. Ver geheiben, my darling son. Climb. Cleave. Attach!"

Yussel was in front. The congregation was with him. They sang when he sang, paused when he paused. Grisha followed Yussel's beat with his fist on the bimah.

As Yussel's voice rang out with "Praised be Thou O Lord our God, Ruler of the Universe Who with Thy word bringest on the evening twilight and with Thy wisdom openest the gates of the heavens," the mercury lights turned on. Yussel watched them through the little window at his shoulder. He liked the coincidence. He felt better. Not great, just better. All he asked was that he could get through this Shabbas.

Yussel finished first, Grisha second. A few struggled on. Grisha turned to the men in the narrow room, beat his fist on the bimah trying to hurry them along. Slotnik's son was way behind. Faster and faster Grisha beat his fist, stared down at him, glowered. Slotnick's son missed something, turned pages backward in his siddur, lost. Grisha stepped down from the bimah, walked over

167

to him, stood above him, looked down at him. "Nu, shlepper, nu?"

Slotnik's son stammered. Yussel wiped under his tallis with a handkerchief and helped him with the Hebrew. The kid's ears were red with shame; Yussel's with hatred for Grisha, who was clearly out for blood.

"Nu, Yussel? The Schema?" Grisha turned to the man in the white cashmere jacket. "Some Rabbi, our Rabbi." He turned back to Yussel, whispered too loudly, "When you talk to HaShem, Yussel, you talk fast. When you listen to Him, then, Baruch HaShem, you go slow."

"Okay, Yussele, work with the rage. Okay. Rage can work. Use anger. It doesn't matter what you ride as long as you go in the right direction." His father was very excited.

"Hear O Israel, the Lord our God, the Lord is One." Yussel thought he sounded a little like Neil Diamond, he was belting out so good. Grisha kept pushing Yussel to go faster. Yussel sang louder, slower, let notes ring, echo. Finally he allowed himself to ride Lillywhite. Why not? His ancestors turned somersaults in the streets of the Ukraine, tested themselves against Russian whores in golden beds. Jewish Rasputins, holy men. Why not? He thought of Lillywhite in a golden bed. Flagellation, starvation, rolling in the snow, song, dance, liquor, chopped liver, maybe even opium, he'd heard. Anything that works. So Yussel decided to cleave with whatever worked. The moment he said he would cleave, he did. He felt it, like little iron bits drawn up by a magnet. By the time the congregation stopped to recite the "Amidah" in silence, Yussel felt such power in his lungs, as if he could suck in stars and spit out constellations. That's how he sang. "Who is like unto Thee? Thou sustainest the living with loving-kindness." His heart lifted, lightened like a matzoh ball in the soup, a nasty little compact mealy-mouthed thing suddenly pops up in the boiling water, expands, bounces around. That's what he felt in his heart: a matzoh ball. He could almost forgive Grisha. He was dancing on the surface. He was walking on the water.

"See? He's feeling it. He's feeling it a little." His father whispered to someone else.

Who in Hell was his father talking to about him?

The matzoh ball turned to farina and spread, warm and sweet, to his toes, to the top of his head, filled him. But as soon as he felt it, it was gone and he was back to a tight compact mealymouthed matzoh ball. Then he thought about Lillywhite and her legs. Instantly he saw something vague flash on his screen. His screen was back? A screw turned in his heart. The clearer the screen, the deeper the pain. Pain equals screen? Who needs it? And what's this? Lillywhite? Again? What does she want from him? Lillywhite in a chocolate brown Porsche parked in the twilight on the outside edge of a hairpin curve in Loveland Canyon and an eighteen-wheeler coming down the mountain on top of her. What's this? A new trick? Just when he was getting a handle on Shabbas, in comes the mishugge universe? He didn't want it. Leave him out of this.

"Okay, okay, it's like pulling teeth," his father said to someone else. A chill went through Yussel. Who? Angels? The Heavenly Court? The Angel of Destruction? *"Yussele, you see anything? Now's the time to pay attention. The computer's working. It's coming up now with the variables . . ."*

"I'm pretty busy now, Totte." He wanted to sing Kaddish. He wanted to be left alone. Looking at Lillywhite was like reading Talmud in the toilet.

His father spoke as if he were announcing a horse race. *"Almost there, Yussele. A woman's out of cigarettes. Your shamas has a visitor, forgets to turn off the sound. Tonight a parking spot, certain winds, a driver named Stuart delivering NASA parts decides to take a little tour on his way to California, see the Rockies. On the rock face of the canyon there are certain configurations. And now a little free will here, there, and suddenly, Yussele, possibility turns to probability, and then becomes necessity. The girl pulls off the highway and parks her car. So you pay attention. You're being shown a direction."*

"She needs insurance? Collision? Liability?"

"Trust me, Yussele."

"Don't get me involved with your computer chazerei."

"Rabbi!" Grisha's face was in his, sarcastic, miserable. "Your congregation is waiting for Kaddish, Rabbi."

"That's your cue, Yussele. Give it all you've got. You hear?"

Yussel gave it all he had. He turned his back to the others, lifted his head to HaShem, sang. And as he sang he heard the voice of an angel piercing the universe. He looked around. It was the Jackalope singing, as the Flower Child had said he would. The Jackalope's voice soared. His words were clear—silver pellets piercing the veils of the universe—his face shining with a fire. This dumb cluck was an angel. If he was, Yussel could be. He joined the Jackalope, soared with him, floated on his back in the clouds. Big, total, potent, like the universe itself, Yussel soared and sang his glory into Grisha's face, Grisha coughed, backed away. Yussel forgot Grisha, forgot his father, saw the orange truck full of NASA parts, Stuart the driver looking around at the Rockies, Lillywhite in her little brown car on the edge of the pass, and he started to hurt. Up his arms, down his legs, in his chest, a vise. It was the kind of pain his father must have had all the time. He sang his pain. "Yisgadal, viyiskadash . . . exalted and sanctified be His great Name. . . ." He sang his pain. He remembered the woman in the creamy cashmere with cancer. He sang for her too. He sang for them all, goddamn them.

16

WHEN STEVIE LILLYWHITE was nineteen, a sophomore at Radcliffe, she had a terrible fight with her father and told him she'd never speak to him again. She had been studying medical anthropology, discovered the chemicals her father sold to Third World nations were pesticides that could cause abortions. She flew to New York, took a limo to his warehouse in Hoboken, stalked past a phalanx of Puerto Ricans on forklifts, and in front of all his employees, called him a murderer. Her voice echoed in the big warehouse. "Murderer!"

Her father pulled her into his office. "What are you, crazy?"

"You're president of the temple. You're a religious man. You brought me up to be religious. How can you do this?"

The bookkeeper, Kate, a single Irish woman, shooed two pale girl typists out, snapped down the shades in the cubicle.

"Do what?"

"Murder babies."

Her father and Kate looked at each other, relieved. "My daughter walks in here and calls me a murderer to my face?"

Kate said to them both, "Now, don't get excited. Stevie, keep your voice down. Don't upset your father."

"You're murdering babies, Daddy. You're supposed to be a good Jew."

Kate raised her eyes to the ceiling, shook her head. Her father's face swelled, turned red. "Listen, Little Miss Lily White. My customers are happy because my pesticides are increasing their food supply. And if they're decreasing the population, they don't mind that either. That's the way the world works, kid."

"You brought me up to be Jewish, to obey the commandments. You want me to marry a Jewish guy and have Jewish kids." Stevie started to cry. Kate brought Kleenex. Stevie shoved Kate's hand away. "I don't understand you. I don't know what to do, Daddy. I don't know what to believe in."

"You can start by believing in some respect, in who puts food on the table and leather coats on your back. One color for every day in the week," he screamed at Kate. He screamed at Stevie, "That you can believe in. Start there. No. Start with respect."

Kate screamed, grabbed Stevie's arm, pulled at her. "He's getting very upset. You want him to have a stroke? Why don't you leave him alone?"

"What business is this of yours?"

Then Kate put her arms around Stevie's father. Her father was shaking, threw Kate off so hard she landed in his swivel chair.

"Daddy! How can you do this?"

"You're breaking my bones, Stevie."

"You're breaking my heart, Daddy."

Stevie's father wept. "Just get out, Stevie. Just go back to your fancy school with your fancy ideas real people can't afford. Go!"

"Daddy . . ."

"Go!"

"I—I—I'll quit being Jewish. I'll quit being your daughter."

"That's what you want? You got it. I disown you. You're dead."

"I disown *you! You're* dead!" Stevie tore at her knapsack, threw credit cards at her father. "I don't need you. I don't need your filthy money or your hypocritical Judaism."

Kate tried to quiet Stevie. "Your father's very upset."

"Yeah, and what's your story, Kate?"

Kate flushed.

"Big shot! Big independent big shot!" He swept the credit cards toward himself, found a pair a scissors, cut the cards into pieces. "Saks, Ann Taylor, Bloomingdale's, Bergdorf." He spoke the names with the same voice he listed God's curses against Pharaoh at Passover. Frogs, locusts, plagues, death of firstborn. The pieces dropped onto his desk. "You wanna see suffering, Miss Lily White? I'll show you suffering."

"Should I cancel the accounts? Should I write letters?" There was something hopeful and savage in the way Kate asked.

"What's between you and your little Irish friend here, Daddy?"

Kate stood between her and her father. "You better leave. You better go away. You're killing your father. You better leave him alone."

Stevie yelled over Kate's shoulder to her father. Her father had his hands over his face. His hands were trembling. "I'm not speaking to you. Ever again. I want nothing to do with you." And went back to college, had her Daddy's lawyers change her name to Lillywhite. One week after she told him she'd never speak to him again, after he told her she was breaking his heart, her father had a stroke on the floor of the warehouse, went into a coma, and never came out of it. Ten days later, Stevie had to give permission to pull the plug. Her mother was drunk. Two cousins took over the business. Kate disappeared.

By the time she was a senior, Stevie Lillywhite had learned that nothing was so simple, that she could never forgive herself for what she'd done to her father, what she'd done to herself. In her junior year she'd discovered real sex with Tom, an architectural student at Harvard. Tom looked a little like Warren Beatty. They were engaged. Lillywhite lay next to him in the attic room she rented, thought about sex, watched a streetlight sketch oak leaves and grapevines with the wind on her ceiling, thought maybe she should marry a dentist, live a normal life, give all the money to Save the Whales. There was already a lot of money. Lillywhite tried to think about Tom. There was nothing to think about. She wanted her father. She didn't want to marry anyone. She graduated with honors, sent back Tom's ring, called Gabriella, her mother's personal shopper at Neiman-Marcus, ordered lots of khaki stuff, climbed Annapurna, called her mother's housekeeper every month or so, hung around Katmandu, played jazz piano in a restaurant, tried to forget about her father's grave, studied architecture, numbers, music, geometry in London, measured cathedrals and Egyptian temples, read, drifted, sought, avoided Israel, avoided Jewish men, knew all along she was looking for an answer to the big question: Did I kill my father? Men fell in love with her. They didn't have any answers for her.

She felt special, even chosen, but she didn't know what for or what difference it made until she visited a Tibetan refugee camp in India, heard the cry of a newborn, and decided to be a midwife. She went into the camps when she was twenty-six. She biked to hill stations, hitched rides in beer trucks to other camps, climbed mountain paths, tried to make up for her father's sin by bringing into the world as many babies as he'd sent out. A Tibetan monk in the camps taught her how to think fire and burn leaves at a distance. It took hours and wasn't worth the trouble. Then he told her she'd never bring enough babies into the world to make up for the dead ones, that she should go home and make her own babies. The child she had would have her father's soul and that soul should work out its own karma. But Stevie wouldn't forgive herself. She had hepatitis. She walked to a village where there was a telephone, called her lawyers, was three or four times richer than she'd been when she first came to the camps, bought half a mountain in Colorado, and called her mother who'd moved from Montclair to Houston. Her mother had been living on Valium and scotch the way Lillywhite had been living on the cries of newborns. Her mother mumbled something, dropped the phone. Lillywhite listened to the phone bouncing, swinging against the night table in descending chords until a man picked it up and said, "Hello, hello . . ." Lilly-white hung up, headed home. She wanted to stop in New York, visit her father's grave, make peace, but it was too late. By that time she'd lost her courage or knew too much about herself. Or both.

She was thirty-three when the cab drove her up the long drive-way to her mother's house. She gave her mother chains of pearls from Hyderabad. Her mother tossed the pearls in the swimming pool. Her mother was fifty-six. Her mother tried to get Lillywhite to drink with her. When Lillywhite refused, she came after her with a kitchen knife. Lillywhite called Tom, grabbed a lot of her father's clothes, and left for Colorado, where, eventually, on the night Yussel was leading his first Shabbas service below the mountain, Lillywhite ran out of cigarettes, turned off her Music Minus

One tapes, tossed on her father's golf jacket with his name on the back, punched Willie Nelson into the tape deck, headed her chocolate brown Porsche down her mountain, pulled up on the outside rim of a hairpin curve on Loveland Pass, cut her engine, killed Willie Nelson in the middle of "All of Me," rolled down the window, threw her head back on the neck rest, and watched the clouds.

Buzzards circled in a column of hot air. The strip of sky was solid turquoise, hard as the face of the rock walls. The peevish cry of a hawk scraped along the sky, a truck shifted gears to make a grade somewhere in the mountains above the canyon. She sang to the clouds, imagined she changed their shapes, could see her father's face, could hear his voice. She saw his face in dreams. She'd be on a train going one way. The train would enter a tunnel. Another train, going the other way, would pass. In the yellow windows of the cars she'd see travelers' faces. One of the faces would be her father's. She'd run to the conductor, tell him the train was going in the wrong direction, but he wouldn't turn the train around. He'd offer to let her drive, but she would be too afraid. Then she would wake up, adrenaline racing into her bloodstream, and know her life was going in the wrong direction. The dream lasted for hours during the day, made her drive too fast.

Tom had a wife and a kid in Santa Fe, lived on a trust fund, inspected chimneys three or four days a week, owned a part share of an airplane, built things from atom bomb parts he found in the junk pile at Los Alamos. Tom said he'd been waiting for her to call. She said she'd been waiting to call. He said he knew that. Tom didn't have a weapon in the world. Lillywhite had them all. Tom and Lillywhite didn't have to say much more. He still looked like Warren Beatty, still had a sexy crooked grin, still rolled along when he walked, still had a smooth slim body, still was good and grateful in bed. Lillywhite was relieved to have him around again. She wished she could feel more.

Tom designed a sprawling house of twelve-inch rough timbers, glass, nose cones, missile parts for her on the mountain, set up the sound system so she could make all the noise she wanted to, built a skylight so she could sleep under the stars in her own bed, and used orange plastic strips, which were meant to detonate hydrogen bombs, for the light pulls. It didn't matter much to either Tom or Lillywhite that he'd married. He'd fly up, land his plane on the main road, stay two or three days, wait for her to ask him to stay longer, ask him to leave his wife. She never asked. Then he'd fly home. Sometimes he called. Sometimes he punished her by not calling. He begged her to make a decision. She said until she figured out if she killed her father, until she could forgive herself, she couldn't go on with her life.

The last rays of the sun shot up over the canyon walls, smeared cosmic graffiti on the rock face. Lillywhite knew if she could open her heart a fraction more, she'd be able to read the bloody letters pulsing on the rocks, get the message. A gust of sand blew across the highway. She shivered, rolled up the collar of her father's jacket, found a pack of cigarettes in the pocket, lit up. The turquoise turned to wine, poured down over the rock walls, filled the letters. Mica chips in the rock face clustered into stars, pairs of elk eyes blinked at the top of the cliff. She took a deep breath, closed her eyes. And then, on some perverse vector, the wind came up the mountain from the desert floor, lifted itself to Loveland Pass, found her car, found her heart, like an arrow, like a direction. And Lillywhite heard, on that perverse shift of wind, instead of her father's voice, Yussel Fetner's voice singing Kaddish, which was close enough.

She knew it was the Rabbi. Up, down, deep, high, breaking now and then with pain, sweet, joyous, sexy. As if he were making love to God. Lillywhite heard babies and lovers and fathers all at once. And death. She knew how dangerous it was for her head to listen to someone singing Kaddish. She'd been tricked and trapped before and she wanted no part of it. So she turned on the engine, ripped the Porsche onto the highway, wiped the face of the night with rooster tails of dust and sand and rock, didn't see the eighteen-wheeler loaded with NASA parts tearing around the curve, wanted to kill the Rabbi because he reminded her she was still afraid that she'd killed her father, that she didn't know how to make peace with him.

She didn't hear anything behind her until she pulled off into the parking lot of the Riverside and the eighteen-wheeler screamed past her, brakes sparking, trying to slow. Stuart, the driver, gave her the finger. She never knew he'd been behind her. She threw her hand over her mouth. A minute more, the bloody letters on the rock face would have spelled her name. She shot pool, drank beer the rest of the night with the boys, wondered if she should go climb in the back of a truck, take a walk down by the river with one of the boys, didn't have the heart for it.

LATE FRIDAY night, after kiddush, Yussel piled dirty dishes in the dishwasher. His father vamped around the kitchen, flapped a dish towel like a stripper. *"How about these, Yussele? Am I the Maharajah of Pajama or not?"* One of his doors was now louvered. The other door was still solid wood. He wore tie-silk pajamas with tiny green crowns on a shimmering gold background and a tie-silk bathrobe with tiny gold crowns on a shimmering green background. The cuffs and the collars were piped in gold. His slippers were green silk, a large gold crown on the fronts. *"Yom diddle yom diddle ai diddle dai dai."* His father grabbed him, pulled him into the dance. *"First thing tomorrow, I'm going to get you four kibbutzniks, so you'll have a permanent minyan. It's going to work, Yussel. It's going to work. You keep this up, I'm going to Heaven. Yom diddle yom diddle ai diddle dai dai. I'm going to sit at the throne, enter the gates, breathe the perfume of paradise. And my son, my beautiful caring loving saint of a son will put me there."*

"What worked?" The Jackalope had worked and Yussel couldn't find him. First thing after everyone walked out and said it was a wonderful Shabbas, they'd been transported, Yussel looked for the Jackalope and he was nowhere. All his things were gone.

"What worked? What worked? Listen to him. Is this humility? You changed a decree of the Almighty, that's all. You changed a decree. Your blood has come alive, Yussele, and it's good blood and it can change a decree of Heaven. You have the blood of a zaddik, my darling." His father pulled Yussel out of the kitchen, out into the bar, down the length of the Arizona, polkaed with him in front of the altar. *"Also because I did a favor for a friend, he's going to give me his place on line."*

"On line for what?"

"To get favors, to help, to intercede if you need anything, if your

kids, God forbid, get sick. You'll see. Oy, Yussele. I am so happy."

Yussel sat down at the kitchen table. "You really think that's what happened?"

"I know it." His father beat both fists on Yussel's back. *"Yom diddle yom diddle ai diddle dai dai."* On the kitchen table, on the refrigerator door.

"I'll have to think about it." He looked for the Jackalope on his screen, but his screen was gone again. He knew it would come back if he could feel enough pain. He didn't want the pain. He didn't want the power. He didn't want to change the decrees of Heaven. He wanted to be left alone. He wanted to go to bed and think dirty disgusting thoughts about Lillywhite Stevie. As soon as Shabbas was over, Yussel picked up the phone to apologize to Lillywhite Stevie, lost his voice when the information operator came on, called Shoshanna to tell her he was staying a little longer.

17

ANOTHER DAY AND Yussel didn't go home. How could a man of such filth go home? He borrowed Slotnik's truck, drove out to the Great Sand Dunes, which stretched white, silver, silent for miles along the base of the mountain range. There was no wind. The sky was a deep blue. A jeep named Rosebud was parked under a stand of birches. Yussel thought about pouring sand into its engine. A wide swift river ran just beyond the birch trees. He'd have to cross it to get to the dunes. Two sets of footprints, one small, one large, crossed the dunes. Someone had survived the crossing. He couldn't imagine swimming such a width, in such a current.

His father was curled up, fast asleep under a birch tree, his cheek resting on his hands. He wore silly Dr. Denton's pajamas with horizontal lines of little blue ducks. Over them he wore a white terry-cloth bathrobe with a big blue duck on its pocket and little blue waves all around the borders. Yussel held his breath, walked around him. His father spoke as if he were speaking in his sleep, *"If HaShem puts a river in front of you, He puts it there for a reason. So plunge in."*

Yussel plunged into the river, not because the river was there but because his father was there. He hit the bottom too soon because the river was maybe four inches deep. The riverbed was ridged like snakeskin and tore at his belly. Yussel flattened into the water, made believe he was swimming, dragged himself along the rough bed, scratched his skin, made big splashing strokes.

"Don't swallow, Yussele! It's a fast day!"

Yussel made believe he climbed up a high bank, scrambled, slipped back in, hoped his father was impressed, then collapsed on the sand. With great fake gasps he called to his father at the far bank, "You put one foot in the water, I'm in Far Rockaway!" Then he crawled, crouched, ran up the dunes. Within moments his feet were scorched. Still he ran to get out of his father's sight. The air was thin, the sun brutal. Breathing was rough. Someday he'd stop smoking. His chest heaved for real.

Yussel picked up the tracks of Rosebud and Company. Rosebud had a girl up here. Yussel imagined her in kneepads. And couldn't imagine how such an alien idea came into his head that a woman should wear kneepads for a perverted act. The idea made a frenzy in his head, like insects. He hoped he wouldn't come across them riding each other. He reached one ridge, walked along it, descended into its shadow side, lay down in the arm of the dune, heard a man say, "I'm the thunder. And I'm going to make lightning between your legs." A girl giggled.

Yussel walked along another ridge, descended into its shadow side, lay down in the arm of the dune, curled up, took a deep breath, shuddered at the pleasure, closed his eyes, thought about lightning and thunder. The curves of the sand under him, around him, felt like the curves of a woman, belly, thighs, bosom, her. When he moved, she moved with him. He stroked the sand. It was cool to the touch, like Shoshanna's skin after a bath. He made a small mound. His blood leaped, swelled. He stuck a finger into the sand. Deeper it was warmer, fleshier. He whispered, "Gottenyu," to no one. On his knees, Yussel dug, pressed, shaped Lillywhite out of sand. When she was complete, he stuck tumbleweed on her head for her hair, two quarters for eyes, covered her parts with his handkerchief. He looked down at her, walked away, returned, knelt by her side, stroked her cheek as she'd stroked his, said, "I'm sorry." The wind lifted and blew tears across his face. He stretched out over her, covered her nakedness, wept at his weaknesses.

Other men knew. Other men went through this, other men have felt this rage, grief, guilt, hunger. God help them, that they weren't married men with kids and congregations and fathers who were caught somewhere in their own private father-sins who needed their sons to get them out of whatever hell they were in.

Then Yussel heard the soft movement of cloth, the sweep and brush of robes drifting like small winds across the dunes. He heard the velvety padding of slippers, smelled linseed oil. Yussel leaped up, off her, stepped on her face, kicked her, stomped all of her out into nothingness, made believe he was dancing, forced a couple of bars of song. "Yom diddle yom diddle ai diddle dai dai."

"I flew. I'm dry. See? I flew."

The Rabbi's bathrobe was now black velour—gorgeous, hooded, deep rich velour down to the ankles. It had orange bands along the front and an orange belt. The sleeves dangled by the knees, six inches too long. Underneath the robe, he wore white silk pajamas with little black diamonds and in the center of the diamonds, half-inch orange suns. A large orange sun was embroidered on the pocket of the bathrobe and in the pocket a handkerchief to match the pajamas, except the diamonds were orange and the suns were black. He wore an ascot of orange silk.

"You went all the way back to change your pajamas?"

His father snapped his fingers. *"They didn't even have time to get me matching slippers."* Like a ballerina, he pointed a toe to show Yussel a brown slipper. *"Your mother never let me wear black with brown."* He cocked his head, appraised the color combination. *"Because, Yussele, I was up all night doing a job which you should have done so they didn't have time even to shorten the sleeves, never mind matching the slippers."* He rolled back the cuffs. The lining matched the orange silk ascot. *"Feel the goods."*

Yussel rolled the velour between thumb and forefinger. "You care to tell me what I didn't do you had to do?"

"When you figure out what you didn't do, you'll know what I did. Some goods, huh?" Then his father cocked his head at Yussel the same way he'd looked at his slippers. *"Don't fardrei me with your games, Yussele. I could see under my Hasidim's blankets. I knew when they left their houses to come to me. I knew what they wanted before they even knocked on my door. So you're not fooling me. Here, help me off with this."* The Rabbi slipped off his robe. Yussel helped him with a sleeve, held the sleeve. The pajamas had little pleats at the waistband. His father paused in the

middle of disrobing and looked at Yussel's watch. *"Ten oh four."*

And then the bathrobe was over Yussel's head and pulled tight around his neck, over his mouth, his nose, his eyes. His father did not intend Yussel should breathe. Yussel struggled. What is this? Some kind of joke?

Yussel kicked, grabbed, couldn't make contact. He thrashed. His head felt ready to blow. He sucked black velour up into his nose, down into his throat, his lungs. He was going to suffocate. His father was trying to kill him.

And then his father released the robe. A minute longer, maybe seconds, Yussel would have been dead. "You mishugge son of a bitch."

His father was humming. Now Yussel recognized the tune. *"Take me along, if you love-a-me, take me along."*

His father grabbed his arm, looked at his watch. *"Ten oh six."* He seemed mildly satisfied with the time. Yussel ran.

He ran, slid, fell downhill, the sand collapsed in front of him, sucked him in, pulled him along. He ran downhill until he thought his knees would crack, and then turned uphill. The sand pulled him back downhill. His heart tried to get out of his body, through his throat, through his lungs, through his ears. A great antediluvian bird-man shadow that was his own father drifted over him, covered him, blotted out the sun. The lead door was slower, lower than the wood door, so his father was flying at an odd angle, like a biplane with a broken wing, spinning in lopsided circles. And singing, *"Yom diddle yom diddle ai diddle dai dai."* Everybody needs such a father. Yussel swung sideways and ran along another ridge. He didn't know where he was. He zigged and zagged until, far below, he caught a glint of Rosebud's hood in the birches along the bank.

He lumbered along the crest of the dune. He told himself not to believe this, that it probably wasn't really happening, that he wasn't going to die this way, this day. He couldn't convince himself.

"Yom diddle yom diddle ai diddle dai dai." His father sang, swung, spun over him. At least he blocked the sun from Yussel's back. *"C'mon, Yussele, c'mon. Death's nothing."* Yussel could think only of air. He would give his life for a breath of air, to stop

and take a deep breath. . . . Maybe it wasn't his father. Maybe it was a demon who looked like his father. Nope, it was his father who looked like a demon. If a guy can dance without his feet touching the ground when he's alive, certainly he can do better tricks when he's dead. Yussel yelled, "Rosebud, help! Rosebud!"

Yussel ran along the ridge, kept his eye on the glint in the birches below. Suddenly the sand gave out in front of him and he was slipping over/into the edge of a precipice of sand, a long steep drop, hundreds of shifting feet into which he was about to fall and be swallowed. Just before Yussel went under, his father swooped down, grabbed him up, carried him to another ridge, threw him back on the sand, stood over him while an avalanche of sand thundered toward the river. Dust swept around them. When it cleared, the Rabbi looked at Yussel's watch. *"Ten twenty-seven. Terrific, Yussele, twenty-three minutes!"*

Once Yussel had dropped a watermelon from the fourth floor of the Yeshiva. The way that watermelon looked on the sidewalk, Yussel's chest now felt. Yussel's guts tore with each breath he tried to take. He bent over his pain, gagged. "Why are you trying to kill me?"

"I see you have pain. I didn't break your natural bones. I broke the supernatural ones. They hurt more and take longer to heal, but this way you can function as if you were whole." His father removed his robe, smoothed out the velour, swung it around, let it float to the sand, and then folded himself on it, cross-legged. He pushed his hat back off his head, patted the robe, invited Yussel also to sit on it. Yussel crept away. *"You want to talk about women, Yussele?"* His father crept after him.

"I don't want to talk."

"Good. So once a Hasid comes to his Rabbi. He's tearing out his hair. 'Reb, Reb, what can I do? I'm obsessed with money.'

"'Give it away, my son.'

"'I do. I give. That's not the problem, Rabbi. I just can't help thinking about money. That's all I think about.'

"'When you daven?'

"'When I daven.'

"'When you eat.'

"'When I eat.'

"'And when you're with your wife?'

"'Every minute, Rabbi.'

"So, the Rabbi throws on his coat. 'Come with me.' They go straight to the mikveh. They both climb into the pool. 'You ready?'

"'Certainly, Rabbi.'

"So the Hasid goes under and while he's under, he feels the Rabbi's hand on his head, heavier and heavier. So he tries to come up, to breathe, to see what's what. He can't come up. The Rabbi is keeping him under water. He struggles but the Rabbi is suddenly very strong. The Hasid is dying for air. Suddenly the Rabbi releases him. Up to the surface he pops and gulps for air like a fish on land. 'You trying to drown me Rabbi? I come for help, you try to drown me?'

"'Of course not,' says the Rabbi. 'But tell me, while you were down there, did you even once think about money?'"

Yussel looked at his father, looked at him good. "Son of a bitch! You couldn't have just told me the story?"

"You spent twenty-three minutes thinking only about air. Twenty-three minutes you didn't think about your redhead."

Yussel flopped back, looked up at the sky. "So I suppose we're now talking about women?"

"Women? Moi? Who would bring such a thing up? Women?" His father addressed an invisible congregation. *"An eternal future is at stake, I should talk about such trivia? Women?"* His father walked around in excited circles.

"Women," Yussel sighed.

"I have it in mind, Yussele, the day of the flood that maybe you talked to HaShem, that maybe you addressed Him directly for the first time in your life? And that's a good thing to talk to Him directly. Don't get me wrong." His father stopped, waited. *"Nu?"*

"I did."

"And?"

"Listen, Goyim talk to Yoshke, they get bliss. I talk to HaShem, I get tzuros. I mean tzuros."

"He answered . . ."

"I need such answers? A flood? A woman heating my blood until it boils? Ain't bliss, Totte."

His father started to walk around again. *"I also have it in my mind that maybe when you talked, when you asked HaShem to make sure you got water, maybe you also asked Him to get my Flower Child off your mind?"* His father looked up from under his eyebrows. *"With all due respect, Yussele."*

"Maybe."

"And maybe you made a little complaint He didn't give enough to you, to the chickens, to the world?"

"Maybe."

His father clapped his hands. *"So."* Then he started with his right thumb, arguing, making points, every time digging down with the question and up with the answer, arguing, agreeing, understanding. *"So. The question is, can Yussel Fetner handle His abundance? My second wife was not abundant enough. You could endure her, you could handle her, you managed to get rid of her, and, I hope soon, you'll find her and take care of her. With all due respect, my Flower Child angel is second team compared to your Lillywhite in the shmata jeans. So HaShem finds out you can handle my Flower Child and he sends in his first team. Lillywhite is a challenge you can't handle."* Yussel's father clapped his hands. *"So far, so good, Yussel?"* He didn't wait for an answer. Now he used his left thumb also in the argument. Both thumbs agreed with each other. Both came up at the same time. *"So. Lillywhite is sent to you because she is a challenge you can't handle."*

"I thought HaShem only sends you what you can bear."

"The kind of person you are now, you have more than you can bear. The kind of person you might become, Yussele, maybe . . . maybe . . . you can overcome this challenge. You know what Carlyle said? 'In order to reach your inner being you must find a great love or a great tragedy.'"

"Given a choice, I'd take the great love and forget the tragedy."

"Carlyle forgot a great love can also be a great tragedy." His father wrapped his arms around his legs. *"Farshteist, mein kindt?"* His doors caught the last light of the day. *"You understand, my child?"*

Yussel dug a finger into the sand to see if it was still warm underneath. It was. His blood jumped. God knows it was a better feeling than respiratory arrest on the dunes.

"He's showing you what it is to want. I understand how you

*want, Yussel. Because that's how I want HaShem. It's the same
hunger. He's giving you a dose. The closer you get, the more you
want. Sex, God. It doesn't satisfy you. It just makes you hungrier.
That's what happens when you start climbing the rungs. I think
maybe now He intends you take some steps. It's very dangerous,
such steps. That woman . . ."* His father shook his head. *"Maybe
she's a way to your inner being?"*

Yussel sighed. "I'm a married man, a pious man."

"Yeah, yeah. Me too. Twice."

Yussel shivered. The wind picked up. The dunes shifted,
changed shape. His father stared off into the great silent distances,
into nothing Yussel could see. Strange shadows formed, reformed,
drifted along the crests beyond the sunset lights. The river turned
black. A dog/wolf/something howled. Coyote. There would be coyote here.

His father's voice was soft, subdued. *"My whole Yeshiva class is
in Gan Eden. They look around. They say, 'Hey, look who's missing. Would you believe Fetner, that cuchem, with his lineage? He's
down there with Pecky Storch. Hah hah.' My whole Yeshiva class,
laughing. 'He doesn't have a son?' they ask. 'Who, Pecky?' 'No,
Fetner.' 'Sure he's got a son. But he's no good.' Pecky Storch was
the worst kid in my Yeshiva class. I am with Pecky these days, a
murderer."*

"Your sins aren't exactly equal. A kitchen door isn't the same as
murder."

*"Doesn't work that way. For my kind of soul, what I did to give
another human being pain is as much a sin as what Pecky did for
his kind of soul."* His father stood, stretched.

"He get pajamas?"

*"Naah, cigars, English shoes. Pecky can't come back because of
his temper. The poor shmuck doesn't even have a son. Thieves,
murderers, men without sons, that's what I have to while away
eternity with. And every time I turn around you've done something. You've ignored this, forgotten that. There's just no way out
for me. Me and Pecky. Forever."* His father brushed sand from his
bathrobe, sighed deeply, started to take long sliding steps down the
hill. Yussel followed. *"Right now they're matching up the lead for
the new door. Right now. One more lead door coming up. Next
maybe a ball and chain."*

186

"Totte, first you say she's intended. Then you accuse me of sinning? Is it intended I sin?"

"*Intended, maybe for a challenge. Also we don't know which side intends her, or for what purpose. I don't know yet who took your screen. Maybe from the Other Side, the Sitra Ochra, maybe from the Yetzer Hara, the devil. Maybe the good guys and the bad guys are working together to break you down. Who knows? What I do know is you're being asked to pay attention, to make important decisions. Something's put in front of you, you better pay attention.*"

His father had trouble going down to the river. His doors couldn't keep up with his feet. Two piles of sand, one for each door, grew higher every time he took a step. Yussel moved effortlessly. Now and then he'd stop, kick the piles of sand away from the doors to free his father.

Halfway down, his father had to rest. He spread his robe. Yussel stood beside him out of arm's reach. "*I'll try to protect you from yourself. I can't make any promises. Also I'm sending four kibbutzniks so you don't have to daven by Chaim.*"

"Listen, Totte, as long as I hold my head under water, you shouldn't even give it a thought. I'll be fine."

His father stood, walked sullenly behind Yussel. Yussel kept kicking sand away from his father's doors until he reached the banks of the river. There his father took off his slippers, put them in his bathrobe pockets, gathered the hems of his robe, rolled up the cuffs of his sleeves, the bottoms of his pajamas. Yussel sloshed ahead into the river. His father wasn't coming. Yussel turned back. His father was waiting on the sand. Robe, slippers, dangling sleeves, silk-lined cuffs were all too much for him. So Yussel picked him up in his arms. His father put his hat on Yussel's head, curled up, tucked his head into Yussel's shoulder, like a little kid. Tears welled up in Yussel's eyes; his throat contracted he loved his father so much.

18

ON ROSH CHODESH, on the new moon, the first of Tammuz, when Joshua caused the moon and the sun to stand still until Israel was avenged, the month of calamities, Yussel called Shoshanna because he knew she'd be upset another month was beginning and still they weren't together. A man wants his wife to be predictable so he feels safe and then he's mad at her for being predictable. For being boring.

Shoshanna finally answered. "What's wrong?"

"I wouldn't tell you if something's wrong?"

"You're eating?"

"Of course I'm eating."

"You're fasting?"

"On fast days I fast," he lied and didn't lie.

"You sound . . . your voice is thin, Yussel."

"I'm fine. Why are you crying?"

"I'm not crying."

"Were you crying?"

"Yussel, you're making me crazy."

"I'm sorry. I won't call you anymore." He could see her little hand on her throat. What was he doing?

"Are the kids okay?"

"Yussel, you're frightening me. Is something going to happen?"

"That's how the world works. Something's always going to happen."

188

"To us?"

"Of course not."

"I thought you'd say that." There was a long pause. "I had a letter from Ruchel. She's coming out soon. She hopes and prays every night that all of us will always be friends no matter what."

No matter what what? Chaim was up to something. "Is that why you're crying? Over Chaim?"

"No." She didn't elaborate. She didn't have to. She wanted to come down.

"If it makes you happy, you should know I go to Chaim to daven because I haven't got a minyan here. I see him twice a day and all Shabbas."

"I heard. But still you don't talk to him. I also heard Natalie ran away."

"I didn't know that."

Shoshanna sighed. "You're supposed to know. She needs guidance."

"Who told you?"

"The same person who told me you do nothing but fast and take naps."

"It's a trick I learned from my father," Yussel lied. "The weirder you act, the more prestige you get."

"Yussel, when are you coming to get us? It isn't right we should be apart so long."

"Maybe you should take the kids home to your mother until I'm ready for you."

There was another long pause. Yussel was familiar with those long pauses. Sometimes they were followed by days of exaggerated silent servitude, as if she were mimicking someone she really wasn't. He didn't like long pauses.

"Don't start trouble, Shoshanna. Don't play smart with me." He meant dumb. He didn't know what he meant. When his mother challenged his father, that's when their troubles began. He'd always had a sneaking suspicion that when women wanted to get along with their husbands, they played dumb.

"I'm not playing smart, Yussel. I am smart. You don't want to know I'm smart. You don't want to know from my being smart. You think I'm only smart about coupons for diapers and instant coffee? You look at Babe, you say, sure, she's smart, but she can't make a man happy. You look at Natalie, you say she's nuts. You always have an excuse not to look at us. We're nuts, we're bitter. We're too fat, too little, too big, too weak, too strong. Any excuse not to look at us as humans, not to listen to us. You always have an excuse not to look at me, not to hear me. I'm little, I'm sweet, I'm innocent, I'm dumb. Hey, Yussel, dinner's ready and I'm pregnant again. Then you look. Then you hear."

"God protect me from your mouth. I don't want such trouble from my own wife." He knew she was trembling all over like a butterfly flying against the wind.

"I have the right to ask why your family is not yet with you. I have that right."

"Okay, soon."

"Yussel! It's been since Shavuos. In seventeen days it's the fast of Tammuz. I won't be able to travel from then until after Tishabav. That's almost the whole summer without you. What are you doing to me?" Shoshanna dropped her voice melodramatically and quoted, "'Her enemies have her between the fences.'"

"Don't quote at me, Shoshanna. I'm not your enemy and it's me who's trapped. Not you. Look, this is my problem, Shoshanna. Leave me alone. Let me resolve it."

IN THE SAND he'd built her too small and too zaftig. In the grocery store, he found out he'd made her legs too short. In the bank, he found out he'd made the breasts too big. In Woodpecker's Hardware, he found out her waist was longer, narrower. In the Rexall he realized she was bigger, leaner, taller all over. When Adam fashioned Eve, who was his second wife, he fashioned her the way he wanted her to be and then, for the rest of time, yearned for something else. Yussel, in the sand, had made the same mistake as Adam: creating a woman he could handle, making her soft, round, small. The real Lillywhite was something else. He wondered for a moment how much he'd fashioned poor Shoshanna to suit himself or how much she'd fashioned herself to suit him. Maybe he was the monster. Maybe that was why he was yearning for Lillywhite, because he'd forced Shoshanna to remake herself to please him. Yussel dismissed the idea because it was too awful.

Each time Lillywhite was placed in front of him, he didn't look on her face. Even if his father of blessed memory, even if HaShem had put her in front of him, although the Angel of Destruction was more likely to have arranged such meetings, he didn't look on her face. Also he didn't breathe. He kept his eyes fixed on the floor, on the sidewalk, raced back to Bingo's cab, roared off, forgot everything he'd come to town for, had to go back, would see her again. He had the feeling she was waiting for him, strutting around in crotch-tight pants and high-heeled boots. Once he saw her in the Rexall sitting in a booth with Indian Joe. That day, the sidewalks empty, her Porsche parked behind Bingo's cab, Yussel picked up a garbage can filled with chicken wings, dumped it onto the front seat of the Porsche. A Publisher's Clearinghouse Sweepstakes mailer stuck to the bottom of the can. You may have just won ten million dollars. Yussel replaced the garbage can precisely on the sidewalk.

ONE MORNING his father was outside by the lake, feeding a half-dozen deer little square leaves from his pocket. The deer were crowding him. He waved them off, turned to Yussel, leaned on his lead door. The wooden door now had thick iron grates. *"You ask me why grates? Things are getting worse. You aren't paying attention. You must pay attention, Yussele."* Under the grates, he wore a white satin bathrobe with gold embroidery, as rich as the Torah covers, with Lions of Judah the size of housecats embroidered, thick and crusty, on the back, on each front panel. His father, this poor soul locked into Hell, trying to get into Heaven, as if he were walking down Oleg Cassini's runway, put a hand on his hip, turned from the hip like a model, chin high, eyes half-closed, turned, swiveled his doors ever so slightly and approached Yussel. *"How about these?"*

The pajamas were white damask with borders of small gold lions on the cuffs, the lapels, the collar, and the pocket fold. He loved his father. He really loved him, and when he was human, like now, showing off his pajamas, coy, vamping, a little embarrassed, wanting Yussel's approval, Yussel adored him.

"They're you, Totte."

"*I had a message you needed to ask me a question. I came right away.*"

"Totte, you talk to Him, to his angels, to someone. You're standing in line. You said you stand in line, right?"

"*Well, not exactly. I stand in line but talking . . . don't forget I'm not exactly up there with the rest of my Yeshiva class. The closest I can tell you, it's like a big room full of spaghetti, or spiderwebs. Something living, maybe protein. You tell someone your problem or your complaint. They discuss back and forth, back and forth, and if they grant you the decree, they point out you should pull on one of the lines. Then the whole place starts to quiver because the line you touch is connected to every other line. Of course I'm talking in metaphor.*"

"I don't want to know. I want you to ask a question for me."

"*Sure.*"

"Find out what HaShem wants me to do. Why He keeps putting this redhead in front of me."

"*Yussele, for shame. That's looking at answers in the back of the book. That's cheating. You have to do the problem by yourself. Otherwise, what's the point? Vey iz mir. I can't believe I was ever so dumb.*" His father was out the door, stuck his head back in. "*Am I to understand you are giving some consideration to the possibility that the redhead is intended?*"

"I'm examining possibilities."

"*There is only one possibility: everything is intended.*" Then went off singing his yom diddle yom diddle ai diddle dai dai.

YUSSEL TRIED to keep busy, tried not to get involved with anyone. He found projects. He put in a toilet. He put in a sink. He dug holes where he didn't need holes. He stretched Plexiglas across wooden frames and made storm windows. He tarred a path from the highway to the front door of the Arizona. Babe, all the time, would remind him. "Yussy, you didn't call her yet? She could ruin us all, Yussy. She owns everything around here. You owe her an apology. Maybe if you said you were sorry, she'd turn off the music. It's getting louder and louder, her music. Maybe she's just waiting for you to call. It wouldn't hurt to call, would it, Yussy?

Listen, all you have to do is say hello. Watch my lips. Hel-lo. You say, I'm sorry. You invite her for Shabbas, tell her it would be interesting. Try to be nice, Yussy. It wouldn't hurt to be nice, would it? How could it hurt, one phone call to a neighbor?" He didn't bother telling her what one phone call to Chaim had precipitated.

Another day his father sat alone in the kitchen, drinking a cup of coffee, sorting through a pile of requests to HaShem on little cards, from his grave. Some kvitls he put in his left pocket, some in his right. He wore a Milk of Magnesia bottle-blue dressing gown with Chinese gold medallions and a mandarin collar. The belt had long black silk fringes. His black felt slippers had a gold Chinese medallion on each toe. *"A little over a month, you're still here, and you've accomplished all this. This is terrific."* He gave Yussel a long hot look. *"And maybe that's why HaShem sent the redhead to you . . . to make certain you stayed. Intended. Intended. Intended."* He offered Yussel a square leaf from the pocket of his robe. *"On Shabbas they let us pick fruit. But this . . ."*—his father reached deep into his robe and withdrew a large and perfect pineapple with bright green leaves—*"this we grow locally. We have a guy who hates to grow pineapples."* Yussel tasted a square leaf. Juice sprung from it—it was like chewing Chiclets. He spit it out.

His father took the remainder of the pulpy leaf from Yussel's hand, put it back in his pocket, put the pineapple on the kitchen table. *"A fruit from Heaven, he spits it out. Boy, when you're ready, you're ready. When you're not, you're not. Thank God for the redhead."*

ALL THE MEN, except Slotnik, who was studying, formed a Building Committee. Feldman had a fight with him, said he had to contribute. Slotnik offered to pray for the success of the Building Committee. Feldman gave up. The Building Committee made plans. By fall, before the holidays, the dormitory on the north end would have a dozen beds for women, a separate place for families, another section for men. Every day trucks dropped off bags of mortar, loads of siding, kegs of nails, Sheetrock. Babe thought they were from the people who were putting kvitls on the grave, which meant their prayers were being answered. yussel kept saying, "there's no free lunch." grisha kept saying, "sure there is. if you're eating at HaShem's table." On the south end of the Arizona, next to Grisha's room, they added another room big enough for a single bed. Yussel told everyone the new room with the single bed could be for his mother-in-law or maybe his stepmother, someone. He moved into it before it was finished because that room was for him and Lillywhite. If she's intended, Yussel decided, my imagination may as well be comfortable, have some privacy.

"Yeah, well," his father said from noplace. *"I don't think it's intended you're comfortable, Yussele. You better watch out. There's a paradox here. Don't forget, He gives you free choice but He's the only one Who knows the consequences of your choices."*

They wouldn't leave him alone in his room. "In case you forgot, Yussy, I'm Babe. Today's Wednesday. How many times a day do you have to take a nap? Over a month you've done nothing about the water rights. You don't have the deed; you haven't apologized to Lillywhite. What's the matter with you? What are you doing in there anyway? You should call her. She saved my life, Yussy."

"We all make mistakes."

"Very funny." Babe waited for Yussel to answer. He didn't. "Don't say I didn't warn you about the water rights, Yussel. Your father also did this with the bed when he wanted something. You want something, Yussy?"

"I'm not my father."

"Look, if there's something we haven't done, something someone's said to you. You want us to call you Rabbi, we'll call you Rabbi. You want Nova and bagels, I'll fly them in from L.A. Just tell us what you want."

Natalie came. "There are people here to see the lake. They want you to pray for them. I don't want to interrupt your meditation, but they want to give you money, building supplies, join. They say you're bringing good luck and prosperity to their town. They thank you. Also would you like to join the Rotary Club? And there's a man here who wants a blessing for his tennis elbow."

"Tell him to ask God. I'm busy."

Yussel heard trucks arrive, unload, leave. Heard building sounds, a cement mixer, Lillywhite's music sneaking in under Ernie's tapes. He dreamed of her dancing in the dark, taking a slow boat to China, singing in the rain. She played. She sang. He ached.

Ernie banged on the door to the little room. "They brought a truckload of two-by-fours. You mind if we start some sub-flooring for the dormitory? Also someone sent over cement. Do you mind if we start pouring for the mikveh?"

Yussel didn't answer.

"He doesn't mind," Ernie shouted to somebody, "so let's go!" Yussel had never heard Ernie excited in his life. Hammering started that afternoon, went on forever.

Natalie slipped a handful of kvitls under the door. Yussel read the little notes. "Dear Rabbi, pray for my mother who is crippled. Gloria Figuero." "Dear Rabbi, pray for good luck on my new Martinizing business. Claire Alvarez." "Dear Rabbi, pray for Chaim that he should love his wife. Mendl."

"How did you get these, Natalie?"

"From your father's grave. Now everyone knows who you really are."

"Excuse me?"

"The lake. You can't deny what you did."

"Natalie, if anyone's responsible for the lake, it's the shmuck Indian, Rosebud. Not me. Let them take their requests to him."

OUTSIDE, the cement truck rolled around. It was bright red and had ROSEBUD painted on its door panels. Babe ran from crew to crew giving orders. Her name-in-diamonds bracelet and her name-in-diamonds necklace flashed in the sun like artillery. The mikveh walls already had tiny high windows for light. The first floor of the men's dormitory was complete. Bingo and Slotnik's son danced over the trusses. The Blondische had become a concrete mavin. Ernie knew all there ever was to know about cutting glass. Indian Joe, wrapped in a faded blanket, sat on the Rabbi's grave, laying out his bundle of sticks. Natalie was shouting mantras to increase productivity, menus to improve everyone's sex life. Rosebud, with a shirt on, was taking orders from Babe. Two dozen seagulls Yussel knew had flown in from Far Rockaway were roosting on the Shanda, cleaning their feathers, carrying on. Sometimes Yussel found himself stroking his cheek the way she'd stroked his cheek, and he shuddered under his own touch. He began to imagine things he had never dared imagine. And up on the mountain, she played her music with a vengeance. She played "All of Me" until Yussel felt he had to climb out from his skin. Yussel immersed himself in the mountain pool every day for the dreams he had every night. Also he hoped to see her there, on the horse, hoped this time she'd kill him and he'd be done with her. Yussel wondered if anyone he knew had ever been in love, decided maybe his father, no one else. He thought maybe he should talk to someone, read a book, but what could he read? Who could he talk to? Grisha? Chaim? Oh, Chaim would tell him all right. And then tell everyone else. Also Chaim would go after her himself. He thought seriously about calling his uncles, decided it would be a terrible mistake.

YUSSEL CALLED Chaim. "Chaim, meet me at the drugstore."
"Why the drugstore?"
"What I want to discuss doesn't belong in the sanctity of our homes."
"I'm pretty busy."
"Chaim, I'm asking."

THE DRUGSTORE was next to Woodpecker's, which was having a summer sale on blade sharpeners. The drugstore had pink-and-brown marble tables, mahogany walls, lots of sexy magazines in plastic wrappers, postcards, video tapes. Kids who needed haircuts fondled toys. Square-jawed mamas painted rough hands with lipstick samples, thumbed through movie magazines, told their kids not to touch anything. Chaim wore his cowboy hat, smelled of Brut. His shoulders were hunched over the table. He still looked like a victim. Yussel felt a surge of warmth in his chest. Chaim might help him.
"Your car needs new struts, Yussel."
"You drove it across the country. That's a rough trip."
"You sell me something in good shape and suddenly it needs major work?"

"I didn't sell it to you. You bought it from Bernie."

"You got money for it, didn't you? Any court would say you sold it to me."

"Now you're taking me to court, Chaim?"

"When I get the bill, I'll send it to you. Then we'll see."

The waitress brought two coffees in Styrofoam cups. Yussel and Chaim wrapped their handkerchiefs around them to hold them. A family of blond kids came over from the toys to watch them. One carried a kitten in a basket. The little sister stroked Yussel's fur hat.

"Listen, Chaim. I have to talk to you. I have to talk about . . ." Yussel gulped. ". . . love."

"What about love?" Chaim shot back.

"Have you ever been in love?"

Chaim glared at him. "You accusing me of something?"

"No, no. Believe me, Chaim, I'm asking you."

"You're accusing me."

Yussel let the kid try on his hat. "I'm not accusing you of anything. What are you so defensive about?"

"I don't like you accusing me."

"I told you . . ." The little girl put the kitten in Yussel's hat. Yussel took his hat back, handed the kitten to the girl.

Chaim's voice rose. The kids backed away. Their mother swooped over, hustled them to the sidewalk.

"Chaim, listen, you're accusing me of accusing you," Yussel tried to explain. He didn't want Chaim to leave him.

"Just stay away from me. Just keep off my property."

Yussel was bewildered. He put his hat on, patted the kitten in its basket, paid for both coffees, followed Chaim out the door. "How can I keep off your property if we have to go to you twice a day to daven?"

"Then to daven only. Otherwise, I don't want to see you. Understand? I don't want to see you."

HE CALLED his uncles. Moses from Abnormal Psychology said, "It's perfectly natural. You had erections in your mother's womb, so what are you worried about? Just don't do anything about it and

197

it should go away." Gimbel from Humanities said, "Come home. The desert's no place for a Jew." Nachman from Law asked Gimbel, "What are you telling the kid, Gimbel? Moses shouldn't have been in the desert?" Then he told Yussel to make sure his leases were in order. Moses said, "You should defuse her. Invite her over to meet everyone. Your wife, your kids. Let her know who you really are." Gimbel added, "And take sleeping pills so you don't lie in bed too much at night. We've all been through it." Yussel and his uncles were not/could not possibly be talking about the same thing.

ONE TERRIBLE night, near midnight, Yussel, light-headed from hunger, dry-mouthed from the thirst of yet another fast, was trying to run a wire to attach an outlet for the Eternal Light above the altar on the dance stage. Nobody was around. Grisha was snoring his great moist snores in his little room off the bar. Yussel stapled the wire along the woodwork, once into his own thumb. It came to him, what if he called her? Yussel paused with the staple gun in the air. What if he called her? What if you called her? Are you crazy? What if he just picked up the phone and called her? What would happen?

Yussel put the staple gun down, removed the staple from his thumb, went outside, was surprised it was raining. It was raining so hard he couldn't hear any music. The rain beat on his shoulders, ran down his face, splashed above him in the water tower, fringed the mountains. Yussel sucked his thumb where the staple holes were. And asked himself, Are you crazy? And answered himself, Yes. Then he went back in, listened at Grisha's door, heard the steady snores, tiptoed to the phone, stood over it. It was so small. It's two A.M., Yussy. You're a married man, a pious man, a Jew. You're crazy to call her.

So he picked up the receiver, dialed information, told the operator he wanted to talk to Lillywhite Stevie. He whispered into the mouthpiece, had to repeat himself twice, louder each time. Sweat dripped from his collar down inside his shirt. "Lillywhite." A Mountain Bell computer voice gave him a number. He punched the number.

She answered. Her voice was clear, polite. "Lillywhite."

"Listen, what do you want from me?"

"Aah."

"You make me deaf with your music. You beat me up. What do you want?"

"Who is this?"

"Very funny. I asked you what do you want."

"I want you to know I exist."

"Okay, you exist. Leave me alone."

"You called me. You see me and you don't even look at me. I exist as filth and evil to you. I know you guys."

"I'm a married man."

"I'm not talking about marriage. I'm talking about existence."

"Philosophy isn't my field."

"If you called me up at two in the morning, you have something to talk about with me, don't you?"

"I asked you, what do you want? Why are you making me crazy?"

She sighed. "You look like someone I once knew."

"Redford it's not." Yussel sat down. "All right, I'm listening." He sounded exactly like his father. "I'm listening."

"You rented a room in Cambridge. We had to share a bathroom. You were Orthodox, forty. You weren't a Hasid, but you wore a yarmulke. You were studying something at Harvard with permission from your Rabbi. That's what the landlady told me. My father had just died. We weren't speaking. I'd walked out on him and everything Jewish. You probably didn't even think I was Jewish. You were right. I'm not. I wanted to tell you about my father, how he was a religious man, how he brought me up to be religious, how he sold pesticides that caused abortions in Third World countries, how I called him a murderer, how he had a stroke, how he died. I wanted to talk to you. I wanted to tell you that I never said goodbye to him, or I love you, or I'm sorry. Or anything. I just pulled the plug. And there you were, a religious man, with answers, in the room next to mine. You never came out of your room except to go someplace to pray, use the bathroom, get the mail. I wanted to ask you about pulling the plug. I wanted to ask you if I killed him. Once you came into the kitchen and saw me cooking sausage.

"What's that?" you asked. You looked at me as if I'd shit on the floor and was frying my stool. "Sausage," I said. "Pig." From then on you ate cornflakes with grape juice in your room three times a day and raw vegetables and never came near the kitchen. I heard you in your room next to mine, singing, praying. You washed your clothes out every night and hung them in our bathroom. I wanted to talk to you. I needed to talk to you. I wanted to go with you to synagogue, to ask you if I should have pulled the plug, to ask you where souls go, to ask you why things happen. You looked like you knew. Once when you went for the mail, I looked in your room. It was filthy. It smelled of old socks. I saw the broccoli and the paper bowls of soggy cornflakes purpled in grape juice. One morning I followed you to a synagogue to pray for my father. It was a big mistake. I was climbing the steps to the women's section. They were concrete steps. I had to pass a dozen dry old men in the men's section. One pulled up his pants leg and showed me that his flesh was still firm on his ankle. You know how old men smell in the morning? I fell on the concrete steps, on my face, right next to the old men. Not one saw me. Not one helped me up. I had blood all over my face. Not one stopped to help me. I didn't exist. One day you knocked on my door. I thought the moment had come, you'd heard me, you knew. 'At night,' you said, 'when you use the toilet,' you said, eyes on the radiator behind me, 'could you please put the seat up so when I go to use it in the morning, I don't have to touch it before I pray?' I took your boots and burned them in the incinerator. Remember your boots were missing and no one knew where they were and you kept accusing everybody? You were right. You refused to pay your rent until you got your boots back. Finally the landlady kicked you out."

Her pain clung to him like a garment of fire. Yussel wanted to hang up right then and there. He didn't want to hear pain. He heard pain. He remembered his great-great-grandfather in Kiev who had the hiccups, who didn't feel the white-hot iron on his back. He thought about the Cossack who felt it and jumped out the window. He wanted to jump out the window, roll in the snow, run home. The only trouble was, he was the Jew. The Jews stay. They can't help it. "I want you to leave me alone. I'm a married man."

Her voice dropped. "Then let's not talk about marriage."

"Who's talking about marriage?" Yussel snapped. "I'm talking about sex." Yussel hung up.

NOTHING HAPPENED. Grisha was still snoring. The world was still turning on its axis. The rain was still splashing in the water tower, filling the mikveh pool. She'd turned on Ella Fitzgerald so loud Yussel could hear them both singing over the beat of the rain. In the morning, Grisha knocked on his door to wake him up. There were no reports of his kids terminally ill, no car accidents, no wife leaving him. Nothing happened except in the morning, two things. His Uncle Nachman called, said "Yussel, it's almost the fast of Tammuz. For the next three weeks, from now to Tisha-bav, you know to avoid situations of danger." And the other thing, mid-morning, when he looked out the kitchen window, he saw Chaim standing in front of the mikveh, towel slung over his shoulder, whistling.

Yussel blocked his way to the door of the mikveh. Chaim stopped whistling, smiled his visit-to-the-dying smile. "Ask Babe." Whistled.

Ernie was tying string around a square of stakes. Natalie pounded the stakes into the ground with a soup ladle. Some local men who might have been Figueras and Alvarezes were delivering large wood joists. Grisha sat on his stool, singing psalms. Babe and Bingo were smoothing mortar in Ernie's square with new trowels. "Like sheep you stand there while this wolf pollutes our mikveh?"

Bingo touched Yussel's arm. "We took a vote."

"I voted against, Rabbi," Natalie called to him.

Mendl from Rikers Island walked out of the mikveh. Chaim walked in. Mendl dried his hair with a towel in front of Yussel. "Mendl, tell Chaim only for Shabbas, once a week, Mendl, and you have to call first."

"A man could have an emergency, Reb Yussel."

Yussel lifted his hands in front of him, which meant go no further. "In an emergency, of course." A flush moved up around his neck. Everyone went back to work. Yussel took a walk around the new lake.

THE NEXT NIGHT, almost midnight, just as Yussel was picking up the phone, Grisha came out of his room to go to the bathroom. His pajama tops were safety-pinned to his pajama bottoms. Grisha asked him who he was calling at such an hour. Yussel told him he was calling his broker but he wasn't answering.

"He lives in China he's open for business at such an hour?" Grisha shuffled to the bathroom where he stayed forever.

Yussel finished the wiring for the Eternal Light, dusted the bookshelves, thought he should see if Grisha was okay, sanded the bottom of the front door, which was swollen from the flood, sanded it until it swung closed easily, knocked on the bathroom door, asked Grisha if he was all right. Grisha growled, grunted. Finally Grisha came out scratching his behind. "You reach him yet?"

"Who?"

"Your broker. The one who dances naked in a room full of books."

Yussel punched a bunch of numbers, hoped it was the right amount. Grisha shuffled past him, slammed his bedroom door. Yussel yelled, "It's still busy," at the door. When he could hear Grisha snoring, Yussel dialed the number, said, "Hi," very softly. "Guess who."

"I know you," she said to him as softly. "You were my father's doctor, when he was dying. You stormed into the room with ten students following you. You filled the room. The nurses retreated. The students had notebooks, took down every word you said. You pulled the sheets from my father's body and examined my father, put your hands on his body. You wore a ring from Yale. There were tufts of black hair on your knuckles. I could imagine the tufts on your body. Maybe you were fat. I didn't see that. You were big, oxlike, a peasant-king. Strong, powerful, with that gorgeous Jewish mouth. You were Chief of Internal Medicine at Albert Einstein. You looked like those old sketches of Semites drawn by anti-Semitic anthropologists. The strong sweep of nose, the soft lips, the deep black eyes, the wings of brows, the beard, Oh God, the beard. You put your hands on my father's body, explored, listened, touched, rolled him over, bent down, listened to his heart. Suddenly I'm in the bed being touched, listened to, explored by those hands, by that knowing arrogance, by that wisdom that knows death. You look up and say, 'Your father is dead.' All I wanted was that you would touch me with those hands. I followed you from the room. You turned, looked at me. Tell me things with those hands. Listen to my heart with those hands. 'Yes?' I didn't know what to say. 'Did I kill him? Did I do it?' Your lip curled up. Your students surrounded you, held notebooks, pencils in the air. 'You should talk with his attending physician. We're paging him. Excuse me.' And you turned to your students. 'Now, where was I?' Where are you? The man who knows why my father died, why we die, whose hands will touch me and know my destiny, where are you? Are you that man? I hope for your sake you aren't, because I've known since I've been looking for you, I would rip you apart for ignoring me. And I would love you until I died."

"This is what you want from me? To tell you why your father died?"

"I want you to show me something moral." They were both silent. Then she asked, "What do you want from me?"

"My world would be destroyed. I'm a married man, a pious man."

She shifted suddenly, revengefully. "Is it true you guys use a sheet with a hole in it?"

"No, we use the sheet to cover up your faces." When he heard himself say this, he understood why he'd punched her the day of the flood.

He spent that night in the narrow bed in the small room off the kitchen with Lillywhite, listening to her heart, pulling off her blankets, rolling her over, listening to her heart, listening to her sing out his name. He lay awake until the sun rose. What she said she wanted and what she sang she wanted were two very different things.

In the morning, Grisha asked, "So how's your broker?"

"Fine." Yussel tried not to swallow.

"I thought last night maybe he was sick."

"Brokers, Grisha. You know how the market is."

"Yeah, yeah. I know all about the market."

The women lined up outside the mikveh with towels over their arms. They sat outside in the afternoon sun, made the men leave, lifted their hair off their necks to let it dry. By sundown, thunderheads piled up like freight trains over the mountains, her music came on.

HE CALLED HER from the Texaco. "Talk to me. I'm listening."

"I know who you are. You're the past coming to get me. You're five thousand years old. You won't look at me. I see you every place I go and you won't look at me. I'm the future and you're the past and the world would split in half if we touched each other here, here in my bed, here in the present."

"How did this happen?"

She whispered. "You called. You stay up all night. I stay up all night. I sing to you. You sang to me." Her voice changed, softened. "The first day up in the mountains, at the pool, I saw your eyes when you smiled. Your smile lit up your face. It lit up the woods. And then you sang in the canyon and I heard your heart. I hate you guys. I always have. But you have something I want."

19

IT WAS THE seventeenth of Tammuz, the fast of the fourth month. Shoshanna had reminded him already that it was a day in which he should examine himself and undertake repentance from wrongdoing because it was still the month of calamities for the Jews, maybe for his family. "And the Lord saw their actions, Yussel."

"That's enough, Shoshanna. Don't quote. Listen, what have you been doing with yourself? Are you keeping busy? Did you find someone to take your wigs to? Have you been shopping? If you're dieting, I decided I think you should be a little fat. I wouldn't mind a little fat."

"Also this is the day Moses broke the tablets, the day his people worshiped the golden calf, the day the walls of the temple were breached, and the day I can't travel for the next three weeks, until Tishabav. What are you doing to me, Yussel?"

"I'm doing what you want me to do. I'm being a rabbi."

"A man isn't whole without his wife."

"Tell me about it."

"This is the day Noah sent out the dove, Yussel." She spoke very slowly. "And it could find no resting place in the flood. Do you hear me?"

"I hope you're teaching all this to the children."

"Who else is here to teach them? Their father?"

"Lay off, Shoshanna."

"My place is there with you, Yussel. Shame on you. Oh, Yussel. I forgot. I found the deed. In the Chinese checkers. You bought only the surface of the land. No mineral rights, no water rights. Is that what you needed to know? Yussel? Yussel? I hear the kibbutzniks came. You don't have to daven by Chaim anymore. Yussel? . . ."

YUSSEL PARKED Bingo's cab by the SL in Chaim's driveway, kicked the side of the SL, walked up to Chaim's front door.

Chaim yelled to Mendl. "Please inform Reb Fetner Mincha services don't begin for another hour. He can't cross my threshold until seven-ten. He should remove himself from my property."

"I'm not exactly asking, Mendl, can I enter the Gates of Heaven," Yussel yelled, loud enough so Chaim could hear.

Mendl shook his head no, slowly, from side to side, lowered his eyelids until they were slits, blinked once, snapped a shade shut over the shower-glass window. Yussel leaned on the bell and listened to the first six notes of "Ain Kaloheynu" maybe a hundred times until someone pulled the plug on the chimes.

When Yussel walked around to the back of the house to find an open window, the dogs hit the fence with G-force. Yussel pulled himself up to the windowsill.

The kitchen ceiling was so low it almost came down to the top of the refrigerator, which was big enough to freeze four grown men. The kitchen looked like pigs had left in a hurry. On the kitchen table was an open can of Heinz Vegetarian Beans with a fork stuck in it, a can of sauerkraut with a spoon stuck in it, a bag of hot dog rolls, a pile of half-filled paper plates, open mustard, schmutz. Yussel tiptoed, held his breath, didn't see the crayons on the floor, went sliding, stumbling, arms out, past the turquoise bar, past the triple-strand ficus trees, and into the living room where his supernaturally broken shoulder hit the floor eye-level with the toes of Chaim's Tony Lama lizard cowboy boots.

The Miracles of Creation growled. Then Chaim made a joke. "Look at this. We don't let Fetners in through the door, they come in through the windows. This must mean we're doing something right when the Fetners can't stay away."

Mendl helped him up. The others laughed at Chaim's joke. Even bent over double in pain, Yussel towered above them. "So, sit, Reb Yussel," Mendl from Rikers Island invited. "You want a glass of tea? A cookie?"

Chaim's house smelled of sauerkraut and gas. The gas hissed from a small fire burning fake logs over a little spigot. "You have business, Yussel? Maybe you came to sell me some homeowner's? You need a loan?"

"Chaim, I have business to satisfy."

The Miracles of Creation swelled up, moved away from Yussel, toward Chaim. Yussel took a deep breath. "I ask you point-blank, Chaim, do you own my water rights?"

Chaim kissed the tips of his fingers, then touched them to the prayer book on his lap, looked up at the ceiling for the answer. The Miracles of Creation looked sideways at each other with sly smiles.

"No, Yussel, I don't own your mineral rights."

"I said water rights. Do you own my water rights?"

"No. No. What makes . . . of course I don't own your water rights. Why should I own your water rights?"

"Emes Adonoy, no?"

"Emes Adonoy, no."

Yussel thundered. "On your children's lives?"

"On my children's lives, Yussel."

This Yussel couldn't argue with.

Fifey the Kluger walked up too close to Yussel, stuck his face in his, covered him with a fine spray of sauerkraut. "So your business is satisfied? We'll see you back here for Mincha?"

"You stand there with your hand on the sefer, Chaim, and you say no?"

"Yes."

"So who does?"

Zipper joined Fifey, then Velvl the Shecter. Together the three of them, like a greasy wall, slid into Yussel's space. Yussel backed up. They moved him in this way into the kitchen, toward the window.

"I'll call you, Yussel. I'll call you," Chaim called. "I need homeowner's. Don't forget."

Yussel, forgetting, climbed out the kitchen window. Mendl,

from inside, whispered, "You okay, Reb Yussel? You need anything?" Yussel shook his head no, told him to wait a minute, ran to the car, returned with the pineapple, passed it through the open window to Mendl. Mendl whistled in approval, pulled down the window, pulled down its shade, then all the other shades as Yussel walked around the house. So who owns the water? Yussel moved his yarmulke back and forth, cracked himself on the head. He could see nothing on the screen.

YUSSEL COULDN'T start Bingo's cab. He looked under the hood, wiped off the battery, checked the oil, kicked the tires, flooded the engine. Chaim stuck his head out the door, offered to call the Texaco. Yussel ignored him. Yussel tried the engine. Nothing. From noplace his father said, *"The paradox is, He gives you free choice but He's the only One Who knows the consequences. I told you."*

Yussel ignored his father, told HaShem what he thought of Him. "You think You're the only One who knows consequences? I also know some consequences! The consequences are, someday I'm going to kill Your friend Chaim unless You give me a little something too! You hear me?"

At that instant, like a clap of thunder, Bingo's cab turned over by itself, scared Yussel out of his mind.

20

A FIRE-ENGINE RED BMW 735 with a magnetic sign on the driver's door was parked in front of the Arizona. The sign read OFFICIAL TRIBAL CAR. The moon shone placidly on the new lake. Yussel could taste mud in his mouth from his fast, from his fear.

Indian Joe sat at the bar, drinking coffee with schnapps, making Babe giggle. He was as shiny and alert as a clean spittoon. Babe was having a flamingo pink day. She leaned over the bar, giggled. Indian Joe looked like a friend of Frank Sinatra's, with a tanning-salon special, a hand-tailored Western-style gray flannel suit with pink stitching, pink shirt to match, a three-inch solid-gold kachina doll with turquoise eyes, a Rolex watch that could be fake, snake-skin boots with silver points on the toes.

Yussel rubbed his nose, pulled at his beard, wondered if his mother was giggling someplace for somebody. Indian Joe looked up, grinned at Yussel, shot a pink cuff, examined his Rolex, which moved around so smoothly Yussel knew it was a $1,500 Rolex because the second hands on the thirty-five-dollar Hong Kong knockoffs jerk around.

"You go on, Mrs." Indian Joe pointed to the kitchen. "We gotta talk man to man."

Babe ran out of the room in a quick little dog trot. Indian Joe shrugged, pulled a sheaf of legal papers from inside his pink-stitched breast pocket, flattened them out on the table, and pushed them quarter-inch by quarter-inch toward Yussel as he talked. The universe was tightening up. "I promised your father I'd take care of you. Number one, he didn't touch her."

"Who owns my water rights?"

Yussel tried not to wonder who he, who her, tried to stare the Indian down. The Indian kept sliding the papers closer.

"First, he never touched her." Indian Joe leaned forward, so close his eyes crossed when he looked at Yussel, their noses almost touching. Yussel could see the little hairs at the ends of his nostrils, like Spanish moss.

Yussel knew at that very moment, as he looked up Indian Joe's nose, he was going bankrupt. He didn't know how; certainly he didn't know why, but he knew it was happening. Yussel tried not to look up into Indian Joe's nose.

"So, you believe me, my son he didn't touch her?"

"Rosebud's your son? I paid for all those trucks?"

"He takes her to his house. I admit that. She's gotta massage him and rub him with oils and then she's got these little plastic bags of sagebrush shit and she burns it all over his house, spices, and tells him how he's going to give her the Messiah that night in the full moon and she's saying these prayers with her eyes closed, getting ready, she says to him. My son, he's a simple kid. He says, 'I'll get you ready.' She says, 'I mean inside.' He says, 'That's what I mean.' She says, 'That's not what I mean.' He says, 'Inside, outside, what's the difference?' She says, 'Inside, as in spirit.' He says, 'Oh.' What's he gonna say? What would you say? Then she wants to give him an enema, a coffee enema. She's gobbling like a turkey, her eyes closed, rocking back and forth, getting ready, and the sage is burning, and the whole house stinks, so he takes off his shoes and sneaks out of the house, doesn't go back until she's gone. It took him all week to get all that shit out of his house. For three days we laugh when he tells it. But he's scared. Believe me, that one's loco. The Messiah."

Yussel saw the two sets of footprints in the sand on the dunes. Natalie's gone. Natalie's back. Natalie's kneepads. And his father was busy all night protecting Natalie. You didn't pay attention. A lot of things he hadn't paid attention to, like where is the Flower Child and where is the Jackalope and why isn't your wife here and what does Natalie need that would keep her away from

Rosebud. The papers were almost across the bar. They were legal papers. Very smoothly Indian Joe maneuvered a ketchup bottle and a sugar shaker out of the path of the papers. Yussel wouldn't look.

"And number two, I said there would be a sacred lake on your property. You didn't believe me then. You believe me now?"

Yussel said, "It's a lake. You also said the world would come to an end when we got the lake."

"Give it time."

The papers were almost at his fingertips. "So now, here." Indian Joe tapped his manicured fingers on the papers. "Free and clear. Your own house. You believe me?"

"Okay, Cochise, who owns the water rights to my land?"

"Eight bedrooms, two baths, apple trees, full modern baths, free and clear. Two stories."

"The water rights, Cochise."

Indian Joe smoothed out the deed, cocked his head. "You don't believe me. Your father believed me. I told you there would be sacred water, didn't I? You have valuable land now. My tribe trusts you with our sacred land and our sacred lake." He beat at his heart. "My tribe trusts you." The kachina doll danced on his diaphragm.

"My tribe doesn't trust your tribe." Yussel lifted Indian Joe up by his lapels. He was light-boned, tumbleweed blowing around in the desert. The inside of his mouth could have been a display case at Tiffany's.

"DBM." Indian Joe's nose hairs moved rapidly. "A tribal corporation. My tribe," he said softly.

Yussel dropped Indian Joe into a chair. "Okay. I'm going to your tribe. Where is it? I'm going to tell them how you and your son spent all their money. I'm—"

Babe yelled from the kitchen, "You're talking to his tribe. Plus his son."

"I have to pay *you* extra for the water?"

Indian Joe shook his head no.

Yussel stalked the perimeters of the room.

"We leased them out to another party. But I'm giving you a house free, eight bedrooms, full modern kitchen, two baths. Free." He flagged the papers at Yussel.

No one had to tell Yussel who had leased the rights from Indian Joe. Chaim, who, like death, couldn't get enough.

"So if he owns the water, I have to pay him to use it, right?"

"You're getting a house for nothing, Yussel."

"Whose side are you on, Babe?"

"I'm just explaining it."

"You think I don't understand? Is that what you think?"

Yussel stopped in his tracks, turned on Indian Joe. "How much do I have to pay?"

"Whatever she wants."

"I thought you leased it to Chaim."

"He did." Babe moved between Yussel and Indian Joe. "Chaim subleased."

Someone was drilling a hole in his stomach, draining out his fluids, embalming him. Yussel looked at Indian Joe. Indian Joe jerked a thumb up toward the mountain. And that's how Yussel found out where some of Chaim's money was coming from. And where the rest of whatever Yussel had left to live on could go.

"Come on, Yussy," Babe shrugged, spread her hands. "It's not that bad. So you'll call her. You'll make nice."

INDIAN JOE DROVE the Official Tribal Car. They took Ray-Vac lanterns. Yussel sat in the front seat, Babe in the back. The moon was high and big. Indian Joe said the house wasn't quite finished yet. They crossed Moffat, drove onto a dirt road, past the cemetery, past the town dump, pulled up in front of a battered, paintless, two-story house. Doors banged in the wind. A gray filthy wisp of curtain blew out of the broken window of an upstairs bedroom.

"Babe," Yussel whispered, "this is the old whorehouse!"

"The new one is occupied."

"How can I put my family in such a place?"

"The shul's in a bar. You bring to it; you don't take from it. Also, tell me where else you're going to find eight bedrooms, enough for all your kids plus your in-laws, plus Shabbas guests. It's perfect."

They walked among old apple trees, a well, an outhouse that was one of the two bathrooms, piles of shipping cartons containing kitchen cupboards, bathroom sinks, one master bedroom Jacuzzi. Yussel kicked the Jacuzzi box. It wasn't a dummy.

"You can't tell much from the outside," Indian Joe apologized. "So, let's go inside."

"You can't tell much from the inside either. But my son, he'll have it fixed inside out in no time. Another two weeks you could move in. My son he works like lightning."

"Thunder."

It was a big house, a rambling house, with the apple trees, probably a good view of the mountains, a little stream behind the apple trees. It wouldn't be so bad. A swing on the old tree, the kids learning how to fish.

"Shoshanna picked out the wallpaper and the kitchen already."

Yussel thought about a whore wiping between her legs with the curtain in the upstairs window. Yussel thought about all the bedrooms. "We better get it really clean if my kids . . ."

Indian Joe grinned, said to Babe, "He likes it." They drove back to the Arizona.

Yussel curled up on the backseat. His father made himself small and curled up next to him. He was wearing a silk jacquard robe in beige with dark brown piping, pajamas in beige tussa, with the same piping, a brown-and-beige polka-dot ascot at his throat. His father took out a notepad from the Palace Hotel in Madrid, read a list to himself Yussel couldn't see, shook his head.

"How's it going with the redhead?"

He didn't know how much his father knew, so he told him. "Terrific. I think she's in love with me."

"With you?"

"What can I tell you?"

His father put his hands behind his head, leaned back into them, looked somewhere behind his eyes, sighed for what had been. Yussel was dying to ask for names. *"When I was your age, women were hanging all over me. Of course I was better looking than you. But later when I started losing my hair, my teeth, they were still hanging around so I figured it wasn't me they were after. It was God. This one mention God to you?"*

"No. She talks about my lips, my hands, eyes, nose, beard. Mostly my beard."

"What could something like that see in you?" He shook his head. *"She's got to be intended. There's no other explanation."* He folded his notepad up, slipped it into his bathrobe pocket. *"So just don't*

touch. You're being offered choices, challenges. Just don't touch. Unless of course that's intended too. We'll see." He snorted. *"They never sent me such a sexy challenge. They never sent me to the Other Side either. They're really serious about you. This is some trip they've got you on."*

"She's smart."

"That makes it worse, much worse. You must be getting closer to HaShem, He gives you such punishments." His father went back behind his eyes again, shook his head dreamily. *"All those lovely broken hearts heading in the wrong direction."*

Yussel woke up as the BMW bumped down the spur, pulled up in front of the Arizona. Babe had covered him with her coat. The deed to the whorehouse was in his pocket. He stumbled into bed with his clothes on, dialed her number. "Lillywhite, do you ever think you're heading in the wrong direction, that maybe you're looking for God, not for me?"

"I won't know until I get there, will I? Listen, I know who else you are."

Yussel curled into the pillows, made himself deliciously comfortable against her feathery thigh, her goosedown breast. "Who else am I?"

"You're the Rabbi they were sorry they invited to the conference on consciousness. You'd written about old Jews in cellars who were mystics, filthy mystics. You followed me around. I went to buy a belt and you followed me into the store and pinched my ass. Once when I was secretary of the student government in college, there was a dwarf who later became a famous actor, although he died young. He used to follow me up the stairs to the student government offices on the second floor of the student building, and he'd pinch my ass on the way up. I felt about you as I felt about that dwarf. You were too small to hit, too poor to insult, and part of me was you and didn't belong on the second floor with the big shots but downstairs with the dwarfs and the misfits. So when you pinched my ass in Southampton in the belt store, I hated you because I hated me, and I couldn't say anything but ask you if you liked the belt. You shrugged. Later that day, most of us sat on the floor of a big room and meditated with Pir Vylat Khan. Two hours I sat with my tongue at the roof of my mouth trying not to think of anything. What a way for a Jew to spend two hours. You knew. I walked out onto the porch in a half-trance, sat down on a wicker chair overlooking the bay. You were standing beside me and put a square of Hershey's bar into my mouth. You forced me back to where you were. You reminded me who I was. I didn't want to know I was also the dwarf from the lower floor. I wanted to be up there with the guys in white on the second floor. If you hadn't pinched my ass, maybe I would have understood the earth of what you were putting in my mouth. I just thought you were the clod. Years later I watched you marry two young children at Waterside. It was raining. It cost three hundred bucks a couple to stand in the rain and eat Nova. And there you were. And I was so sorry I hadn't taken the rest of the Hershey's bar. But I was trying to get rid of the dwarf in me. I think it's called Kill the Jew."

The pillows were hard and lumpy. He was being asked to redeem her soul? His body was asking other questions.

"What do you think? I don't hate Jewish men. It's just that they let me down. I expected so much. I wanted so much. I want so much."

"I think I wish you were here."

"Why?"

"I'll feed you chocolate, Lillywhite. I'll . . ."

"I thought you were listening to me."

He knew she'd hang up. He wanted her to. He wanted to be alone with her, without dwarfs and rabbis, directions, meanings and significances. Just for a while, until Shoshanna came with the wallpaper.

21

IT WAS THEN the first of the month of Av, almost August, the day Aaron, the priest of Moses, died. Shoshanna didn't have to tell Yussel it was the beginning of a terrible month, the month of punishment, the month of the fathers. But she hadn't passed up such an opportunity. In nine days, she reminded him, it would be Tishabav, the day of calamity. In ten days, he reminded her, he'd bring them down and would she please lay off. The new moon snapped on and off inside the clouds like a strobe light. Another month or so, summer would be over. Soon the tents would have to come down, the women would move into the new dormitories. Snow dusted Crestone Needle, Crestone Peak, Kit Carson. Herds of deer clustered in the cottonwoods, stole through the high grasses, wandered closer and closer to the Arizona. The moment the sun was gone, the air turned cool, the evening sky flattened out like an old bed sheet, wind-wrinkled, stained with the bloody splashes of night, and Yussel wanted Lillywhite under him, singing out his name, begging for more. Lillywhite played her music, sang her heart out, called to him like whales call each other under oceans, wolves across forests. Yussel phoned Lillywhite every night as soon as Grisha went to bed. Grisha studied later and later at a table next to the phone, midnight, one, sometimes two A.M.

"It's past midnight, Grisha. You'll get sick staying up so late."

"What's out there, Yussel? It's all in here." Grisha patted the siddur he was reading. "Come, Boychickl. Come."

Yussel sat at a study bench in front of Grisha. Grisha wheezed like a leaky bellows. He patted the book again, lovingly. "This here is the real treasure."

Yussel's chest ached from Lillywhite's music. He tried to study.

"You could stop tapping your foot, Yussel. You could concentrate better."

"I can't concentrate like you can."

"Of course you can't. I was conceived without passion."

Yussel started to tap his foot again. Grisha banged his fist on his study table. Yussel heard something outside, went to the window.

Natalie paddlewheeling her arms in the air, turning in thoughtful circles. She wasn't making her turns in time to the moonlight or the music. She wore a glossy shirt over blue jeans, a striped satiny belt tied in a huge foolish bow at her waist.

Yussel tapped on the window, opened it, leaned out. "Hello, Natalie. Where are you coming from, Natalie? In pants."

She stopped mid-turn, one arm pointing to the sky, the other to the ground, looked at him, didn't answer. Natalie had the fishy smell of a woman who'd been with a man.

"Natalie, there are now four nice Israelis here for you. Stay away from the Indian."

"I love Rosebud. He loves me."

"He's not Jewish."

"He's kind to me and good-natured. He can become Jewish."

"Why should he become Jewish?"

"So he can marry me."

"That's the wrong reason. I wouldn't convert him for that reason."

Yussel remembered her up in the tree, demanding to know how many garbage cans she needed in a kosher kitchen. She still had no understanding, yet she was smarter, more certain of herself, still screwing around, but no wounds and scars, no blue and orange marks. "And so, Natalie, because you can't marry him, I have to forbid you to see him."

"Oh, come on, Rabbi. You sound like your father. Don't you

guys ever learn? You're full of new ideas, but the minute an old idea is threatened, you forget everything new."

"You're part of this community or you're not. No separate laws. You can't rewrite the laws, Natalie."

"Someone should. Someone really should. You guys have a romance with God . . . who am I supposed to have it with? What do I have to circumcise? I'm going to see Rosebud. You've already kicked two people out. You want to kick me out, go ahead."

Natalie the Nut, who expected to give birth to the Messiah, paddled off toward her tent, moonlight flashing over her head as if she'd already been chosen. And Yussel held his head, knew Natalie was right.

"Grisha, if a woman can't be circumcised, can't be Bar Mitzvahed, can't daven in a minyan, how does she participate as a Jew?"

"By doing women's things. Kids, food, a peaceful home."

"It's a man's religion, isn't it? We're supposed to love HaShem the way we love a woman . . . the Shabbas Bride. Why does a new Torah get married under a chupa? Because the Torah is a woman. I'll bet the Torah is a woman. You take off her dress, you take off her jewels, you spread her legs, you read her, you know her. You carry her up and down the shul so all the men can kiss her."

"Bite your tongue, Yussy."

"Women can't read Torah. They can't welcome the Sabbath Bride. They can't be a part of a minyan. They can't go to the Wailing Wall. They can't say Kaddish for their parents. They can't carry the Torah at Simchas Torah. Maybe that's why there are so many Catholic women . . . at least they can take communion."

"You want to hand out crackers, hand out crackers."

"What are Jewish women supposed to do? Make a religion out of housework and raising kids?"

"Something's wrong with that?"

"Would it satisfy you?"

"How should I know? Do I look like a woman?"

"Seriously, Grisha, you know the ruling if a man goes to a beast the beast should be killed because it might have had pleasure. But if he goes to a tree, the tree doesn't have to be killed because the tree took no pleasure. You know this?"

"Of course I know this."

"And all the references to cutting down the Asherah groves. Asherah wasn't a kind of tree. It was the name of a goddess. So the Jews were doing something like sex, like worship, with the trees."

"Boychickl, I didn't go to Yeshiva?"

"It follows. And what they were doing, Grisha, was davening."

"Tripe."

"I'm telling you. We daven now without the tree, without the woman under us. What are we doing—cleaving, attaching, going into ecstasy as we shookel back and forth? Where do these concepts come from? We're standing up because we're used to trees. At home, with our wives, we lie down."

"You sound like your father. Worse than your father."

"My point is that women have no one to worship, no way to worship, because our religion is rooted in men worshiping some old idea of a woman. That's the ring around the pecker . . . we're dedicated to—"

"Genug. Enough, Yussel. Crazy talk. You want to change the religion? You want to destroy the past?"

"Change doesn't have to destroy belief, Grisha." Yussel walked around the room, twice past the telephone. "Who can women worship and adore? I ask you."

"Us. That's who." Grisha cackled, stood, shuffled to his bedroom.

Yussel followed him. "It's a man's religion. Who can women love the way you, my father, men like you, love HaShem?"

"You know why God gave women two sets of lips, Yussy? So they can piss and moan at the same time."

"You really think about it from their point of view . . ."

"Five thousand years it's been okay. You want to rewrite the Torah?" Grisha shut his door.

Through the door Yussel answered. "We're worshiping the past. Why can't we turn it around and worship the future?"

"Sweetheart, the past, we know what it is. The future, we don't know from."

"Think of it from their point of view, Grisha."

"Why should I?"

———

JUST AS YUSSEL reached for the phone, Grisha came out of his room, sat at the study bench, opened his book. Yussel sat down at his, turned pages for another half-hour. At last, Grisha's shoulders were higher than his head. The pocket watch dropped, startled Grisha, who looked at Yussel as if Yussel had fallen out of the sky, looked at his pocket watch as if he'd never seen it before, shook from his head whatever of the Upper Worlds or mercury vapors were in there. Yussel undressed him, pinned his pins, tucked blankets under his beard, around his bony shoulders. In moments, Grisha was snoring steadily in his little storeroom and Yussel was holding the phone as long as the cord would extend because the music was playing on the mountain and he could hear her loneliness beating in his head like a bird trying to escape. He thought people were happy when they were in love. For him, love pressed in as heavy as grief.

"I dreamed about you, Rabbi. Do you want to hear?"

"Anything you say, anything you think I want to hear."

"I wish that were true. But I'll tell you this dream. I dreamed it right after the flood, the day I met you, which is putting it lightly. I went home. I was furious. I came back down to tell you off. You saw me as filthy. I knew the bigotry. As if no one but you has a soul, no one but you knows God, no one but you exists, except as an obstacle in your path. I hate that bigotry. I want to be in the world, not in the ghetto. So I drove down to tell you that I'd watch you, and if I didn't like what you were doing, I'd force you off your land and your friend out of his houses. There you were by the side of the road digging your father's grave. I who didn't/don't even have the courage to go to my father's grave watched you bury your father's corpse. I saw how easily you understood death. How you put it in its place. I drove home, took a sleeping pill, and just before I really fell asleep, I had this dream, which wasn't really a dream. We were on a boat." She laughed. "It must have been all that water from your flood. All that water. My father steered the boat. There was a construction in the middle—housing—so he couldn't see us. You and I sat on the deck leaning against the back of the boat. You kissed me with your tongue. You said you were showing me the parts of your mouth, making shapes. I woke up in a cold sweat, shame, fear, all that for having thought such thoughts about you. I was kissing you. I *thought* I was kissing you. I mean from my level of understanding that's all I could understand. When I woke up I realized the correct meaning was that you were teaching me how to make sacred sounds."

"What do you want? You want to dig graves? You want to learn? You want me to teach you?" He heard his own voice from a distance. It was cruel and sarcastic.

"The day you had the flood you were talking with your hands. I wanted you to talk to me with your hands. Yes, I wanted you to touch me, to teach me. I'm not sure of the difference. I wanted you to teach me about death, to take me to *my* father, to help me make peace with him."

Yussel thought about her sitting near him, turning pages, asking questions, watching him, judging him. It was an unbearable thought. "I'd like to teach you. I'd like to make lightning between your legs. I'd like to be the thunder and make—" She hung up. The music came on very loud. It was heartbreaking. He held her. They danced to "Unforgettable" in great white circles on new snow at the top of her mountain. What did she want from him?

HE CALLED BACK. It was almost light outside. "I'm sorry, Lillywhite. I can't help myself. I'm fighting myself. You touch my heart. I have to push you away. Meet me tomorrow at the Rexall."

"At the Rexall? Come here."

"You know I won't come there."

"I can't talk to you about death at the Rexall."

"I have to talk business."

"I want to see you, to be with you. I want to be alone with you."

"We can't."

HE HAD TO ask how much she planned to charge him so he could budget ahead. Yussel had cramps in his stomach. Babe had to go to the Rexall for him, came back with bad news. "She won't talk business until you give her a face-to-face apology. She's right."

"That's all she said? You were gone over an hour."

"Women talk." Babe shrugged. "Men, money, loneliness, free-

dom, pain." Babe thought for a moment, tapped her long nails on
the table. "She's smarter than I am. First woman I've ever met
who was smarter than me. All she has to do to ruin you and Chaim
is to pull in her chips and charge you for the water. That's all."

"What about men?"

"She wants one."

"She couldn't have anyone she wants?"

"Aah, Boychickl, it's the old problem. She has a whole heart. If
she finds a man, she'll go back to half a heart."

"Marriage wouldn't work?"

Babe shook her head. "You tell me." Babe stood, smoothed her
skirt. Something in the movement reminded Yussel of his mother.
He knew Babe and his mother had talked about this, probably
over coffee in the kitchen, both weeping, wiping their eyes with
their aprons. "You find a man, you fill up one kind of loneliness,
but then you get lonely for yourself and that's the worst kind of
loneliness in the universe."

"I never heard that."

"Yeah, well, it's our oral tradition."

"You think Shoshanna has half a heart?"

"All I said was your friend has a whole heart. That's all I said."
Babe sighed. And maybe Shoshanna sat in the kitchen with Ruchel
and talked about whole hearts and half hearts, broken hearts and
lonely hearts, wondered what love was, wondered what passion
might be, dreamed about dancing naked in a roomful of books.
Babe swung around. "She was Jewish. She quit."

"Maybe that's why she's letting me use the water."

"I doubt that."

THE THREE Little Kings called. "A man shouldn't be without his
wife so long. You and Chaim, the both of you without your
families. You're just like your mother, running off."

"One, nothing's going on. Two, Chaim I think has his family
here. Three, this is between me and Shoshanna. Three, go sell
shoes."

His Uncle Nachman said, "You mean four, go sell shoes. Are
you okay, Yussel? You haven't touched her, have you?"

SHOSHANNA CALLED early in the morning, before the kids were up. She couldn't sleep. "Your uncles called me."

"I hear you called them."

"They think I should be there too. Ruchel thinks I should come back with the kids too and maybe . . ." Shoshanna left out something important.

"Ruchel's in Far Rockaway? I thought she was here."

"You saw her?"

"No. Chaim's acting weird."

"You're both acting weird if you ask me. Yussel, you know why I called."

"I can't come to get you now, not until after Tishabav. You know that."

"I'm driving the bus down after Tishabav."

"Driving? You can't drive that bus! What if something happens to you?" He hadn't meant to yell at her.

"You told me nothing would happen to me. You told me."

"Shoshanna, you want to kill yourself and the kids?"

Very quietly, almost patiently, she repeated, "I can drive the bus and I'll be down after Tishabav."

Yussel could not imagine that sweet little thing, that girl with the tiny hands, the butterfly eyes, the little foot on the huge pedal, maneuvering that bus, swinging around dangerous curves, sharp corners, oncoming tour buses. "I don't want you driving that bus. You hear me?"

"Don't yell at me, Yussel."

"What are you scared of? A little noise? Have I ever lifted a hand to you? I just don't want you taking any chances." Worse than that she trusted him. Worse than that he was depending on her stupidity and her trust so he could . . . could what? Could listen to a lonely woman, could wonder?

"It's okay, Yussel."

He didn't want her to come. On the other hand he'd die if she left him and went home with the kids. Maybe she knew she had to learn to drive the bus because she had to live without her husband, because she couldn't depend on him anymore, because he was out of his mind over another woman. Maybe she was coming to say good-bye.

IT WAS ALMOST light out when he called Lillywhite. The moon was still pale in a herring-belly sky. Two deer nibbled outside the kitchen window. "Lillywhite, talk to me."

"Ask me a question. You never ask me questions. Ask me anything. Say you just met me. First time. I'm a new student. What would you say to me?"

"Probably, I'd ask you what your father's Hebrew name was."

"I don't know."

"And your mother's?"

"She's Lutheran."

"You're not Jewish?"

"That's not a question, is it?"

"I guess not. I thought you were Jewish."

"I am."

"Not if your mother's not."

"I was raised Jewish."

"The law is, if your mother's Jewish, you are. It has nothing to do with your father."

"It has everything to do with my father. God, don't you understand?"

"Lillywhite, Lillywhite, what do you want from me?" Yussel cried out. He heard his own anguish, felt her pain.

"Once I brought my boyfriend Tom to my grandfather's house. My father's father, who had kicked my father out when he married my mother. Okay? So I brought Tom. My grampa took one look through the screen door, said I was just like my no-good father, and slammed the door in my face. Don't slam any doors on me. Do whatever you can to keep from slamming doors on me. Please."

"My wife is coming soon."

"Please."

"You're forcing me to see you, aren't you?"

"Babe said you would. Tomorrow night, eight-thirty, at the Paradise on the other side of the mountain."

"It's already tomorrow."

THE PARADISE had probably put the Arizona out of business. It had a big parking lot, a neon sign advertising a seventy-two-ounce steak free if you finish it, wings, Chinese food, live music after ten P.M. Yussel pushed open the double doors. He was used to people hiding cards and piles of money when he walked into a room. Nobody noticed him at all.

Chinese lanterns hung from low ceilings. The concrete walls had been painted in early awful South Pacific without perspective: thatched roof huts, dancing natives, sky-blue sky, sea-blue sea. Lillywhite leaned against a gambling table in a side room. She stood between two cowboys who had longer beards than Yussel's. Yussel made believe he didn't see her, walked to another table to watch the betting. His hands were ice cold.

Lillywhite wore a silvery lamé shirt, a silver belt studded with hunks of turquoise, worn jeans, high-heeled snakeskin boots with the same silver toes as Indian Joe's boots. Yussel leaned over the dice, something snapped in his head, his screen flashed on full blast, and he knew what everyone should bet on.

"Hey, hey there," she called, waved. He nodded, walked over, stood behind her. She said very softly, "Hello," laid a handful of chips on the six.

"The four." He couldn't help it. A huge living neon four was pulsing in his head. What had suddenly revived his screen? A sexy woman, God forbid? A gambling den? The smell of Chinese pork from the kitchen? Numbers flashed in front of his eyes. Rabbits, greyhounds, horses ran in circles. The four played. She grinned, swept in chips, wiped her hands on her jeans and said, "Let's go for a walk." Now people noticed him because he was walking with her.

So she led him outside to the parking lot. He wouldn't look at her face. Her hair was caught up in a comb that flashed under the parking lot lights. He could see the nape of her neck. Little red tendrils curled on it. Her boots clicked on the cement of the parking lot and echoed in the mountain stillness. She sounded like a creature with claws. Yussel reminded himself to remind himself to take deep breaths.

"How'd you know about the four?"

"It came to me."

"You really are one of those rabbis, aren't you?"

He shrugged. "I don't do prophecy."

"We could go in and try it again? I'll split with you."

"We don't gamble."

"But you take chances."

"What do you mean?"

"Coming up here."

"I don't gamble. It's not taking a chance."

It wasn't what she meant. It wasn't what he meant.

Two young men walked down the stairs of the Paradise toward them, past them, looked back over their shoulders. Suddenly Yussel and Lillywhite were a couple under a streetlight. As if they were both guilty of a private act in public, as if they had something to hide, they stopped talking. When the men drove away, their headlights drew a circle around Yussel, around her, around the light pole, left them in a darker moment.

She reached up, put her hand on his cheek, breathed egg roll onto him. "I saw you once at Purim. I went with some girlfriends to your synagogue in Brookline. They didn't belong but the young adults from their congregation were invited. It was like an All Fools' Day. They said you drank to get closer to God. I'd never seen Jewish men really drink. Your people were in costumes. Men were women, women were men. Someone was dressed like death, in long burlap rags and pregnant with a pillow stuck under the burlap. It was in the basement of a Victorian house. It was hot and noisy. Even the women were drinking. You wore a long white gown with a Roman striped belt that kept unwinding. Your face was bronzed. Your hair, your beard, your eyebrows were big, red, bushy. You were the burning bush; you were Moses. You stood on a picnic table, chugalugged a bottle of wine, a green bottle, tried to balance yourself with a shepherd's crook. I'd never seen such power. It was everything I wanted . . . joy, wisdom, strength. I wanted a man like you. Between gulps, you'd look up to Heaven, beat your heart with your fist. You danced on the table, sang at the top of your voice. I don't know why the table didn't break. Bottles of vodka and scotch were lined up on the table. Sometimes a bottle fell off, sometimes they'd break, but no one would stop you. You'd pour a drink into a paper cup, shout for someone to come forward, pull him up on the table, put your arm around him, make him drink and dance, beat your heart, sing to the ceiling, weep, hug him. You were gorgeous. Then your men helped you down from the table. You broke two bottles of scotch coming off. No one cared. You fell into a chair. You looked at me and said something. I didn't understand what you said. I was twenty-two, a senior at Radcliffe. You said to my girlfriend, 'Don't have children.' Then you said to a man in a yellow-striped sweater, 'Four years.' He threw a hand over his mouth, paled. He knew what you meant. Then to a young boy with a white face bubbling with pimples and whiteheads, you said, 'You have six generations. Ask and it shall be revealed.' Then you looked at me again, annoyed that I was still there, and spoke more clearly to me. 'I said,' you said, 'you have no generations. I said you will have generations of disciples.' Remember? I was a senior. I knew a lot. I understood more. I said something. I didn't mean to say it out loud. I said to you, 'I know.' It rolled out. I did know. I hadn't known until that moment, but I knew as surely as you knew, just as the man to whom you'd given four years knew. I'd never known anyone who had God's ear. You did. You climbed up onto the table, danced, beat at your heart, snapped your fingers, clapped your hands, shot out your fingers, shouted, made everyone drink. I was frozen to the spot. My friend was leaning against a bookcase crying her eyes out. 'We don't belong here,' she kept saying. 'It's too scary.' When you saw her crying, you called her over, gave her a paper cup of vodka, smiled. She said to you, 'What did you mean?' You asked, 'What did I say?' 'That I shouldn't have children.' You shrugged. 'I don't know. I don't remember anything I say on Purim. Don't worry about it.' Then you hit the table with your foot, started to dance again."

Yussel choked on his tears. "Lillywhite, the prophecy wasn't important. You saw the joy, the life, the strength. That's what I would give you if I could. That's what. But I can't. I can't."

"Are you crying?" Lillywhite asked Yussel.

Yussel cleared his throat, blew his nose. "Did he really say 'generations of disciples'?"

"It's not something you forget."

"You remember his name?"

"No."

"I have a cousin in Boston. Maybe that was my cousin. I wonder what he saw."

"Not my tits, for a change."

Yussel shuddered at the words. "Maybe he was trying to impress you."

"You won't let me have it, will you? You think he was trying to impress my cousin? Or the guy with four years?"

"I just wonder what he saw."

"I told you what he saw. Why don't you do a little prophecy? Tell me what's going to happen with us? Why do we feel this way about each other?"

"I don't have to do prophecy. I just have to be realistic. Nothing can happen."

She leaned against the lamppost, put one leg up against the pole, comb flashing, eyes burning like candles. He could see the shape of her breasts in the silk shirt. She saw him looking at her breasts. She threw her shoulders back so he could see more.

"I came to talk business with you."

She cupped her breasts, lifted them toward his eyes, his hands, his mouth. "How is it you can look at these but not in my eyes? What's the matter with you guys? Listen, I'm not going to charge you for the water, if that's what you want. You just have to tell me what you want."

"I want . . ." Yussel lifted his shoulders and took a deep breath. It was like drowning. If this wasn't the Other Side he couldn't imagine what else it could be. Any minute she'd take out a little book and make him sign his name in it. Yussel whispered. "Why did you lease the water rights if you didn't want to charge me?"

She tilted her chin up, looked at the stars. "I like to control things. I wanted control over the water. I told you I own all the land around you. Someday I may need water. Someday I might need something from you. Right now I don't need water so you've nothing to worry about." She stopped talking and looked very directly at him. He had to look at her face. "I don't like to gamble either, Rabbi. Most of the time."

He grabbed her hands from her breasts, held her wrists, shoved her arms above her head and pinned them behind the lamppost. "You're too real, Lillywhite. You're too real. I can't take it." He was only protecting himself from her. The raised knee pressed sharply into his leg. He squeezed her wrists tighter.

"I wait all this time for you to touch me and your hands are freezing." Then she dropped her knee and Yussel fell against her. That's when he felt her. Her body was like iron, muscular and stiff. He was leaning against her, holding her arms above her head and she was fighting to get loose. She was very strong. A car flashed headlights over them, tooted.

Someone shouted, "Go for it!"

She stopped fighting. He felt her soften, loosen. Her mouth opened. He felt her breath on his face, her breasts, her hips, belly, her legs against his, the heat of her body through his clothes. Everything fit just as he'd expected, even standing up. How long had he stayed there against her, silent, the both of them, except for their deep breaths.

She whispered, "Your hands are getting warmer," moved against him as if she were swimming.

"Don't touch me," he whispered in her ear, against her hair. "Ever again. Do you hear?"

Electric blue numbers flashed on his screen. He knew what would win the New York State Lottery, which Exacta would come in at Roosevelt Raceway, the odds at Monticello, everything. She rolled her hips around him in a circle like the headlights, asking big questions. Yussel was filling up with big answers. He gripped her wrists tighter to stop her movements. "Do you hear me?" he yelled at her. For a split second he moved against her.

That's when Yussel wanted to kill her, bang her head against the pole until he stopped feeling her. When he realized that the lump in his pants was becoming a murder weapon, he ripped his hands from her wrists, his body from hers. Somehow he found his car. Balloons of his own breath floated away from him, as if his soul were leaving. He didn't blame his soul. He'd like to leave also. His headlights lit her up. He hadn't saved her soul. He'd cut out her heart to save his own. He couldn't see through his tears. He had to make it up the road home, remind himself of the turns, the sharp shoulders. It was all right that he couldn't see. He wanted to die.

First he went to the mikveh, seriously considered drowning himself. His body trembled so much he made waves. He looked down at his sex, floating small and innocent, telescoped, in the holy water. I didn't do it. Me? Never. I make little Jewish babies. "You're a liar," he told it.

His father came in a blue terry-cloth robe, little blue terry-cloth slippers, climbed into the mikveh, patted Yussel. The lead doors displaced great amounts of water. *"Two lead doors now. Thank you very much."*

His father splashed with his hands. *"Well, that's why HaShem might make you suffer—for protecting your own soul. You won't get Brownie points because you denied yourself a pleasure; you'll get punished for protecting your own ass at the expense of someone's soul."*

"Totte, find out. You talk to someone up there. You stand in line. Find out what I'm supposed to do. . . ."

"I told you, Yussele, that's not how it works. You have to be free to choose. You can't make choices if you know the answers." His father made waves with his doors. *"Let me explain to you the nature of suffering. God makes you suffer so you'll come closer. When He sees you're too far away from Him He brings you to Him. He makes you pay attention. The pain you feel is the correction you're making in your soul. Everything depends on the correction you make."*

"My home? My money? My job? My car? Maybe my wife."

"Maybe my wife, Yussele."

"My heart, my identity. What's left? How much more do I have to give? Can't you ask? Can't you find out?"

"Don't second-guess. It all depends on the choices you make. Just think hard about those choices when they're presented to you."

Yussel left his father blowing his lead doors with the hair dryer. In his room there was a message from Shoshanna to call right away. Twice he dialed the wrong number.

"Dinela has a little fever and she wants to talk to you so she'll sleep better." This fast? Yussel's heart turned over. He started to weep. "She wants to talk to you. Hold on."

Grisha yelled from his room about the phone waking him up, yelled, "Can't you stay away from each other?"

"My Dinela's sick," he yelled back to Grisha.

"Nebbuch. I thought it was your broker still sick."

Dina was on the phone. Yussel cried, "Dinela, Dinela."

Shoshanna got on the phone. "You'll upset her. What's the matter with you?"

"When did she get sick? How sick is she?"

"It's okay, Yussy. It's nothing to cry about. Stop crying. It's only the chicken pox. They all had it. She's just taking a little longer to shake it off."

"When did she get sick?"

"Maybe two weeks ago."

"What does the doctor say?"

"He says it's chicken pox. I should build up her resistance and she'll get rid of it."

"Take her to another doctor, Shoshanna. Find an expert."

"Kids get sick, Yussel."

The knife turned in Yussel's heart. Blood should come from his eyes. Is this the punishment he was waiting for? He grabbed Grisha's arm. "Grisha, what does that mean, my kid's sick?"

Grisha was eating a crust of challah dipped in cigarette ashes for Aaron the Priest. "Don't ask me. Ask your broker."

HIS FATHER came so fast he wasn't even wearing a bathrobe, just red-and-white-checked flannel pajamas, rumpled, a little stain on the fly. *"Gevalt, Yussele. You see what you've done? You see? Now you want something from Him. Now He's got you where He wants you."*

"You leave me alone too. You too. Get out of here. Look what's happening. Look what you've done! My baby."

His father gave a long and painful sigh. *"You look, kid. You look."*

Two nights and two days Yussel stayed in his bed except for necessities. He wouldn't eat. His heart was stone. By the afternoon of the second day under the covers, he decided maybe he was overreacting. Men have affairs; kids get sick. These things don't have to be connected. It doesn't mean the world comes to an end. It doesn't mean a kid, God forbid, dies. Also who said he was going to have an affair? As soon as Shoshanna came, it would be all right. He'd forget. Bingo came, knocked. "Can we get you anything?" Then Natalie, Grisha, Babe, others. One of the kibbutzniks had to go to New York. His grandmother was dying. Grisha gave him permission. Was it okay? They'd have to go to Chaim's for Tishabav. Yussel didn't answer. He wouldn't answer knocks on his door, supplications from Babe, advice from Grisha, a chain of phone calls from the Flower Child, who needed to talk to him, it was an emergency. Yussel would only agree to call her back, but she didn't know where she'd be, wouldn't say where she was. Still he wouldn't talk to her, to anybody. Lillywhite called twice. He wouldn't talk to her either. Nothing could rouse him.

Finally on the morning of the third day of his depression, they told him Shoshanna called: the tetracycline was working on Dina. He made a deal with himself. He wouldn't call. He made a deal with HaShem. "Make her better. I won't call." Babe came to his door and told him Grisha was missing. Yussel got out of bed, called Lillywhite, told her he could never see her or talk to her again as long as he lived because God was punishing him by making his daughter sick, and hung up before she could call him a medieval son of a bitch.

22

TWO BY TWO the men went out in the dark along the road to the base of the mountain, along the highway, looking for Grisha. Yussel called the police. Babe cried, beat her chest. Everyone stayed up, took turns going outside, blamed themselves that Grisha had gone. Yussel reprimanded them. "You blame yourselves for the bad things and thank God for the good things. What's wrong with you?" Yussel knew exactly why Grisha had gone and knew also to blame himself. At four in the morning someone with a Mexican accent called from the clinic on the other side of the mountain to say Grisha had been brought in. Yussel and Babe drove to the clinic. The clinic was a one-story adobe with two beds, a male nurse, a state trooper. The trooper took Yussel aside, held his hat against his chest as if he were pledging allegiance. "Might be a little mental, sir."

Grisha had walked down the center of the highway, so a truck would hit him, so Dina would live. Yussel tried to sound like the trooper. "Might be some medication he's on. We'll make sure he stays on the property."

"Can't have him wandering."

And Grisha, like a piece of butcher paper, stiff and waxy, struggled to take off his oxygen mask, did, pulled Yussel to him, waved Babe off.

"You must be very close to HaShem, Yussel." Yussel could

hardly make out the words. "That he punishes you so soon for your sins."

"Listen, Grisha, HaShem must love you a truck didn't hit you."

"Maybe. Maybe he refused my offer."

"Dina's getting better. She's responding to the new drug. She's going to be fine."

Grisha squeezed Yussel's arm, whispered. "Nu? Maybe He heard."

The male nurse, Ruiz, a small brown man, obsequious, concerned, said to Babe. "Your husband he needs oxygen. We keep him here. It's all right. Just to make sure. Too much liquid in the lungs. Three, four days, maybe."

After the trooper left, Babe said, "He's trying to kill himself."

"Why should he kill himself?" Yussel asked, because if he didn't Babe would know he knew why.

"I know how a man's heart works?" Babe closed the clinic door behind her.

YUSSEL WALKED around the phone a thousand times. Lillywhite's songs sailed down the mountain, over the desert, into his blood. That night, for the first time, he didn't have to wait for Grisha to go to sleep. Once he picked up the phone, started to dial. Once it rang as he went to lift it and he tore it from the wall and looked at it in his hands, surprised. It's okay, he told himself. Your Dinela's getting better. It's okay. Do what you have to do.

He called her from the Texaco.

"Lillywhite?"

"You medieval son of a bitch. You promised not to slam the door on me."

"Lillywhite. Lillywhite." Yussel groaned. "My baby's sick, Lillywhite, maybe dying. It might be connected. I touched you that night. They called that night and told me my baby was sick."

"And I'm killing your baby? What an asshole you are."

"I'm being punished. Lillywhite. I can't see you. I can't look at you. I made a terrible mistake. What do you want from me?"

"I don't know. I'm not sure anymore."

"I'm sorry, Lillywhite. I'm . . ." he whispered into the phone, "I'm so afraid."

BABE BROUGHT Grisha home for Tishabav. His eyes were as big as boiled eggs. The north wind whistled in his chest.

Before the last meal, before the fast began, Yussel called the congregation in to hear the rules about the night of the fast and the fast day. They sat around tables, drank coffee, ate cake, said nice things to Grisha, which he wouldn't acknowledge. "First of all, we're again short of a minyan so we have to go to Chaim's." This was Yussel's fault because he'd ignored Grisha. Grisha looked over Yussel's head at the wall. Babe kept covering him with a pink lambswool stole. Grisha kept throwing it off his shoulders. Ernie propped his chair against the wall and slept. Everyone else, except for the kibbutzniks who had no understanding of what was happening, watched Yussel with hostile anticipation. "I guess it's my fault. I shouldn't have let him go to see his grandmother before she died. Right?" No one said anything. They were wishing he was his father. So was he.

Yussel told them exactly what his father used to tell them. "By ritual we re-create the past. The fast begins before sundown. It lasts until after sundown tomorrow. So you shouldn't eat too much salt tonight because you can't drink water. No more washing than the tips of your fingers. No brushing your teeth, no sexual relations."

Ernie's head rose from his chest. "Who wants sex if no one brushes their teeth?" Ernie's head dropped back on his chest.

"Sometimes people who fast twenty-four, twenty-eight hours reach a different plane, a different level of perception. If anyone needs special dispensations for illness, you should discuss that with me. Women wear white clothes. No one wears leather shoes." Yussel desperately wanted them to feel the fear he felt, to pay attention so they wouldn't suffer. He didn't know how to tell them.

"What do we wear?"

"Sneakers." The next line would be, "But my sneakers are leather." It was.

"So put a tack in your shoe or get some dried peas from Babe. The point is you should be uncomfortable. In the days of the Temple, leather shoes meant your feet were comfortable. So wear something that isn't comfortable. We're trying to recapture the essence of that awesome day."

"Rabbi," Natalie was waving her hand in the air like a school child, "if we're really going to try to recapture the essence of Tisha-bav, why don't we invite the Indians to come and burn down the Arizona, rape the women, kill the men, and I myself will cut off the hand of a child and cook it. Like they did then back in Jerusalem."

"That's cute, Natalie. What amazes me is how you can know so much and get it so wrong."

"I just want to know who decides what applies and what doesn't apply. I mean one day you guys are absolutely literal and the next day you interpret. So who decides when to be literal and when to interpret. I'd like to know once and for all. A cow is meat and gives milk. Suddenly it's a sin to have meat with milk? Is the cow committing a sin? Who makes these things up?"

Yussel banged his fist on the table. Bingo fell off his chair. The silverware jumped. A fork flew from the table. Yussel roared. He sounded to himself the way his father had sounded to him, to his mother, to his congregation. "What's the matter with you? Tomorrow's the ninth day of the fourth month, the most dangerous day in the year. The Temple was destroyed. Tishabav is a day of punishment, of bad luck. You don't take chances on Tishabav. You don't mess around. You don't swim. You don't drive. You don't bathe. It's a dangerous day, so don't take it lightly. Next day, God willing, you'll wake up in the morning. For the same money, you won't wake up in the morning. You'll wear sneakers or you'll go barefoot. Natalie, I want you at Chaim's. The other women, it doesn't matter."

"I can't sleep on the bus with you guys. I can't sleep in a house where there are no women."

"You like to walk. You'll walk over in the morning. And you'll wear a skirt."

"Why just Natalie?" the women objected.

"Ask Natalie," Yussel answered. Everyone looked at Natalie, who, this time, didn't have an answer.

Babe said, "You don't have to go, Natalie. It's five miles."

"Natalie knows what she has to do and why. Leave it alone, Babe."

Natalie was crying into Babe's shoulder. Babe gave Yussel a

look he had gone too far with Natalie. Everyone else filed out. Babe called out after them she had peas for their shoes if they needed any.

BEFORE SUNDOWN, they ate a light, tasteless meal of hard-boiled eggs, cold chicken, cold farfel kugel. The men tossed their sleeping bags into Babe's bus and left. The women wanted to stay home. They didn't want to sleep in the houses of Chaim's Miracles of Creation.

The men davened by Chaim. Yussel thought he heard noise upstairs. Chaim said he thought he had raccoons. Yussel asked Chaim if Grisha could sleep inside his house. Chaim said it was inconvenient, suggested they go by Mendl. Yussel didn't bother asking Mendl. Chaim offered to take the dogs inside so they wouldn't wake up Yussel's men. That Yussel accepted. After services, about midnight, everyone from the Arizona climbed into the bus that was parked outside Chaim's house, pulled their sleeping bags over their heads, and slept.

Yussel stretched out on the long backseat of Babe's bus, his arms wrapped around a pillow, his face stuck in the softness of Lillywhite's belly, dreaming about God, her. When he pressed the pillow, he smelled egg roll. Moonlight streamed along the floor, lit up the faces of the sleeping men, some curled up on the floor, some on the foldout couches. Except for Grisha, the men looked like boys. Grisha still looked like butcher paper, stiff and waxy.

In his sleep, Yussel smelled something burning, a cigar. A pale figure stood above Yussel, cleared his throat. Yussel clutched his pillow, pulled his knees up to his chest to make room on the backseat. But he couldn't feel him sit. It wasn't his father. His father had weight, bulk. Even in a dream this thing scared him. It was a shadow of a figure, shifting, small, like a bantam-weight boxer on a bad TV set. Moonlight passed through its shroud like a flashlight. He wore Church's oxfords. Yussel watched the red dot of the cigar tip move up and down. Yussel sat up straight.

"I'm your father's friend. Pecky. Maybe he talked about me?"

"Where's my father?"

"Fighting a decree, a terrible decree. Poor soul, how he suffers

for all of you. Listen, it's better if you make believe you're sleeping. I'm only supposed to come in a dream to you."

Yussel lay down, closed his eyes. Still he could see the red point of the cigar moving around in the dark.

"You know the story about how Rabbi Akiba meets a man with a black face, shlepping wood, and he finds out the man is shlepping wood to the fire and it's the fire in which he is roasted every day for eternity because he's being punished in Hell? You know that story?"

Yussel nodded, in or out of his sleep. He could smell the wood burning. He clutched the pillow, buried his face in Lillywhite, smelled egg rolls.

"So, because he was a cruel tax collector, he was in Hell and the only way out of this punishment was if his son would say Kaddish for him, but his son wasn't even circumcised, didn't go to shul?"

"I say Kaddish, Pecky. I go to shul."

"Shah, I'm not talking about you. Shluf, sleep. So then Rabbi Akiba goes to the town the man came from, where he had been a cruel tax collector and had made everybody suffer, and Rabbi Akiba finds this uncircumcised son and teaches him, and gets him circumcised. Finally the son stands before a congregation, says Kaddish, and his father goes up to Heaven." Pecky sighed, blew out a ring of smoke, was a ring of smoke. *"You know the story?"*

"I *am* the story."

"I don't have a son." Pecky tapped Yussel lightly on the thigh. *"Your father says, I should ask maybe you'd include me when you say Kaddish."*

"My father thinks I can elevate a murderer into Heaven?"

Pecky tapped him on the thigh once again. *"Your father also says . . ."* Pecky tossed his cigar out the window, pulled a fortune cookie from a pocket, snapped it open, held a little piece of parchment up to the moonlight. He read with difficulty, *"God weaves your destiny from your choices. Now shluf, sleep. Tomorrow's a tough day."*

In his dreams, Yussel smelled the wood burning, the egg rolls burning, the cigar, maybe fresh roasting, feathers. He slept better because outside it sounded like Far Rockaway, with sirens, dogs, people yelling, tires screeching. He dreamed the strange dream. He saw the long line of people. His father was standing in the line holding a piece of paper, waiting to see the king. His father wore a silver fox fur coat down to his ankles over black pajamas. A strong wind rippled the fur of the coat like waves. His doors were folded against the wind, his father huddled inside, his face rippling with terror. He banged very hard on his doors for attention.

THEN NATALIE was banging very hard on the window of the bus. It was morning. She was covered with dust, tears streaking through the dust on her face. She stood on one foot, then the other. Yussel had a terrible pain on the spot on his thigh where Pecky had touched him. Flames danced on Chaim's red tile roof. Cars and pickups with revolving blue gumballs were parked behind three gleaming new fire engines in front of Chaim's houses. The fences around the houses were burning like a wall of fire. The strings Chaim had strung around his neighborhood were wicks for a thin line of flame. Firemen in yellow rubber pants and slickers leaned against their trucks, drank coffee from paper cups. One fireman ran around with a bullhorn yelling, "All personnel accounted for? All personnel accounted for?"

Yussel had seen it all before, on his screen, the first day.

Yussel's men were already awake and off the bus. He saw Velvl and two others carrying out the couch, its leather sides curled and crisp, its yellow padding melted like cheese, dripping over iron mesh. They carried out the smoke-blackened slab of turquoise. Mendl came with one of the onyx tables and a pile of smoking siddurs. Torahs and tallisim and all the silver from the fancy breakfront were piled up on the roofs of cars. People were dragging Chaim out the front door. Chaim was screaming he had to go back in, pummeling the backs of firemen, spilling their coffee. They tried to ignore him. Chaim's court were embellishing on Chaim's argument. It did no good.

The fireman with the bullhorn stopped Mendl. "All personnel accounted for? Everyone out?"

Mendl looked around for a long moment, counted heads, Chaim's men and Yussel's men, said, "Yes. No personnel." Something was wrong with the way he said it.

Yussel grabbed his arm. "Mendl, your brother-in-law who sold Chaim's house? Is he in there?"

"Pinchas? Na-ah. What would Pinchas be doing in there?"

Yussel still smelled the cigar smoke on the bus. Chaim was screaming, "Let me in! I have to get something! Let me in, for God's sake!"

The firemen were stony-faced. They offered both sets of Jews coffee and chocolate-covered cream donuts, which of course no one could accept because it was Tishabav. Chaim's men were now holding Chaim back by his arms. Chaim's feet tread the air double-time. He held his hands above his head, shaking them like propellers. He yelled gibberish about money in the ceiling, blood on their hands. Yussel cornered a fireman, took a cup of coffee he offered, just held it in his hands.

"I've got water," Yussel said very quietly to a fireman with a ruddy face and a handlebar mustache. "I'll replace whatever you use."

"It's not the water, Reverend. Your friend doesn't have membership, so we won't put out the fire. We're only saving lives. It's a by-law. There's no one inside." He shrugged. "We're legal."

"You wouldn't let him have membership? How much is membership? I'll buy his membership." Yussel went to take money from his pocket, remembered he didn't carry any on a holy day. "I'll send you a check."

"He can't have membership unless he has homeowner's and he doesn't have homeowner's. Association rules."

"You can't change the rules?" Yussel tried to negotiate, sounded he thought, like Natalie. "You made the rules. You can't change them?"

Chaim yelled. "And I don't have homeowner's because that son of a bitch Fetner wouldn't sell me any. This is your fault, Yussel. I'm ruined and this is your fault. The blood is on your hands, Yussel. You hear me?" Velvl held Chaim in a hammerlock.

"What's with blood, Chaim? Money's not blood."

"Reb Yussel, how do you hold?" Mendl yelled.

"How do I hold what?"

"Can he go in there and get his money?"

"How do you hold, Reb Yussel? What's the ruling?"

240

"Let Chaim decide!"

Natalie sat on the steps of the bus and pulled off a hiking boot. Her face was ribbed with pain.

"Reb Yussel, he has all our cash in the ceiling."

"In the ceiling, Mendl? Cash?"

"Yussel, if I don't go in there, you'll have to support me in the manner to which I'm accustomed. You'll have to take care of me and all my people if you don't let me go in." Chaim's hands were going around so fast Yussel was getting dizzy.

The bottom of Natalie's sock was red. The top was white. She screwed up her face and pulled it off. Yussel looked away.

"Everything we own is in the kitchen, Yussel! Everything!" Chaim was crying. "You don't understand." The tears on his face had fire in them. It looked like his eyes were bleeding.

Natalie's sock was wet with blood.

"It's your fault, Yussel. You wouldn't sell me homeowner's. So they wouldn't give me membership so now they won't put out the fire and it's your fault. There's blood on your hands, Yussel."

"That's a lie, Chaim. You're telling a lie!"

Natalie wrung blood from her sock. Then she shook out her boot. Red peas spilled out.

"Nu, Reb Yussel?" Mendl asked. "How do you hold?"

"It will endanger his life?" Yussel asked. Natalie wrung blood from her other sock. It was Yussel's fault. Everything was Yussel's fault. What have I missed this time? What haven't I paid attention to?

"Once the roof goes . . ."

"It's your fault, Yussel. Let me go in."

"How could I sell you? I don't have a territory. You should have bought from someone else. It's not my fault, Chaim. It's your fault."

Natalie took off her other boot very gently, then the red-and-white sock, wrung blood from it, shook out the red peas. "Look at that, Reb Yussel. I guess I circumcised my feet. I found something to circumcise after all, didn't I?"

"Reb Yussel, please." There they were, the Miracles of Creation and his own men looking up at him with the faces of children, begging him to be a rabbi, to be a Solomon, to tell them the law, to apply the law. If Chaim didn't get all his money out, Yussel would be responsible for him and all the families in Chaim's court. It would have been the same if Yussel lost everything. Then Chaim would have been responsible. Although Chaim, Yussel knew, would find a way out.

"How much money you have in there, Chaim?"

Grisha took him by the arm, hissed. "Shmuck. The amount matters?"

The more blood Natalie wrung from her sock, the more ran from Chaim's eyes. "This was your idea, Yussel. I hold you responsible."

Yussel's leg was killing him. The spot Pecky made on his thigh pounded as if a butcher knife were stuck in it. "Okay. Okay." Yussel took a deep breath, made his voice strong. "You can't endanger a life for anything less than another life. Chaim can't go in."

Velvl released Chaim. Chaim sprang toward Yussel, ran around him in circles, pulled at his lapels. "You've got to let me go in, Yussel. Please. Protect yourself, Yussel. Protect your portion in the World to Come. Protect your poor family. I was a rich man. You'll have to make me a rich man again. You'll be ruined. You don't know what you're doing!"

"You can't go in."

"All our lives, you and me, Yussel. Don't do this to me. Don't do it to yourself! Your father will murder you for this."

Then the roof collapsed and Chaim fell against Yussel, buried his face in Yussel's chest, howled from his heart without words. As much as Yussel hated to, he put his arms around Chaim. Maybe because the firemen were there watching.

"Mendl," Yussel said over Chaim's shoulder, "how much money did he have in the ceiling?"

"A lot, Reb Yussel. It was a terrific decision you made. You should live to be a hundred and twenty."

"There's not enough money in the world for him to go so crazy. Chaim isn't stupid."

Mendl shrugged.

"Your house okay?"

Mendl nodded. "Baruch HaShem."

"Take him to your house, sedate him." Yussel jerked his chin toward the crowd. "They shouldn't see us like this."

242

YUSSEL STOOD in front of the firemen. "I want to ask you a simple question. You couldn't break a stupid rule? You couldn't put out the fire and forget the rules? Think of the loss."

The firemen looked at him. "A rule's a rule, Reverend. We don't question your rules." Yussel shook his head in disbelief, asked the firemen for a pail of water, and sat on the steps of the bus beside Natalie while she rinsed her feet. The red peas were on the ground in front of him. He wished there were another woman nearby to rinse Natalie's feet, to comfort her, to put an arm around her. The firemen brought bandages, but she wouldn't let them touch her. Yussel sat and held his head in his hands. "You circumcised your feet?"

"What else do I have?"

"How can you have sex with Rosebud but not let the firemen touch you?"

"I'm married to Rosebud."

Whether the fire that burned down seven of Chaim's houses was caused by Pecky's cigar, or the fire caused Pecky's appearance, or Pecky brought the fire from Hell, or one of the Miracles of Creation tossed a cigarette into the gas fireplace, or the raccoons in the attic were chewing on matches, or maybe Chaim and his Miracles of Creation had reached such a high plane of ecstasy, the wheel of time stopped and the fires lit by the Romans in the Temple two thousand years ago started up in Chaim's house, no one would ever know. His father, of course, would say you can find a million logical reasons after the fact, but the fact is HaShem intended it. After that, just pick a reason. Yussel would find out tomorrow how much money had been in the ceiling and how much it would cost him to support Chaim's mortgages on eighteen houses and the main-frame empire. One thing Yussel wouldn't find out tomorrow was where he would get such money from.

Firemen stretched ropes around the seven houses, hung No Trespassing signs. Yussel's men, Chaim's men came over to congratulate Yussel on his decision, stepped over Natalie, who was wrapping bandages around her feet. They shook Yussel's hand, hit him on the back, the shoulders. Even the firemen, who couldn't have understood the ruling that when a member of the community has a loss you have to take care of him in the way he lived before, even the firemen came to shake Yussel's hand.

Grisha whispered, "Good decision, Rabbi."

Yussel answered, "A rule's a rule. I had no choice."

"Still it was good. Your father would be proud."

"You called me Rabbi, Grisha?"

"Today. Tomorrow, who knows?"

Yussel didn't know what to do with Natalie. He needed a woman to get her into the bus. In the end he picked Natalie up and carried her up the bus steps himself. She put her arms around his neck, whimpered into his chest like a little kid. "You're breaking the rules, Rabbi."

"Natalie, Natalie. When I first came out here you said to me, 'I know who you are.'"

She nodded. "I do. I knew who your father was too."

"I don't know who you are, do I?"

"I'm somebody."

"I'll say."

"We're not formally married, Rosebud and me." She smiled up at him, closed her eyes, let him put his fresh socks on her feet, wash her face, cover her with a sleeping bag. She'd sleep on the bus with the men. It didn't matter. The rest of them went to Mendl's house to daven and fast. Mendl forced a sleeping pill down Chaim's throat, held him down until he passed out on Mendl's bed.

23

THE DAY AFTER Tishabav, the morning sun slid over the lip of the mountain like a rotten egg. The flagpole clinked. The wind was still hot and dry from the south, smelled of yesterday's ashes. Yussel sat on his father's grave, prayed Shoshanna would have a safe trip, wept at the thought of losing them, knew he deserved to lose everything he loved, wondered how he was going to get money for Chaim. His father's grave was littered with dozens of slips of papers, now all the same size, flapping around under stones and pebbles.

"*You! Yussel!*" A call, an accusation, a condemnation. Both doors were double-lead bank-vault doors, studded with wheels, locks, clocks. They groaned open. His father wore a black coat over black silk pajamas, a black shtreimel of a lustrous flat fur, maybe sheared beaver, maybe some creature from the World to Come. Red fox tails hung from the brim. His face was high-cheeked, slant-eyed, severe, like a mandarin, alien.

Yussel felt a cold slice of terror in his soul. "He could've bought homeowner's from someone else. I don't even have a territory. Why are you blaming me?"

His father picked up the kvitls, stuffed them into his pockets, replaced the pebbles, took his beard in his hand, twisted and curled the bottom of it. "*Listen to me,*" he said in a monotone. "*A Jew comes to the Besht and the Besht says, 'What do you need? What can I do for you?'*

"The Jew says, 'I need nothing. I have my health, wealth, a family.'

"And the Besht says, 'Really? You need nothing?'

"'Nothing.'

"The Besht says, 'So let me tell you a story. Two friends grow up together, go to Yeshiva together. They're inseparable. They get married together. And then they drift apart. Chaim becomes very wealthy. Yankel doesn't. Yankel tries a dozen things. Everything fails. Finally he's destitute. He's borrowed from everybody. He's facing ruin. He sits down with his wife. 'I have no place to turn.' His wife says, 'You know, Yankel. I heard about Chaim. He's doing very well. Maybe you should go to him?' Yankel says, 'Go to a friend I haven't seen in years? How can I go to him?'

"There's nobody else so Yankel goes off to find Chaim. He comes to a beautiful house, people walking in and out. He walks in. Chaim comes down the stairs, sees Yankel.

"'Yankel! How are you?'

"'Listen, Chaim, I'm very uncomfortable. We haven't seen each other in years. I've been very unlucky. Could you help me?'

"'Of course. What are friends for? How much do you need?'

"'I don't know . . . I . . .'

"'Never mind. I'll give you a blank check. Make it out. Thank God I have what to give you.'

"So Yankel takes the money and invests it and thank God he is very successful. But as he becomes more successful, Chaim becomes more unlucky. Now Yankel is a wealthy Jew. Chaim sits down with his wife. 'You know, Yankel came to me and I lent him money. I'm sure he'll help me.'

"So off goes Chaim to find Yankel. This time Chaim comes to a beautiful house. But there are guards, gates. You have to have an appointment. Chaim tells the guards their master, Yankel, would want to see him, they're childhood friends. It would be a terrible mistake not to let him in. The guards send him around to the back, to the servants' entrance. Chaim sits and sits and thinks to himself, 'If Yankel knew I was here, he'd come out to greet me.' Then he sees Yankel.

"'Yankel! It's your old friend Chaim.'

"'Hello, Chaim.' He isn't so excited to see him.

"'Yankel, I come to you for help.'

"'Look, Chaim, when I became successful you became poor. Our fates are interconnected. If I help you, you'll become wealthy and I'll become poor. I'm not ready to become poor.'

"So Chaim works and slaves and toils to make money and he does. And again the tables are turned.

"This time Yankel is poor. He goes to his wife. 'We're destitute, poor, hungry. What should we do?' She tells him to go to Chaim. 'How can I? I turned him away. Like an enemy.'

"Anyway he goes. Chaim greets him at the door of his beautiful home. 'Yankel, my friend! How are you? Sit down. What's the matter?'

"'I'm embarrassed to ask.'

"'What are friends for? Only when everything is so rosy between us we should be friends?'

"So once again Chaim gives Yankel a blank check. Yankel gets rich; Chaim gets poor. And now Chaim has to go to Yankel.

"Yankel stands at the top of the stairs and doesn't come down. 'Remember what I told you last time? I'm not interested in being poor.'

"Chaim says, 'Yankel, I'm shocked.' Chaim is so shocked he has a heart attack and drops dead at the bottom of the stairs.

"Well, God decrees that Yankel should also be taken at that moment for having caused the death of his friend. So the both of them stand before the Court. 'Yankel,' the Almighty Judge says, 'you are a cruel and mean man. You will go through Gehinnom.' And to Chaim, 'And you, Chaim, will go to Heaven for your generosity and your kindness.'

"Chaim refuses. 'I should go to Heaven while my friend goes to Hell? I refuse. He goes to Hell, I go with him.'

"'He caused your death.'

"'No,' says Chaim. 'If he doesn't go into Heaven with me, I don't go. A friendship is a friendship.'

"So the Almighty Judge says, 'All right. This one time. Both of you will be sent back down to earth. This time you will not know each other. Chaim, you will be born into a wealthy family. Yankel, you will be born into a poor family. Yankel, if you don't do the right thing this time, Chaim will go to Heaven without you.'

"*Chaim says, 'I know my friend. He'll do the right thing.'*

"*So the two souls are sent down to earth in other bodies.*

"*The Besht sits back, looks at the Jew who is visiting him. 'That's the story.'*

"*The Jew says, 'How does this concern me?'*

"'*Today these two souls came together. Chaim had barely enough strength and he came to Yankel today begging for help and Yankel turned him away. By the end of the day Chaim will die from hunger and Yankel will go to Hell. It is almost sundown.'*

"*The Jew leaped up, alarmed.*

"'*Where are you going?' asked the Besht.*

"'*Rabbi, I'm Yankel!' And he runs out to find his friend.*

"*The Besht calls out after him, 'See, you thought you didn't need anything.'*"

Yussel's father squeezed Yussel's face between his hands. His hands were icy and strong. Yussel thought his eyes might pop. "*Yussele, I don't have to tell you you're Yankel, do I?*"

"I'm not Yankel."

"*Not only are you Yankel, God is Yankel. Not only man, Yussele, but God. You get it? HaShem needs you as much as you need Him. God is Yankel.*" And his father slapped him across the face, one side, the other side. Yussel's cheeks burned. It wasn't an insult, his father's slap. It was the slap a doctor gives to a newborn. "*Wake up! Pay attention!*"

"Pay attention to what, Totte? I saved Chaim from the fire. I didn't lay a hand on your wife. I've committed no adultery, stolen no money, told Lillywhite off. What do you want you should come from Above and slap me on the face? Dina? Is that the message? Be kind to Chaim, save Dina's life? Okay, from now on I'll treat Chaim like a brother, better than a brother."

His father said nothing, sat on his grave, sorted through the kvitls, put certain ones in certain pockets of his coat and his pants. Then a small whirlwind of dust and kvitls swept over him, encircled him, and lifted him away.

Yussel went to Mendl's to see Chaim the afternoon after the fast. The day had turned crisp and blue with picture-book clouds. Yussel went to tell Chaim he could have the Arizona, the deed to the land. "Take my land. Take my shul. Take my congregation. Mortgage the land, pay off your mortgages. I can't take it anymore. God's testing me. I don't want to be tested. Take, Chaim. Take anything I have."

He rehearsed it as he drove into Moffat. "You see, Chaim," Yussel would say, "I've talked to God and I told Him, 'You leave me alone. I'll leave You alone. I won't bother You for anything again.' Chaim, I'm offering you on my word a piece of property worth maybe two million bucks. Free. Sell subdivisions with lake rights, bring in a K-Mart. You'll make a fortune. I'll go home and sell insurance. You get a fresh start. What can you lose, Chaim?" That's what he would tell Chaim. "I want to go home. I'll never leave Rockaway again. I want to get carried out feet first on the Shabbas table from my house by the ocean when I die."

CHAIM'S HOUSES still had puffs of smoke coming out of them as Yussel drove by. His SL was a shell, his leather sofa a grilled-cheese sandwich. He understood Chaim. Chaim was too human. We're all too human.

Chaim wasn't at Mendl's. He was at his own house. Mendl walked over with Yussel. On the way over, Yussel told Mendl, "I came with an interesting proposition for Chaim."

"You think today's a good day for a proposition, Reb Yussel?"

It wasn't a good day. They heard something terrible: Chaim shrying. His cries drove through Yussel like nails, leaving holes. Chaim was howling as the dogs had howled. A fireman let them over the ropes, shook his head. "He's having a bad time over his dogs."

Chaim was filling in a deep hole behind the dog kennels. Mendl stopped Yussel, whispered. "Let's leave him."

"Maybe we should help, Mendl?"

"I'm not his gabbai? If I thought we should help him, you don't think I'd be helping?"

They sat on two kitchen chairs in the yard where Chaim couldn't see them and watched him shovel dirt, listened to him howl.

"This is over dogs?"

Mendl shrugged. "You didn't have an uncle who saw the skull of a cow in front of a tannery and stayed the rest of his life in his room? That was over cows. This is over dogs. Cows, dogs, women. A man breaks, a man breaks. God has weapons. For this man a shout, for this man a song, for this man a whisper. Who knows?"

"I thought he was trying to save his money last night. I thought that was why he wanted to go back in."

Mendl shrugged. "There *was* money. In the kitchen ceiling. From New York."

"Donations?"

Again Mendl shrugged. Chaim was almost to the top of the hole. A hot sharp wind from the south came up suddenly, covered them with ashes from the fire. They pulled their coat collars up for protection. Chaim's face was streaked with grime, sweat, charcoal. He looked like the tax collector from Hell in Rabbi Akiba's story. Chaim wept, wiped his nose and his eyes with his sleeve.

"Rentals?"

"You'll ask him."

"What was wrong with a bank, Mendl?"

Mendl scratched his head.

"Then something was wrong with the money?"

"You'll ask him."

"Okay, I won't ask."

Yussel took a deep breath. Dogs, cows, women. A man breaks. A great tragedy, a great love affair. Both. If God wants to break him, He'll find a way. For Yussel He was using a shotgun method. "So how can I help, Mendl?"

"A fourteen-hundred-dollar mortgage payment by next week is how you can help."

Chaim dropped his shovel, tore his shirt with his hands, threw himself facedown on the grave. Mendl turned away, covered his face, wept. Chaim beat his fists on the dirt. Yussel shook his head in disbelief. His father in the same elegant black silk and fur of the morning stood next to Chaim over the grave. Yussel watched Mendl. Mendl didn't see Yussel's father, nor did Chaim seem to. But there was his father, taller and more angular than Yussel had ever seen him, drawn out in grief, standing above the grave, above Chaim, beating on his chest while Chaim beat his fists on the ground. It couldn't be dogs and it couldn't be money. Maybe his father was mourning for Yussel who had betrayed Chaim. Yussel couldn't figure it out, any of it. His father's landscape was chaos.

Yussel called out to his father. "Totte?"

His father turned, looked at him, his face black with fury, turned his back, disappeared.

"Mendl, have you talked to Ruchel?"

"They're not speaking."

"Call her. See if she's okay."

The fireman's yellow rubber slicker flapped in the wind. "First sign of summer's end, a wind like this." He let them out with great courtesy. "A man gets attached. They're only dogs, but you get attached."

AS IF RAIN had cleansed the world, Shoshanna arrived that night. She tooted the horn on the bus again and again. Yussel raced to her. His children's faces were shiny apples. Yussel held each child in turn, starting with the youngest, held them so tight against himself they squirmed loose from his need. Dinela he held longer than the others. She was incandescent, felt like a handful of tinder and feathers. Scabs speckled her face and legs. She clung as if she'd crawl inside him if she could find an opening. Over the heads of the children, over Dina's head, Yussel wept. Shoshanna wept. He couldn't hold Shoshanna, but they drank the tears from each other's eyes and it was just as good as holding. Schmulke ran to the bus, came back with Kleenex. Everyone blew their noses hard and laughed. His Shoshanna was peace. Why would he want torment? Why would any man want torment when he could have this? Who was this other terrible person in him who wanted, yearned for torment? What was wrong with him he should do such a thing, such a thing would happen to him?

"We're staying, Yussel."

"Sure. Sure. As long as I'm staying, you're staying. Of course. Listen, Shoshanna, Chaim's house burned. We have to support him."

"Vey iz mir."

"Where will I get the money from?"

"God provides." It rolled off her tongue. What do women know?

Yussel sweats. His wife says, "God provides." His hand shakes on the calculator. "God provides."

"Yussel, I said we're staying."

"Fine. Fine."

"Gutzadunken. I thought you'd be mad at me. We'll stay on the bus until the house is ready."

"How can I be mad at you? How can I be mad at a person like you?"

What was wrong with him? To hurt this beautiful family? Chaim's howl rose in his chest. Yussel prayed that when he went to his wife, God would keep him from thinking of Lillywhite. Apparently the answer was no. When he touched Shoshanna, he touched Lillywhite. When he closed his eyes, he saw Lillywhite. When he tried to enter Shoshanna, he was entering Lillywhite, and, for the first time in his life, he found himself unable to perform his duties to his wife. Shoshanna said, "This is what comes from being apart too long."

He sat on the edge of the bed. "We'll never be apart again. I promise you."

"It was wrong, Yussel."

"Tell me about it."

24

THE WEEK AFTER Tishabav there is an odd little holiday left over from the time of the Temple, even before. It was a holiday in which all the unmarried men and women went into the fields. It was the time of the joining together of male and female. If Tishabav was the fast of endings, Tu B'Av was the time of beginnings. Mystically it was the time of the joining of the letters of HaShem's name, a fertile time. It was good, Shoshanna said, that Yussel was building the new house with the men. It was a good beginning. She did not say that anything had ended.

Rosebud arrived at dawn every morning, hung around while the men davened, ate breakfast, took Ernie, Bingo, Slotnik's son, and the Israelis off to the whorehouse. Yussel spent the mornings with his family, took the kids for walks up the dirt road, drove Dina to the pool in the mountains, heard hoofbeats, knew it was his heart, carried Dina in his arms when she was too tired to walk, cut wallpaper dolls from the sample books Shoshanna brought home from Woodpecker's, bought everyone cowboy boots, cooked, cleaned, helped Shoshanna, drove her to see the mountains, to the shops in Alamosa, even to the sand dunes.

After lunch, Yussel drove over to the whorehouse. From there he couldn't hear the music, couldn't turn white when the phone rang, didn't have Shoshanna watching him as if he were a new species. The men returned to the Arizona for afternoon services, ate supper, went over again, worked late into the night, strung lights so they could paint outside, tore down ceilings, put up ceilings, tore down plaster, put up plasterboard, added a wing, extended the whores' front parlor into a long dining room so Shoshanna could have lots of company for Shabbas and holy days, doubled the size of the kitchen, installed a dairy end, a meat end, put in a storage room for freezers, put in freezers, a trash-masher, a Jacuzzi, sky-blue slabs of Brazilian granite for the kitchen counters, better then Chaim's turquoise slab. Yussel threw himself into the work. It was such a relief to read an instruction book and know what to do. You do this; then you do that; then it works. Yussel only wished in his real life he could have such an instruction book, and realized, in shame, he had the Torah. He learned more about electrical wiring than he wanted to know, installed one stove three times, wouldn't climb a ladder, wouldn't help on the new roof, took apart the furnace they installed, did it over again by the instruction book. Slotnik's son had the air vent in wrong and would have killed them all with carbon monoxide. Golems. Yussel saw the shipping cartons, the new appliances, asked seriously who was paying for this. They laughed as if he were telling a joke. It was no joke. UPS came every morning with boxes—little ones from the front of the truck, big ones from the back. Rosebud told him this was the Hopi version of the Jewish version of "God provides," which meant Indian Joe was using Yussel's money to build Yussel's house, which made it easier to accept, so when Shoshanna came to inspect, kvelled with pleasure, asked how they could afford such luxury, Yussel said, "Simple, Shoshanna. God provides." He provides a gorgeous house, another woman, a sick child, a polluted husband. Simple.

SHOSHANNA WAS worried they hadn't heard from the Flower Child. Yussel told Shoshanna the Flower Child was a free agent, a grown woman. He questioned the Blondische, who hadn't heard anything, was also worried. The Blondische reminded Yussel he'd hurt her feelings terribly and that's why she'd left.

"I didn't make her welcome," Yussel explained to Shoshanna.

"Shame, Yussel."

Yussel shrugged it off. "It wouldn't work. I told her . . ."

"Yussel, she had no one. She had nothing. What will happen to her."

"She's young. She has her looks, a good head. She keeps a nice house. She'll marry again soon. Maybe she's in San Francisco. She has friends in San Francisco. Maybe she's in a commune."

"Yussel, we're responsible."

"She's a big girl, Shoshanna. In no time she'll have a husband, a rich widower. She likes alte cockers. There was nothing for her here. And it wouldn't have worked between her and you."

"You decided that? You don't think she and I should have decided that?" Shoshanna looked away, shook her head. "What do you know about women?"

"Nothing. Okay? I know nothing about women and sometimes I think I know nothing about you. Coming down here before I told you to. Driving by yourself with the kids in the bus like a crazy woman."

"You're right." Shoshanna threw her hands up in the air. She spoke in a tone Yussel had never heard before. "You know nothing."

"And you know everything? You don't need doctors for Dina?"

"Chicken pox I understand. Four of my children had it. I know it. You I don't understand."

"I want her to go to a doctor. I want you to find one in Denver."

"What are you so hysterical for over the kids?"

"I want her to go to a specialist."

"You know something I don't know? You're doing prophecy?"

"I'm not doing prophecy. I'm just concerned."

"Let me take care of the children, Yussel. You have enough on your mind."

THE MUSIC WAS louder than loud, sadder than sad. It wrenched his gut, made his body heavy, filled his pants. He didn't call. He didn't answer her calls. Still Dina ran a fever in the afternoons between four and eight. Shoshanna started to talk about calling their doctor in Far Rockaway, called him. He sent a prescription by overnight mail, gave Shoshanna the name of a doctor in Denver he'd gone to medical school with, advised her not to worry, advised her to build up Dina's resistance, suggested chicken soup, meant it. Grisha sat by Dina's bed, told her the stories about lost princesses and kings' sons he'd told Yussel when he was a kid. Grisha gave up playing cards so Dina would get well. Babe made him special meals, watched him like a hawk. Yussel talked to God, "Listen, I'm not calling her. Make my baby better." He lay in bed at night, said to his father, "I'm staying away from her. What else do they want? Can't you find out what they want from me?" His father wouldn't talk to him. Chaim wouldn't talk to him. Yussel dreamed an old dream about eating the wax from his ears and how it tasted like ginger. Yussel dreamed a lot of old dreams. Worse, he dreamed new ones. Pecky came once, still in his shroud, still smoking his cigar, told Yussel his father stood in line, night and day, fighting terrible decrees, everyone wants something from him, everyone has such tzuros. *"Your father sent me to tell you something."* Pecky read from a scrap of parchment. *"Two Jews are in a rowboat. One is drilling a hole. The other says, 'What are you doing, drilling a hole in the rowboat?' The driller answers, 'Leave me alone. I'm only drilling on my side.' That's the message."* Pecky left. Yussel got out of bed, looked around for fire, found none. Yussel prayed, fasted, wept. When he davened he strained for attachment, strained to bring Dina back to health the way he'd made the eighteen-wheeler slow down when he'd saved Lillywhite's life. Now when he davened, he didn't have to make up tears, desire, sorrow. It was all there. Shoshanna said he yelled out in his sleep all the time.

The tetracycline stopped working. Yussel and Shoshanna begged Dina not to scratch her chicken pox. They made her sleep with mittens on her hands. Still there was blood in the morning. She said she didn't scratch. Yussel finally held up the sheet one morning, yelled at her. "Where is this from? Where is this from? If you didn't scratch."

Shoshanna stopped him. Dina wept, choked on her tears, "Emes Adonoy, Totty. I didn't scratch, Totty. I don't. I'm a good girl, Totty." She pulled Yussel's head down to hers, opened her palm, showed him a square leaf. "It's a secret. Don't tell, Totty." Yussel burst into tears. Dina's eyes glittered with death.

Shoshanna pulled Yussel out of the bus, pinching his arm hard, "Don't get her upset."

Yussel hid in the cottonwoods, pulled hair from his head, lay on the ground, and beat on it. "Don't take her. Don't take her. I'm staying away from her. What do you want? What are you doing to my baby? Take the blood from me. Give me the fever. Give me the itch. Leave my baby alone!"

Shoshanna took Dina to sleep with her in their bed. Yussel called his uncles on a conference call. There was a long silence after he asked to borrow money, reminded them they'd offered.

Moses from Abnormal Psychology said, "We offered so you wouldn't go out there."

Gimbel from Brown, the Dean of Humanities, said, "The kid needs money. Who are we to deny his request?"

Nachman from Yale in Law said, "You know how much money we sunk in there for his father."

Moses corrected him. "For our brother."

Gimbel from Brown said, "It's a bottomless pit, Yussel."

"Tell me about it," Yussel said.

Nachman from Yale asked, "What happened to your money?"

Yussel said, "I put it all in here."

"And that wasn't enough?" Nachman from Yale asked.

"You see," Gimbel from Brown said, "nothing's enough for them."

"That's not a personal remark, Yussel," Moses from Oxford interrupted. "We've been through this with your father for years. You hang up. We'll talk."

They called back. "Yussel, if you come home, we'll set you up again, pay your expenses, buy you a Ben and Jerry's, anything you want. If you come home."

"Maybe after the holidays."

"When you do," they all said, "you'll call us."

HE CALLED Chaim again to offer him the Arizona property and his congregation, free and clear, so Yussel could take his family back to Rockaway. Chaim wasn't taking calls. Mendl said Chaim said Yussel should call when he has the fourteen hundred dollars, until then he doesn't want to hear from him. Mendl then whispered into the phone that Chaim couldn't listen to any propositions except maybe how to commit suicide and did Yussel want that on his hands also? Yussel restrained himself from answering.

He called his friends. They'd give him any amount he wanted, a blank check, but not for the shul. As a favor to Yussel they didn't want to give him a debt he couldn't repay. Loans like that ruin friendships.

He thought about the numbers flashing on his screen when he went to the Paradise. Hadn't Someone put the numbers on his screen? If he had been given the numbers, maybe he had been told to gamble. Men have done worse to save a family, to save two families, his and Chaim's, maybe more, maybe Mendl and his family, maybe all the court, who could tell? And so, finally, Yussel put on regular clothes, new cowboy boots, drove up and over the mountain to the Paradise, prayed on the way that Lillywhite wouldn't be there. As soon as he walked in, *4* and *7* flashed on his screen. The place was filled with cowboys, polka music, a few women, no Lillywhite. The cowboys drank hard, danced with each other. Life in the Ukraine must have been like this—the women at home with the kids and the cows, the men together. In the Ukraine they wore bark shoes. Here they wore boots. Didn't the polkas come from the same earth as his father's music? Hadn't he heard the same tunes at his grandfather's table? Yussel slugged down one vodka, two, slapped a hundred-dollar bill on numbers *4* and *7*, picked up fourteen hundred-dollar bills, drank two more vodkas, polkaed to the sounds of Charlie Weaver and his Chicken Man Polka Band with a cowboy named Lunchmeat, who was also very drunk. It felt like Simchas Torah. It smelled like Simchas Torah. Yussel leaped down on the floor, stomped, sweated, yelled, beat his heart with his fist, sang, raised his arms over his head, made horns with his hands through his hair, charged like a bull. The cowboys made a circle and watched him dance. They clapped, hooted, cheered him on, bought him drinks, made horns with their hands through their hair and charged Yussel like a bull. When the Chinese lanterns in the ceiling were also drunk, Lunchmeat stuffed Yussel into Bingo's cab.

Yussel drove slowly up the mountain to her house, turned off his lights in front of her house, looked around, saw nothing in the dark, drove slowly home down the mountain to the Arizona, wrapped fourteen hundred-dollar bills with aluminum foil and freezer tape, labeled the package: LOX, Y.F. DON'T TOUCH, stuffed it toward the back of the freezer, went to sleep. In the middle of the night his screen came back. He saw Lillywhite sitting in the front of a pickup truck, kissing someone. He couldn't see if it was another man or himself because her hair was in the way. He tried not to watch.

"What's the matter, Yussel?"

"Shoshanna?"

"Who else?"

"I can't sleep."

"You yelled out."

"What did I yell?"

"Just a sound, not a word, but a yell."

"I'm sorry."

Shoshanna woke him up at noon. She was smart enough not to ask any questions. Her husband was drinking and gambling, and, if she knew, she also knew to wait it out. Maybe.

Three times that week he went up to the Paradise. He drank a little, danced a little, lost a little on purpose, won a lot. By Shabbas, he had just under five grand in the freezer. Now he was a sinner, Shoshanna had grocery money, and Chaim could pay his mortgage. If he weren't a sinner, Shoshanna wouldn't have grocery money, Chaim would lose his property and his business. Also Someone gave him the right numbers so it couldn't be too terrible what he was doing. He tried to figure the cause and effect, the odds, the probabilities. He does this, HaShem does that. He couldn't figure anything out. He was in his father's universe and he was lost. Dina was getting sicker. Shoshanna now talked about taking her back East. Not calling Lillywhite wasn't helping Dina. Wasn't helping Yussel. He called her from the Texaco.

"I thought we weren't speaking. I thought you weren't calling me."

"I'm calling."

"What do you want?"

"You." He heard her sigh, knew she'd lit up a cigarette, looked out into the desert night. He looked out at the same night.

"I don't know what to say. Anything I say is wrong."

"I'm sorry I called, Lillywhite. I tried not to."

"Try not to again."

THE SECOND week of gambling, he drove over the mountain to the Paradise, went in, bet, won, leaned against the wall to watch the dancing. It was couple's night. The polka band had been replaced by a pale thin couple in Hawaiian shirts, who played canned country music, pressed buttons, swung maracas, hummed along, told dirty jokes between numbers.

Lunchmeat pummeled Yussel on the back, pulled him into the room, pointed to Lillywhite, who was on the floor with Warren Beatty, throwing her body around like she wanted to get rid of it. He did this; she did that. He held her out, she took three turns, he brought her in. She ducked under his arm. He twisted her arms, this way, that way. The timing was perfect. They had blank faces, looked beyond each other as if they were reading the instructions off the South Pacific walls. Then Lillywhite saw Yussel, met his eyes, lost her footing. It made him sick, that bolt of lightning that went through him when she looked at him. Warren Beatty caught her before she fell.

His screen flashed *9* and *13* urgently. Still he left.

"Hey!"

Mercury lights haloed her from behind. She was running after him in high-heeled boots, clicking on the tarmac. She gulped air, grabbed his sleeve. He shook her off. "You know how they tortured white men out here in the old days? They slit their stomachs, pulled out a piece of gut, nailed it to a tree, and made the guy run in circles around the tree until he died."

"You want to do that to me?"

"You're doing it to me."

A man stood on the steps, looming in the light. "Honey, you okay?"

"That's Tom?"

"Listen, just don't look at me like that again. Okay? It's not fair.

I'm only human." She turned and walked back to Tom, who put his arm around her, looked back once over his shoulder at Yussel.

He remembered opening the car windows under the black night, the smell of pines, sweat drying up in the wind. He hit a jackrabbit. It flew up onto Bingo's hood, looked at him, astonished. Yussel swerved along the road until the rabbit slid away.

AT HOME HE wrapped another package for the freezer, climbed into his bachelor bed next to Grisha's room, couldn't sleep, saw Lillywhite and Tom on the futon later that night, didn't want to see what he saw. Once she said to Yussel over Tom's heaving shoulder, "Don't look at me like that." Yussel walked outside up and down the road until the night faded, until Babe's lights went on. He knocked on her door. Babe hadn't put in her teeth, looked like a shrunken apple. He felt very sorry for her. She made coffee, came back with her teeth in. Together Babe and Yussel worried about Dina, whether she should go back to Far Rockaway, to a good doctor, worried about money, about the water rights, about Chaim, whether Babe should stay, where her life was going, where his life was going, what they really wanted. She offered him money. He said he couldn't take it.

Yussel wanted desperately to tell her about the square leaf, to ask her if she thought it was a sign Dina was to die. He was tempted to tell her everything, knew it would harm her to know these things. Would harm him, all of them, because after the leaf he'd tell her about Lillywhite. Near daybreak, he fell asleep in the La-Z-Boy. At seven Babe woke him to go daven.

Babe sighed, leaned toward him. "Listen, menschele, if it's going to kill you, you should quit. I'm here to tell you that. It's what your mother wanted me to tell you. You and Shoshanna are walking around like zombies. Schmulke's a wild animal, wild with fear, I think. Dina needs a doctor. Go home, Yussy. Get your life in order. Go home."

"We'll talk about it. Maybe after the holidays. After the holidays. Maybe then."

She didn't believe him. "You're just like your father. Let me at least give you the money for Chaim."

"No. It's my problem."

So he stayed away from Lillywhite, from the telephone, from trips up into the mountains, from drives past her house. And every day she played her music longer, louder, lonelier, sadder, calling him, surrounding him, blinding him, like fog. He wanted to climb the mountain on his knees, on his belly. Once in a while he'd see Shoshanna looking at him in an odd way and he'd ask her, "What's wrong?" She'd say, "Nothing." Sometimes she'd ask him, "What's wrong?" and he'd say, "Nothing."

#

ONE NIGHT AFTER supper Shoshanna said she wanted to talk away from the children. They walked down the road toward the mountains. Yussel tried not to look for horses or redheads, tried to stay with Shoshanna, hear her, respond to her, talk. Guilty people with torturous secrets listen very carefully. The air was cool, the sky big. Great sheets of air stretched and snapped between them. He pulled. She pulled. Choya cactus grabbed at their clothes. Except for the snow-crested mountains, the landscape looked like a dust bowl Depression movie: the sad couple, heads hanging, kicking up dust, a light wind in their clothes, something wrong between them, walking the same path, going in different directions, weighted down. The mountains loomed sharp, sullen, treacherous. Yussel yearned for a clean salty breeze from the ocean, wet sand at low tide. Shoshanna tied her scarf backward over her mouth and nose, made a joke about being a cowboy.

"Everything's a joke today?" He was sorry as soon as he said it. She kicked a rock in front of her.

They turned onto a logging road, hit a field of hay spotted with the red splashes of Indian paintbrush like the spots on Dina's body. Shoshanna didn't notice. She picked a few stems, held a little bouquet in front of her. As they entered the dark coolness of junipers, Yussel sensed something moving behind them near the hay field. He could see nothing. They stepped over old skidways, a broken wheel, a rusted pan, rotted planks.

"You've changed, Yussel."

So this was how it would happen. This is how she'd begin. What was following them? Something black that cracked a twig. Maybe the Yetzer Hara, slipping in and out of the junipers, shadow broken here, light broken there. "Me?"

"I'm alone?"

"How have I changed?"

"You're thinner, stronger. You listen. You're more thoughtful."

"I guess the fasts helped." He could see nothing behind them. But he knew something had crossed the hay fields with them and entered the woods. "Shoshanna, the other day when you came over to the house, I said something to you. I want to apologize."

"For what?"

"I was making fun of you. I said, 'Simple, God provides.'"

"So?"

"Forget it."

"For some things you owe me an apology. To tell me God provides, you don't owe me an apology. That's a change also. You never in your life apologized to me. Another change is your body looks ten years younger."

"You look at my body?"

"You don't look at mine?"

"When I think of you as a woman, it's, Baruch HaShem, with the same emotion I feel when I put on my tallis."

"I couldn't ask for more." They were both lying to each other, repeating what they'd learned as kids.

Yussel walked along, wondered if he should ask her, did ask her. "So, uh, how does it look?"

"What?"

"My body."

"Fine, especially from the rear." Shoshanna blushed.

Yussel's face burned.

She walked a little ahead of him, finally said what she'd come to say, "I'm going home."

Yussel didn't dare ask why. "You're moving into the new house next week. You have everything you want in it. You . . ."

"Ask me why."

"Jokes, games. Just tell me."

"Because of Schmulke."

"Dina I could understand. She should get to a good doctor. Schmulke, I don't understand. What's the matter with him?"

Something large fell, made a human sound. Shoshanna looked around also. It didn't deter her. "He's not learning."

"I haven't had time. Also he fights me. Every idea, he fights. Why do I have to have a kid who wants to take on the world? He has to be the last of the just? Why can't he just be a kid?"

"Two weeks you haven't sat one minute to teach him."

Because I'm lying on my back dreaming about Lillywhite, trying not to call her, talking to her in my head the minute I'm left alone. I'm fighting a fight you should never even have to understand. Two weeks I haven't called her, except once for a minute. Give me credit for that much. "Shoshanna, let's turn around. I don't like it in here."

"So it's someone's dog. Don't avoid the subject. It breaks my heart I want to be here with you so much, but Schmulke has to learn."

"You aren't a rabbi's daughter? You can't help him a little until I have more time?"

"His father should teach him. A man should teach his son what his father taught him. That's the way it should be. So you better start teaching him. Or I leave." She turned and faced him. "So what should I do?"

Yussel knew he should leave, leave and take them all home with him. He couldn't leave because he couldn't leave Lillywhite. "Mendl's bringing out his boys and Chaim's boys and a teacher." It wasn't true. It would however be true tomorrow. He'd find the airfares. He'd find the teacher.

"Why didn't you tell me? This is wonderful news!"

"My son should go to school with those bums?"

Shoshanna looked at something behind him. Yussel swung around, jumped. Darth Vader stood with his hands on his black poly hips. "I'm not going to cheder with those bums. I'm going back to Far Rockaway with my mother."

Yussel pulled him off the ground by the collar. "You want to give me a heart attack? What are you doing out here? Spying on us?"

"You were going to talk about me," Schmulke whined. Shoshanna giggled. Yussel let Schmulke go, hit a fist into a hand. He always suspected Shoshanna of using Schmulke so she could compete with Yussel, pair up against him at moments like these. Had his mother done that with him? Used him as a weapon against his father? Their giggles infuriated him. He wanted to bang his head on the ground, Schmulke's head.

Shoshanna said very softly. "I want him to be with a teacher. I want him to have Shomer Shabbas boys to be with, observing boys."

"He'll go to Mendl's."

"Not with those bums, not me."

"If Totty says you will, you will, Schmulke. That's all there is to it. It's that simple."

Schmulke raced off before them deeper into the forest, shouting, "Not me."

"Get him back, Yussel. I don't like him in the woods by himself. He'll get lost."

"Him? The trees will get lost."

She yelled into the woods, "Schmulke, come back."

"Two weeks, we'll try it, Shoshanna. He can sleep there. They've got a woman coming from New York to cook for the boys and do the laundry. Just try it." He would have to pay so many fares from New York he could charter a plane.

"We'll try the cheder, Yussel. If it doesn't work, I'll take him home."

"Come on back, Tottele," Yussel yelled into the woods. "You can go to Far Rockaway with your mother. Come on back."

"One condition," Schmulke, who couldn't be fooled, yelled from the woods.

"What?"

"I wear what I want."

Shoshanna shrugged. Yussel yelled, "Okay."

Schmulke plunged down through the junipers, jumped around behind them as they walked home. They knew he'd go to cheder every day of the week as Darth Vader. "Except on Shabbas," Shoshanna added without turning around. Schmulke gave her no argument. Yussel thanked God she was staying, whatever it cost him, wondered how she could have lived with a man all these years who didn't know how to apologize.

RUIZ WAS COMING to visit Grisha. Grisha was very excited, swept his room, hung his blankets out to air. Babe was making stuffed cabbage for them in her bus. Grisha was examining cabbage leaves for bugs, one by one. Babe was mixing rice and hamburger with her hands. Her knuckles were stuck with raw meat.

"I don't know why he's coming. I'm not sick."

"You weren't sick. You made yourself sick over Dina."

"Somebody had to."

"This is the *world*, Grisha. There's doctors and medicine." Babe rolled the meat mixture in soft large cabbage leaves, secured them with toothpicks. "You know why Ruiz is coming? Because he likes you. Did you ever think someone could just like you, Grisha?"

"You think Shoshanna would let Ruiz look at Dina?"

"She'd let him look, but she won't listen. Since she came here I've been telling her to take that poor little thing to a decent doctor in New York. Shoshanna just keeps waiting for the chicken pox to go away."

"That's not all she's waiting for to go away."

"She knows?"

"Who doesn't?" Grisha peeled the outer leaves from another head of cabbage, dropped them in the pot, splashed water on the stove. Babe shook her head over the splash, over Shoshanna, over the shame. Grisha shook his head the same way, clucked the same sounds. "She won't mind me bringing company?"

"A rabbi's wife with a showcase house? A magazine's coming to take pictures. Of course she won't mind." Babe gave Grisha a new head of cabbage, leaned with her elbows on the counter, looked out at the distances. "Grisha, you've known me since I was a girl. Let me ask you a question. Yussel let Indian Joe pay for everything in that house. It wasn't cheap. I would have helped. Yussel wouldn't take a penny. What's the matter with my money?"

"With your money, nothing. With you, you'll forgive me, something." Grisha spread his hands in apology. Water dripped from them. "You don't feel good unless you give, but when you give you want control. Yussel wanted it to be Shoshanna's house, not yours."

"You just came up with that?" Babe handed him a towel.

"Nah."

"You've been thinking about that?"

"For a while." Grisha dropped more cabbage leaves into the pot but this time they didn't splash. Babe said nothing, turned her back, smiled to herself.

"Why don't you marry Indian Joe? You shouldn't be alone."

"You just come up with that too?"

"He could convert."

"Yeah, yeah, an old bag like me."

"A sixty-year-old in good shape? Who wants a sweet young thing?"

"Everybody."

"You want me to mention something to him?"

"I'm not interested."

"So who are you interested in?"

"My husband ran off with another woman. That's enough of a message. I control too much, Grisha?"

"Don't take it wrong. You're also very generous."

Babe poured tomato sauce over the cabbage rolls, sprinkled them with brown sugar, banged around with trays, oven doors, can openers. Grisha was right. Last week when Shoshanna hung curtains over the garage windows, Babe told her that only goyim hang curtains in the garage. Shoshanna said nothing, but she must have told Yussel, who must have told Grisha, who had just told Babe. Babe shrugged. He was right. Grisha washed his hands. "I have to get dressed. You sure it's okay to take Ruiz to Shoshanna's?"

"I'm sure. Listen, troublemaker, if you say one word to Indian Joe, I'll hang you from the ceiling like a chandelier." Without using her hands, Babe pushed him out the door, splashed cold water on her face she was blushing so much.

At supper, Grisha wore a fresh shirt and a fedora Babe hadn't seen before. Ruiz wore white shoes and a Mexican wedding shirt. He poured salsa on the stuffed cabbage, ate two big portions. Grisha beamed, kept shoving food at him. After supper Ruiz and Grisha sat in the bus and played gin rummy. Babe couldn't believe her eyes. She managed not to tell Grisha it was against the law, leaned over Grisha's chair, kibbitzed, made tea. Finally she sent them to Shoshanna's before it was Dinela's bedtime. She decided not to go with them because she might get there and try to control things. She looked in the mirror for a while, wished she could control her chins, went to sleep a little happy. The next day Grisha told her Ruiz said it didn't look like chicken pox. It looked a lot worse. Babe said, "Anyone who plants half a bathtub on its end in his front yard and sticks a Madonna in it, what does he know from medicine?" She said it because she wanted to protect Grisha from himself.

AFTER RUIZ'S visit, Grisha's face started dropping until he looked like a starving bloodhound. He stopped playing solitaire again. Babe bought him a new plastic deck of cards in a carved wood box. He wouldn't touch them, wouldn't respond to her or Yussel. But when the phone rang, if Yussel was in the room, he'd leap to get it first. One day Yussel heard him say, "He's not here." It rang a second time. "I told you he's not here."

Yussel knew it was Lillywhite because after the second phone call the music came down from the mountain louder than he'd ever heard it. Her voice was strident, ugly. The third time the phone rang that day, Grisha said, "I'll look for him," and left the ear piece swinging against the wall. He didn't come back. Yussel walked by the phone a dozen, a thousand times. He chewed blood from his lip. When he left the Arizona, he saw Grisha in his room, lying on his bed fully dressed. The phone at the bar was still off the hook.

Three times a week Yussel went to the Paradise, brought home just enough money for Mendl's expenses, his own, airfares and salaries for Steinberg the new teacher and Steinberg's teacher's wife, who would cook. Once a week he made sure to lose. If the Porsche was in front of the Paradise, he drove away, came back when it was gone. He drove Natalie's wreck, Babe's Lincoln, Slotnik's truck, anybody's car except Bingo's. Lillywhite called Babe. Babe went to find Yussel. "It's Music Minus One. She says its urgent."

Yussel waved Babe off.

Babe hissed, "Yussel, be reasonable."

Grisha said, "He's being reasonable." Yussel took the phone. He leaned his elbow on the counter so Babe couldn't see his hand trembling.

"It's urgent. I'm sorry to have to . . ."

"I'm a little busy. I'll get back to you."

She swore and hung up.

Babe asked what Lillywhite wanted. Grisha said, "She wants to convert," and set himself off into a bout of laughter. Yussel felt as if someone had punched him in the stomach. He knew he'd hurt her and it was a terrible feeling.

LILLYWHITE CALLED Mendl. Mendl called Yussel.

"How's it going, Mendl?"

"Baruch HaShem, the school is fine. The teacher is patient. Mrs. Steinberg is happy with the boys and cooks decent food."

"Schmulke give you the check?"

"Yeah, yeah. Your kid's a regular Fetner, a born leader with a mind like a trap. It cost me five bucks to get the check from him. And with my five bucks he bought everyone ice cream, even the teacher. I spent time on Rikers Island and still your kid put one over on me."

Yussel knew Schmulke was going to get in trouble soon and Shoshanna would have an excuse to leave and take Schmulke home. "And Chaim?"

"Ruchel calls from New York. He won't talk. She puts his girls on the phone. Still he won't talk. But he now comes out of his room to see his boys."

"That's something. Listen, Mendl, Schmulke's learning?"

"We're doing our best."

"Is he?"

"To tell you the truth, Reb Yussel, yesterday he climbed out the window, went to the regular school with a couple of boys who climbed out the window after him, and picked a fight with some goyim in the playground. It wouldn't hurt if you talked to him."

"Mendl, anything else like that, tell me, not my wife. Okay?"

"I heard she's upset. That's terrible your Dinela's not getting better."

"Dinela isn't getting better *fast enough* for Shoshanna," Yussel lied. "That's all. You know women. So why did you call, Mendl?"

His voice dropped. "You alone?"

"If it's so secret maybe you should come over."

"I don't leave Reb Chaim alone. Listen, Reb Yussel, this is between you and me?"

"Depends."

"This woman called for Reb Chaim. I take his phone calls. She said to tell Reb Chaim she knew." He dropped his voice. "I told her to leave us alone. She told me if I want her to leave us alone, I should tell the other rabbi he better call her and take care of the problem. Reb Chaim's face turned black, but he wouldn't tell me anything. So I guess you're the other rabbi. Maybe you'll call? I wouldn't ask for myself."

"Okay, Mendl, for me it's between us also. Also for you. I'll take care of it." He forgot to ask for her name. He forgot to ask for her number. Mendl, Baruch HaShem, wasn't so smart, also not so suspicious, called back and gave Yussel Lillywhite's name and number.

"IT'S EXTREMELY private," Lillywhite said.

"I said all right, didn't I? You want an affidavit?"

"When?"

"When? Why wait? Let's do it right now. Right now. I'm leaving my house right now and I'm driving up to the pool."

Shoshanna was in his way as he flung his coat on. "What's the matter? Where are you going?"

"On business. About the water rights. I'll be back in a half-hour."

"Yussel . . ."

"Get out of my way."

"I don't understand . . ."

"Who are you kidding, Shoshanna? Of course you do."

She flung her hand over her mouth.

26

FOR A LOT OF reasons Yussel drove up into the mountains. His body strained at his clothes. His breath steamed up the windshield. "You couldn't make my flesh crawl when I look at her? My stomach couldn't turn upside down? Why did You make her so beautiful? Do me a favor. When I look at her, let me see pimples, warts, hairs on her nose. Not even real ones. I don't ask so much from You. Why do You torment me with temptations? Why do You set this package in front of me and say, 'Take, take'? I'm not a married man with a lovely wife and a precious daughter who might be dying? Why are You doing this to me? One terrible canker sore, a harelip, fangs. That's all I ask. Unless You want me to be tempted? Unless You want me to take? What do You want? Do You know what You want from me? You can't tell me? Give me a clue?" Yussel had to stop the car, blow his nose, dry his eyes.

She marched around the pool, under the roof of pines. Her eyes were candle-bright, the red hair illumined by the sun behind the pines. He felt what he always felt when he saw her. Something gathered itself inside him, gathered up from all points like little bits of iron filings, drew upward into his mouth like hunger. He shivered. "Make it short. My wife knows I'm here."

"Cute." She wore a rough brown wool sweater jacket with big deep pockets, held a hand in one pocket as she marched. Yussel wondered if she had a gun. That would be all right with him.

Just once if he could hold her face between his hands, kiss her, lay her down by the pool. Just once, if he could have her just once, he'd be done with her, with all of it. How long could it take? A couple of minutes? He could go on with his life and he'd really be finished with her. This was a good place, a great place. They'd never been so alone before. Is this what's intended? Is this the other side of the Other Side, the reward, the final river to plunge into? Why is she put before me? Maybe it's the end of the path? The last drop into evil? Hadn't it begun here? He could end it here. Over by the flat rock, he could end it. On the rock he could spread her legs, cup her breasts, listen to his name, be done with her. "I have nothing to give you. My father quotes Carlyle. 'In order to find your inner being you have to have a great love or a great tragedy.' Well, I found my inner being. It's garbage."

"You told me that once, when you filled my car with garbage. You're wrong."

"We're finished, Lillywhite. I can't see you."

"Abraham's tent had four doors, right?"

Yussel panicked. Who had she been talking to? His father? Who else was in on this she should have Talmudic weapons? "So?"

"So a person could enter his father's house no matter what direction he came from. Open another door for me."

"How do you know that?"

"Someone told me."

"I'm Abraham? I have no other doors. I have no tent. Between us there's only one door . . . the door between a man and a woman. It's closed, nailed shut."

"You promised you wouldn't slam the door on me. You're slamming the door." Lillywhite turned her face away from him for a moment. From her back he could see her take a deep breath. "All right. Okay. Before you slam the door, I want you to take me to my father's grave."

He didn't know if the sorrow in his heart was for her or for himself. "You don't know how to get on a plane? I'll tell you. You get on the plane in Denver. You get off in New York. You take a cab. You go to the cemetery. They're all in the same place. You go into the office, tell them your name. They give you the . . ."

"I can't do that. Don't you understand? I told you, I can't do that. You have to come with me."

"They give you a map. You take the map . . ."

"I saw you put your father's body into the grave. Your father's corpse. I saw that. I saw you predict the winning numbers at the Paradise. I saw you touch death. Why won't you help *me?*"

He heard his father's voice. *"Yussele,"* his voice was low. *"Didn't I tell you you couldn't hide your heart forever? Didn't I tell you someday someone would figure you out?"*

"You want to ruin my life? You want to kill my baby?"

"I want you to take me to my father's grave. I want to speak to my father. How will that kill your kid?" Lillywhite took a paper from the pocket of her sweater. "These are your water rights. If you take me to my father's grave, I'll give them to you. If you don't, I'll ruin you and your friend and all your people and all his people." She thrust her lower lip forward, watched him.

Lillywhite was the first woman he'd ever been in love with. He couldn't dismiss her. How many other women had he pushed away? Leave me alone. I'm comfortable. Leave me alone. Natalie he dismissed as nuts, Babe as bitter and barren, his mother as revengeful. Shoshanna, God forgive him, as dumb. All of them he'd found a reason to dismiss. This one stood in front of him with her hands on her hips and he couldn't dismiss her. And all the rest of them were lined up behind her. For what he'd done to Shoshanna, that she should hide herself all these years to keep him happy, he could cut out his heart. And Natalie who was filled with sparks and devotion, he'd made her feet bleed. And the Flower Child? What was his excuse for her? That she was after him? Was she? Maybe she was after something else? Like a place to stay, an understanding heart? And this one? This one in front of him with his livelihood and Chaim's livelihood and the welfare of all their families and their congregations' families shaking in her hand? He could find plenty of reasons to dismiss this one. This one wasn't Jewish. This one was a sexpot, a whore, the work of the Yetzer Hara. On the other hand, also maybe possibly Lillywhite and he were fragments of the same soul. Why else would they have snapped together like puzzle pieces? Why else would he be in agony without her? Someone, for good or evil, had put in front of him a woman he couldn't dismiss. *"I've been to see your mother, Yussele. She's taking the baths in Switzerland. She was covered with mud. I thought she was dead. I think I got through. She smiled. I think she's going to marry again. Someone rich. Where could she get the money to take mud baths in Switzerland?"*

His father wore the Milk of Magnesia blue mandarin silk pajamas, with the black-fringed belt, the blue slippers with gold Chinese medallions on their fronts, carried a soft overnight bag of Pierre Deux fabric, which Yussel recognized because Shoshanna once bought such a bag for her mother and Yussel couldn't believe how much it cost. His father's left door was a jalousie blind, slatted, enameled, electric blue aluminum. The other was the same lead door. He looked drained.

"I'll ask Babe. Listen, Totte. I'm in a situation."

"I know. Gevalt."

"I don't think I have any choice."

"He's taken away your free choice. So now you know free choice is intended."

"Shoshanna wants to leave, take Schmulke. Dina's very sick."

"I know."

"My money's gone. And this woman . . ."

"You're suffering. He's correcting the distance between you and Him. You're feeling the correction. The purpose of suffering is to correct the distance between you and HaShem. You get exactly the right amount of suffering for the same amount of correction. No more, no less."

"What if he takes my Dinela?"

"What if he takes any of us? Death is a miracle just like birth. He gives; He takes. He knows what He's doing."

"Totte," Yussel groaned, "what am *I* supposed to do?"

"Trust." His father pulled his hat down over his forehead. Yussel couldn't see his eyes.

"Okay, Lillywhite, I'll think about it."

"There's a train out of Denver on Sundays at six."

"Why a train?"

"So we can be alone."

Terror squeezed his heart. "I said I'll think about it."

"You can't see my soul for my tits, can you?"

Yussel knew why she'd been given to him. She was here to break his heart. He let her drive down the road first, watched the dust behind her car. When the dust cleared his father was leaning against Bingo's cab. His aluminum slats caught the sun.

"You got a new door?"

"*Lightweight. What a relief. It gets worse for you. It gets better for me. You're almost halfway there, Yussel.*"

"Totte!" Yussel groaned. "What's going to happen to me?"

He shrugged, brushed pine needles from his silken shoulders. "*You'll see. They don't want me to tell you anything. I can tell you stories. That's all. So come.*"

His father put the Pierre Deux overnight case on the flat rock, sat next to it, pointed for Yussel to sit with him, put one thin arm around him gently, held his own beard in his right hand. "*Once a Jew was sentenced to twenty-five years hard labor. For twenty-five years he stood grinding something. The grinder and the wheel were on one side of a wall. He had no idea what he was grinding. He just turned that wheel, day and night. He imagined maybe he was grinding wheat to feed a family, two families, a whole village. Maybe he was grinding stones into sand for building. Twenty-five years, he had a lot of maybes. At the end of the twenty-five years, his jailers released him. He was a ruined man. There was no strength left in him. He walked around the wall. He thought, now he would find out what he was grinding for all these years. He wouldn't mind if it had been grain, stones, as long as he was helping someone, accomplishing something. He got around the wall— there was nothing on the other side.*"

His father turned the handle on his jalousie, the louvers opened and closed. "*That's all I can give you. You'll get around to the Other Side, you'll see.*" His father pulled a handful of wax candles from the overnight, gave them to Yussel.

"What if He takes Dina?"

His father looked into Yussel's eyes. Yussel could feel the burning. "*I don't know, Yussele. This is a very complicated computer He has. If He takes, He takes. Who are we to question? My platform isn't high enough. It's only high enough to know He has a reason for everything and everything's intended.*"

"So he ruins my family, makes my kid sick?"

"*He gives you choices. Your choices determine your destiny. Only he knows the consequences. You told the young lady you'd think about it. I think you better think about it.*"

"What He asks is I should climb into bed with a strange woman?"

"Listen, he asked Abraham to kill his son, didn't He? Let's put this in perspective. This is what I mean by sublime: not to save Chaim's life would be a worse sin than a little yentzing, a little mixing it up with some wet muscles."

"No wonder you never had a respectable congregation."

"It surprises you I'm human?"

"Okay, Totte, say I sin. You know what worries me?"

"Your breath?"

"What if I like it?"

He ran his fingers up and down the jalousie like a keyboard. *"Yeah, well, that's the danger, Yussele. That you might stay over there. The slippery path gets narrower and narrower until there's no way to turn around."*

"It feels like there's no way to turn around now. It feels like He's asking me to kill my daughter."

His father shrugged. *"I don't know, Tottele, I'm attached. I do what He wants. You're not attached. You have to make the choices."*

"I'm really on the Other Side?"

"You expected a change of scenery? An intermission? I think when you gambled you went over."

"Totte," Yussel groaned, "I had to get the money."

"Maybe before."

"When?" Yussel cried out.

"When you figure that out you won't be there anymore."

27

THE BEDROOM AND bathroom were like a honeymoon suite at the Marriott Inn. Yussel was in the Jacuzzi when Reverend Bismark of Moffat phoned. "My adult education class? Mutual understanding?" Yussel yelled when Shoshanna repeated the Reverend Bismark's request. "Let Bismark teach his kids not to beat up my Schmulke."

Shoshanna had her hand over the mouthpiece. "Schmulke started it. You know that. Kids get mad. They use their fists. You can't blame them."

"Chaim started it by cheating half the people in Moffat."

"Yussy," she hissed, "he wants to know how many you can send?"

"My scalp diseases? Like Castro I should empty my asylums and send Bismark my crazies? Natalie? Grisha?"

"He'll send his bus over."

"Paper cups, coffee only. Nothing to eat. Not in his church. In his home. And he's not to mention Yoshke's name once. If he does, we get up and leave."

"He wants to know who Yoshke is." Shoshanna giggled.

"*I* should teach *him* who Yoshke is? Yoshke, Yoisel, the guy on the cross, tell him."

Very carefully, Shoshanna said, "Your gentleman on your cross." She was afraid of saying Jesus.

Yussel was sending seven plus the four kibbutzniks who couldn't understand a word of English. Babe took Grisha's suit to the cleaner's in Alamosa, ironed a white shirt. Shoshanna and Babe stood on each side of the door of the Assembly of God bus, checking fingernails and shoes. The Blondische wore her hiking boots but that was okay around Moffat. The four kibbutzniks wore terrorist camouflage gear. Babe wore all beige and no jewelry, not even her pearls. Grisha looked like he had been laid out. His suit two sizes too big, his skin two sizes too small. Natalie had to be sent back to change into a skirt. Shoshanna wanted to go only if Yussel would go. Yussel wouldn't. The bus was to pick up Mendl and Steinberg in case Bismark said anything Yussel's people shouldn't hear, couldn't respond to. Yussel stayed home. When Shoshanna went to the bathroom, he called Lillywhite, said very fast, "Not this Sunday and next Sunday I have to teach," hung up.

Later Yussel drove to the Arizona to meet the returning bus. His people were hoarse from singing "Yankee Doodle Dandy," talked only about forgiving their enemies, loving their neighbors, turning the other cheek. Yussel smoked, pushed his hat back off his head, listened, nodded. When they were finished, he said very softly, "Let me tell you something. If Schmulke had turned the other cheek, he'd have two black eyes."

There was a long embarrassed silence. Finally Yussel said into it: "Five thousand years Jews have learned something goyim don't know. You don't forgive your enemies. You forgive your friends."

Again a long silence. Ernie broke it. "Maybe it's time you started teaching us, Rabbi?"

There was another long silence. This time Yussel was embarrassed, finally said, "You're right."

WHEN IT WAS Yussel's turn to teach the Reverend Bismark's adult education class, Shoshanna again had to make the arrangements over the phone with Yussel yelling in the background. "What's the matter with you, Yussel? It's a wonderful challenge."

"Let Chaim's Steinberg do it. Let Chaim do it."

"Chaim can't put two words together."

"No covered dishes, no cameras. This isn't the Indian reservation. And you'll serve the cheap instant coffee, not my Zabar's French Roast. And tell them I don't shake hands with women."

Shoshanna made a sweet kugel from leftover challah, canned fruit salad, lots of eggs. She made the French Roast coffee, defrosted rugelach her mother mailed from Toronto. Yussel wore a black sweater over a white shirt, thought he looked a little like a college professor, brushed his eyebrows out from his forehead so he could examine everyone from underneath them.

Bismark sent thirteen, like a hostage exchange. Yussel took down the divider, let men and women sit together, greeted everyone at the door, pulled at his beard like a patriarch, examined them one by one from under his eyebrows. Three cheery ladies smelling of baby powder arranged themselves on the seats in the front row, smiled at him, took out needlepoint. Behind them the others took out notepads. Some he'd seen the night of the fire, also in the supermarket, in the bank, at the Rexall. They were, in a strange way, all neighbors. Part of him wanted to reach out, be neighborly, maybe enlighten and illuminate. The other part of him wanted to get even for what their kids had done to Schmulke, even though Schmulke deserved it. Rosebud, scrubbed and shiny in a three-piece western suit like his father's, smelling expensive, shook hands with Yussel too energetically. The ladies poised in their needlepoint, smiled little contemptuous smiles at one another. Indians and Jews, two of a kind.

Yussel knew what the Reverend Bismark's adult education class was thinking. They were thinking he killed Yoshke. They were thinking the Jew in front of them could be five thousand years old. They were thinking maybe that's what Moses looked like. Maybe even what Yoshke looked like.

Bismark wore a navy blue suit. He was very tall and thin. He might have been the mechanic from the Texaco, but he was so clean Yussel couldn't be sure.

He felt Lillywhite in the room before he saw her. He moved away from the crowd at the front, stood at the coffeepot. She came over. He growled, "What are you doing here?"

She smiled a surface smile. Her eyes were hot. "I'm looking for another door."

"There aren't any more doors, Lillywhite."

"I'm waiting for an answer about the train."

"I told you I had to think about it."

She drew her forefinger back and forth over her lips, weighed something, said almost under her breath, "There's a boy at my house. He says two words: Mama and fire. All day long, Mama and fire. I took his mother to your friend's house after you kicked her out. Be on the train or I'll start asking questions."

The ashes of his father's wife filled his mouth.

And then Shoshanna stood next to them holding a tray of cups and spoons. "Is this the famous Ms. Lillywhite?"

Yussel cleared his throat so he wouldn't choke on the ashes. Buried like a dog in Chaim's backyard, buried because Yussel threw her out. "Shoshanna, my wife. Lillywhite, our neighbor."

Shoshanna put the tray down very carefully, said, without looking up at Yussel or Lillywhite, "The Rabbi's told me a lot about you."

"Nothing bad, I hope," Lillywhite answered lightly.

"Oh, no. The Rabbi would never tell me anything bad." Shoshanna smiled brightly at Lillywhite and Yussel. "Well, enjoy the lecture. He's a wonderful storyteller."

With a terrifying frosty little smile on her face, Shoshanna watched Lillywhite fold herself into a children's desk chair in the back row, said to Yussel through her smile, "So maybe it wasn't you who told me about her. Maybe it was someone else."

His father stood at the grave, slapped him across the face. Chaim howled, buried his dogs.

"You have your speech, Yussel? You wrote it out?"

"They want to hear how the Jews killed Yoshke. That's what they came for. For that I don't need notes."

"Yussel! You're acting like Schmulke. Pull yourself together, Yussel. Act like a Fetner."

"*You* want to act like a Fetner? Be my guest. Don't tell *me* how to act."

Natalie came, bright-cheeked, sat beside Rosebud, swiveled around to stare at Lillywhite. Lillywhite looked only at Yussel, who sat in the front of the room, facing the chairs. Yussel looked at the light bulb, thought to Lillywhite, You want to know what makes us tick? You dare to come into my shul, talk to my wife, sit on seats my children sit on? But Lillywhite continued to sit in his shul, in the same room as his wife, in the same chair his children sat in, sat there, looked at him, rubbed her forefinger across her lips, said from behind it, he knew, You better be on that train.

What do you want from me, Lillywhite? My left ball or my right one? I didn't kill Jesus. I didn't kill your father. You didn't kill your father. Things happen. Take your tzuros and leave me alone. His speech to Lillywhite completed, Yussel gave a short formal welcome, told Reverend Bismark's class that it must have been intended their children were fighting because God wanted them all to get together and try to understand each other as long as they had to live in the same town, which induced nods and benign smiles. Then Yussel told them a little history of the Jews, paused now and then as he'd rehearsed, stared at them from under his eyebrows, gazed at the ceiling as if for inspiration, sprang his side curls boing boing against his ears, saw the Flower Child with Chaim, saw her hiding in the attic, heard her screaming, saw Chaim running around trying to go back into the house. All personnel accounted for? Mendl running around, counting. Mendl hadn't known either. All personnel accounted for. They were fascinated by the side curls. He pulled them out to their full twelve inches, right side, then left side, rolled them up in little anchovies, tucked them back in. Except for the three cheery ladies whose heads were bent over their needlepoint, the adult education class took diligent notes. When Yussel asked for questions, Bismark stood, cleared his throat, pulled at his collar, took a little notebook out of his pocket. Yussel watched his Adam's apple bob up and down. "We made up these questions, Reverend, before we came." He looked around, got approving nods. Yussel thought he might have seen him at the fire. He might have been one of the firemen. Chaim would go to jail for murder, for hiding the woman, for not telling anyone she was there.

"Question one." He was nervous and sincere. "We understand you all don't believe in the Messiah. Is that true?"

"*Believe* in him? My great-great-great-grandfather *saw* him."

"Saw Him?" It was Lillywhite. "What do you mean saw Him?"

"Yeah, saw him. I see you. He saw him."

Lillywhite pursed her lips, looked down, away. Shoshanna stood by the coffeepot, scowling. Knowing Yussel wouldn't stop her in public, Natalie was elbowing Rosebud. Bismark stood. "Your folks tell you what He looked like?"

Yussel shrugged. "What should an old Jew look like? A white beard? In a bad mood? A big nose? Overcharging? He said to my great-great-great-grandfather he wasn't coming because his generation wasn't ready for him."

Some chuckled, some sat silently offended. Yussel wanted blood. He wished Shoshanna would leave, which was maybe why she was staying. "You have some more questions on your list there?"

"Question two." The Reverend Bismark's voice was shaky, his Adam's apple was now a yo-yo. "Why did God make evil?"

He saw their heads bent over their notes, pencils ready for his truths. He wanted to enlighten and illuminate. He forgot Lillywhite. He forgot Shoshanna. He forgot Dina. He forgot Schmulke. He was in Yeshiva again, soaring like an eagle, the answers rolling out, his father's words, his father's father's words, commentaries, commandments, stories, meanings. "Let me tell you about evil. Once the Jews prayed to God to get rid of the evil inclination. So God answered their prayers and got rid of evil. The next morning when the Jews went down to the marketplace, they couldn't find a single egg." Everyone laughed. Yussel was elated. "So they went back and begged God to bring the evil inclination back, they'd learn to live with it. That's the difference between Christianity and Judaism."

The Reverend stood again, smoothed his hair, calmer, as if he'd won something. "Have the Jews learned to live with the Holocaust?" Bismark was the mechanic after all.

Yussel stood, snapped out one side curl, then the other. "Well, it goes like this. You heard we were the chosen. Let me tell you what we were chosen for—in case some of you thought it was for something terrific. A Jew is someone whose disobedience or obedience of the Torah's commandments determines the history of the world." Lillywhite raised her hand. He ignored her. To his routine of looking up at the ceiling for inspiration, examining them from under bushy eyebrows, and springing his side curls, he added a patriarchal stroking of the beard. "So if we disobey our command-ments, the whole world is in trouble. If you were to think about what it really means to be chosen, you'd know it wasn't so terrific. A Jew is responsible for everything that happens. Therefore, to answer your question, we're responsible for whatever happens to us. And to you. Maybe even the Holocaust. My father says we live in a universe where everything's intended." Lillywhite's head jerked up. Their eyes met. "No act, no event happens unless God wants it to happen. My father says everything is intended." It was the closest he had come to telling her he loved her. Someone else noticed, turned around to see who he was speaking to. Yussel forced himself to look away from her.

They wrote, underlined. Yussel soared. Maybe he was illumi-nating, enlightening. Maybe. In the rear a woman closed her note-book, dropped it into a shopping bag at her feet, took out a red-and-white checkerboard sweater, started knitting, moved her lips to count stitches. Suddenly Yussel realized how many thou-sands of other fools had tried to teach them, tried to explain, begged them for pity, pleaded for a child's life. How few Jews had ever succeeded in changing their minds, in winning a little pity, a little mercy, a place to live, a little land, a little sympathy, a shred of understanding. How many stand-up-comic saints had stood before them, hoping for a spark, a breakthrough behind the cataracts of distaste, begging for their lives. They nod, say Je-ew in two syllables, and murder you in your bed. Go home, ladies. Play duplicate bridge, make tomato aspic, hang curtains in your garage windows. "How many of you here think the Jews killed Jesus? Raise your hands."

Faces froze.

"So." Yussel glanced at Shoshanna. Her little mouth was opened in a silent scream like the jackrabbit on the electric fence. But he couldn't stop himself. "And how many of you here think the Romans killed Jesus?"

Hands shot into the air. Everyone was relieved. You want to see power, Lillywhite? I'll show you power. Watch. Shoshanna was now watching Lillywhite as if no one else were in the room. Lilly-white watched Yussel with the same intensity. You think, Yussel thought, a wife catches you kissing someone, looking at her body, whispering into a telephone. No. A wife catches a husband in love—she sees the deep pain on the other woman's face. It seemed, at that moment, less important a secret than that of Chaim and the Flower Child.

"Well, you're wrong. The Jews killed Jesus. You want to hear how?" Needles and pencils hung in midair.

"You ever meet a Jewish kid who's a wise guy? Like maybe my son? Well, two thousand years ago a very famous Rabbi in Jerusalem had a disciple who was a wise guy who always gave his teacher a hard time. He was a brilliant kid, no question. The Rabbi's sister was the queen and he said something to her she didn't like so she threw him out of the country and of course his disciple, this kid, Jesus . . ." Yussel heard some gasps. ". . . we call him Yoshke . . .went with his teacher. They went into Egypt and this kid for years gave his teacher a hard time. A million times his teacher tried to get rid of him, but he didn't because Jesus had all this potential."

"I never heard such a thing," the Reverend Bismark protested.

"Don't forget, we were there. You were in a cave in Europe chewing on your neighbor's cheekbone." Oh, Lillywhite, did you pick the wrong rabbi. And you too, Shoshanna. And you too, Totte. You got the wrong horse.

"So finally after many years the queen dies and the Rabbi starts out to return to Jerusalem. He and Jesus stop at an inn and the Rabbi says to Jesus. 'Look, isn't the wife of the innkeeper beautiful?' And Jesus answers, 'No, she has crooked eyes.' Well, that's the last straw. The Rabbi says, 'Leave me. You are no longer my pupil. I am talking about her soul. All you see is the outside of her, that her eyes are crooked. I do not want you for a pupil any longer.'" Yussel watched his audience cringe. Shoshanna hadn't taken her eyes off Lillywhite, maybe didn't hear, maybe would have stopped him if she'd been listening.

"So he kicked Jesus out. Now he couldn't be a rabbi. Maybe the Rabbi couldn't take a joke. Maybe Jesus wasn't joking. Who knows. Anyway he kicked him out. Well, your Jesus, he was furious. It was like being kicked out of medical school because you argued with your professor. And he's going to show them. So on Yom Kippur, which is the holiest day of the year for us, he goes to the temple in Jerusalem and he takes with him a pin. On Yom Kippur in those days, the holiest moment was when the high priest went into the Holy of Holies and spoke the secret Name of God. All the people heard the Name and they became like angels. At sundown they passed out of the temple between two gold lions that roared and the people forgot the secret Name and were again ordinary people. But when Jesus heard the Name, he scratched it on his knee so when he went out between the lions he still had the name. So Yoshke, even though they wouldn't let him be a rabbi, was still like an angel. And he flew around the courtyard over everyone's head so everyone could tell he still had the Name. Then he went out and healed people and did wonders with the Name that only the high priests were supposed to do. It was like the Rosenbergs stealing the atom bomb secrets and handing them out in the supermarket. So the ruling body went after him. They gave him forty days to prove he hadn't used the Name of the Lord in vain, but of course he couldn't prove it, nor did he want to prove it, so they stoned him to death. That, folks, is how the Jews killed Jesus. Instead of crossing yourself, you should be hitting yourself on the head." Yussel banged on his head with his knuckles.

The Reverend Bismark was the first to shake himself, look around, stand, put his arms around two of his flock, lead them out. The others followed. Rosebud paused, caught Yussel's eye, smiled, left. No one said good night. In moments the room was empty except for a lot of kugel, the gurgling coffeepot of Zabar's French Roast. Shoshanna looked at him sideways, poured a cup of coffee, handed it to Yussel, unplugged the pot, said, "Whatever Chaim started, you finished. You've exposed us all. I'm taking the children home." And walked out of the room.

After they could no longer hear Shoshanna's footsteps, Lillywhite said softly, "What else does your father say?"

"My father says there's an angel behind every blade of grass and each angel whispers to each blade, 'Grow, darling, grow.' I have never believed that. My father says . . ." Yussel couldn't stop. Tears burned his cheeks. "My father says everything's intended. My wife's leaving. That's intended. I'm in love with you. That's intended. I kicked the Flower Child out and sent her to her death.

How can such things be intended?"

From her child's chair, Lillywhite said, "Your father's dead. Why do you say 'my father says'?"

"Because we talk. Because he tells me everything. I don't listen. I can't hear. He tried to tell me about the Flower Child of blessed memory. I didn't listen." They sat facing each other, Lillywhite and Yussel. "He told me to pay attention. I didn't see what I should have seen. I stepped on the angels. I didn't look."

"You and your father talk to each other?" There was something ferocious in the way she asked the question. "And he's dead."

Yussel remembered Chaim howling, remembered him yelling that blood would be on his hands, remembered his father slapping him across the face. Lillywhite stood above him. "I want to talk to my father. I don't want to tell anyone about people dying in fires. So be on the train."

Once Yussel was selling single-life premiums to his cousin Asher. Asher's kids were watching the Atlanta 500 on a six-foot TV screen. The cars and the drivers were larger than life. Yussel and Asher shouted fixed rates and variable rates over the scream of engines. Finally Asher's wife came in and told the kids to turn the TV off. They turned the sound off. In the moment Yussel watched the silent race, a red car pulled into the pit, four mechanics surrounded it, one spilled gas on the fender, the fender ignited, the mechanic jumped back into the track and another car killed him. All without losing a beat. There could not have been a vengeance more precise, a heavenly intention more perfectly delivered. Yussel put the Flower Child in Chaim's head. Chaim fell for her. Yussel threw her out, put her into Chaim's house, didn't sell him homeowner's, couldn't convince the firemen to put out the fire, ruled Chaim shouldn't go inside. And now the woman his father said was intended was holding the evidence that Chaim murdered the Flower Child, certainly allowed her to die. It was the same chain of events. He had no way out. This he'd brought on himself not because he'd lusted for the Flower Child or fallen in love with Lillywhite, but because he'd ignored them. He'd made Yoshke's error, just as Lillywhite said. He couldn't see their souls for their tits. "Sunday," he said to Lillywhite, "I'll be on the train. Sunday."

Yussel closed the door after her, rammed his hand through the wood, heard the popping of bones and cartilage, felt the pain sweep into his heart, saw the hole he'd made, knew he'd broken his bones, wanted them broken. He was broken. He looked up to the ceiling. "You win. You hear me, HaShem? You win."

28

THE NEXT DAY Ruiz took him to a large animal clinic that had the only X ray for hundreds of miles. Yussel lay in a room next to a black-and-white calf with a broken leg and a nozzle over its face while the vet X-rayed Yussel's hand and arm. Ruiz made a cast for his hand. Dinela drew pictures of cats and dogs and square leaves from Paradise all over it in blue Magic Marker. Shoshanna wasn't speaking to him. He told Shoshanna's back he was taking them all home. First he told her he was going back East to talk to his uncles, get money, set up a business, maybe buy into a Weight Watchers franchise, talk to Ruchel, see if he could help. He'd be gone a week, no more, then he'd come back, get them, and they'd go home. He called his Uncle Nachman at Yale, told him he'd be there at the end of the week, told Shoshanna he was taking the train because he needed time to think, time to himself. She seemed to understand, said she'd drive him to Denver because she'd decided not to wait any longer to take Dina to a doctor. They didn't speak to each other. They just said the things they had to say. The car needs gas. Do you have enough cash? I put food in your briefcase. Yussel didn't even try to talk her out of driving him to the train, decided if it were intended she should see Lillywhite, she'd see Lillywhite. It was that simple. She never mentioned his cast.

When he told Babe he was leaving for a week and she had to

take Grisha to live with her on the bus, she said, "You're crazier than your father," stormed around the bus, slammed doors. "Where will I get undressed?"

Yussel let her storm, then said, "He's got to be watched. You'll figure out where to get undressed."

"You think he'll want to?" Babe asked softly.

Yussel shrugged. "He has to."

"So if he has to, he has to." Babe gathered courage. "I'll tell him. I'll *make* him!" Babe called after him from her bus door so everyone could hear, "I want you to know, I never heard of such a thing!"

Then he went to Chaim's, yelled at Mendl loud enough so Chaim could hear, "I came to say good-bye. I insist on seeing Reb Chaim. I insist. I need his blessing for my trip."

Mendl and Yussel stood at the bottom of the stairwell, watched the doorknob turn slowly on Chaim's door, watched the door open a half-inch, an inch. Yussel climbed the stairs, let himself in, nearly fainted. Chaim had lost twenty or thirty pounds. Under his eyes the skin was black like cannonballs. Yussel hugged him so he didn't have to look at him, said over Chaim's shoulder. "I understand. I know and I understand." Chaim wept in torrents. Yussel felt Chaim's tears on the back of his shoulder, sinking in. "I'm doing everything I can no one should know. When I get back, we'll talk. We have to talk, Chaim. You understand? You're not alone."

"No."

"We'll talk. Give me your blessing."

Chaim mumbled something, drifted off.

Yussel said, "Amen," anyway, squeezed Chaim hard. Mendl led him out. They couldn't look at each other.

BABE MADE them take her Lincoln to Denver. Yussel wrapped Dina in a quilt, tucked her into the front seat of the Lincoln, pulled his hat down over his face, sank into leathery depression in the backseat. Shoshanna drove. Dina curled up, put her head in Shoshanna's lap. Shoshanna sang to her. When they stopped at the Texaco for gas, Shoshanna held her head high, spoke crisply and politely to Reverend Bismark. Yussel made believe he was sleeping. By ten that night they'd get to Pueblo, sleep over, drive to the train station first thing in the morning. Yussel's father sat next to him in the backseat, pushed his hat off his forehead. In flashes of light from oncoming traffic, Yussel saw two aluminum jalousie doors. His father clicked the slats of his doors open and closed. Yussel shook his head in the dark. "Am I doing this because I'm supposed to or because I want to?"

"Maybe both." His father put his hand on Yussel's knee. Yussel remembered his mother's touch on his forehead when he had a fever. *"Listen, I knew other guys on earth . . . an extra wife in Utica; another family in Hempstead. They didn't get struck down. They led long and productive lives. A little busy."* His father patted Yussel's knee, spoke intensely. *"It's only a day and a half on the train, Yussele. Big deal, a day and a half. I'm looking at eternity."* He leaned over the front seat, over Dinela, sang along with Shoshanna, soft lullabies, prayers. Yussel slept, prayed, slept. His father shook him awake once. *"Yussele, wake up. I have to tell you something. No matter what happens, on the train, I'll always be near you. Your world, my world, any world you're in, we're side by side, like envelopes in a dark drawer. Not even, not that separate, but I don't know how else to explain it. I can move round from envelope to envelope in the drawer. I even went to Horodenka!"*

"No! You saw everybody?"

"It wasn't so terrific. Filth, cold, murder, disease, hunger, humiliation. The people wore rags, bark on their feet. Fools, saints in long white gowns, dancing, begging, drinking, studying, praying. Their wives weeping, their kids starving. I'm sorry I went. Maybe the reason HaShem destroyed the Jews in Europe was so we shouldn't look backward any more. Maybe that's why we're in America. So we look forward."

"What's forward."

"That's what I want to tell you." He nodded, agreeing with himself, some inner voice, God knows who. *"You know how many words are in the Torah?"*

"Millions."

"One. Listen. One long word, the name of God, written in dark fire. No grammar, no punctuation, no sound. It's the blueprint for creation. But until men give it sound, it means nothing. Until it's

brought into human affairs, it waits like yeast, someone should come along and give it a new shape, add the light, add the white space between the letters to make words. The shapes from our past . . . maybe they don't fit into our time. Maybe this is for your generation to do. Maybe that's why Europe is in ashes. Baruch HaShem."

"You should have been a rabbi."

"Very funny."

"Who can make the new words?"

"The sages said the Torah has seventy faces. Seventy interpretations. It's time." He held Yussel by the shoulders, looked above him toward the mountains. *"Who but you would understand this?"*

"Totte, you hear about the old Jew who walked into the SS recruiting office before the war? He comes in half-blind, crippled, palsied. He goes up to the Nazi recruiter and says, 'I just came in to tell you, on me you shouldn't count.'"

THE PEOPLE in the room next to theirs at the Pueblo Ranchero were making love. Their pressed oak headboard banged against the wall behind Yussel's head, shook his pressed oak headboard. Shoshanna slept peacefully on the other bed, Dina snuggled alongside her. Probably Shoshanna heard the same noises he heard but was faking sleep, being brave. Yussel held the pillow tightly over his ears, tried to think about the future. Berel had written that the new agent who had Yussel's territory was a Reform Jew, so nobody was taking from him because a Reform Jew in the eyes of Yussel's friends and relatives was a Christian, which meant Yussel could now get his territory back. He'd borrow enough from his uncles to set up the business, get his family. In a couple of years he'd be liquid again, walking along the boardwalk, sitting out on the jetties watching the waves, lying in his bed with the windows open, listening to the roar of the ocean in a storm, walking over to Edgemere Avenue for fresh bagels and the Sunday *Times*. That's all he wanted. He tried not to hear the woman's cries, the man's rough groans, tried not to think about the train ride, not to think about Lillywhite, tried not to think whether he would, should, could, whether Lillywhite would demand he do things he wasn't allowed to do, things they'd whispered about in Yeshiva, things nobody would believe anybody in their right minds would do to each other or allow to be done to themselves, things they were doing in the next room in the Pueblo Ranchero. He wiped his hands on his pajamas. "This is what You want?" he asked HaShem. "This is really what You want from me?"

THE AMTRAK station was a grand old high-ceilinged building falling to pieces. Pigeons flew in and out of the broken glass panes in the ceiling. "The first stop, I'll call."

"I won't know right away. He'll take blood tests, maybe X rays, maybe biopsies. I won't know."

"I can call anyway, can't I?"

He bought a ticket on the California Zephyr with a connection to the Lakeshore Limited in Chicago, forced himself not to look around for Lillywhite, picked up Dina, squeezed her tight. She whimpered, "Totty, Totty!" A drop of Dina's blood stained his cuff. He looked over Dina's head at Shoshanna who stood so small, so scared, her butterfly wing eyes wet, her eyelashes glistening. "Listen, Shoshanna, I'll be back in a week. I'll call every minute I can. If you can't reach me, you'll call Uncle Nachman at Yale. If you have a problem, you'll call Mendl. If you need money, you'll borrow from Babe. Everything will be okay. I promise you, Shoshanna, in less than a month, we'll take a walk after supper on the beach. You hear me? I'll buy you an ice cream sandwich and we'll take off our shoes and walk on the beach." Leaving her was like cutting his own veins. "Totty! Totty!" Dina screamed at his back. In her scream he heard the woman's cries at the Pueblo Ranchero, Chaim's howl at the Flower Child's grave.

The first time his father had come to him after he'd died, he'd asked, *"Yussele, do you feel pain?"* Yussel had answered no. Now he didn't know what it was like not to feel pain. Look at Shoshanna. Listen to Dinela. Her cry is glass breaking in my heart.

His father boarded the train with him, took his arm. The aluminum slats of his doors glinted in the morning sunlight. He wore safari-style khaki pajamas, khaki mules, and a quilted calico jacket, an Abercrombie and Kent safari flight bag, took a runway turn, hand on hip, smiled coyly. *"I told them I was taking an overnight trip, so they give me a smoking jacket and safari gear. The jacket's okay, isn't it? I mean without the safari stuff? You think it's too busy in Pierre Deux?"*

"I'm about to lose my portion in the World to Come and you're talking smoking jackets."

His father clicked his jalousies like castanets. *"There's a paradox for you, Tottele. You get stripped, I get covered."*

YUSSEL DIDN'T see Lillywhite on the train as he walked through the cars. He found his compartment: greasy walls, a narrow bunk, a crisp white linen napkin pinned to the pillow. Yussel put his things neatly overhead, stuck the ticket in his pocket, tried to breathe. He slid his briefcase under the seat, gave the conductor his ticket, went into the corridor to find some water, found Lillywhite in a gorgeous white silk suit. She pressed against the wall of the narrow aisle to make room for him. He flattened himself against the corridor like a fruit tree gardeners train to climb walls. Even so, his body swelled, stretched out toward her. People with luggage, porters with trays pushed past them.

"Let's get inside," Yussel suggested smoothly.

Lillywhite opened the door behind her, sat on the lower bed. Yussel closed the door, turned a chair around so the back faced the bed, straddled it so the back caged his business. "So?" he said, meaning nothing. "Here we are."

"I had to do this."

"How did this happen to us?"

Her legs looked silky. Lillywhite put a pillow behind her, lay back against the wall, curled up a little more. Her skirt rose above her knees. She sighed.

"What do you want?" He could see the outline of her belly.

"Teach me," she whispered so softly Yussel had reason to hope he'd heard "Touch me."

Yussel let go of his breath enough to say sure. The word escaped from him like steam from an engine. "Sure." So she was being coy. "So, what do you want?"

She curled up on the bed. Yussel unwound his legs from the chair. "What do you want?"

"Make believe I'm your son and it's the first day and you're teaching me. Teach me the first day."

"This is what you want?" Maybe this was teasing. Frum women don't know about teasing. They wear perfume and think they're teasing. They make a kugel and think they're flirting.

"We have all day and all night. So I'll ask to begin at the beginning. Teach me as you'd teach your son."

He sat down next to her. Lillywhite took a little curl toward him, slight, but in the right direction. Yussel wondered if they both had their feet off the floor would that constitute the act and therefore, without him doing anything really, could his father then go to Heaven?

"We take our sons to cheder on the first day. For each letter he gets a little honey so he knows learning is sweet."

"That's it. Wait. Wait here." She left the room, left the door open. Yussel sat on the bed, tried to catch his breath, relax, figure out what she really wanted, how she would tell him, how he'd agree, whether he had it to give to her. She came back with a handful of little white-and-gold packets of honey, red spots on her cheeks, closed the door behind her, sat on the bed beside him.

"Give me honey with each letter." She handed him the packets. "As if I'm your son."

"For this I have to run away from home? For this you have to blackmail me, ruin me, my friend?"

She stuck her tongue out. It was astonishingly naked. You want a little skirt for it, Yussel? It's just a tongue. "Okay, okay." Yussel squeezed a drop of honey on her tongue, watched it retreat, watched her lick her lips, licked his. "Okay, first letter. Watch my mouth." Maybe this was her way to get him to relax. He opened his mouth and said, "Aleph." She opened hers and said, "Aleph." He squeezed more honey on her tongue. Her breath tickled his lips. He made a little kiss to show her bes. She made a little kiss and said, "Bes." He fed her another lick of honey. He could taste the inside of her mouth. He decided to get her on the lamed. He moved quickly through gimmel, daledh. She followed. Her face was inches from his. "Lamed. You touch the roof of your mouth with your tongue." She stuck her tongue out, then touched the roof of her mouth with it.

She smiled up at the ceiling, her chest rose and fell. Yussel's clothes felt tight all over. His breath was short. Lillywhite's face was an inch from his, maybe less. She was very excited. He wanted to feel her come, to sing out his name, that's what he wanted.

"Go on," she insisted. "Lamed, then what?"

He went on. It was torture. He loved it. At the end she repeated the alphabet for him, hesitated, let him fill in, did it finally by herself, grinned, clapped her hands. "I love it. I love it. Thank you. I love it. Now tell me about the letters. Tell me about Torah."

"Lillywhite, this is what you want?"

"Let me tell you another dream I had. You put your arm around my shoulder. We were in an elevator. In my dream I couldn't understand why you were touching me, but then your arm became bread, a long bread arm holding me, nourishing me. You just told me what the dream meant."

He put his arms around her, leaning toward her, felt the soft fat pressure of her breasts against his arm, her hair brushing his cheek. "Take a bite. See if it's bread."

She sat up, pulled her skirt back over her knees. "You're not listening to me."

"I'm listening to every breath you take, to every beat of your heart, every rustle of . . ."

She didn't move. She stared at him, reading him, "You said that door was closed. Leave it closed." She pushed him away. "The eyes of the innkeeper's wife are crooked."

He remembered what his father said about shame versus cancer. If they offer you a choice between shame and cancer, take the cancer. "I . . . thought you wanted . . . what the hell am I doing here? Why did you make me come on the train? What the hell are *you* doing here? I better go." Yussel went into his compartment, locked the door, slid the chain across it, climbed into his bed, pulled the pillow over his face. The honey was still on his fingertips.

IN CHICAGO, in the evening, they had to change trains. She walked with him to a bank of telephones, waited as he called Shoshanna, lit a cigarette. He couldn't look at her. There were no results yet, but Dina's color was a little better. And her appetite.

He should call tomorrow. They boarded the Lake Shore Limited, took their separate compartments. Lillywhite asked if he wanted to sit with her in the dining car while she ate dinner. He said no.

She said, "Listen, I just figured it out before you did. It's not that . . . that it wouldn't have been wonderful."

He said, "I don't want to talk about it. I'll see you in the morning." He closed his door, turned the key, slid the chain across it, turned his face to the wall, heard her close her door, was grateful, furious, ashamed, grieved. In his mind he went through the aleph bes with her, couldn't get to the toff. He slept on and off during the night, rocking between panic and fury.

HE HAD NO idea how she got into his compartment. She was sitting on his bed, touching his face. He woke up. She reminded him for a moment of Pecky. "I'm scared to be alone tonight. I want to be with you."

"Wait. Let me get up and wash my hands."

She stood by the sink, watched him pour water, from a blue plastic pitcher with two handles, over one hand and the fingertips of the broken hand. She held out her hands. He spilled the water on his pajamas, refilled the pitcher, poured water on each of her hands, made the blessing. He saw her smiling in the mirror as he dried her hands for her. She repeated the blessing very slowly, whispering. Then he laid down on the bed and she sat down beside him.

"I had a terrible dream about graves and suffocating and then a wonderful dream. I'll tell you my wonderful dream. I dreamed of dancing with you in your long robes and golden slippers and that beard in a golden room, waltzing around and around with you, breathless, someplace high, glorious, a palace with gardens and waterfalls and magical lights and tiny white deer. You took me into the paths, down the lanes of gardens with fruit trees. The trees had square leaves. I knew I was someplace else. Around and around you turned me until I couldn't see and I just clung to you and you were smiling that smile I saw the first time I saw you and your eyes were filled with light and I loved as I'd never loved anyone, anything, any idea in my life, and yet it felt as if I always had.

You wore golden shoes and I remember thinking they had to use a lot of gold because your feet were so big. We danced in the gardens all night. Once I saw couples coming from a grove of apple trees. They weren't human. Two by two, these very delicate couples walked toward me from under the apple trees . . . a long line of them. They were pale and small, like aliens from a movie, unformed, maybe gray, although the grass and the trees were clearly green. They were coming from the tree and I think I knew in my dream that it was a Paradise tree. I knew for sure in my dream that they meant heavenly marriages."

"Souls travel while you sleep. Your soul went very far."

"I'm sorry we didn't make love. It was wrong. It isn't why I wanted you to come."

"I didn't know that."

She lay her head on his chest. "I did. I've known that . . . that's why I wanted you to open another door." She lay her hand very lightly on his. "For a long time I'll be making believe it's you when I'm with someone else. You know that."

"I can't. That's not the way to conceive."

"That's okay."

"My baby's really dying, Lillywhite."

"Because of us?"

"I'm not sure. Because of me, maybe."

"Teach me to say Kaddish."

"Here? At two in the morning?" No one would believe this one. "Will you?"

"Sure. It won't matter, you know. Women don't say it. It won't mean anything."

"I want to say a prayer for my father."

Yussel let out a big breath, put his hands over his head, hit his cast on the wall by mistake, flinched with pain, wondered if it were a sign. Signs. So what. He was finished with signs, with all of it. He was finished. The only sign he expected was a train crash. They'd find the both of them burned to death, lying in the same bed. "Kaddish isn't a prayer for the dead. It's an exaltation of God."

"I don't want to be scared tomorrow. I don't want to lose it. I don't want to be afraid. I want to talk to him."

"Kaddish raises the soul of the dead to higher rungs. But a son has to say it. It doesn't do anything if a woman says it. But I'll be happy to teach it to you." He gave her his pillow, made a pillow for himself out of his bathrobe, wished his pajamas weren't soaked, wondered why he wasn't excited, why his parts weren't popping out of his pajamas, was grateful, felt gracious. First she learned it in English, word for word. Then she learned it in Hebrew. She wept the first time she said it by herself in Hebrew. He wiped her eyes with the corner of his bathrobe. She said it again and again and again. Yussel fell asleep while she was saying it. When Yussel woke up she was gone. He was sleeping on his bathrobe. The pillow was still warm next to him where she'd been. He washed his hands, made a blessing, talked to HaShem. "All right? You'll leave me alone now? You'll let me go home to the ocean? I did it. I didn't do all of it, but some of it. That's what You wanted? That's what You got. I'm finished. We're finished."

The train was rocking along the Hudson. He saw sailboats and barges, utility poles, other trains along the tracks. He knocked on her door. She was dressed in her white suit.

"I thought you'd never get up," she said. "Let's get some breakfast."

Yussel followed her through the train, swaying, grabbing the backs of seats, toward the dining car, sat in front of a vase with a yellow rose in it. She ordered an enormous breakfast. He drank coffee, watched her, waited for her to say something about sleeping in his bed. Finally, he asked, "Lillywhite, last night. How did you get into my room?"

"Me? I never left my room."

"I poured water over your hands and I spilled it on my pajamas and my pajamas are wet."

"I never left my room."

"Did you dream?"

"No." She blushed. He'd never seen her blush.

"Tell me the truth."

"Yes. I had frightening dreams about falling in a grave and suffocating and then I dreamed I was lying next to you and I felt better. I told you a dream and you washed my hands and taught me to thank God that He returned my soul to me."

"You told me about leaves."

"Square leaves. Yes. I saw square leaves on a fruit tree. How would I get in your room?"

He'd slept with her soul. She left her animal soul in her room, came to him with her Neshama. She looked up at him over a fork-ful of pork sausage. He shook his head.

"What's the matter? The pork?"

"I saw your soul."

"It's about time. Listen, before we get in, would you write out the Kaddish so I can read it over in the cab?"

29

THEY TOOK A cab to Queens, double-parked in front of a Greek bakery on Woodhaven Boulevard. Lillywhite bought a bag of almond cookies, counted the cookies in the bag, ate three. Sugar hung on her lips. He still wanted her. At least his animal soul still wanted her. It also wanted the cookies.

"Three weeks ago my baby held a square leaf in her hand. That's why I stopped calling you. Soon I'll visit her in the cemetery." Yussel pressed his face against the glass of the cab window, watched his tears roll down the glass, slip into the ashtray.

"Maybe the square leaf means she's being cured."

Yussel took Lillywhite's hand, held it until the cab pulled up at the gray fieldstone office of Mount Lebanon Cemetery.

FROM BEHIND a wall of computers, a big-shot clerk examined Yussel suspiciously, agreed to let them store their luggage for an hour, ignored Lillywhite. Lillywhite waited. Yussel tried to reach home. There was no answer. He called Babe, watched Lillywhite writing out a name for the clerk that Yussel knew wasn't going to be Lillywhite. She looked the way Yussel had first seen her, crackling with neon fear. She shook her hair defiantly, shifted from foot to foot, tapped her boot on the stone floor. Babe didn't answer. It didn't matter. Yussel knew the answer. The clerk brought up the name, gave Lillywhite a map, made an orange x on it, pointed up the road. "Block fifteen, Gate A."

She walked ahead of him in big strides, her boots banging on the cobblestones of the road, echoing. He knew she was being brave. Armies of headstones crowded each hill: marbles for the rich, markers for the poor, black granite tree trunks for the young men cut off in their prime, little gray stone sheep for dead babies. When Lillywhite was too far ahead of him, she turned, marched back, circled him again. He tried to think of her agony, tried not to think of his, smiled at her each time. Once she said, "When I met you, you were as afraid of life as I was afraid of death." She was filled with light as she had been in the flood. But this time it wasn't angry light. It was softer, golden. They climbed through a weave of iron gates, stone columns, arches, winding roads, little dolmen hills, past a work crew planting a headstone into the ground, nailing the pain of life back into the earth. The crew leaned on their shovels, watched Lillywhite swinging up the path. She opened the rusted Victorian wrought-iron fencing to Block 15, Gate A, waited for Yussel to catch up. Yussel caught up, read the sign on the gate. "I should have known. Damn him. I should have known. We're related, Lillywhite Stevie. I never heard of you. We have no redheads. But you're from Horodenka."

"I never heard of you. We have no rabbis. Horse thieves."

"Baruch HaShem, I hope it's not too close. Incest is worse than fornication."

"We didn't do anything."

"Some of us slept together."

"Yes, but I forgot to bring my tits." She was right. He was no longer afraid.

The rules of the Horodenka Burial Society were incised in Hebrew on a bronze plaque on one side of the gray stone arch. On the other side of the arch, in English. It didn't surprise Yussel that Block 15, Gate A was the property of the descendants from Horodenka, that Lillywhite's roots were in Horodenka, that she was a relative, or almost a relative. Nothing surprised Yussel about her. A great oak trembling with wrens fanned the hill. The afternoon sun cast diamonds on the headstones, coals on their backs. Yussel followed Lillywhite up a footpath of broken slabs. Lillywhite drew her hand over every stone she passed. City sounds rose, blended with the chatter of the wrens, a drill on stone, someone shrieking, someone blowing his nose, soft weeping behind a gravestone. It was his father—a study in a jacquard silk maroon-and-gold-striped shawl-collared bathrobe to the floor, under it, silk notch-collared pajamas of traditional gold-flecked maroon challis. His father walked beside him. *"Look around, Yussele. Pebbles on the graves from a thousand visitors, a million visits, scattered like seed on the graves for new generations. All this behind you."*

Lillywhite's name was Storch. It meant nothing to Yussel; he'd never heard it. The monument was the largest on the hill, a black marble building with columns, portico, matching bench for visitors. No pebbles. Yussel picked up pebbles, put one on a shelf of the monument, handed one to Lillywhite. She kept the pebble, put her bag of cookies on the shelf, sat on the bench in front of it. His father sat down next to Yussel.

"That's some monument." Her legs were still silky, her hair like spiderwebs against his cheek. He could smell the sharp liquid soap from the train.

"It's for all the babies he killed." She turned on the bench, looked up at Yussel expectantly. "There I go again. I can't help it. You better tell me what to say."

"Ask him to forgive you. Tell him you forgive him."

"That's all?" Lillywhite covered her face with her hands, whispered, "Daddy." Stood up, walked around the bench, challenged Yussel, "Aren't you going to do anything?"

"Talk to him. It doesn't matter what you say. What matters is that you came."

"Daddy . . . I want to say, if you're listening, forgive me. Forgive me. Okay? I'm sorry." She shook her head from side to side, snapped at Yussel, "It's not enough. Why can't I say what a son would say? Why do daughters have to be without words? What if your daughter doesn't die? What will she say for you?"

Yussel shrugged. "My son says Kaddish for me. For my daughters there's nothing else."

"Tell me what to say."

"I told you, there's nothing."

"Where's the napkin?"

Yussel dug into all his pockets, couldn't find it. "It must be in my briefcase. Look, Lillywhite. You need a minyan to say Kaddish. Also you have to be a son. I told you. It wouldn't mean anything. We could find a shul someplace, with a minyan." He looked at his watch, blushed at his impotency. "In a couple of hours."

"That I could do by myself." She grabbed him by the arm. "I want the words. Forget the rules; tell me the words."

Yussel shook Lillywhite off, walked around the Horodenka hill, wives, sons, daughters, husbands, sorrows, young men, young wives, infants. His father walked with him. *"Look at her, your Lillywhite. How have we done this? What have we done to our daughters, Yussele, that they have no words for their sorrows? They don't have the same sorrows?"* Then Yussel's father cocked his head, held his heart, listened. Very deliberately Lillywhite recited the alphabet in Hebrew, over and over again, in a strong voice, like an actress.

"Aleph. Bes. Gimmel. Daledh. . . ." She spoke with agony and passion, her forehead pressed against the marble, her arms extended, her palms flat on the cold side of the monument, and called out the sacred letters. Her letters echoed around the gravestones.

Yussel stood beside her. A cold wind picked up, blew leaves around the stones. Lillywhite shivered, kept saying the aleph bes. Yussel put his arm around her, whispered, "Remember the taste of the honey," recited the letters with her. He knew he'd never touch her again. He said the letters with Lillywhite, for her, for Dina, for Shoshanna, for the agony of this awesome soul beside him who had no words because the men in the generations behind him had kept the words to themselves.

Yussel pressed his forehead against the freezing marble. "Two days ago, Lillywhite, I thought you'd break my heart because I couldn't make love to you or I tried and you laughed at me. Or I'd left my wife and kids for you and then you left me. I didn't imagine you'd break my heart with something you didn't have, you who have everything. I watch a daughter at her father's grave and she has no words to say. This is the law, the way it must be. And for this, my heart breaks."

Yussel's father, his hands shoved into his bathrobe pockets, stood next to him, shook his head from side to side. *"I can hear your heart breaking, Yussele. The angels can hear it. Like a tree cracking in a storm."* He waved his arm over the Horodenka dead, toward the city below and then, oddly, included Lillywhite. *"Well, Yussele, what was, was. What will be is up to you. Pay attention to what is being asked of you now."*

"You know I'm going to your brothers to get money to take my family home. You know I'm quitting."

"That's tomorrow. Pay attention to this moment. The lady wants to say Kaddish."

"What meaning can it have?"

"The world is created by the letters and answered by the sounds. Give her the sounds. Let HaShem decide what He wants to hear."

Pecky came up the path. Yussel saw the cigar, the Church's oxfords, the thin shroud. He came like an old king, dragging a white fringed satin canopy from a grave, nodded at Yussel, shook ashes from a cigar with his forefinger, nodded at Lillywhite, who didn't see him. Tears streaked his face.

"Pecky? Hello, Pecky," Yussel said. "What are you doing here?"

"My daughter." He choked on his tears, lifted his hands toward Lillywhite. *"My little baby girl, praying for me. How about that?"* Pecky opened the bag of cookies on his grave, ate.

"Pecky, Totte? Lillywhite?"

"Once you make the deal, Yussele, everything becomes intentional."

"She's not praying, Totte. She's reciting the alphabet."

Pecky looked up. *"We heard prayer. I say she's praying."*

His father adjusted the canopy on Pecky's shoulders, tied nervous knots in the fringes. *"Yussele, go teach her the Kaddish."*

"For what?"

"If she can bring her father up from Hell with the alphabet, just think what she could do with the Kaddish. Go."

So Yussel sang the Kaddish to Lillywhite as he had sung it on the first Shabbas. In a graveyard with all your ancestors listening, even if only another branch, with your own father and another soul listening, with a love for Lillywhite that broke his heart, Yussel, in what he knew would be his last act as a rabbi, sang the Kaddish slowly for her, "Yisgadal, viyiskadash . . ." His voice cracked and broke, rose and fell. Lillywhite sang along, then she sang alone, softly at first, then louder, then so loud and strong, leaves rose and tumbled around her boots. Yussel remembered his first

Sabbath at the Arizona when he'd sung Kaddish, when his voice soared as hers soared now, when he'd saved her from the eighteen-wheeler. Something very bright in her face looked like what he had felt that Sabbath. "Exalted and sanctified be His great Name in the world which He created according to His will and may He rule His Kingdom—"

"Hey, Reb," a workman called from the other side of the hill. "Tell her to stop. We're not supposed to listen to a woman sing."

"She's saying Kaddish."

"I don't care what it is. Just tell her to shut up."

"Go on, Lillywhite, go on."

"May His great Name be blessed forever and for all eternity," Lillywhite sang. The stones rang around her.

An old Jew in a long coat stood in front of her, beat at her arm with a prayer book. "Are you mishugge, girlie? You can't say Kaddish. Are you mishugge? Why are you letting this woman say Kaddish, Rabbi? You're not going to stop her? You want we should report you?"

"I'm not singing for you," Lillywhite said to the old Jew. "I'm singing for my father."

Two workmen came from the other side of the Fetner hill, yelled at her, threw a few pebbles near her feet. They were frightened. Yussel stood next to Lillywhite. The workmen tossed more pebbles. A small crowd gathered from other plots, shook their heads, tried to persuade Yussel to make her stop singing, tried to make the workmen stop throwing stones. A pile of leaves smoked in a corner of the monument, burned. Yussel stomped out the fire. It smoldered and relit itself like a trick birthday candle.

"Blessed and praised," Lillywhite sang, "glorified and exalted and uplifted . . ." She shoved the old Jew off with her elbow. ". . . and extolled. Name of the Holy One, blessed is He, above all the blessings and hymns, praises and consolations which we utter in the world—and say Amen."

"Amen," Yussel said, as strong and as loud as Lillywhite had.

And then the universe held its breath. The air in the graveyard changed, took on an edge. The wrens were quiet, the wind absolutely still. The workmen looked around, dropped their stones. Yussel's father held his arms above his head as if he were tossing a child into the air, higher and higher. Pecky was gone, the satin canopy thrown carelessly on the ground, a small black cloud rising from it toward the oak. "Don't stop, Lillywhite! Don't stop."

The sooty little black cloud floating upward, hesitantly, caught itself in the oak tree, shook loose itself or was shaken loose by Lillywhite's words, out of the oak limbs, upward. When the cloud lifted out of the oak tree—just like the time he'd pressed against Lillywhite in the parking lot of the Paradise and everything in Yussel had moved toward his center like iron filings toward a magnet—everything in Yussel moved now. Something big like sorrow broke loose, banged at him from inside. Yussel Fetner, who had refused since the day of his Bar Mitzvah, had at last attached himself, had at last circumcised his heart. He wanted God the way he'd wanted Lillywhite.

The wrens swept in one wing from the oak tree to the monument. A soft fog, a cloud passing over the hill, dropped on them, filled the empty spaces with mist as if the universe, having held its breath, exhaled. Something was happening behind the monument. "Keep singing, Lillywhite. Keep singing."

Yussel walked closer, wiped his eyes, saw flashes of the bottoms of black frock coats flying, worn boots leaping behind the marble. Yussel walked around to the back of Pecky's monument. Rabbis danced in a circle, arms raised to Heaven, eyes rolling, madmen singing, dancing, drunk with grief, glory, knowledge, who knew? Their feet never touched the grass. One looked at him. *"Look, here's Yussel."* They pulled Yussel into the circle, made him dance. *"Look, Yussel, our limbs are so sanctified in the circle, each step weds worlds together. Come, dance."*

He saw the Fetner who saw the cow's skull, he saw the one who made it rain in a drought, the one who sold the tefillin for an esrog, the one who saw the Messiah, the one with the hiccups—uncles, grandfathers, great-grandfathers, all the crazy Fetners. Some looked like his father, small fiery wiry zaddiks. Others looked like Yussel, big and burly like a butcher. His father sat on top of the monument, waved at Yussel, clapped his hands to the fiddle music coming from someplace, wiped his eyes with his sleeve. *"Yom diddle yom diddle ai diddle dai dai."* He had no doors. His wings were long and thin, diaphanous, like the dragonfly's wings. *"Mazel tov, Yussele. Now you won't have to ask because when you're attached, your ears hear what they should hear and your mouth speaks what it should speak and your heart feels what it should feel. You're attached, Tottele. Mazel tov."*

A big grin sprang up from inside Yussel's heart, spread out on his face. Yussel took his hand from someone's shoulder, waved vigorously at his father until someone grabbed his hand again. Yussel yelled over his shoulder, "Hey, Totty, write when you get work." Then the circle flung him around and he sang his heart out with them, dizzy from the sun and the heat. Light flashed inside his eyes. His heart pounded. His feet burned. Still he danced, still they flung him. And then suddenly in a whirlwind of dust, pebbles, hats, oak leaves, they were gone.

Where they'd been—a grand-uncle, a great-grandfather, even the Baal Shem himself, all dancing behind Pecky's grave—everything was the same. Wrens chattered in the trembling oak. Workmen watched Lillywhite. City sounds rose up to the hill. The sun cast diamonds on the headstones, coals on their backs. Everything the same. Everything changed. The wind roared up from below. The people watching Lillywhite wrapped their coats around themselves, shivered in the wind, turned away. The gravediggers looked up at the sky, went back to work. Lillywhite stood at the edge of the hill, looking down at the city, eating from her bag of cookies. Yussel's father sat on the bench in front of Pecky's monument.

"Totte? What are you doing here? Why didn't you go with them?"

"Listen, Yussele, I've been thinking. I need to talk to you about that."

"You got your ticket. You made your deal. What's the problem?"

"I've been thinking. You know here in . . . here where I am, I told you . . . nobody but murderers, sinners, goniffs. On the other hand, in Heaven, they've got more zaddiks than they know what to do with. But in Hell, I'm the only one."

"So?"

"So I decided. You see, this way, I can go back and forth, I get these gorgeous pajamas, I can see you whenever I want. I can always argue over decrees from wherever I am. So I decided I think I'll stay. You understand, Yussele?"

"You put me through this and then you decide to stay?"

"Sending me to Heaven, it's like cupping the dead. What good can I do? One more saint in Heaven? You think they're short of saints up there? In Hell, I'm needed."

"I don't believe you've done this to me. You tortured me for nothing? You tortured me, my wife, my children, my friends? You promised you'd leave me alone."

"Yussele, try to understand. They need me here."

"I understand completely. You'll never change."

"Listen, Yussele," his father said, as gently as Yussel could remember his father saying anything, *"maybe you'll need me also?"*

"What do you mean?"

"I don't know. You're the Rabbi. Figure it out."

"Hey, wait for me." Lillywhite was running around the gravestones toward Yussel. "Someone ate the cookies. Someone . . ."

Yussel waited for Lillywhite to catch up, headed home. On the plane to Denver he told her the story about how his ancestor sold the tefillin for an esrog and when he bought the esrog home, his wife threw it against the wall. Lillywhite said, "I would have thrown him against the wall. I think it's time to make up some new stories."

Coronado, having found gold, went home to look for more.